SKY FIRE

Liam Lafferty was in the process of pulling in his fishing lines when the night sky seemed to momentarily catch fire. The blindingly bright flash originated high in the previously pitch-black heavens, and for a few startling seconds it was as if the sun had miraculously dawned. Yet the intense, mysterious light was snuffed out as abruptly as it arrived, and as night rushed in to prevail once more, a muffled, explosive boom echoed in the distance.

And then it began to rain. This shower didn't consist of droplets of water, but was made up of thousands of pieces of shredded metal that clattered down upon the deck and bombarded the surrounding waters. Once more Liam looked to the heavens, but the only thing he saw was a huge, billowing object that floated down from the sky with a feathery lightness.

He rushed to the pilot house to start up the engines. He was absolutely certain this object held the secret to the great mystery that had befallen him this fated evening, and if luck was with him, he'd be there when it came to rest in the sea.

THE FINEST IN SUSPENSE!

THE URSA ULTIMATUM (2310, $3.95)
by Terry Baxter

In the dead of night, twelve nuclear warheads are smuggled north across the Mexican border to be detonated simultaneously in major cities throughout the U.S. And only a small-town desert lawman stands between a face-less Russian superspy and World War Three!

THE LAST ASSASSIN (1989, $3.95)
by Daniel Easterman

From New York City to the Middle East, the devastating flames of revolution and terrorism sweep across a world gone mad . . . as the most terrifying conspiracy in the history of mankind is born!

FLOWERS FROM BERLIN (2060, $4.50)
by Noel Hynd

With the Earth on the brink of World War Two, the Third Reich's deadliest professional killer is dispatched on the most heinous assignment of his murderous career: the assassination of Franklin Delano Roosevelt!

THE BIG NEEDLE (2776, $3.50)
by Ken Follett

All across Europe, innocent people are being terrorized, homes are destroyed, and dead bodies have become an unnervingly common sight. And the horrors will continue until the most powerful organization on Earth finds Chadwell Carstairs—and kills him!

RICHARD P. HENRICK

SEA DEVIL

ZEBRA BOOKS
KENSINGTON PUBLISHING CORP.

ZEBRA BOOKS

are published by

Kensington Publishing Corp.
475 Park Avenue South
New York, NY 10016

First printing: August, 1990

Printed in the United States of America

The real threat to society is not the launching of bombs between the U.S. and the U.S.S.R. . . . The real threat is a terrorist orientated country or group gaining possession of a nuclear bomb. They are not responsible people and have nothing to lose in using it to further their goals.

—*defense expert Dan McKinnon*

Out of Ireland have we come
Great hatred, little room
Maimed us at the start
I carry from my mother's womb
A fanatic heart.

—*W. B. Yeats*
28 August 1931

Chapter One

Three hours out of Oahu the weather began to deteriorate. From the jump seat of the specially configured AV-8B Harrier, Commander Brad Mackenzie anxiously scanned the line of dark clouds that seemed to fill the entire southwestern horizon.

"Looks pretty ominous," broke the gravelly voice of the pilot over the intercom. "From what the weather boys back at Pearl say, that low-pressure system has all the makings of a full-fledged typhoon. I sure hope it keeps tracking to the north."

Brad Mackenzie, who was known simply as Mac to his friends and coworkers, could see only the back of the pilot's head as he responded. "I was thinking the same thing. Two years ago I rode out a typhoon while I was stationed at Guam. And believe me, it's not an experience I'd like to repeat."

"I read you loud and clear, Commander," returned the pilot. "Just hang in there a little bit longer. We should be sighting some of the islands of the Ratak Chain shortly. From there on, Kwajalein is practically around the corner."

A pocket of turbulence shook the Harrier. For a sickening moment the jet plunged downward. The cockpit filled with the throaty roar of the aircraft's single Rolls-Royce vectored-thrust turbofan engine as the pilot

7

fought to regain the altitude they had just lost.

It seemed to take an eternity for them to reach more stable air. Only then did Mac issue the barest sigh of relief. Even under ideal conditions, flying played havoc with his nerves. He was the type of individual who liked to have complete control of a situation. And since he didn't know how to pilot an aircraft, whenever he was airborne he was forced to put his destiny into someone else's hands.

Back on terra firma this obsession was particularly noticeable, especially when it came to driving. He could never relax in the passenger seat of an automobile. He thus avoided taxis whenever possible, and did all the driving when it came time for commuting, shopping trips, and the family vacation.

Yet another gust of unsettled air shook the aircraft, and the thirty-six-year-old naval officer's grip on his handrest instinctively tightened. Sweat lined his forehead as he guardedly turned to peer out the cockpit in an effort to see how the Harrier was meeting this punishment.

He could barely see the wing, which was mounted into the central portion of the upper fuselage. It was a stubby structure that held a pair of elongated pods slung beneath its length. Stored inside these external drop tanks was the extra fuel that allowed the Harrier to attain this unusually long range.

As he watched the tanks quiver slightly, a familiar voice sounded from the intercom. "We've got land dead ahead of us, Commander. It's not much, but I'll stake a week's pay that we've arrived in the Marshalls."

Mac diverted his gaze in time to see a small, circular-shaped island pass down below. He could just make out the protected lagoon of the atoll and its surrounding reef.

"Most likely that was Ailuk Island," added the pilot. "If so, that would put us at our rendezvous point in another ten minutes."

"How's our fuel situation?" Mac asked.

The pilot answered a bit hesitantly. "I'm not going to b.s. you, sir, but the way it looks, we should just make it. I figured that it would take all four external tanks to get us here. Fortunately, we had a tailwind for most of the trip, though this turbulence that we've just encountered could make things interesting."

Mac spoke up while watching yet another minuscule coral atoll pass below. "At least we can always land this baby on one of those islands if our fuel state gets critical. That would sure as hell be better than dropping into the drink."

As the Harrier shuddered in the grasp of another pocket of rough air, the pilot replied, "Don't worry, sir. As long as that storm keeps its distance, I'll get you safely to your destination. Besides, I've got a date back in Honolulu tomorrow night with this Thai chick who's really a looker. I sure as hell wouldn't want to stand her up."

Again the airplane shook violently. This was followed by an abrupt drop in altitude that caused a nauseating knot to form in Mac's stomach. Instead of pulling the Harrier out of this unexpected dive, the pilot allowed it to drop a full 10,000 feet before leveling out. This put them only a few thousand feet from the ocean's surface.

Their forward velocity was much more noticeable at this height. The surging blue waters of the South Pacific passed in a blur as Mac's gaze returned to the horizon, where black stormclouds continued to gather.

Less than five hours before, the mere idea of a visit to such a remote corner of the globe had been unimaginable. In fact, Mac was still at his condo on the North Shore of Oahu, sipping his morning coffee, when the fated call arrived that was to send him rushing off on his current assignment.

Marsha was seated beside him on the porch when the

telephone began ringing. His wife intuitively sensed that whoever was calling would be the bearer of bad news, and when Admiral Long himself somberly greeted Mac, he knew that her guess had been correct.

Mac had only just returned from a three-week stay at the Mare Island Naval Station outside San Francisco. He had a week's leave due him and was planning to take his family on a driving tour of the big island of Hawaii. All he needed to do was type up a report detailing his stay on Mare Island before this much anticipated leave was to begin.

If things had gone as scheduled, the report would be just about completed by now. Unfortunately his superiors had other plans for him.

The call sent him packing for the Marine Corps Air Station at Kaneohe Bay. Here he was met by Admiral Long and given a rushed briefing. Though the details were sparse, Mac knew the admiral had no choice but to send for him. For if the marks found on the seafloor outside Kwajalein indeed proved to be manmade, his long trip would certainly be justified.

With his gaze still locked on the cloud-filled horizon, Mac contemplated the implications of his mission. Though he hated to have to disappoint his family once again, he found himself with no alternative. As project manager, it was his duty to personally inspect each suspected sighting as soon as they were reported. Only in such a way could the pieces of the puzzle that had taken him over a year to gather together be finally assembled.

"Harrier one-zulu-alpha, this is Iwo Jima control. We have you on radar lock. How do you copy? Over."

A static-filled voice emanated from the intercom. With his thoughts abruptly brought back, Mac listened as the Harrier pilot answered.

"*Iwo Jima* control, this is one-zulu-alpha. You're a bit fuzzy, but we copy that. Over."

"Roger, one-zulu-alpha. You're free to begin your approach. You'll find us on bearing two-six-zero, on the other edge of that squall line in front of you, approximately three-five nautical miles distant."

Mac peered out the cockpit just as the first raindrops began pelting the plexiglass. Seconds later they were completely enveloped in a shroud of thick gray clouds. The fuselage began to vibrate, while outside a blinding bolt of lightning cut through the black heavens. This was accompanied by an ear-shattering boom of thunder that all but swallowed the straining whine of the Harrier's engine.

"Hold on, Commander," offered the pilot. "I'm afraid it's going to be a bit on the rough side. It shouldn't last long, though."

Mac's gut tightened as the airplane smacked into the most unstable air yet encountered. The entire fuselage began to quiver madly and shake with such a violent intensity that he didn't know how the plane could stay in one piece. He began mentally re-creating his hurried instructions in the workings of the Harrier's ejection system, all the while placing his right hand on the side-mounted console where the eject trigger was located.

Like an out-of-control roller coaster, the aircraft plunged downward. Held in place by his shoulder harness, Mac found himself possessed by nausea, and he was thankful that earlier he had passed on the pilot's offer to share a box lunch.

A resonant crack of lightning split the heavens, and for one chilling moment the entire cockpit seemed to be aglow with a pulsating iridescence.

"It's St. Elmo's fire!" cried the excited pilot.

Though he hadn't been a practicing Catholic since high school, Mac began silently mouthing a frantic Hail Mary. With his left hand he reached up to touch the silver crucifix that still hung from his neck. The cross had been given to him by his grandfather, who surrendered it on his deathbed at the ripe old age of eighty-seven.

The plane canted hard on its right side. As another lightning bolt lit up the cockpit, Mac wondered if he'd have the nerve to eject in such a storm if so ordered. The fourteen-year naval veteran never learned the answer to this disturbing question; the Harrier broke out of the squall line as suddenly as it had entered it.

A sunlit, bright blue sky greeted them. Wiping the sweat from his soaked brow, Mac peered out the plexiglass canopy and spotted a large vessel serenely floating on the blue waters below. Though the ship looked much like an aircraft carrier, Mac knew it was properly classified as an amphibious assault ship; its primary mission was to carry helicopters.

"Harrier one-zulu-alpha," broke a voice from the intercom. "This is Iwo Jima control. We have you on visual. You are clear to land at station number three."

As the pilot verified these instructions and initiated the landing sequence, Mac's thoughts returned to his last visit aboard this very same vessel over eighteen months ago. Mac had been working at the Naval Ocean System Command's laboratory on St. Thomas in the Virgin Islands when the *Iwo Jima* made port in Charlotte Amalie. While he was in the midst of a routine tour of the ship, it was learned that an F/A-18A Hornet belonging to the aircraft carrier *Coral Sea* had gone down in the waters north of St. Croix. Since Mac's expertise was in the field of marine salvage, he was ordered to remain on board the *Iwo Jima* as it immediately set sail for the crash site.

An exciting week's worth of work followed. Mac was glad to get out of the stuffy laboratory and enjoyed his brief excursion into the Caribbean Sea. Yet before he knew it, the Hornet was located and pulled from the clear blue depths. This signaled the end of his temporary sea duty, and the last he saw of the *Iwo Jima* was from the flight deck of a Bell Huey helicopter as he was

12

being whisked back to St. Thomas.

He couldn't help but be pleasantly surprised when Admiral Long mentioned the name of the ship that Mac was to be flown out to this afternoon. Though this was a long way from the Caribbean, it was a sort of homecoming all the same.

A throaty roar filled the cockpit as the pilot adjusted the Harrier's vectored-thrust engine. The plane had all but stopped its forward movement, and was hovering over the forward flight deck. The banshee-like whine of the engine further increased to an almost deafening crescendo as the AV-8B began gradually losing altitude.

The Harrier landed with a bare jolt. As the engine was switched off, the relief from the persistent roar was immediately noticeable.

"I told you I'd get you here in one piece, Commander," boasted the pilot lightly.

"That you did," replied Mac, who managed a relieved grin as the plexiglass canopy was removed. The scent of warm salt air met his nostrils as he added, "Thanks for the lift. Enjoy your date tomorrow night."

"I certainly will, Commander," replied the pilot. "And good luck to you, sir."

An alert seaman on a portable ladder appeared at Mac's side and helped him out of his harness. After removing his helmet, Mac stood and gratefully stretched his cramped limbs. He wasted no time exiting the tight confines of the Harrier and climbing down to the deck below. Here he was met by a khaki-clad officer with a tanned face, bright blue, inquisitive eyes, and a full blond moustache.

"Welcome aboard," shouted Commander William Hunley, the ship's executive officer.

Mac accepted the XO's firm handshake. "It's good to be back. Is Captain Exman still the CO here?"

"That he is, Commander. The Captain's waiting for you up on the bridge. If you'll just follow me, I'll escort

13

you up there. How was your flight?"

Mac answered while following the XO across the flight deck. "It was going pretty smooth until we hit that squall line a couple of minutes ago."

"We just passed through it ourselves," added the XO, who was leading them toward the large superstructure located amidships starboard. "I just hope the main body of the storm stays well to the north of us. Even with a displacement of 18,000 tons, the *Iwo Jima* is no match for a Pacific typhoon."

Mac noted the puddles of rainwater that still stained the deck. He was also aware of the rolling motion of the ship beneath him. It was apparent that the sea was much rougher than it had appeared from the air. Massive swells were crashing into the carrier's hull in irregular sets, making the mere act of walking a challenge.

They ducked through a hatch and began their way up a twisting stairway. Two flights up, the XO turned and led them down an open passageway. This afforded Mac an excellent view of the entire flight deck. He briefly halted and watched as the deck crew swarmed around the Harrier.

The XO noted Mac's interest and offered a brief explanation. "From what I understand, that flight from Oahu was just about at the limit of the AV-8B's range. Our boys will top off those external fuel tanks and make certain that the Harrier is in shape for the flight back to Kaneohe Bay."

Mac's line of sight shifted to the collection of large, banana-shaped, dual-rotor helicopters positioned on the forward a deck. Again the X0 provided the commentary.

"Those are Boeing-Vertol CH-46 Sea Knights. If I remember correctly, during your last visit with us, the Marines weren't embarked. We're presently carrying an entire battalion landing team of approximately 1,700 men. Those helicopters are utilized as assault transport vehicles that can hold up to 25 equipped troops, or

14

4,000 pounds of cargo each."

Mac looked on as the massive hydraulically powered platform set directly opposite the superstructure activated. A single dark green Sikorsky Sea Stallion soon appeared, having been lifted up from the ship's enclosed hangar bay.

"I believe you'll be most familiar with that particular helicopter before the day is over," offered the XO.

Before Mac could get the commander to explain what he meant by this, the man turned for the enclosed bridge. Mac took one last look at the chopper that had just arrived from below deck, shrugged his shoulders, then continued forward.

The *Iwo Jima*'s bridge was the nerve center of the ship while it was at sea. Mac entered the spacious glassed-in compartment and found it bustling with activity. Most of this action was centered around the plotting table, where the vessel's commanding officer could be seen hunched over the charts, all the while barking out orders to a nearby lieutenant j.g.

Mac remembered Captain Kenneth Exman well. Back in the Caribbean eighteen months ago, they had hit it off splendidly. The *Iwo Jima*'s broad-shouldered CO looked fit and vibrant. His baseball cap covered a mop of bristly brown hair, and the captain's full, rounded jaw and flat nose reminded Mac of his favorite coach back in high school.

It was the XO who informed the captain that their guest had arrived. Without hesitation, he looked up from the chart that he had been immersed in, met Mac's stare, and smiled.

"Good to see you again, Mac," he said warmly. "Has it really been a year and a half?"

Mac walked over and accepted the CO's firm handshake. "It's good to be back, Captain. Believe it or not, I genuinely missed this old lady."

The CO affectionately patted the nearby bulkhead. "I

15

know we have plenty to gripe about, but for a thirty-year-old vessel, the *Iwo Jima* can still get the job done."

"Are you still based out of Norfolk?"

"That we are, Commander. I gather that your next question is what in hell we're doing out here in the middle of the South Pacific."

Mac nodded, and the captain continued. "We've been stationed in the Mediterranean all fall. When those Iranian pirates hijacked that Brit oil tanker, we were sent down the Suez Canal and into the Persian Gulf to show the flag. Once the crisis was resolved, Command decided to make our life interesting and send us home the long way. We had just finished a port call in Subic Bay and were on our way to Pearl when we got the word to expect a visitor. I only learned your identity an hour ago."

Mac seemed confused. Taking the Captain aside, he spoke cautiously. "But how did you get involved with the find in the waters off Kwajalein?"

The CO's wide brow tightened. "I see that your briefing was as cursory as my own. To tell you the truth, Mac, I don't know anything about any find. All I've been instructed to do is act as your transfer point and provide you chopper transport further southward."

Mac was suddenly aware of the meaning of the XO's cryptic comment earlier. "I think I'm starting to see the big picture, Captain."

"At least someone around here knows what the hell is going on," said the captain, whose attention was diverted by a call from the air boss.

"It looks like we're stuck with you for awhile, Mac." The grinning CO hung up the telephone. "Seems that Harrier driver of yours is hot to get back to Oahu. Would you care to watch him lift off?"

Without bothering to respond, Mac followed the captain over to the port observation window. Below on the flight deck, the AV-8B looked sleek and deadly in its camouflage paint. As the pilot switched on its jet en-

16

gine, a throaty, high-pitched whine filled the bridge with intense sound. The roar intensified steadily until it reached almost deafening proportions. Appearing much like some sort of prehistoric beast, the Harrier proceeded to lift off vertically, straight into the air. Then, with a slight dip of its stubby wings, it gracefully turned its nose to the northeast and shot off in an incredible burst of forward speed.

Awestruck, Mac continued watching the aircraft until it was but a speck on the horizon. It was a gentle hand on his shoulder that brought back his thoughts.

"That's quite a sight, my friend. No matter how many times I see it, it never fails to astound me. Now, how about joining me in my quarters for some chow? I should be able to get a decent meal into that belly of yours before your whirlybird's ready to fly."

Mac readily accepted the captain's gracious offer. It was while washing up that he realized that he had left home so hurriedly that morning that he had neglected to shave. While pondering whether or not to borrow a razor, he stood before the mirror and momentarily studied his reflection.

He had inherited his full head of blond hair and his pale blue eyes from his mother. From his father he got a dimpled chin. The one feature that was distinctly his own was his nose. Broken during a collegiate football game and never set properly, Mac's nose was unique. Even Marsha referred to it as his "personality." Because of his fair coloring, his eyebrows and beard were fairly nondescript, and he knew that he could easily miss a shave without anyone but his wife noticing. With this in mind, Mac decided to forget about obtaining a razor, and after soaking his face in a handful of hot water, continued on to the captain's stateroom.

As he had proved during Mac's previous visit, Captain Kenneth Exman was an excellent host. There was a genuine warmth to the CO's smile as he greeted his guest and led him over to the table set for two.

"I think we'd better get going with the chow. There's another squall line approaching, and we'd like to get you airborne before it hits."

No sooner did they seat themselves when an alert orderly appeared with their salads and some hot rolls. This was followed by a platter filled with grilled chicken breast, noodles, and a helping of broccoli in cheese sauce.

The *Iwo Jima*'s CO had originally been an aviator. A graduate of the Naval Academy, he'd flown the Grumman A-6 Intruder in Viet Nam, and had over 3,500 flight hours and over 700 carrier-arrested landings. Two and a half years ago he'd reported to the Naval Education and Training Center at Newport, Rhode Island, where he was enrolled in the prespective commanding officers' course. Upon graduation, he assumed command of the *Iwo Jima*.

Mac liked the man's no-nonsense attitude. He genuinely cared about his shipmates and wasn't afraid to candidly express himself. This was the case as he described the *Iwo Jima*'s current deployment.

"I don't have to tell you that I was worried as all hell when Command ordered us home by way of the Pacific. Our steam plant is over thirty years old. It needs some major overhauls. Yet to make matters worse, not only did they cut our funding, but they rushed us through our last refit as well. I've got over 2,600 men currently on board this ship. With only a single shaft to propel us, we can't risk even a brief interruption of power. So far my boys have managed to keep us going, but the Lord only knows how long our luck is going to hold."

Mac polished off his broccoli. "I still say that your crew deserves a lot of credit, Captain. The gator navy might not be glamorous duty, but just look who's called upon when there's trouble brewing. If you ask me, we've got our priorities all wrong. Nuclear-powered aircraft carriers and high-tech cruisers are great for world-wide conflicts, but for the low-intensity threat operations that we'll most likely be facing during this upcoming decade, it's vessels like the *Iwo Jima* that will lay down the law."

"Well said, Mac. I'm glad to hear that someone out there calls it like it is. Now if we could only get the backing of Congress and the Pentagon."

"You're not asking for much, are you, Captain?"

A wide grin turned up the corners of the C.O.'s mouth. "Here I go and invite you to chow, and all I do is bore you with my problems. So enough of my belly-aching. How's that family of yours doing? If I remember correctly, you've got a set of twins about five years old. At least those two should keep your mind off the Navy."

"Actually, Andrew and Michael will be six next month," said the proud father. "And yes, when I'm home they keep me occupied every minute of the day. Their new love is baseball. Marsha got them uniforms, and now they're pestering us to let them join Little League."

"Six is a little young for that, isn't it?" offered the captain.

Mac was quick to answer. "That's what Marsha says, but I kind of wonder. Michael's got an unbelievable arm. Why, that little devil can already throw a curve ball. Andrew's specialty is hitting. He's already cost me a kitchen window and a new skylight. How's your son doing?"

The Captain's eyes sparkled. "Ken Jr. will graduate junior high school with honors this June. That kid's a mechanical genius. Just last month he took apart our personal computer and replaced a defective chip. Now he's writing his own programs. He plans to eventually attend the Naval Academy, where he wants to study nuclear physics."

A ringing telephone interrupted the captain. He

reached for the handset at his side. While he initiated a conversation, Mac finished his chicken breast and took a second to survey the stateroom. Behind them was a comfortable sitting area — of a couch, a magazine-filled coffee table, and two upholstered chairs. Next to this was the captain's desk. One could easily forget that such a setting belonged in a warship, though a CO's duty hardly allowed one a moment's respite.

"That was the XO," said the captain, who had already hung up. "It looks like that weather is moving in quicker than we'd anticipated. Our senior meteorologist recommends that we get you airborne pronto. Your chopper's just about ready, so I'm afraid you'll have to take a raincheck on dessert."

Mac patted his stomach while following the captain's lead, and pushed his chair away from the table to stand. "That meal was more than adequate, Sir. I've had nothing all day but a half cup of coffee, and it really hit the spot. Thanks again for the hospitality."

"You're most welcome, Mac. And don't be such a stranger. We'll be back in Norfolk at the end of the month, and I'd love to have you stop by for a proper visit. Who knows, maybe by then you'll be able to tell me what this mysterious excursion of yours is all about."

Doubting that he'd ever get the clearance to talk about the project that had called him these thousands of miles, Mac nodded politely and followed the captain up the flight deck.

The weather topside looked menacing. Thick dark clouds blotted out the sun, while a rising wind made the mere process of walking difficult. They were halfway to the open fuselage of the Sea Stallion when the rains began falling in a torrent.

"Good luck to you, Mac," offered the CO as he escorted his guest to the helicopter's side. "I sure hope the weather is better down south where you're off to."

"You don't happen to know where that might be, do you, sir?" asked Mac as he climbed into the doorway.

The captain had to hold onto his cap and practically shout to be heard over the howl of the gusting wind. "Afraid they didn't bother to share that with me. Command will relay the exact coordinates to you once you get airborne. All that I know for certain is that you're headed somewhere south of Kwajalein. Have a safe trip!"

"You too, Skipper," returned Mac, who saluted and then allowed a jumpsuited airman to lead him further into the helicopter's rather cavernous interior. There was room inside for at least three dozen passengers. Yet Mac was alone except for the single attendant.

No sooner did he sit down and buckle his restraining harness when the Sea Stallion's dual turbine engines coughed alive. As its six-bladed rotor began madly spinning, a large drop of hydraulic oil fell onto Mac's forehead. He disgustedly wiped the smelly fluid off and addressed the airman seated across from him.

"I think something's leaking up there!" shouted Mac.

"Welcome aboard a Sikorsky, Commander," replied the airman stoically. "It's when this baby *stops* leaking that we've got serious problems."

Mac could only shake his head and sit back as the helicopter began its ascent. They rose vertically. Except for a slight vibration, the wind didn't seem to play a factor as the Sea Stallion turned to the south, all the while continuing to gain altitude.

Strangely enough, during the entire ascent Mac was unusually at ease. In fact, he was so relaxed that he fell asleep soon after they reached their cruising altitude.

Mac's sound, dreamless slumber was broken by a loud buzzing noize. As he groggily opened his eyes, he watched as the cabin attendant picked up a bulkhead mounted intercom handset. The cabin was lit by a muted red light and Mac realized with a start that it was

21

apparently night already.

"Good evening, Commander," said the airman, who had completed his phone conversation and noted that Mac had awakened. "How'd you sleep?"

"Like a baby," Mac answered as he yawned and glanced down at his watch. "Have I really been out for two hours?"

The airman nodded. "That you have. You didn't miss anything but a little lightning and thunder."

"How's the weather now?" quizzed Mac.

"It's clear as can be. We left all the heavy stuff up north. So it looks like we can complete your transfer with a minimum of risk."

"Transfer?" repeated Mac.

Mistaking Mac's puzzlement as an inability to hear over the chopping sound of the spinning rotors, the airman shouted, "I just got word from the cockpit that you'll be leaving us shortly. We'll be dropping you onto the deck of a submarine. Have you ever used a rescue hoist before, sir?"

Mac was genuinely dumbfounded. "I can't say that I have," he managed with a heavy sigh.

Noting his anxiety, the airman's tone softened. "Well, you have nothing to worry about, sir. I'll be fitting you into a harness, and then utilize a winch to lower you by means of a steel cable. All you have to do is hit the release mechanism once you touch down on the deck."

Mac looked up when a loud electronic tone sounded. It proved to be the attendant who identified this noise.

"It's showtime, sir. Just follow me over to the doorway and I'll get you fixed up."

Mac reluctantly did so, and was soon sitting on the edge of the now opened hatchway. The roar of the Sea Stallion's turbine engines filled the cabin with a deafening grind. Outside the air was warm and clear, and Mac could see a myriad of stars glistening in the heavens. Conscious that the helicopter was now hovering, he looked down and could just make out a single dim red light. As the Sikorsky began to descend, this light intensified until soon Mac viewed the distinctive, teardrop-shaped outline of a submarine floating on the surface of the sea. When several individuals could be seen on the forward deck of this vessel, Mac heard the attendant cry out behind him.

"So long, Commander. Just ease your way off the ledge and we'll take it from there."

Mac managed a brave salute and after inhaling a deep calming breath, scooted off the helicopter's hatchway. He found himself dangling in midair now, his weight supported by the steel cable attached to the harness at the back of his shoulders. He could feel the downdraft of the Sea Stallion's rotors as the cable began playing out, and he began to drop.

So rapid and smooth was this descent that Mac had little time to contemplate his precarious position. The submarine continued to grow larger, and Mac spotted two individuals perched in its sail. Behind them, mounted on the aft portion of the vessel's deck, was a large, cylindrical object that Mac identified as being a deep submergence rescue vehicle. He was no stranger to the workings of a DSRV, and supposed that this would be the platform that would be conveying him to the seafloor itself.

He found himself being guided forward of the sail. Here a pair of brawny sailors succeeded in grabbing his legs and stabilizing him. The moment that he touched down on the deck, he hit the harness release mechanism as instructed and felt the pull on his back lessen. The last he saw of the harness itself was as it was being hoisted back up into the hold of the still hovering helicopter.

"Commander Mackenzie, welcome aboard the USS *Billfish*."

This greeting came from a wiry, khaki-clad officer

who stood at Mac's side. He continued, "I'm Lieutenant Commander Jenkins, the sub's XO. Captain Holden is up in the sail and sends his respects. I'm afraid that time is a bit critical, so if it's all right with you, we'd like to get you loaded into the DSRV and get on with the dive."

"Lead on, Mr. Jenkins," replied Mac, who was relieved that his long journey was finally about to end.

As they proceeded around the sail, Mac noted that the chopping roar of the helicopter was no longer audible. This racket was replaced by the splashing sound of lapping water as it gently broke against the sub's rounded hull. The warm night air was fresh and smelled of the sea. Quite happy to be back in this familiar medium, Mac traversed the vessel's spine, finally coming to a halt beside the DSRV. Here he spotted an individual dressed in dark blue coveralls, in the process of inspecting the mini-sub's forward thruster ducts. It proved to be the XO, who provided the introductions.

"Commander Mackenzie, I'd like you to meet the DSRV *Avalon*'s pilot, Lieutenant Richard Sullivan."

Mac accepted the pilot's cool handshake. The lieutenant was well into his forties and displayed a lined, weather-worn face as he looked Mac directly in the eyes.

"The *Avalon*'s ready to go whenever you are, Commander."

Mac sized him up as a man who had worked his way up through the ranks. He exuded confidence, and Mac felt instantly at ease with him.

"Were you the one who made the initial discovery?" asked Mac.

"I'm the one," the pilot answered. "I'd be happy to give you a complete briefing once we get underway."

"I'd like that, returned Mac. He followed Sullivan as he climbed a portable ladder that was propped against the DSRV's side.

A humped casing on the *Avalon*'s upper deck hid a

narrow hatchway. As Lieutenant Sullivan opened the hatch, the XO of the USS *Billfish* called out to Mac.

"Have a safe voyage, Commander. If you need anything, just ring us up on the underwater telephone."

Mac returned his salute and then followed the *Avalon*'s pilot down into the DSRV's interior. A short climb led to the main pressure capsule. The air was cool here and smelled of machine oil. By the light of a red lamp they moved forward. This put them in the central command module. While the pilot settled into the padded chair on the port side, Mac squeezed into the seat beside it. Following the grizzled veteran's example, Mac fastened his safety harness.

"I take it you're no stranger to a deep submergence rescue vehicle, Commander."

"Actually, I spent some time on the *Mystic*. And please, call me Mac."

The pilot continued while addressing the various switches and buttons of his console. "You wouldn't happen to know Matt Crowley, would you?"

"I certainly would," answered Mac. "Matt was my driver during a dive off Kauai."

"Good ol' angles-and-dangles Crowley," reflected the pilot. "He taught me the business, and was almost responsible for getting me to muster out of the service early. That guy's scared of nothing."

Mac grinned. "So I've noticed."

The intercom activated, and they were informed that the *Billfish* was standing by to dive. Only when he was absolutely certain that the *Avalon* was properly pressurized did the pilot notify their mother ship that they were also ready for the black depths below. A raucous blast of compressed air signaled that the dive was on. Still anchored piggyback-style on the deck of the *Billfish*, the DSRV slid beneath the surface of the sea.

"How long until we disengage?" asked Mac.

"A couple of minutes at most."

"Does that give us time for that briefing you promised me?"

The pilot nodded. "The *Avalon* was in Sydney when I received my current orders. The Aussie Navy is thinking about building a couple of DSRVs of their own, and they'd like to use *Avalon* as a prototype. Since I was ordered up here ASAP, MATS sent in a C5-A that subsequently carried *Avalon* to the airstrip at Kwajalein. From here we were mounted on the back of the *Billfish*.

"The *Avalon*'s primary mission was to search the waters surrounding the atoll for any recently deposited debris. It seems that the Air Force lost some sort of warhead in the area after a successful test launch from Vandenberg, and it was hoped that we would be the ones to sniff it out for them.

"After scouring the lagoon and finding not a trace of the warhead, we expanded the search to the surrounding ocean. It was while examining the waters directly south of the lagoon's entrance that our bottom scanning sonar registered a minor irregularity on the seafloor, at a depth of six-hundred and seventy-eight feet. I decided to bring the *Avalon* down to eyeball this anomaly, and that's when I made the initial discovery."

A soft electronic tone began sounding in the background, and the pilot excused himself to begin the disengagement process. He utilized the underwater telephone to coordinate this process with the USS *Billfish,* and soon afterward the *Avalon* was free from its mother vessel and totally on its own.

With the assistance of an airplane-type steering column, the pilot guided the DSRV downward. At a depth of five hundred feet he hit a clear plastic button on the sonar console. Almost immediately a repetitious, soft warbling ping began sounding from the elevated intercom speakers.

"That sound that you're hearing is from a set of homing beacons we placed at the site. It will lead us straight

26

to the area in question."

Mac sat forward excitedly. His pulse quickened as they passed below six hundred feet and the pilot activated the *Avalon*'s powerful bow-mounted spotlights and its video camera. Now all Mac had to do was gaze up at the monitor screen to see for himself what secrets the ocean had in store for them.

A startled grouper darted into the blackness beyond, while a curious gray shark stared into the camera as if it was considering it as a possible food source. After adjusting the monitor's fine-tuning knob, the pilot continued.

"I don't really know what I was expecting to find down here. But I'll tell you this much, in my ten years of work on DSRVs, I haven't ever seen anything like what you're about to see with your very own eyes. Why, it just doesn't make any rational sense!"

Mac's mouth was bone dry as they dropped below six hundred and fifty feet. On the monitor screen, the gray shark was no longer visible. In its place was a faint blue beacon whose strobe seemed to be synchronized with the pinging tone that was still emanating from the *Avalon*'s intercom.

"That's the homing beacon," observed the pilot. "The site is only a few meters from its base."

It seemed to take forever for the DSRV to cover this distance. As they passed the strobe, the pilot took manual control of the video camera and aimed its lens straight at the seafloor.

An expanse of smooth golden sand filled the monitor screen. Yet as they sped over a nesting starfish, the character of the sand abruptly changed. Its previously glossy surface was now pockmarked by a set of alien tracks. This trail seemed manmade, the individual treads appearing much like that which would be left in the wake of some sort of subterranean tractor.

Mac noted the shape of the treadmarks and the width

of the track itself. Though he would need to take exact measurements, there was no doubt in his mind that Admiral Long's suspicions had been correct.

Only three weeks ago, Mac had seen an exact duplicate of this same track on the seafloor beneath San Francisco harbor. The previous month, he had examined another similar trail off the coast of Norfolk, Virginia, in Chesapeake Bay. Earlier in the year, other tracks were found in the Mediterranean Sea near Sicily, and on the seafloor of the Baltic opposite the Swedish city of Karlskrona. Each of these sightings pointed to the presence of some sort of mysterious vessel that used a tracked drive to prowl the seafloor. What made this supposition all the more chilling was the fact that each of these sightings occurred in the restricted waters adjoining a variety of the West's most sensitive military installations. It was Mac's current mission to determine the nationality of this vehicle, and to figure out a way to stop future incursions before America's very security was compromised.

"If you ask me, it looks like someone's been driving a Caterpillar tractor down here. Who knows, maybe the guys who were driving it are the same ones who made off with our warhead," offered the pilot.

Such an idea caused goosebumps to form on Mac's forearms, and as he was about to respond, the DSRV's underwater telephone activated. The pilot put the receiver to his ear, and after a brief conversation he handed it to Mac.

"Commander Mackenzie, this is Lieutenant Commander Jenkins on the *Billfish*. I'm afraid we're going to have to get you topside on the double. We just received a priority flash from COMSUBPAC requesting your immediate presence in San Diego. Air transport will be awaiting you on Kwajalein."

His eyes still glued to the monitor, Mac wondered what had occurred to necessitate his immediate presence

28

in far-off California. The only thing he could be certain of was that it was most likely somehow related to the mysterious set of tracks that were still displayed on the screen before him. Not looking forward to yet another long commute, he wearily instructed the *Avalon*'s pilot to break off the scan and rejoin the mother ship.

Chapter Two

The sun set over the Irish Sea with a deceptive swiftness. From the transom of his battered fishing trawler, Liam Lafferty watched the twilight. The western horizon was aglow in breathtaking color. Rich bands of orange and golden yellow merged with the gathering violet of night to produce a unique, ever-changing canvas. Absorbing every detail, the grizzled fisherman prayed it was an omen of good fortune.

For an entire two-week stretch, they had had nothing but one angry gale after another sweep in from the North Atlantic. During this time, only the most desperate fishermen left Dundalk Bay to ply their trade. Most of these individuals returned home with nothing but smashed equipment and a severe case of seasickness to show for their efforts.

Even though his family was already down to half-portions of cod, Liam wasn't one of those fools who challenged the windswept tempests. Better to go hungry than lose one's life to the elements. This was a lesson that the old-timer learned the hard way, for he had lost his father and his only brother to just such a storm.

Less than three hours ago, the red pennant was lowered from the harbormaster's flagpole. Shortly thereafter, the dark canopy of low-lying clouds that had been with them for the past fourteen days began to clear. Liam was working on his lines in the shed behind his cottage when a neighbor excitedly conveyed the good news. Without wasting a second, Liam gathered his line and hooks, and rushed from his cottage to get his seabag. He was able to get his trawler to sea just as the tide began to change.

He had been out for a good two hours now and already had several fat fish in the hold. Soon it would be time to once more pull in the lines to add to this catch. But before he did so, he decided to have a smoke. He packed his trusty briar pipe with tobacco and lit the bowl with a wooden match. The aromatic scent of rum and vanilla wafted upward as Liam exhaled a long ribbon of smoke.

With his gaze still locked on the western horizon, he watched the vibrant colors of twilight begin to fade. The night was swiftly taking over, and a sharp crescent moon crowned this inevitable triumph. Almost directly beneath this celestial orb, Liam spotted the distant, flickering directional beacon at Dunany Point. Since he had no navigational equipment of his own to speak of, he preferred to keep this light in sight at all times. As long as he knew in what direction it lay, not even the arrival of a sudden gale or fog bank could disorientate him.

His son Sean was forever pestering him to buy one of the new-fangled Loran directional finders. Such a device would allow him to find his way home even without the assistance of the Dunany Point beacon. In this way, argued Sean, he could vastly increase his fishing territory and assure his future safety as well.

Liam wanted no part of such expensive, wasteful contraptions. He was a traditionalist who much preferred to work with as few mechanical devices as possible. Fancy equipment was always breaking down. Besides costing a fortune to repair, it only made life that much more complicated. Though the territory he could cover was limited without such gear, he could still get the job done just as his forefathers had for seven generations before him.

If Sean was so anxious to help him increase his catch, the very least he could do was give his father a hand once in a while. Sean was his only son, and Liam had hoped he would take an interest in his father's craft. As a child, Sean seemed to love the sea and accompanied Liam on many a fishing trip. The boy was bright and inquisitive, and was a great help when it came to baiting the hooks and hauling in the catch.

It was when Sean dropped out of upper school that he seemed to lose all interest in both his family and fishing. Bored of life in provincial Dundalk, he moved to Dublin, where he got a job at the Guinness brewery.

Though Liam hated to lose him, at least the boy had gotten himself a decent job and was taking care of himself. Content to let him do his thing, Liam made the best of the situation. Even though he was pushing sixty-five, he was in decent health and could still manage his affairs quite capably.

His wife Anne wanted him to hire an apprentice. Liam would have no part of such a ridiculous thing. Even in bountiful times, fishing was a poor man's occupation. Liam's profits were meager, and bringing in an outsider would only dilute them that much further. Besides, he honestly enjoyed working by himself. At least during his time at sea, he could be guaranteed genuine peace and quiet. Clever small talk and gossip were not for him. Like his father and grandfather before him, Liam was a loner. Bringing an apprentice from outside the family would make serene evenings such as this one impossible, and as far as he was concerned, it just wasn't worth the bother.

Taking a contented pull on his pipe's worn stem, Liam redirected his gaze upward. The rapidly darkening sky was unusually clear, and the evening star could be seen close beside the new moon. Further up in the heavens, a myriad of twinkling stars greeted him.

With his gaze still locked skyward, the old-timer muttered a prayer to the gently blowing wind. "Heavenly Father, I realize that I'm not one of your most devout subjects, but I really do try to live within your gospel even if I don't make it to church every Sunday. So with that in mind, could you please see to it that this good weather holds, and that I'll return home with a full hold before my Annie's forced to eat the last of the cod. That woman's an angel if I ever met one, and it's for her sake alone that I issue this prayer. For yours is the kingdom, and the power, and the glory, forever and ever. Amen."

Hurriedly crossing himself, Liam took one last look at the twinkling expanse of stars that covered the black heavens before sticking the stem of his pipe back in his mouth and turning to get back to his fishing.

Thirty-eight thousand feet above the Irish Sea, the Boeing B-52G Stratofortress bomber, whose call name was Red Dog two-niner, was about to complete the second leg of a twenty-five-hour-long mission. Eighteen and half hours ago, the aircraft had taken off from Barksdale Air Force Base, outside of Shreveport, Louisiana. Manned by a crew of six, Red Dog two-niner headed due north on the first leg of its flight. It was over the northern tip of Greenland that it rendezvoused with a KC-135 tanker and took on 25,000 gallons of kerosene jet fuel. Over the frozen Arctic island of Spitsbergen, the B-52 initiated a racetrack-shaped course for eight hours. At this time they came to the very edge of Soviet airspace, patiently awaiting the "go" code that would send them on the mission for which the aircraft had been designed—the nuclear bombardment of the Soviet Union.

Captain Lawrence Stockton had made dozens of these alert patrols before. Only thirty years old, Stockton already had over 2,000 hours behind the controls of a

B-52, and was presently Red Dog two-niner's senior staff pilot. At his side in the cockpit, he had a rectangular black satchel marked with red stripes and the words *Top Secret* bodly emblazoned in big yellow letters. This was the Combat Mission Folder, or CMF, for short. It held the precise identity of their target, and could be opened only on direct orders from the President. Fortunately for all of them, a CMF had never been opened in the air; hopefully it never would be. For such an act would be contrary to the motto of the Strategic Air Command, which read, Peace is our profession.

As a veteran cold warrior, Lawrence Stockton understood SAC's role as a deterrent. As a B-52 pilot, he participated in only one leg of the so-called triad, which also included ground- and submarine-based missiles. Each of these delivery systems was developed to ensure that the United States could respond in case of a surprise nuclear strike by the Soviets.

In the event that such an unthinkable attack was to take place, Stockton's mission was to deliver four hydrogen bombs to their targets. Each of these weapons was stored in the forward bomb rack and could produce an explosion equivalent to 1,000,000 tons of TNT. To give him a better idea of its true nature, it was once explained to Stockton that such a blast would be about seventy-five times stronger than that which destroyed Hiroshima.

When he was off duty back home in Louisiana, the Michigan State graduate tried not to think about his awesome responsibility. At such a time his family became the center of his life. Married for nine years now, he had three healthy children and another on the way. Since his wife had been an Air Force brat, she understood the demanding nature of his work, and made certain that his time at home was as free from needless pressures and petty hassles as possible.

Only a few days ago, he had learned that with the

conclusion of this mission, he was to be taken off the flight line and made command post controller. Though he loved to fly, this new ground position would be more like a nine-to-five job, and thus allow him a more stable home life. It would also give him a chance to take his family on a long overdue vacation. His kids had already picked Walt Disney World in Orlando. He didn't dare veto them, and left instructions with his wife to begin accumulating the proper maps and guidebooks.

Satisfied that he was finally going to be able to spend some real quality time with his family, Lawrence Stockton anxiously looked up and scanned the dozens of dials and gauges on his side of the cockpit. To his right, his twenty-four-year-old copilot, Lieutenant Michael Ritter, was in the process of monitoring the instruments that he was responsible for.

"How are you holding up, Lieutenant?" quizzed Stockton lightly. "Is your first real deterrence patrol all that you expected it to be?"

The copilot yawned before answering. "It sure beats flying those simulators, sir. Although I must admit that I'm going to really enjoy getting some decent rack time."

The pilot grinned. "You'll get used to it eventually. Of course, you could always call up Major Avila. I'm certain that he'd be more than willing to spell you."

Major Pete Avila was their relief pilot, and was presently curled up in the rear of the plane reading the latest issue of *Popular Mechanics*.

"That's okay, sir. I can handle it," retorted the recent flight school graduate a bit more eagerly.

Stockton remembered well his own eagerness on his first mission, and wasn't about to spoil his copilot's first experience in the big leagues.

"We're getting close to our final refueling point, Lieutenant. All we need to do is top off our tanks, and then we can turn this eagle home to its nest. Why don't you see if First Lieutenant Geller has our KC-135 on the scope yet."

While the copilot initiated this call to Red Dog two-niner's navigator, the Boeing KC-135 Strato-tanker that Lawrence Stockton had been referring to had just taken off from its nearby base at Mildenhall, England. Built around the same basic airframe as a commercial 707, the KC-135 was in reality nothing but a cavernous flying gas station. Though its mission was far less glamorous than the fighters and bombers that it was designed to refuel, the KC-135 Stratotanker was one of the most important platforms in America's military arsenal. Without such dependable vehicles available to fulfill their mission, the range of the country's strategic and tactical airborne response would be drastically cut back.

As the sleek tanker streaked across English airspace and headed toward the Irish Sea, its four-man crew settled in to their jobs. In the cockpit, Major Gene Aikens, a forty-five-year-old veteran of the Vietnam conflict, was at the controls, while Captain Paul Standish sat beside him as his copilot. In an adjoining cabin, the plane's navigator, First Lieutenant Lee Rothman, charted the exact coordinates where they were to rendezvous with the thirsty B-52. In the rear of the aircraft, Master Sergeant Lou Moretti passed the time reading a two-day-old copy of *USA Today*. As boom operator, Lou would not begin his work until the initial rendezvous was completed. Only then would he continue on into the tail portion of the plane, where he would take control of the actual transfer of the fuel.

As the master sergeant scrutinized the sports page, he came across an article showing the results of the latest NFL draft. A decade ago, Lou had been an All-American defensive tackle for the University of Missouri Tigers. During his senior year, he was scouted by the Dallas Cowboys, who were so interested in his potential that they actually made him an offer. Coach Landry had been a childhood hero of Lou's, and the Cowboys were one of his favorite teams. Yet it was a prior commitment with the United States Air Force that kept him from accepting. As a participant in the ROTC program, Lou received assistance towards his tuition at a time when a football scholarship wasn't available. So upon graduation, instead of beginning a career in the NFL, he began one in the military.

As it turned out, the Air Force had been good for him. Though he could have made more money playing football, his training was superb, and he genuinely enjoyed working with the service's quality personnel. He was also soon to learn that above all, he loved to be airborne.

A slight case of nearsightedness kept him from going for his pilot's wings. Instead he did the next best thing and qualified as a boom operator. This allowed him plenty of flying time and placed him as one of the elite few trusted to handle this difficult and demanding task.

What really bugged him, though, was the fact that today, a fellow could be both a professional athlete and in the armed forces at the very same time. Why, he had just read about a recent graduate of the Naval Academy who was allowed to do his duty aboard a ship from Monday through Friday, and then on weekends played professional football for the Raiders. In Lou's day, such a thing was unheard of, and as far as he was concerned, it shouldn't be permitted even now.

Astounded by the salaries the NFL was offering its latest bunch of recruits, Lou disgustedly threw down the newspaper and dug into his jacket pocket for the Snickers that he had hidden there. Because of his diet, he knew he shouldn't have even taken it along. But he had so few pleasures left in life, and one little candy bar certainly wasn't going to hurt him any.

He carefully unwrapped it and took a second to savor its chocolaty aroma before taking a biteful. The bar was fresh and tasted of roasted peanuts, creamy nougat, and rich milk chocolate. Only after he had completely devoured it did the first pangs of guilt possess him.

Four months ago, he had made a New Year's resolution that he would go on a strict diet and lose at least twenty pounds. At six-four, he was a naturally big man who had developed a lot of muscle as a young football player. His duties in the Air Force were mostly sedentary, and slowly but surely his muscles were turning to flab. To counter this deterioration, he decided on a diet and a strict exercise program.

For the first two months he carefully monitored his diet, cut out all sweets, and exercised regularly. By the end of February he had lost seven pounds. Then, on March first, he was transferred from the States to the UK. The hectic move played havoc with his workout schedule, and the rich English food did the same to his diet. By the end of March, he had gained the seven pounds back and then some, his resolution all but forgotten.

With the taste of the Snickers bar still fresh on his lips, Lou wondered how he'd ever find the willpower to resist such treats. He had to do something drastic, or soon he wouldn't even be able to fit into his uniforms. His excess weight was even beginning to get in the way of his present duty. As boom operator he was required to lie on his stomach and crawl into the cramped passageway at the tail end of the airplane. It was here that he directed the boom down to the refueling aircraft. If he kept gaining weight, he wouldn't be able to fit into this narrow section of the KC-135, and his days of being a boom operator would be over. He'd then most likely be grounded and forced to wait out his retirement at a desk. Such a future didn't appeal to Lou, who wondered if the base hospital could help him find a compatible diet program and force him to stick to it. Promising himself that he would at the very least give this option a try, he sat forward. His intercom headset suddenly activated.

"Master Sergeant Moretti," greeted the distinctive bass voice of the pilot. "We've got our thirsty customer on radar, twenty miles ahead of us. Intercept will be in five minutes. Do you think that you can handle them?"

"We aim to please," returned the boom operator, who then pivoted, and after sucking in his bulging waist, began his way further into the KC-135's tail.

To accomplish the refueling process, it was necessary for Captain Lawrence Stockton to bring his B-52 down to 30,500 feet. This was some 2,000 feet below the tanker, that was in the process of initiating a sharp banked turn, to put itself several miles ahead of Red Dog two-niner. It was as the bomber began slowly closing this distance that the cockpit intercom rang.

"Captain Stockton, this is Major Tabor. I'm showing a yellow light on the fusing circuit of bomb number four. I'm almost certain that it's nothing but that ol' gremlin at work again, but I'd like permission to go down into the bomb rack and check for certain."

"I copy that, Major," replied the pilot. "We're just about to begin refueling up here. Couldn't that eyeball check wait until we've finished this process and turn for home."

"I'd rather get on it right away, Captain. If it's something more serious than a bad circuit, I might have to open it up, and that could be a lengthy process."

Lawrence Stockton deliberated a second before responding. "I understand, Major. Go ahead and check it out. I'll get Major Avila to relieve me and meet you down in the bomb rack. If it is that gremlin again, maybe this time we can catch him redhanded."

Stockton unplugged his umbilical, and as he began removing his restraining harness, addressed his copilot. "I'd better get down to the bomb rack and see what's upsetting Major Tabor. I'll send up Major Avila to take my place. It's about time he earned his keep around here."

"Can I still handle the refueling, Captain?" asked the eager copilot.

Stockton answered the rookie while slipping out of his ejection seat and carefully climbing over the console that held the throttles. "I don't see why you can't, Lieutenant. Make certain our friendly flying gas station cleans those windows while they're at it, and checks under the hood as well. And if he asks for your charge card number, remind him to put in on Uncle Sam's tab."

With this the veteran pilot playfully winked and turned to make his way out of the cockpit. As expected, he found the relief pilot sound asleep on the narrow bunk that lined the fuselage. He put his hand on Avila's shoulder and shook him awake.

"Rise and shine, Major."

Pete Avila groggily stirred. "Are we home yet, skipper?"

"We won't be back in Barksdale for another six hours. And we won't be getting home at all unless you get your keister up into the flight deck and make certain that our tanks get filled. And by the way, I told the lieutenant that he could handle the controls when we link with the KC-135. He's a sharp kid, but keep your eyes on him all the same."

"Will do, skipper," replied the relief pilot as he stiffly sat up, yawned, and scratched his beard-stubbled chin.

"I'll be in the bomb rack with Major Tabor if you need me," added the pilot, who continued on down a narrow passageway lined with snaking cables and electronics gear.

A ladder brought Stockton to the deck below, where the B-52's primary cargo was stored. Here he found the bombardier seated at a computer console, busily feeding a series of requests into the keyboard.

"Find anything yet, Major?"

The bombardier took a moment to scan the monitor screen. "It doesn't look like that short is located on this side, Skipper. Even with an auxiliary circuit, it's still flashing yellow."

Crossing the compartment to check this screen himself, Lawrence Stockton reflected. "If it *is* an internal short, then I bet it occurred when we initiated that practice run over Spitsbergen."

"That's very possible," returned the bombardier. "But I'm still going to have to open up number four to check that circuit board firsthand."

The pilot nodded. "Then let's do it, Major. I'll open up the rack while you get the test kit."

As a duly qualified bombardier in his own right, Lawrence Stockton replaced the Major at the console. He needed to enter a series of security codes before depressing a large red toggle switch positioned directly above the keyboard. The muted hum of hydraulic machinery filled the air as two steel plates that had formed the floor of the compartment opened with a loud popping hiss. This revealed a large hollow cavity, approximately twenty feet long and six feet wide. Mounted inside this opening was the tubular steel bomb rack. Four cigar-shaped objects were held inside this structure. Each of these cylinders, stored in side-by-side pairs, was seven feet in length and looked much like a fat torpedo. Lawrence Stockton carefully studied each of these objects, which he knew to be their four 1.5-megaton hydrogen bombs.

The underside of the cavity was currently sealed, and led directly to the outer skin of the bomber. This was the bomb bay door, and would be opened only to service the weapons or to drop them.

Major Tabor appeared with a compact tool kit. There was a serious look on his face as he began his way down a steel ladder bolted into the rear part of the rack. This allowed him access to the forward portion of the bomb positioned at the rear of the rack's left side. He carefully used a tapered screwdriver to remove the protective plate that covered the fourth bomb's trigger mechanism. Faced now with a number of wafer-thin circuit boards, the bombardier pulled out a probe and began gingerly searching for the malfunctioning chip.

Breathlessly watching this delicate process, Lawrence Stockton commented, "Take your time, Major. And don't forget that if those boards show clean, we can always temporarily cock the trigger to overload the circuit and then read it again."

Not bothering to respond to this except with a curt nod, the bombardier tried to keep his hand from shaking as he continued inserting the surgical probe deep into the juncture of each individual connection.

It was a call from the tanker's navigator that sent Master Sergeant Lou Moretti into the extreme rear portion of the KC-135's tail. His hefty frame seemed to fill the entire enclosure as he stretched out on his stomach on an elongated red plastic-covered mattress. Before removing the tail's outer plexiglass shield, he strapped himself firmly in place so as not to be sucked out if the inner window collapsed. Only when his bonds were taut did he remove the shield and peer out the viewing port that was cut into the very tip of the tanker's tail.

Less than a mile away he could make out the nose of the B-52 Stratofortress, illuminated by a pair of powerful spotlights. The bomber seemed to be perfectly aligned, and Lou spoke into his chin-mounted radio transmitter.

"Red Dog two-niner, this is your friendly attendant, Master Sergeant Lou Moretti on Troubador Six. I have you on visual. You are cleared to close."

For the next ten to fifteen minutes, Lou would in effect be commanding both planes during the actual refueling process. But first he had to guide the B-52 to the proper transfer distance. He did so by operating a set of red and green guidance lights that were mounted on the tanker's tail.

When the distance between the two planes was less than a half a mile, he activated the tanker's 42-foot-long boom. This telescoping metallic tube had two stubby wings built onto it that Lou "flew" to a position straight behind their tail. On the end of this boom was a nozzle that would be fitted into an opening just at the upper rear of the bomber's cockpit.

Looking down from his cramped vantage point, the Master Sergeant could almost see the individual faces of the B-52's flight crew as the bomber closed within 200 feet.

"Come closer and elevate your nose slightly," he commanded calmly.

The two planes sped along one beneath the other at a speed of 275 miles per hour. All so gradually, the lower of the two aircraft began closing in.

"Okay," said Lou. "Now just a little bit closer and we've got it."

The nozzle of the boom was just about over the B-52's cockpit when the veteran operator noted a slight inconsistency in the bomber's closure rate. Startled by this sighting, he called out excitedly, "Hey, heads up down there! You're coming in too damn fast!"

What followed next took place with the ponderous pace of a nightmare. For the bomber's flight crew failed to heed his warning, and Lou looked on with disbelief as the boom pierced the B-52's longeron. As this taut metal spine fractured, the bomber began breaking up in mid-air, and a fiery spark shot up the tanker's refueling boom. Master Sergeant Lou Moretti had no time to cry out in horror as this spark ignited the 30,000 gallons of fuel stored in the KC-l35's tanks.

A blindingly bright flash lit the night sky, and in a blink of an eye, the Boeing Stratotanker was blown apart by a tremendous explosion. Lou Moretti and his crewmates never felt any pain, for their bodies were instantly vaporized, while the molten remains of their aircraft's fuselage and wings spiraled downward to be buried in the cool depths of the sea below.

The first hint that something was amiss was when the high-pitched wail of the bail-out alarm filled the bomb bay enclosure with its chilling sound. Captain Lawrence Stockton had little time to react as the plane around him violently shook and canted hard on its right side. Thrown off balance by the force of this unexpected roll, the pilot sensed that something was seriously wrong with his command. Seconds later, the plane rolled wildly in the opposite direction, and Lawrence Stockton found himself pinned to the roof of the compartment, the victim of the forces of gravity as the Stratofortress tumbled wildly from the skies.

It was sheer instinct and the will to survive that kept him from surrendering to his rising panic. Forcing himself to take deep even breaths, he scanned the now darkened compartment and failed to locate his crewmate. The last he had seen of the bombardier was as the Major completed his testing of the circuit boards, and still finding nothing wrong with them, was in the process of activating the device's trigger. This was only to be a temporary process, for he wanted to send a brief electrical charge through the circuit mechanism, and this was the easiest way to do so.

The pilot vainly reached out to stabilize himself when the cabin once more rotated and he fell sprawling to the deck below. He landed painfully on his side, next to the console. As he struggled to right himself, there was a loud popping noise followed by the deafening roar of rushing air. The temperature immediately dropped a good forty degrees and Stockton realized that the bomb bay doors had just been wrenched open. His pulse quickened, for now he had a way out of the crippled aircraft.

As always, he was wearing his parachute. Since there were no ejection seats in this portion of the plane, his only path to safety would be through the bomb bay doors. Yet the cabin was still spinning so wildly that it was a supreme effort for him just to get to his knees.

A momentary vision of his family flashed in his mind, and he began desperately crawling toward the twenty-foot-long opening. Inch by painful inch he moved his bruised body forward until he was able to peer into the enclosure. Looking down toward the four bombs, he could just see the open air beyond, through the struts of the rack mount. He was prepared to try crawling into the space that lay between the rack and bomb number one when the cabin spun upside down and he was once again sucked upward and pinned to the ceiling. Before he could cry out in frustration, another quick pitch of the cabin sent him spiraling back to the deck. He did his best to ignore the excruciating pain that coursed up his right arm as he crawled back to the bomb bay enclosure. Yet this time when he peered downward, he saw that the entire rack, including its lethal load of bombs, was no longer there. Only the spinning night sky greeted him as he wasted no time dropping into this welcome void.

Liam Lafferty had been in the process of pulling in his fishing lines when the night sky seemed momentarily to catch on fire. The blindingly bright flash originated high in the pitch black heavens, and for a few startling seconds it was as if the sun had miraculously dawned. Yet the intense, mysterious light was all too soon snuffed out as abruptly as it had arrived.

A muffled, explosive boom echoed in the distance, and the wizened fisherman scanned the sky in a vain effort to locate the source of this sound. His night vision temporarily lost by the unexpected flare-up, Liam felt his pupils take a full minute to readjust to the blackness. When they eventually did, he viewed a sky full of familiar twinkling stars and exhaled a long breath of relief.

His first concern had been that a sudden storm was on its way. Lightning could play curious tricks on the eyes, and he was certainly no stranger to the resonant blast that only thunder could produce. But a variety of phenomena were present that indicated that this was not the case. First of all, the heavens were still clear from horizon to horizon, meaning that there were no clouds belonging to an advancing storm front present in the area. And since the wind remained negligible and the seas calm, the veteran fisherman seriously doubted that a storm was responsible for the strange sighting.

Several years ago, Liam had seen a movie on the television at his local pub that told the story of the day when a giant comet hit the earth. Of course this was mere fiction, but he did know that such a thing could happen. Why, whenever that rare clear night presented itself, he never failed to sight dozens of shooting stars streaking through the heavens. He had once read that these were caused by meteorites. Usually formed from rock, these meteors became visible only when they fell through the earth's atmosphere, where friction burnt them up.

It seemed logical to Liam that a large meteor could have been responsible for the intense flare-up. Yet that still didn't account for the resounding explosion that followed it. To set his inquisitive mind at ease, he decided to ask Dr. Blackwater about it the next time he ran across the physician in town. The worldly doctor was extremely well read when it came to such matters, and would most likely be able to explain just what had caused the phenomenon.

Liam was all set to return his attention back to his lines when of all things it began to rain. This shower didn't consist of droplets of water, but was made up of thousands of pieces of what appeared to be shredded metal. Only lady fortune kept the veteran fisherman from being struck by this debris, which clattered down upon the deck and bombarded the surrounding waters.

Once more Liam's line of sight went to the heavens to find this shower's source. Yet the only thing unusual that he could view was a huge billowing object that floated down from the sky with a feathery lightness. This was certainly no meteorite, and Liam rushed to the pilot house to start up the engines. If luck was still with him, he'd be able to be there when this object came to rest in the sea. Then he'd make every effort to retrieve it. For he was absolutely certain that it alone held the secret to the great mystery that had befallen him this fated evening.

Chapter Three

It took Commander Brad Mackenzie twelve hours to get from the airfield on Kwajalein atoll to the U.S. Navy base at San Diego. The C5-A that had flown in the DSRV *Avalon* from Australia got him as far as Oahu. Here a P-3 Orion ferried him the rest of the way eastward to the mainland. Mac had less than fifteen minutes ground time in Hawaii. He used much of this time to call his wife and reassure her that he was safe. Marsha knew better than to ask where he had been or where he was going. As a veteran navy wife, she didn't even bother trying to find out the nature of his current duty. All she knew for certain was that he was involved in a marine salvage operation of some type that involved classified technology.

The Lockheed P-3 Orion touched down at Miramar Naval Air Station a little after noon California time. Mac slept during much of this flight, and upon their arrival at the terminal he had to be awakened by the plane's copilot. He felt a bit groggy as he climbed down onto the tarmac. There he was immediately met by a bright-eyed lieutenant jg assigned to the base public affairs office. With a minimum of conversation, the young officer escorted Mac to an awaiting automobile.

It was about a twenty-minute drive to the main naval facility. The weather was excellent, and as they crossed through La Jolla and entered Pacific Beach, Mac got a chance to see how much San Diego had grown since he had last lived there. New homes and businesses had gone up on almost every corner. And with this development came tens of thousands of additional automobiles that jammed the thoroughfares in a perpetual gridlock and tainted the once-clear beach air with noxious fumes.

As they proceeded on to the docks, Mac admired his escort's driving skills. Using a variety of side streets, he got Mac to the base with a minimum of stops. Under ordinary circumstances, Mac would have been very hesitant to take a lift with such a stranger. Yet the young public affairs officer quickly gained his confidence, and not once during the entire trip did he give Mac a real cause for alarm.

Once they passed through the main gate, they went straight to the pier area. It was in front of a sleek frigate that the automobile halted.

"This ship is the Knox Class frigate, USS *Fanning*," explained the lieutenant jg as he led the way outside. "Its commanding officer is Captain William Frawley. In fact, there's Captain Frawley right now."

The public affairs officer pointed to a tall black man dressed smartly in khakis and wearing a blue cap. The CO stood on the forward gangway addressing a group of seamen who were gathered on the pier before the bow mooring lines. Other sailors were visible on the deck of the ship, and Mac could tell from their frantic actions that they were getting ready to go to sea any moment now.

Mac's escort left him at the forward gangway. "Good luck, Sir. I hope that your mission is a successful one."

Mac accepted his salute and turned to board the ship. As he climbed onto the gangway, he was immediately intercepted by the vessel's CO.

"Commander Mackenzie?" quizzed the black officer.

"That's correct," returned Mac, who noted an intense

gleam in the CO's eyes.

"Good, we've been waiting for you. I'm Captain Frawley. Welcome aboard the USS *Fanning*."

Mac accepted the officer's firm handshake and followed him on board. They went straight to the bridge, where the CO initiated a flurry of orders. Mac stood in the corner behind the chart table and watched the Captain orchestrate their departure. From this vantage point, he could just see the ship's 5-inch gun and cannister-style ASROC launcher mounted on the tapered bow.

The *Fanning*'s single shaft, steam-powered propulsion system soon had them on the move. Still not certain of their mission, Mac bided his time until he would be briefed. He watched as Coronado Island passed to their port side. A dual-engine, propeller-driven Grumman E-2 Hawkeye was in the process of taking off from the air station, and Mac took in the airborne early-warning surveillance platform's distinctive, saucer-shaped radome as it roared overhead.

The Point Loma sub base was visible to starboard. During Mac's tenure in San Diego, he had been working at the Naval Ocean System's Command Laboratory, which adjoined the sub piers. He was no stranger to the variety of partially submerged vessels moored here.

He identified the single massive tender as being the USS *Dixon*. Moored alongside this support ship were four submarines. Mac could tell from their sizes that they were nuclear-powered attack subs belonging to several different classes. Since only their sails and the upper portion of their rounded hulls showed, the submarines looked far from intimidating. But Mac knew differently. For largely hidden beneath the water's surface was one of the deadliest warships that had ever put to sea.

The frigate he was currently on was primarily designed to track down such vessels. It did so with the assistance of a LAMPS 1 helicopter and a SQS-26 sonar array. As far as Mac was concerned, ships such as the *Fanning* were nothing but torpedo stoppers. If it ever came to a one-on-one engagement, his money would be with the submarine each and every time.

Mac was forced to reach out to the bulkhead to steady himself as the frigate rounded Point Loma and headed out into the open seas. Within a matter of minutes, the *Fanning*'s geared steam turbine was propelling them along at a speed of 25 knots. Their course was to the northwest, and as Mac was wondering just where their ultimate destination would be, the CO crossed the bridge and joined him beside the chart table.

"Sorry I had to abandon you like that, Commander," said the captain. "But my orders were to get us out to sea as soon as you were safely aboard this ship. Now, how much do you know about the reason for your presence here?"

"Not a hell of a lot," answered Mac. "As a marine salvage expert with NOSC, I expect it could be anything from a sunken vessel to an archeological find of some sort."

The captain looked his guest full in the eyes before lowering his voice and continuing. "Actually, it's neither. Admiral Long gave me the authority to give you the full rundown, so here goes.

"Approximately fifteen hours ago, our SOSUS array located beneath the waters off the north shore of San Clemente Island picked up the sound of an unidentified underwater intruder approaching from the west. A P-3 was scrambled from Miramar, and after sowing an extensive sonobuoy field, picked up the signature of what was believed to be a Soviet India class submarine."

The mention of this particular class of vessel caused Mac to interrupt. "Did you say India class, Captain? On what evidence did they base such a presumption?"

Prepared for just such a reaction, the CO directly re-

51

sponded. "As you know, the India class is rarely encountered in the open ocean, especially near our own coastline. Supposedly designed as an auxilliary salvage and rescue vessel, such a diesel-powered sub is characterized by a predominant humped casing that extends from the rear of the sail all the way back to the mid stern. This casing is lined with free-flood holes, and has two semi-recessed wells cut into its surface. A pair of mini-subs are believed to be carried in these wells. Since little is known about the propeller signature of these rarely seen craft, Command was able to identify it by the characteristic turbulence produced as seawater washed through these wells and free-flood holes."

For an entire year, Mac had been trying to accumulate as much knowledge as he could about this very same class of vessel. So far, his study had produced little of consequence. Yet now to have possibly tagged such a submarine right in their very own backyard was an astounding accomplishment, and Mac urged the captain to continue.

"Once it was positively identified as being an India, Command decided to discreetly follow its movements before moving in to intercept. A Spruance and a trio of frigates were called upon to do this job, and instructed to silently loiter off the coast of Catalina while the P-3 continued sowing sonobuoys in the bogey's path.

"Because of the nature of this submarine, Command believed that a Soviet attack sub could have gone down in this same area without our knowing it. Such a find would be the intelligence coup of the century, and we continued playing our cards most carefully.

"It was at about this same time that yet another SO-SUS array stationed off the southern tip of San Clemente triggered. The hydrophones of this array relayed the signature of a totally different type of submersible. This particular craft had no noticeable propeller wash, and seemed to be moving along the seafloor on mechanically-powered treads of some type."

This suprise revelation caused Mac to gasp in astonishment. Struggling to control his emotions, Mac fought to keep his voice from quivering as he asked, "And just where is this second bogey now, Captain?"

The C.O. sensed his guest's excitement, and answered while pointing to the chart spread out on the table before them. "We believe right here, off the southwest tip of San Clemente, only a few miles from where we originally tagged them. It looks like we really caught Ivan with his hands in the cookie jar this time, Commander. As you very well know, these are heavily restricted waters, where it just so happens we'll be testing the new ADCAP torpedo sometime next week."

"Such coincidences never cease to amaze me," reflected Mac facetiously. "Has Admiral Long mentioned how he'd like us to deal with this matter?"

The C.O. nodded. "He certainly has. In fact, we were just waiting for your arrival to get on with setting the trap.

"The *Fanning* will be proceeding directly to the waters off San Clemente's southern tip. As we arrive in this sector, our other ships will be closing in on the opposite end of the island. Their quarry is the India class vessel, while we drew the smaller, tracked submersible. Once we're in position, we'll attack concurrently, using whatever means necessary to get the trespassers topside."

"I doubt if they're going to just ascend and surrender, Captain," offered Mac.

"I hear you, Commander. We'll do our best to convince them that this course of action is in their best interest, short of blowing those Red bastards out of the water."

Mac was glad to hear this. He had come too far to merely sit back and watch the tracked submersible be blown apart for expedience sake. For one solid year he had been on the trail of this elusive vehicle, and he certainly wanted to have more than just a charred hunk of bent metal to show for his efforts.

The frigate's deck trembled under the force of a good-sized swell, and Mac reached out to the table to steady himself. Beside him the Captain did likewise.

"It's going to be another hour until we're in position, Commander. Why don't you go down to the wardroom and grab a cup of java and a sandwich. I'll make certain you're up here when the fun starts."

Though his physical concerns were far from his mind, the Captain's suggestion sounded good to Mac. A seaman was recruited to lead Mac below deck, and he willingly followed.

The *Fanning's* wardroom contained a small, comfortably furnished lounge. With a mug of black coffee in hand, Mac seated himself on a leather couch. Thankfully he was the only one present and thus had the perfect opportunity to put his jumbled thoughts in order.

Mac seriously doubted if the frigate's CO knew how vitally important this mission was for him. Twelve long months of frustrating, exhaustive work was about to come to fruition. When Admiral Long initially gave him this assignment, he never dreamed it would possess his time so. And now his hundreds of hours of hard work were at long last going to pay off.

It all started innocently enough, when the Swedish Navy came to them with the first photos of the tracks themselves. These shots were taken in the waters off the Swedish naval facility at Karlskrona. Mac was given the job of analyzing them, and he immediately came up with the theory that they were created by a Soviet-made mini-sub. Yet little was he prepared when similar subterranean tracks began popping up in such diverse places as Norfolk, Sicily, San Francisco, and Subic Bay.

Until very recently, all these sightings were merely passive ones. Yet this was to change when the warhead was reported missing from the waters off Kwajalein. There was no doubt in Mac's mind that the Soviets could have been behind such a clever machination. Their past behavior certainly showed that they had both the will and the audacity to pull such a thing off. Yet until the tracked submersible was perfected, they really never had the means to accomplish such an unparalleled mission.

Now that the submersible was operational, the Soviets were taking full advantage of its unique capabilities. Its presence off the coast of San Clemente was proof positive of this. It was common knowledge that weapons such as the Harpoon and Standard missiles had been initially tested here. To Mac's knowledge, the Soviets had never been able to steal one of these prototypes, that had since passed their trials and were now a major component of the Fleet.

The ADCAP torpedo was one of the newest weapons systems about to go into production. Designed to run at speeds topping that of the Soviet's quickest submarines, the ADCAP (for advanced capability) represented the West's latest high-tech success story. It incorporated unique state-of-the-art design elements that cost tens of millions of dollars in R and D.

If the Soviets were able to get their hands on such a prototype, not only could they produce one of their own at a fraction of the development costs, but they could learn how to counter it as well. A cheap decoy could be made that would be utilized to draw the torpedo away from the original target, and all America's effort would have been wasted.

An effective tracked submersible could have other uses as well. During times of crisis such a vessel could be used to cut transoceanic phone cables and disrupt the West's SOSUS arrays, those lines of high-tech hydrophones that America relied on to reveal the location of enemy submarines. It could also be utilized to land special forces teams, mine harbors, and attack ships even as they stood in port.

Mac was surprised that the U.S. didn't have a similar sub in development. It would be an invaluable platform to have during times of war. Of course, there were still many in the Pentagon who doubted that such a vessel even existed. To these pig-headed skeptics, the pictures and reports meant absolutely nothing. What they demanded was solid, concrete proof. This evidence was presently situated on the seabed only a couple of miles distant. And if all went well, soon Mac would have an actual working model to show to these doubtors.

It had taken an entire year for Mac to come this close to proving his theory once and for all. During this time, there were moments when even he doubted himself. Yet in these times of weakness, Admiral Long was always there to guide him back on track. Mac had known the kindly, silver-haired flag officer for less than two years now, but he already respected the man like a father. His suggestions were intuitive and timely, and he always made time in his busy schedule to return Mac's queries. The Admiral was also adept at using the system to effectively further their investigation.

When dealing with top secret matters such as this, they had to keep knowledge of their efforts contained within a small circle of "need-to-knows." Admiral Long was an expert at this, and helped develop a curt, enigmatic method of transmitting communications. Though he was often forced to read between the lines, Mac knew that this system worked, for knowledge of their project had yet to be leaked. This was all-important, for once the press knew of their activities, the Russians would also. A severe cut-back in the operation of their tracked submersible would surely follow, and then Mac's job would be all but impossible.

Mac finished off his coffee, and had time to polish off a turkey sandwich as well, when the seaman who had originally escorted him down to the wardroom arrived to take him back to the bridge. It was as he arrived back in the *Fanning*'s glassed-in control room that Mac saw the fog. Like a ghostly white shroud, the swirling mist completely enveloped the frigate. So thick was it that the bow-mounted ASROC launcher and 5-inch gun were no longer visible.

"When did we hit this soup?" asked Mac as he joined the captain at navigation.

"Another sunny California afternoon," mocked the CO. "We encountered the first bank about fifteen minutes ago. It's so thick up north that we had to pull the P-3. But don't worry, we're used to this infernal stuff. The operation's going to take place just as planned. The only difference is that we're going to have to use radar as our eyes."

"Captain, you never did mention how you're going to convince our bogey to surrender itself," said Mac. "If the crew is Spetsnaz, the only reasoning that they're going to listen to is a torpedo."

"You're most likely correct, Commander. Yet even Soviet special forces have been known to listen to the voice of reason. So we plan to first hit them with a series of active pings to let them know that they've been tagged. If that's not enough to scare 'em topside, we're going to drop some noise makers into the water. We'll put a wall of sound around them that will soon enough put the fear of Marx in them."

"And if that doesn't convince them?" dared Mac.

"Then it's time for the ultimate weapon," retorted the Captain. "When we got word of our mission, my weapons officer had just enough time to do some brainstorming and then make a quick, unauthorized trip to

57

the surface warfare supply warehouse. He came back with a device that's a tried and true red herring catcher. Sitting on our fantail as we speak is a series of nets. My boys have already sewn them together, and are presently stitching a line of lead weights around the edges."

Mac couldn't help but grin. "So you plan to snag them. You know, that might not be such a bad idea. In fact, I think it's rather ingenious."

"I'm glad you approve of our methods," returned the proud captain. "On a ship this size, we're often called upon to improvise, and the simplest darn things are often the most effective."

"Sir, we just got word from the *Kinkaid*," interrupted the quartermaster. "The *Spruance* and her escorts are in position to begin the intercept."

A look of relief crossed the CO's face as he spoke out to the eight members of the bridge crew. "Prepare for action, gentlemen. Lieutenant Simmons, you may instruct sonar to begin their active sweep of the seafloor. Make certain that they generate maximum volume. I want a ping out there that they can hear all the way back to Vladivostok. Lieutenant Jacquemin, have your men ready those noisemakers. If our sonar sweep doesn't stir 'em up, I'm counting on those explosives to do the job for us."

As his officers began carrying out these orders, the captain discreetly lowered his voice and addressed Mac. "Well, here it goes, Commander. Though I'm still not sure how you fit into all this, one way or the other you're soon enough going to see the exact nature of the vessel responsible for this operation."

"All that I ask is that you get them topside in one piece," returned Mac. "I've waited a long time for this day to come, and I sure wouldn't want to lose them right on our doorstep."

"You won't lose them if I have anything to say about

it," pledged the CO, who addressed his next remark to one of his subordinates. "Lieutenant Simmons, have sonar interface that scan over our p.a. system. I want to hear just what it sounds like to be the hunted at fifty fathoms."

This order was relayed, and less than fifteen seconds later, the bridge resounded with the loud, warbling "ping" of an active sonar projection.

"We've got a solid contact fifty-four fathoms beneath us, on bearing two-four-two. Relative rough range 8,700 yards," observed the quartermaster.

"That's our blessed bogey!" exclaimed the captain as he looked down at the plotting board. He used a red grease pencil and a straight edge to mark these coordinates on the plastic laminated chart.

"All stop!" he ordered the helmsman. "Is he responding, Mr. Simmons?"

The junior officer double-checked his sonar repeater and answered. "Negative, Captain. Contact appears to be hugging the bottom dead in the water."

Another deafening ping filled the bridge. Impatience filled the CO's tone as he barked out his next directive to the weapon's officer.

"Enough of this bs, Mr. Jacquemin. Drop those noise-makers. And put 'em right down their red throats!"

The lieutenant signaled his men to begin launching the pressure-triggered blasting caps from the stern. Soon the public address speakers filled with both the resonant sonar return and the sharp, staccato blasts of a flurry of popping explosions.

A satisfied gleam sparkled in the captain's dark eyes as he turned to face Mac. "I wonder what that racket sounds like from their vantage point? It's got to be pretty hairy, never knowing if the next blast they'll be hearing will be coming from a Mark 16. It wouldn't take much to blow that sucker to hell and back."

Mac looked on impassively as the quartermaster called out. "Contact remains dead in the water. Range now down to 4,800 yards."

"All ahead one third," ordered the captain. "Mr. Jacquemin, I hope that net your boys put together does a better job than those firecrackers of yours."

The weapon's officer wasted no time with his answer. "Just put us over the target, sir. I'll have 'em snagged and pulled in like a tuna in no time flat."

"We have a priority flash coming in from the *Kinkaid,* Captain!" cried the quartermaster. "They're currently dead in the water. They report hitting what appears to be a mine. The damage is limited to the bow sonar compartment, and damage control teams are currently down there making an assessment. Before losing sonar, they reported that their target was on the run at flank speed, headed on bearing one-two-zero."

"Damn it!" cursed the captain. "I'll bet my pension that they're hauling ass down the western face of the island to pick up their buddies in the mini-sub and hightail it back to borscht town. And what the hell is a mine doing in our own waters?"

As the answer to his own question suddenly registered in his mind, the captain barked out loudly. "All stop! Get a detail topside and have them keep their eyes peeled for anything suspicious that they see floating in the water."

"But the fog," countered the weapon's officer. "You can hardly see your own hand in front of your face out there."

"Damn the frigging fog!" shouted the captain. "And damn those Red bastards for having the nerve to lay a mine right in our own backyard."

Mac listened to this spirited exchange and felt a tenseness begin to form in the pit of his gut.

"Sonar reports that our contact is on the move.

They're picking up mechanical sounds on the seabed headed on bearing three-zero-zero."

The Captain looked on impassively, and Mac dared to vent his frustrations. "Are we going to just sit here and let them get away like this, captain? At the very least we can utilize that net to snag the minisub."

Mac's plea was met by a frantic shout of warning from the quartermaster. "Bow lookout reports suspected mine, twenty yards off our port beam!"

"Helmsman, reverse thrusters!" ordered the Captain firmly. "Mr. Jacquemin, get another detail topside on the double. We're sitting out here in a possible mine field and we need every spare hand available to eyeball us out of this damn dilemma."

"But the mini-sub," pleaded Mac. "We're so damn close."

With problems of a much more immediate nature to be concerned with, the captain addressed Mac directly. "Commander, the *Fanning* is going nowhere until I know for certain what's ahead of us. Now if you'd like me to take 'em out with a Mark 16, that's another story."

Mac was tempted to give the Captain the go-ahead, but reluctantly shook his head that such a drastic course of action wouldn't be necessary. For the tracked submersible meant nothing to him blown to bits on the seafloor. His mission was to capture one as intact as possible. Only then would his doubtors in the Pentagon believe that the threat was a real one and move to counteract it.

With his disappointed gaze centered on the swirling fog that continued to shroud the frigate's bow, Mac fought to center his thoughts. Time after time, Admiral Long had preached to him the value of patience, and now was the time to apply this wise advice. Though the Soviets might have won yet another round, Mac's luck was bound to change eventually. And when it did, one of the tracked submersibles would be his to triumphantly show to a world full of skeptics. Somewhere on the planet, the mysterious vessel would once again be sent on a mission. And next time, if the fates so willed it, Mac would be there waiting for it.

Chapter Four

Nowhere on the planet were winters harsher nor spring more welcome than in the Soviet Union. This was especially the case in the Rodina's Baltic region, where the arrival of the spring sun was met with all the joy and festivities of a new birth.

Admiral Igor Starobin felt like a young man once again as he walked along the rocky shoreline that bordered this portion of Korporski Bay. It was a glorious May morning. The sky was a powdery shade of blue, with a few fluffy white clouds gently blowing in from the south. The usually rough waters of the Gulf of Finland looked almost inviting as they stretched out to the western horizon in a glimmering expanse of deep green.

Though it wasn't even noon yet, the sun generated an alien warmth that had been absent for seven long, frigid months. This sunshine had already brought a little color to Igor's previously pale face. Its soothing radiance could also be felt deep in his arthritic joints, where the pain that had been a constant companion these last few weeks seemed to gradually lessen.

At sixty-four years of age, Igor Starobin had seen his better days long since pass. Not that he had much of a youth to speak of. What little he remembered of his earliest years took place alongside the waters of this same gulf, in nearby Estonia. Here on the banks of the Valge river, Igor was born and raised, the only son of a village blacksmith. He never remembered much about his parents. His mother died of tuberculosis when he was only seven, and what few memories that still remained were of a hard-working, hard-drinking father who was content to let his son run wild as the wind.

Igor abhorred his father's dank, sooty shop. He much preferred to spend his time outdoors, as near to the waters of the gulf as possible. As he grew into adolescence, he became an adept beachcomber, whose keen eye could pick out the smallest of treasures hidden amongst the flotsam that inevitably ended up on the shore. His finds included a chestful of raw silk, a pair of battered binoculars, and a blood-soaked life jacket that the authorities in town were particularly interested in.

It was while roaming the shoreline that he met a man who was to be instrumental in changing his life. Father Dmitri was an Orthodox priest who took an immediate liking to Igor. Though he certainly had never been a churchgoer, Igor was fascinated by the elder's tales of the world beyond Estonia, and he agreed to visit the priest at his monastery. Much to his father's surprise, Igor became a regular visitor to the monastery and eventually enrolled there as a fulltime student. By fourteen he could read and write. Yet whatever ambitions he may have had to continue on in the world of academics were forever put to rest by the invasion of the Nazis.

Forty-nine years ago, at the tender age of fifteen, Igor enlisted in the navy. Basic training took him to the fabled city of Leningrad. There he not only became strong in body, but strong in mind as well.

Igor grinned as he mentally recreated those exciting, innocent days that seemed to have occurred in another lifetime. How invigorating it had been to meet his first real comrades from such far off cities as Moscow, Kiev, Sverdlovsk, and Odessa! And how could he ever forget his first visits to the museums, libraries, and symphonic halls that made Leningrad the jewel of Russian culture?

As it turned out, he had all too little time to absorb these many wonders, as the first falling shells signaled that the German threat was a very real one.

It had been much too long since the veteran naval officer had pondered such memories. Affairs of state had kept his thoughts far removed from such fond imaginings, and he was grateful for this brief respite to the shoreline of his childhood.

A flock of ivory white seagulls swooped down from the blue heavens, and Igor watched the graceful birds as they soared only a few centimeters from the surface of the placid waters. Father Dmitri had always said that there was much to learn from the basic laws of nature. And the older Igor got, the truer this advice seemed to be.

City life had dulled his inner vision. For too many years, his duty had kept him locked behind walls of concrete, glass, and steel. Shuffling papers was no way for a man to live. Fresh air and a pastoral setting was a tonic that was as necessary as bread and water. Back in his Moscow-based office, he could picture the ringing telephones and scurrying aides as they rushed to fulfill yet another order of the day. Only last week, Igor had been one of these pathetic creatures.

It had originally been his wife's idea to escape the city. They usually used their seaside dacha only in summer. But when Igor began complaining of spells of dizziness and shortness of breath, Svetlana insisted that they leave Moscow earlier than planned.

Several projects that he had been working on were about to reach their conclusions, and Igor was tempted to postpone this visit. But fortunately Svetlana would hear no such nonsense. As Chief of Staff of Komsomol hospital, she was used to getting her way, and in this case, her diagnosis had been a correct one.

Igor hadn't felt this good in years. Since leaving the city his appetite had returned with a vengeance, and he was even starting to sleep through the night again. Their dacha was comfortable, and was located close enough to a village that they could walk to get supplies, but was far enough away from civilization to ensure seclusion. A recently installed telephone kept both of them in touch with their offices, and they made a mutual pledge to use it sparingly.

A gust of fresh air whipped in from the gulf, and Igor filled his lungs with its salty essence. Now that he was quickly approaching retirement age, his years of continued quality service to the Rodina were numbered. Of course, there was still one very special pet project that he wanted to see to its conclusion before he stepped down from his position of power. It had taken forty years to bring it to its current level of maturity and was already beginning to pay handsome dividends.

The meeting he had scheduled for this afternoon would bring his life's work one step closer to being fulfilled. That was why his Svetlana didn't dare intercede as he issued the invitations to the two men who would be responsible for getting the ruling Politboro's permission to implement the plan that he would soon present to them. If all went as planned, his visitors would be arriving shortly. Svetlana had agreed to prepare a special lunch for them, and afterward, he would make his presentation.

His one worry was how Stanislav Krasino would react to his carefully prepared briefing. The deputy secretary had never been a professional soldier and was known to be a bit soft on defense issues. His position as first assistant to the general secretary made him an all-important ally, and Igor would do his best to convince the bureaucrat of his plan's merits.

His other guest was a different story. Admiral of the Fleet Konstantin Markov was an old friend and co-worker. During the closing days of the Great War, he had been at Igor's side when they captured the German submarine construction facility at Keil, and knew well the great secret that it held. In the years that followed, Konstantin had been an invaluable supporter, always there to lend a helping hand when one of Igor's projects hit rough waters. As a member of the ruling Politboro, the Admiral of the Fleet was one of the most powerful men in the entire country, and he would certainly greet Igor's presentation with open arms.

Anxious to get on with the afternoon's activities, Igor took one last fond look at the surging waters of the gulf before turning around and beginning his way homeward. The path that he was following was little more than a goat track. Its narrow, earthen meander twisted through a series of massive boulders and crossed a sandy peninsula pitted with several tide-pools. A stand of stunted pines lay on the other side of this peninsula, and as he began crossing through them, his thoughts returned in time to the day he completed basic training and was sent home on a brief 24-hour pass.

Though he would have preferred to spend this time wandering the shores of his childhood playground, Igor remained in the village with his father. For the first time ever, they went out drinking together. The tavern keeper was an ex-navy man himself, and kept them occupied with breathtaking stories of his exploits in World War I. It wasn't until the wee hours of the morning that they drank their share of potato vodka and dizzily headed back for home. Igor had to leave early the next morning, and he remembered viewing the tears in his father's eyes as he kissed his son good-bye This emotional parting would be forever etched in Igor's mind, for it was the last time he would ever see his father alive. The muscular, close-lipped blacksmith was to die a hero's death soon afterward in a frozen foxhole, defending Moscow from the invading Nazi hordes.

With no other relatives to speak of, the navy was to become Igor's adopted family. He applied himself to his duty wholeheartedly, and soon gained a reputation as a dependable, hard-working sailor. It was while on convoy duty in the Norwegian Sea that he would see his first action. This came to pass when a German U-boat put a torpedo into the side of the cargo ship that Igor had been stationed on as a gunner's mate. The warhead exploded just at the water line, inside the main hold. Their cargo of Canadian wheat caught fire, and as the crew struggled to control the damage, Igor remained at his post even as the rest of the gun crew panicked and prematurely abandoned ship. It took a maximum effort on his part, but he succeeded in carrying up the shells from the magazine, loading them into the breach, and then sighting the cannon on the hull of the gloating U-boat. Unfortunately, all of his shots went errant, until the senior lieutenant saw his plight from the bridge and personally went down to assist him. The officer arrived just as the Germans were preparing to fire another torpedo salvo. He fine-tuned the sights on the sub's exposed conning tower and signaled Igor to fire away. Miraculously, the shell smacked into its target, and when the smoke cleared, the now crippled sub was seen limping off for safer waters. Igor received an Order of Lenin third class for his efforts. He also assured himself future advancement in the Soviet Navy.

By the war's conclusion, he was a full lieutenant assigned to a Spetsnaz squadron whose mission was to capture as much German naval equipment as possible. It was while serving with the special forces that he first met Konstantin Markov, who held the rank of captain third rank.

Markov was an educated, cosmopolitan man of the world who had been born and raised in the port city of Odessa. As the Spetsnaz prepared to move in on the outskirts of Kiel, Igor was temporarily assigned to Markov's unit. The two hit it off splendidly from the very beginning. For the city slicker, Igor was like a breath of

fresh air, while the worldly Markov represented everything that the young Estonian ever wanted to be.

They were at each other's side on the morning that
the Spetsnaz overran the defenses of Kiel's naval production facility. Together they burst into the cavernous warehouse on pier 13, and viewed the dozens of miniature
tracked submersibles that the Germans were preparing to
deploy in the Baltic and elsewhere. A frightened design
technician who had been hiding in an adjoining office
explained that this 35-ton amphibious midget was to be
powered by a 25-horsepower motor, giving it a submerged speed of 8 knots to a depth of 21 meters. It's
Caterpillar tracks were incorporated to simplify its
launch from special bases, while two torpedoes were to
be carried alongside them. It was Markov who asked the
cowering technician the name of this vessel.

"Seeteufel," he readily answered.

Igor's German was still poor, and he depended upon
his newfound friend to translate for him.

"They call it Sea Devil," said Konstantin. "What a fitting name for such a unique vessel."

Igor readily agreed, and spent the entire afternoon
crawling through the cramped interior of one of the just
completed prototype models. That evening, he shared his
initial impressions with Konstantin Markov. To the impressionable Estonian, such craft held the future of naval special operations. He envisioned vast fleets of Sea
Devils, complete with their crews of highly trained
Spetsnaz operatives, sneaking into enemy waters, cutting
through sub nets, laying mines and other ordinance, and
even clandestinely landing teams of commandoes. All
this would be carried out right in the enemy's own backyard, without him being any the wiser.

Konstantin listened intently, and agreed that the vessel
did have great potential. He promised to bring Sea Devil
to the attention of his uncle, who was the managing director of Sevastopol's Red Banner shipyards. True to his

word, after the conclusion of the war Konstantin did in fact tell his uncle about the tracked submersible. When he showed a genuine interest in his nephew's wartime discovery, Igor was given the job of transferring one of the appropriated vessels down to the Red Banner shipyards. Little did he ever realize it then, but this would only be the start of a relationship that was to last for over four decades.

The deep-throated cry of a boat whistle sounded in the distance, and Igor broke from his deep pondering and looked up into the clear, blue sky. The sun was not yet directly overhead, but just in case the noon ferry was early, the white-haired veteran decided to increase the pace of his hike.

The path took him through a thick forest of birch trees and led downward into a scrub-filled bog. He had to be extra cautious not to deviate from the trail on this part of the journey, for the swamp was rumored to contain quicksand that could swallow a man up quicker than a great white shark.

He was a bit winded by the time he successfully crossed the bog. His sedentary life-style was not conducive to physical conditioning. And besides, with Moscow's soot-laden air, it was healthier to catch a ride in a limo than walk anyway.

As he attained the summit of a small rise, Igor was thankful that he had given up smoking and had kept his weight in check. Other than his arthritis, his six-foot, two-inch frame was in pretty decent shape for one who had lived nearly six and a half decades. Having the services of a full time live-in physician helped, but so did the decent set of genes that he had inherited from his parents. While wondering if his mother and father would still be living if it wasn't for the ravages of war and pestilence, Igor wiped his forehead dry with a handkerchief.

Once again the distinctive cry of a boat whistle

sounded, but this time it seemed to be much closer. Ready to continue now, he descended into a thicket of stunted pines and climbed up a hill formed partially of coarse sand. From this vantage point he could clearly see the glimmering waters of Koporski Bay. His dacha was also visible, perched on a hill with the bay before it. The cottage was simply constructed of native timber and stone. It had a modern kitchen, indoor bath facilities, two bedrooms, a living room, and Igor's very favorite feature, a screened-in porch. Weather permitting, it was here that they would take their meals, watch the glorious sunsets form over the Gulf of Finland, and then linger long into the evening with the stars and the night wind for company. Since the sky still showed no signs of an advancing front, Igor planned to have today's meeting out on the porch as well. But his guests would never even find the place if he didn't hurry on down to the docks to greet them. He hurriedly began his way down the trail that would lead him to the pier.

He was concentrating totally on his stride and almost missed sighting the three distant figures on the trail leading up the opposite valley. This was the route from the village to his dacha, and Igor could just make out the tall, stately figure of his wife leading two men up the graded pathway. The tallest of these two individuals had a big, round-shouldered frame and wore the distinctive blue uniform of a Soviet naval officer. Behind him followed a thin gentleman in a gray business suit.

"Svetlana!" screamed Igor at the top of his lungs.

This cry echoed throughout the valley and soon had its desired effect when the trio halted and turned to scan the countryside for the sound. Igor wildly waved his hands to catch their attentions, and it seemed to be his wife who first spotted him. She waved in return and so did the portly naval officer, whom Igor knew to be his old friend, Admiral of the Fleet Konstantin Markov.

As they continued on toward the dacha, Igor crossed

71

the valley to eventually rejoin them at the cottage. He could walk at a more moderate pace now just knowing that his guests were in good hands. Once again, Svetlana had stepped in to save the day. They had been married for forty years now, and Igor doubted he'd ever be able to live without her. Regardless of her own hectic schedule, she never failed to keep a warm, cozy house. Her cooking skills were superb, and she was one of the most considerate people that he had ever met. He should have known that Svetlana would be down at the docks to greet his guests when he didn't show up at home earlier. He had just planned to go out on a sixty-minute hike. But that was well over three hours ago! Such was the price one paid when one detested wearing a watch, and was a consummate daydreamer.

A quarter of an hour later, Igor was in the process of striding up the stone walkway that led to his dacha's entrance, when the front door popped open and out walked Konstantin Markov. It was the Admiral of the Fleet who issued the first greeting.

"Well, just look what the tide has washed in. I'm glad that you could find the time to join us, comrade."

This last sentence was delivered with such a serious tone that Igor feared that his guest was genuinely upset with his tardiness. Yet when Konstantin's face lit up with a warm smile and he reached out with his arms spread wide, Igor knew otherwise.

"Igor, old friend, it's good to see you. When you didn't show at the pier, and Svetlana explained that you never returned from your morning hike, we were afraid that a bear had taken off with you. But I knew all the time that if it was a bear that was causing your delay, he'd find your hide much too tough for his likes and eventually let you go."

They met with a hug and a series of kisses to each cheek.

"Thanks for the concern, Konstantin, but I think that

you're right all the same. This old hide is getting a bit tough to make a decent meal of."

Igor playfully winked and both men let out a laugh. It was the Admiral of the Fleet who was the first to gain control of himself.

"Has it really been six months since I've seen that ugly face of yours? Where does the time fly to, old friend? Why, it seems that only yesterday we were waltzing through the streets of Berlin with a gorgeous fraulein on each arm and not a care in the whole world between us."

"Where in the world did we go wrong," returned Igor, who led his guest over to a small flower garden. Tulips could just be seen bursting from this plot as Igor continued. "So how did things go in Vladivostok, comrade?"

Konstantin shrugged his massive shoulders. "It's business as usual, what more can I say? I read the riot act to Admiral Petrov, who swore that he knew nothing about the inconsistencies that I spoke of. Yet as I was preparing to fly back to Moscow, I understand that the good admiral really laid it to his staff."

"You can bet that for the next couple of months all of them will be on their best behavior," offered Igor.

"Why of course," returned the Admiral of the Fleet. "That's what these surprise visits are all about. But we know that it's only human nature at work. The greedy ones will get hungry once more, and start stealing supplies just like before. And then it will be necessary for me to again cross the width of the Motherland to make an example of someone."

While kneeling down to get a closer look at the bursting tulips, Konstantin Markov added, "What we need, comrade, is a real war. That will soon enough get the attention of those shirkers in the fleet. This cold war that we seem to be eternally in the midst of is causing us to lose our edge and go soft."

73

"Who knows, perhaps that's what the Americans have planned all along," reflected Igor. "It's time for us to regain some momentum and readjust the world's balance of power."

The Admiral of the Fleet gently stroked the bright red petals of the largest of the tulips as he responded. "My sentiments exactly. I had hoped that the project that you are responsible for would do just that. As I said before, your retrieval of the American Trident II warhead from the waters off Kwajalein was absolutely brilliant work. Even the Premier's usually dour face lit up in a wide smile when he was briefed on the operation. As we speak now, the Imperialist's most sophisticated weapon's system is being dissected by our scientists, who will shortly be able to develop an effective decoy to counter this major component of their nuclear triad. But from what I read in yesterday's briefings, our quest for their ADCAP torpedo didn't go quite so smoothly."

A pained expression crossed Igor's face as he replied. "That it didn't, comrade. I had hoped that your visit here today would have an extra reason for celebration, but unfortunately that isn't the case. At least we didn't lose one of our units, and it appears that the security of our project is still intact as well."

"We were lucky all the same," returned the Admiral of the Fleet with a grunt. "I just wish that we didn't have to resort to laying those mines. The American Spruance class destroyer took a hit right on its bow. Though the casualties were minimal, the imperialists are angry as hell, and rightfully so."

"They still have no positive proof that we were the culprits," offered Igor. "The mines were unmarked, and if they are indeed able to trace them, it will be found that they originated in China."

Konstantin Markov stood up and shook his head. "The Premier's quite upset, nonetheless. From what I gather from Deputy Secretary Krasino, he wanted it to be made absolutely clear that he never again wants to be placed in such a potentially embarrassing situation."

"Our business does have its risks, Konstantin."

The Admiral of the Fleet compassionately patted his host on his back. "You don't have to tell me that, comrade. These foolish young bureaucrats that we're forced to work with don't know what it's like to fight in a real war. And what they refuse to understand is that our struggle against the forces of capitalism is just that. For there can be no compromise in the struggle for the triumph of world communism."

Igor's spirits seemed to lighten. "Well said, old friend. Our esteemed Deputy Secretary inside wouldn't happen to share your outlook, would he now?"

Konstantin Markov looked at Igor as if he hadn't heard him correctly. "Come now, you know better than that. Stanislav Krasino is still on the side of the moderates, just like he's always been. Yet of all those who sit on the Politboro, I believe he's the one that we'll have the best chance of reaching. So tell me, Igor, how have your powers of persuasion been lately?"

"Shall we go in and find out?" offered Igor with a grin.

"I've been waiting for some time now to find out what's been going on in that head of yours," confided the Admiral of the Fleet as he followed his host to the entryway. "After that Trident scheme, I don't know what to expect from you next."

"That mission was only a warm-up," said Igor as he opened the door for his guest. "The one I'm about to propose is going to go down as the greatest clandestine Spetsnaz mission of all time!"

The two naval officers entered the dacha, and Igor briefly scanned the living room.

"I'll bet Svetlana is charming the Deputy Secretary on the patio. Follow me, Konstantin. It's the cottage's best feature."

Igor led the way down a hallway lined with framed landscape prints. They passed by the kitchen, which directly adjoined a large, airy room that offered a magnificent panorama of the waters of the gulf. The screened-in patio was tastefully decorated with rattan furniture. Seated in two of the chairs were the dacha's hostess and Deputy Secretary Stanislav Krasino.

Quick to realize that they had company, Svetlana Starobin looked up to greet the two newcomers. "So you finally made it back after all, husband."

Igor meekly walked over to her side and gave his wife a kiss on the cheek. "I'm sorry, my dearest. As always time has a way of escaping me whenever I take one of my seaside strolls." Turning to address the bespectacled, fuzzy-haired bureaucrat who sat beside her, Igor added, "And I apologize to you also, Comrade Krasino."

The two men shook hands while the Deputy Secretary responded. "There's no need for apologies, Admiral Starobin. Your wife has been the perfect hostess. Why, I never realized that she was the Chief of Staff of Komsomol hospital. My own cousin is a resident there, and she speaks most highly of the organization."

Svetlana caught her husband's eye. "You remember Dr. Olav, don't you, dear? She's the cardiologist who gave you the stress test."

"Of course I do," returned Igor. "She was a most competent physician, and if I remember correctly, a real looker too."

Svetlana gave her husband a disgusted look and stood. "If you'll excuse me, I'll go to the kitchen and bring in the lunch. I hope all of you are hungry."

"I happen to be famished," retorted Igor, who devilishly grinned as his wife exited the porch.

"That one's a gem," he added, as he beckoned the Admiral of the Fleet to have a seat.

Konstantin Markov sat down in the chair vacated by Svetlana. With his gaze locked on the glistening waters visible in the distance, he thoughtfully observed, "You mentioned that the view was superb from this room, but I had no idea how incredible it really was. I bet on a clear day you can almost see the coast of Finland from this vantage point."

"I saw it only this morning," boasted Igor. "Although I must admit that I had a little help with my telescope."

Deputy Secretary Krasino adjusted the fit of his glasses and politely commented. "This is my first visit to this portion of the Rodina, and I must admit that I'm quite impressed. I was expecting nothing but swampy marshland here."

"We have plenty of that too, Comrade," answered Igor. "But as you can see on the adjoining shoreline plenty of seagrass, pines, and birch trees also."

"From what I understand, your czar and founder of the Russian navy Peter the Great was no stranger to Koporski Bay," reflected the Admiral of the Fleet. "I once read in one of his diaries that he kept a small sailboat stored in these parts, and liked to get off here alone whenever the pressures in St. Petersburg got too intense."

Igor seemed surprised at this. "I didn't know that, Konstantin. I wonder where he kept this boat, and where he stayed during his visits. You must show me this diary next time we get together."

"I'd be glad to, Igor. I have a copy right in my own library and would love to share it with you. Our beloved Peter was quite a fellow. Even I've been able to learn a little more about naval tactics by reading his memoirs. That one was years before his time."

"And thank goodness for that," replied Igor. "Otherwise there's no telling how long Russia would have kept its doors closed to Europe and the rest of the world."

Deputy Secretary Krasino was all set to convey his opinion when Svetlana arrived with a tray of food. The bespectacled bureaucrat immediately stood to help her with this platter heaped with all sorts of appetizing delicacies.

"Why thank you, Comrade Krasino," said Svetlana, who readily accepted her guest's gracious assistance. "Could you please set it down on the coffee table?"

"Of course, Comrade Doctor," answered the bureaucrat.

Noting that she had the full attention of her husband and his visitors, she hurriedly addressed them. "I know it's not much, but it should serve to tide you over until dinner. There's smoked salmon, herring with sour cream and onions, fresh tongue, black bread, and some cheese blini that I cooked myself."

"I can personally vouch for the blini," interceded Igor, as he hungrily eyed the platter. "They're as sweet and delicate as a loving wife's heart."

Svetlana couldn't help but smile at this remark. "The plates are right there, so don't be shy. Go ahead and dig in."

As the Admiral of the Fleet and the Deputy Secretary each reached forward to grab one of the bone china plates, Svetlana addressed a question to her husband.

"Shall I serve the tea now or with dessert?"

Igor lowered his voice and winked. "Wait until later, dear wife. And perhaps we'll have something to celebrate, and imbibe a beverage of a bit more substance."

"I've already got the champagne on ice, husband. Good luck to you, and don't eat too many blini."

With this, she left them. Igor joined his guests and loaded up a plateful of food. While the Admiral of the Fleet munched away on a blini, and the Deputy Secretary bit into a tongue sandwich, Igor went to work on a helping of herring.

"My, these blini are tasty," said Konstantin Markov as he spooned up another helping.

Igor nodded. "Svetlana got the recipe from her mother. She says that's how she won my heart."

"You're a lucky man, Igor," reflected Konstantin between bites of the tender sour-cream-filled pancake.

"I'll say," concurred Stanislav Krasino. "Not only is the Comrade Doctor an excellent hostess, but from what I hear from my cousin, an excellent administrator as well."

"I don't know what I did to deserve such a woman," Igor said with a sigh.

The Admiral of the Fleet slyly grinned. "It's your sparkling personality that won her, Igor. Back at naval headquarters, they say that you can charm the wallet right out of a capitalist's pocket."

"And their latest missile warhead right out from under their noses," added the Deputy Secretary. "At the Kremlin they're still talking about your operation in the South Pacific. Even the Premier still boasts of your unprecedented success in stealing the Trident II prototype."

Igor grunted. "Too bad that I couldn't have followed it up with yet another treasure, this time an ADCAP torpedo plucked from the waters off Southern California. But such are the fortunes of war."

The Deputy Secretary put down his sandwich and locked his gaze on his host. "I was alongside the Premier when word of our failure reached the Kremlin. Soon afterward, the American ambassador called. He hinted that we were to blame for the seven sailors who died when their Spruance class destroyer hit that mine. He also mentioned that 25 others were hospitalized with serious cuts, bruises, and burns. Thank the fates that the ship didn't sink altogether. Yet this still puts us in an awkward position, just as we were undermining the NATO coalition by gaining the trust of its members."

"Why is that?" asked Igor. "The imperialists still have no proof that we were the ones responsible."

The Deputy Secretary shook his head. "But what about the sound tapes that the American ambassador mentioned? They supposedly hold the signatures of two of our submarines that had been caught in U.S. waters just when the blast occurred."

"These tapes don't mean a damn thing!" exclaimed Igor.

"Admiral Starobin is correct," added Konstantin Markov. "Even if these tapes were released to the public, who has the ability to analyze them properly? And even then, all we have to do is firmly deny the allegations."

The Deputy Secretary frowned. "It doesn't look good all the same, comrades. Merely inferring that we were involved in this tragedy will produce new doubts in the minds of the NATO ministers. What worries the Premier is that these misgivings come just as NATO is about to vote on whether or not to remove all of the American short-range nuclear weapons from European soil."

Igor briefly caught the glance of his fellow naval compatriot before looking the bureaucrat in the eye and voicing himself. "In your esteemed opinion, Comrade Krasino, do you feel that the Premier would be receptive to a plan that would irrevocably sway NATO opinion back to our side?"

"Most definitely, Admiral Starobin," answered the Deputy Secretary. "The Premier's number one foreign policy priority remains convincing NATO that their American warheads are no longer necessary."

Igor's green eyes sparkled with the same intensity as the waters of the gulf behind him. "If that's the case, comrade, all I'm asking is that you temporarily put our little set back in the waters off California out of your mind, and that you listen to the following proposal."

"If it will indeed help us regain the trust of our European neighbors, I'm all ears," offered the bespectacled bureaucrat.

Igor put down his plate, stood, and initiated his discourse while pacing before the screened-in porch. "Regardless of what recently occurred in the waters off San Clemente, one thing that is absolutely certain is that Sea

Devil has proven its effectiveness time after time. No other underwater platform in the world can equal it when it comes down to stealth, accessibility, and the broad extent of its operational capabilities.

"What I propose is to use Sea Devil to strike a blow against America's most important strategic base in all of Europe, it's submarine facility at Holy Loch, Scotland. With a minimum of risk on our part, we can close this complex, that's capable of servicing both nuclear-powered guided missile and attack submarines for all time to come. As a bonus, our efforts will effectively cause the closure of the British sub base at nearby Falsane also.

"The scenario that I'm proposing is chillingly simple. Sea Devil will be covertly conveyed to Scottish waters in the hold of a specially designed trawler. With a crack Spetsnaz team on board, the mini-sub will be launched and then penetrate the Firth of Clyde, where it will continue on to Holy Loch. Our latest intelligence reports indicate that except for the standard security precautions such as underwater hydrophone arrays and surface ASW patrols, the American base is poorly defended. We've seen this same naiveté when it comes to security matters in most of their naval facilities around the world, and Sea Devil will easily run this pathetic gauntlet of defenses and proceed to its goal, an American nuclear-powered submarine. This unsuspecting vessel will be at anchor as we approach it with a team of divers.

"The task of this team will be to place a shaped-charge explosive device on the hull of the submarine, just below its reactor compartment. They will then return to Sea Devil, where the charge will be detonated. The massive force of the resulting explosion will rip open the American sub's hull and cause its reactor vessel to plummet into the depths below. Laboratory tests show that there's a ninety-seven percent probability that the reactor will melt down at this point, causing plutonium fuel pellets to be directly spewn on the sea-floor. And in such a way, an ecological disaster of unprecedented dimensions will poison the Scottish waters for decades to come.

"An enraged populace will rush to Parliament to express their outrage. Their fellow citizens will unite behind them as they demand that the rest of the submarines be removed and the base closed. In this same manner, the English facility at Falsane will also be forced to shut down operations, and the West will have lost two of its most strategic ports in all the globe, all for the price of a single, shaped-charge explosive."

"Why, that plan's absolutely ingenious!" interrupted the Admiral of the Fleet. "As we learned during the Chernobyl accident, nothing scares the Europeans more than the threat of nuclear contamination. They'll be horrified when they hear of the meltdown. Their scientists will release various studies of gloom and doom, and all over Europe the peace groups will have a field day."

"Can you imagine what the NATO ministers will have to say as they meet in Brussels to discuss this disaster?" asked Igor, his face red with emotion. "Not only will they vote to remove every single American nuclear warhead from European soil, but they'll most likely demand the removal of all of their troops as well."

"Of course they will," concurred Konstantin Markov. "Uncle Sam will be finished on the Continent, and as NATO withers away, the Warsaw Bloc will gratefully move in to fill the void.

"Igor, my friend, you've outdone yourself this time. Though I'd still like to learn more of the details, I certainly don't have any major apprehensions. What about you, Comrade Krasino?"

The bureaucrat's impassive expression failed to display any outward show of support as he sucked in a deep breath and guardedly responded. "In all my years of service to the Motherland, I must admit that this is the wildest proposals I've ever heard. I readily agree that if this operation is successful, the results will be much as you projected. But I foresee two major weaknesses in your train of thought. First, and most important of all, if a Sea Devil couldn't even penetrate the meager defenses around California's San Clemente island, how are we going to be able to successfully sneak one into some of the most militarily sensitive waters in all the planet? And secondly, even if this penetration does somehow succeed, what kind of shaped-charge can penetrate the hull of a submarine, and how can the desired after-effects be guaranteed?"

Igor carefully listened to the bureaucrat's concerns and briefly caught Konstantin Markov's glance before attempting a response. "Your questions are most astute, Comrade Krasino, and I will do my best to answer them. The Sea Devil that was apparently detected off the coast of California had a long history of mechanical difficulties. We believe that it was a defective engine bearing that gave it away to the American hydrophones. The vessel in question is currently being conveyed back to Vladivostok where a detailed examination will determine this fact for certain. But regardless, let me reassure you that in over one hundred previous operations, not once has a Sea Devil been tagged by enemy ASW forces. This leads me to believe that the penetration that I just proposed can readily be achieved by a Sea Devil in first class working order.

"Your other concerns are completely unnecessary. The charge that I spoke of has been available to us for some time now. It is based on a shaped-plastic compound that's been known to easily penetrate the armor plating of a battle tank. Unlike our own double and triple-hulled vessels, the thrifty Americans utilize only a single hull on each of their various classes of submarine. It should be no problem for our intelligence people to determine the exact location of the reactor vessel. We have ordinance and design experts who will then determine the precise locations to set the charges in order to achieve the desired hull damage."

The Deputy Secretary nodded thoughtfully. "And what if the Sea Devil was to be discovered in the midst of this operation?"

Igor was quick with his answer. "If such an unlikely thing were to come to pass, the crew would first attempt to escape. If all routes are subsequently proven closed to them, the vessel will be scuttled, while the Spetsnaz operatives swallow the suicide pills that will guarantee their anonymity. As always, every effort will be made to ensure that the motherland can't be connected to any of the wreckage that may be subsequently salvaged."

"It sounds as if you have thought this plan out most fully, Admiral," offered the Deputy Secretary. "Though covert missions of this magnitude certainly have their risk, it appears that the Rodina has much more to gain than it has to lose in this instance. I too would like to see the pertinent details that the Admiral of the Fleet requested. Yet other than a few technical concerns, I see nothing that would prevent me from supporting such an ingenious plan. My congratulations, Admiral Starobin, on a job well done."

Hardly believing what he was hearing, Igor fought the temptation to cry out in triumph. The Admiral of the Fleet was also caught off guard by the bureaucrat's ready acquiescence. Still shocked by the scope of his compatriot's plan, Konstantin Markov loudly cleared his throat and voiced himself.

"All this discussion has made my throat dry. If only I had something to wet it with."

Taking this as the hint that it was meant to be, Igor called out towards the kitchen. "Svetlana, to hell with that tea, bring out the champagne!"

His wife was well prepared for such a command, and arrived on the porch seconds later with a tray holding a bottle of champagne and four crystal glasses.

84

Igor briefly examined the label of the bottle before twisting off the foil and expertly popping the cork. His hand was shaking slightly as he filled each glass.

Both Konstantin Markov and Stanislav Krasino stood to join their host and hostess in a toast.

"To the Motherland!" said Igor proudly. "Long may she prosper!"

The four clinked glasses and took a sip of their drinks.

"My, that's quite excellent," commented the Admiral of the Fleet as he smacked his lips together. "Is it French?"

"Comrade Markov, I'm surprised at you," scolded Svetlana Starobin. "Don't you think that the Rodina is capable of distilling spirits as good as the French?"

"What my wife's trying to say is that this superb vintage was bottled in our own Ukraine."

"You don't say," mumbled the Admiral of the Fleet, who looked down to check the label on the bottle. Satisfied with what he saw, he raised his glass upward and initiated a toast of his own.

"To the brave men and women of the Rodina, whose sacrifice makes this bountiful harvest possible!"

Again the foursome lifted their glasses to their mouths. No sooner did Igor refill them than Deputy Secretary Krasino offered a proposal.

"And I'd like to drink to the true heroes of the Motherland, the brave men and women of our military, whose selfless toil and extraordinary vision ensures our security today and guarantees the eventual emergence of one planet united by the bonds of communism tomorrow."

"Well said, Comrade," offered the Admiral of the Fleet as he lifted up his glass to salute the originator of these inspirational words. Yet as Konstantin Markov took a sip of his champagne, a sudden thought dawned in his consciousness. He looked to his host and expressed himself.

"Excuse my forgetfulness, Igor, but in all the excitement, I failed to ask you one important question. Have you yet picked out an officer who's capable of carrying out the type of difficult mission that you just proposed to us?"

Admiral Igor Starobin's eyes sparkled as he answered. "Why, of course I have, Comrade. Who else is more qualified that Captain Mikhail Gregorievich Borisov, who just so happens to be out there somewhere beneath the Baltic Sea at this very moment, displaying the type of death-defying bravado that has earned him the nickname of Lion of the Spetsnaz !"

Chapter Five

Sean Lafferty arrived in Edinburgh on a cold, rainy, windswept afternoon. He was met at the Waverly train station by Patrick Callaghan. Both men were in their late twenties, with similar slight, wiry builds, fair complexions, and mops of longish, straight brown hair. Dressed in jeans, athletic shoes, and waterproof jackets as they were, one would have had a difficult time telling them apart from the locals. Yet it was their Irish accents that indicated that these two were definitely not native Scotsmen.

"Good afternoon to you, Sean," greeted Patrick Callaghan, who had been waiting beside the tracks as the Brit Rail train pulled in from Glasgow. "How was your trip?"

Sean Lafferty shouldered his green backpack and followed his fellow countryman out of the station. "I'm lucky I even got here. There was a real gale blowing in Dundalk as we took off, and it was a miracle that my pilot was able to get us airborne."

"For one who despises flying, that must have been a real terror," reflected Patrick as he led them past the taxi queue, up the cobblestone ramp, and onto Waverly Street.

There was a steady rain falling, and neither one of them carried an umbrella. Yet this didn't deter them from joining the line of sodden foot traffic that was headed uphill toward that section of the city known as Old Town.

It was as they crossed Cockburn Street that Sean looked to his right and first viewed Edinburgh Castle in the distance. The massive walled fortress was perched on a four-hundred-foot-high rounded mountain of basaltic rock that afforded it a commanding view of the city on all sides. A Union Jack could be seen fluttering in the wind from one of the tower flagpoles, and Sean contemptuously spat into the gutter.

"Ah, there she is all right," commented Patrick, who was quick to note his countryman's preoccupation. "That structure has stood there in one form or another for over a thousand years, and in that entire time has only been taken by force but a handful of times."

"I can certainly see why," returned Sean. "That mountain of rock that its set upon would have made an effective siege all but impossible. And even if an enemy managed to scale it, those walls that encircle the castle appear impenetrable."

"That they are, Sean. I took a tour of the fortress just yesterday and was surprised to find the walls in incredibly decent shape for their age."

Sean Lafferty pulled up the collar of his jacket and redirected his gaze to the line of ancient brick buildings that were perched on the street before them.

"How much further to the flat, Patrick?"

"We've only got a couple of more blocks to go, Sean. The place is off of High Street. It's not much, but the price was right and the landlord didn't ask many questions. Ironically enough, we're directly behind the building housing the law courts and the constable's headquarters."

"Why, I feel safer already," mocked Sean, who beckoned his escort to lead on.

A steep flight of stairs took them up to the so-called

Royal Mile. This portion of the city was once the focus of daily life in old Edinburgh, and was made up of a variety of antique structures, many of which had stood here since the fifteenth century. As they reached High Street, they passed the gothic edifice of St. Giles Cathedral. When his escort divulged that the church had originally been built in 1385 A.D., Sean shook his head in wonder, for this was just like seeing a living piece from the history books.

A narrow alleyway took them to their flat, which was located on the third floor of a building constructed a mere two hundred years ago. The apartment had only a single room, half of which was filled by a stove, refrigerator, and a round wooden table with two rickety chairs. Several dirty plates and a variety of soiled silverware sat on this table, alongside an assortment of empty food tins and beer bottles. The rest of the flat contained nothing but a disheveled mattress that lay on the scuffed wooden floor beside a sootfilled fireplace.

While Sean removed his backpack and shook the rain from his jacket, Patrick hurried over to get the fire going. Quite happy to finally be out of the raw elements, Sean carefully scanned the room's interior. An astounded look crossed his face as he noted a large poster tacked to one of the walls. It showed a lush green, sheep-filled meadow. A meandering brook cut through this peaceful, pastoral setting, while an arched estate home could be seen on the summit of a nearby hillside.

"Where in the world did you get this incredible poster of Cootehill House?" asked Sean.

Patrick held back his answer until the pile of kindling and dried sod that he had been working on was fully ablaze. "Marie gave it to me when I left. She found it in a Dublin tourist shop."

Patrick stood, walked over to his friend's side, and

added. "Whenever I get homesick, I sit down in front of this poster and imagine that I'm back in County Caven once again."

"Two months is a long time to be away from home, isn't it, Patrick?"

"That it is, my friend. But as long as my memories are still with me, I can manage. Besides, I still strongly believe in the job that I've been sent here to accomplish."

"And it's a good thing for the cause that you do," said Sean, who turned his glance away from the poster to directly meet the gaze of his associate. "Bernard, the Doctor, and the rest of the members of the Brotherhood wanted me to convey their greetings. Marie sends along her love and apologizes for not sending along some of her infamous oatmeal cookies with me. I'm afraid the only bad news that I have to deliver is that Eamonn O'Neill was picked up by the Brits two days ago. He was crossing the border on his way to Armagh when they nabbed him. The last we heard, he was being held in solitary confinement at Long Kesh."

Patrick Callaghan heavily sighed. "That's too bad, Sean. Of all the lads, Eamonn was always one of my favorites."

"Mine too," added Sean. "But he knew the risks. It's not his first visit to the Maze Prison, and it most probably won't be his last. Rumor has it that it was the SAS who picked him up. They've been staking out the border ever since our successful raid on the armory at Newry. If the damned Brits only knew that Eamonn was the one who originally conceived that strike, they'd probably strip the skin right off his body."

"I understand that we made quite a haul in Newry, Sean."

"You don't know the half of it, my friend. We came home with over one-hundred M-16 rifles, a half dozen

90

Browning M-60 machine guns, and a 90mm M-67 recoilless rifle. We also pulled out several dozen .45-caliber pistols and plenty of ammo."

"No wonder they called back the SAS," reflected Patrick. "With a haul like that, when's the blooming war going to start?"

Sean grinned. "We're close, my friend, so very close. The Brits just announced a new round of price increases in the North, and both Catholic and Protestants alike are hopping mad. Unemployment continues to soar, especially in the Catholic slums of Belfast and Derry. It's especially prevalent among the young, who aren't being given any job training to speak of, and have nothing to look forward to but a life of depravation and poverty on the dole.

"To vent their frustrations, they've been showing an increased interest in the Republican movement. IRA recruitment is at an all-time high. Yet the IRA is still as ineffective as ever. They've been continually unable to produce a dynamic leader, and their goals remain unclear, their policy uncoordinated. Increasingly, the Brotherhood has been stepping in to fill this void. Our ranks have also never been as full of able volunteers as they are right now. The lads who join us don't have to worry about petty political squabbles amongst their leaders and unclear policy goals. For our philosophy has remained basically the same since the IRB's founding."

"You know Sean, since I've been living here in the U.K. I'm as sure as ever before that the Brotherhood's philosophy is the only one that will ever be able to produce a unified Ireland. The English system thrives on class discrimination. They depend on their military and their pathetic monarchy to keep the people content and in line. The only thing that they really fear is a force stronger than their own. That's why we're really going to have to hurt them to gain both their attention and their respect."

Thoughtfully nodding head to this, Sean slowly walked over to the flat's sole window. From this vantage point he could just view the upper ramparts of Edinburgh castle through the rain and soot-stained glass.

"And we happen to know just where to hit them to cause the most pain, don't we, Patrick?"

As his countryman joined him at the window, Sean continued. "The Brotherhood has given me the final go-ahead for our operation. Has anything occurred since your last report that would necessitate a change of plan?"

Patrick shook his head. "As of yesterday, I see no reason why we shouldn't proceed as planned. Your work permit has cleared, and my supervisor is expecting you on the site tomorrow morning."

Sean rubbed his hands together expectantly. "Did you have any luck with our armaments?"

"Though our contact here never came through with the H&K assault weapon that he had promised us, he did manage to appropriate a fairly new M-1 carbine and three clips of ammo. It's currently hidden at the site inside an air compressor alongside the blasting caps."

"Excellent, Patrick. Were you able to find us a decent hiding place?"

"The best that I could do is inside the cistern that we're presently excavating. It's a bit smelly, but that should insure that the guards will stay far away from us when they make their evening rounds. And speaking of guards, a new detail arrived only yesterday. They're the 75th Highlanders. They go way back to Waterloo and beyond, and have a tradition of valor on the battlefield to live up to. Their recent arrival at the castle is to our advantage, since for all effective purposes, they'll still be settling in when we strike."

"And the jewels?" continued Sean.

"As of yesterday, they were nestled inside the crown room as they have been for the last century," replied Patrick. "During the day, the depository is left open for the benefit of sightseers. The regalia proper consists of a crown, a scepter, and a sword of state. All are crafted of pure gold and are adorned with hundreds of diamonds, rubies, and pearls. This collection has been valued for insurance purposes as exceeding three million pounds. But as we very well know, their real value can't be counted in money. For tradition says that whoever possesses the regalia has the right to claim the throne of Scotland."

"The throne of Scotland, you say? Well I don't know if we'll go that far, Patrick Callaghan. But I will tell you this, that once the Brotherhood gets hold of this regalia, it's going to take a queen to get them back. What an interesting trade it's going to make, the crown of Scotland for six impoverished counties in Northern Ireland. Why, it's history itself that we'll be making here starting tomorrow, my friend!"

Patrick anxiously looked to his watch. "We're due at the site at 6:00 A.M. sharp. Since you've had a full day already, I thought it best if we ate an early supper and turned in soon afterward. If you'd like, there's a pub right down the street that serves a decent shepherd's pie."

"What's the beer like?" quizzed his countryman.

Patrick grinned. "It's certainly not a Guinness, but I don't think it will poison you."

"That would be a hell of a way to go," returned Sean Lafferty as he put one hand on his comrade's shoulder, and beckoned with the other for Patrick to lead the way.

* * *

Though thick, gray storm clouds completely veiled the western horizon, the kilted piper emerged onto the ramparts precisely at the moment of sunset. Oblivious to the cold blowing rain, the Highlander put the reed of his ancient instrument to his lips and began playing a mournful march, whose origin was almost as old as the cobblestone that his shiny, silver-buckled shoes were treading upon. Down in the castle's enclosed compound, the notes of this dirge merged with those of the constantly howling wind, and the resulting sound was almost ghostly.

Major Colin Stewart was one of those who heard this ethereal symphony. The rugged six-foot, two-inch career officer from Stirling sprinted across the rain-soaked courtyard and gratefully ducked into the main headquarters building. Taking a second to wipe his feet on the doormat and shake the water from his red beret, he proceeded up the stone stairway in bounding strides. The forty-three-year-old commando was hardly winded as he climbed up two whole flights and turned to begin his way down a well-lit corridor. It was before a door marked *Communications — Authorized Entry Only* that he halted. He needed to insert a heavy plastic key card into a metal slot for this door to open with a loud click.

An attractive young woman dressed in the olive green drabs of an Army corporal greeted him from a desklike console. "Sorry to call you away from dinner, Major, but this dispatch just arrived for you from Northwood. It seems to be from the First Sea Lord."

"The First Sea Lord?" he asked as he grabbed the sealed envelope and tore it open. An indecipherable code met his eyes, and he excused himself for his office, which was located on the floor below.

With the assistance of a code book, he translated the

"for your eyes only" message that told of the crash of an American B-52 aircraft off the eastern coast of Ireland. This plane's cargo included four thermonuclear bombs whose recovery was presently the Admiralty's number one priority.

"What a bloody mess," mumbled Colin Stewart to himself.

Only yesterday, his regiment had arrived from a six-week deployment on the Isle of Man, which was smack in the middle of the Irish Sea, and in the same general vicinity that the B-52 had apparently gone down in. He could just imagine the frenzied activity currently taking place on the island as the recovery effort was coordinated. This was one project that Colin would have loved to have gotten involved with, and he cursed his rotten luck.

For the next six weeks his crack regiment would be confined within the thick walls of Edinburgh Castle. There were many who looked forward to such easy duty, that was primarily ceremonial. But Major Colin Stewart was not one of them. The former SAS commando craved action and adventure. He was happiest during operations such as the Falkland's War, when he was able to load live rounds into his weapons and lead his men into battle.

His one regret was that he hadn't been born thirty years earlier. Then he could have participated in the greatest world conflict of all times. As a child, he had read everything that he could get his hands on regarding World War II. He had an uncle who had served with Montgomery in Africa, who thrilled him with tale after wondrous tale about the hunt for Rommel, the elusive Nazi Desert Fox. His own father had served in the South Pacific, and though he was taken prisoner by the Japanese in the conflict's opening days, could tell some spine-tingling war stories of his own when in the mood.

Today the army had little to do but participate in one boring exercise after another. The majority of these were so ill-conceived that they didn't have the least bit to do with real combat scenarios. They were carried out just for the benefit of the generals, and to give the taxpayer the illusion that he was getting his money's worth.

Colin was of the strong opinion that soldiers need actual combat if they were going to keep their edge sharp. Otherwise, they were little more than unarmed policemen waiting for a crime that could very well never even happen.

Their current duty was a prime example of just such a waste. For the next month and a half they would be stationed at the castle, where their primary responsibility would be to act as a security detail. Yet surely this could just as easily be done by a group of "rent-a-cops." Other than a few overvalued jewels and several dusty war museums, there wasn't much inside the castle to warrant a regiment of Scotland's best. But unfortunately every unit in the country was required to make the obligatory yearly stop in Edinburgh, where tourists would gawk at them and ask their ridiculous questions.

Knowing full well that there was nothing he could do to change the situation, Colin dropped the coded dispatch into his shredder. Then, with crisp strides, he returned to the mess hall to finish his dinner.

Sean Lafferty slept soundly beside the fireplace, wrapped inside the folds of the sleeping bag that he had brought along from Dublin. It proved to be his roommate who awakened him. The flat was dark, cold, and unfamiliar, yet Patrick made him feel right at home with a cup of hot tea. By the time Sean finished his toilet, the sky was just brightening with the first colors of dawn.

They went off to work on foot. The miserable weather of the previous day had passed. The sky was a clear blue, the air crisp and cool, as they proceeded down High Street and began the long climb up to the castle.

Patrick had originally gotten the construction job three weeks after arriving in Edinburgh. It fit his needs perfectly, for the company had just signed a contract to initiate a series of renovations on the castle grounds. He started as a simple laborer and soon enough demonstrated his ability to operate a variety of heavy machinery. He was able to get Sean a job with this same outfit when he learned that they were looking for a man experienced with explosives. Though they would have preferred a local, Sean's résumé was the only one to fit their needs.

Ever thankful for his time spent as an explosives handler during the construction of a new Guinness brewery, Sean anxiously anticipated the days work to come. The castle loomed larger than it had appeared from below as they entered it by way of the main guardhouse. Two uniformed, rifle toting soldiers alertly challenged them here. Patrick calmly pulled out his work permit and Sean did likewise. A quick call to the construction foreman verified their identities, and the soldiers politely stepped aside and allowed them to enter.

They began their way up a sloping brick roadway and crossed beneath an arched structure that Patrick identified as being the Portcullis Gate, built in 1577. They briefly halted to catch their breaths beside the Argyle Battery, which was added on in 1750 and contained a display of muzzle-loading cannon of this same period.

"Well, what do you think Sean?" quizzed Patrick as he scanned one portion of the awakening city of Edinburgh visible four hundred feet below.

His associate was busy studying the layout of the ramparts behind the battery as he responded. "I'll tell you what I think, my friend. Unless those sentries have some bullets in their pockets, this job is going to be easier than I ever dreamed. Those H&K assault rifles that they were carrying didn't even have any clips in them."

Still engrossed in the spectacular view of the city, Patrick shook his head. "Aw Sean, you always were the practical one."

"Thank goodness someone around here is," added Sean as he walked over to join his associate. He followed Patrick's line of sight and patted his co-worker on the back. "It truly is a magnificent sight, Patrick. This city just reeks of history. Now, what do you say to us going and making some of our own?"

Patrick answered his friend's wink with a nod, and turned to lead them further up into the castle's interior. They passed by a gift shop and an infirmary that had a fairly modern artillery piece set up beside it.

"That cannon still looks operational," observed Sean.

"You'll hear for yourself at one P.M. when it's fired. They say folks all over the city set their watches by it."

"No one ever said that the Scots weren't practical people," offered Sean.

Their route now curved upward, and they passed through a compound dominated by a fairly modern barracks. A group of enlisted men stiffly stood at attention outside this structure, in the process of being inspected by a tall, muscular officer in a red beret.

Yet another ramp took them past a small chapel that Patrick mentioned was one of the oldest surviving parts of the fortress, built in the eleventh century. It was beside this simple building that a series of construction barriers were set up. A corrugated steel trailer was placed beside the wall here, with various heavy equipment parked nearby.

"This is the place," said Patrick who led the way inside.

The interior of the trailer smelled of cigar smoke and fresh coffee. It was filled with several vacant drafting tables and a single cluttered desk. Seated here was a portly individual sporting a full red beard, with thick eyebrows to match. He didn't bother to stand as he spoke out with a deep, booming bass voice.

"Good morning, Patrick. And this must be your cousin, Mr. Lafferty. Welcome to Edinburgh, lad. I'm the foreman here, Angus Ross."

Sean accepted a viselike handshake and watched as his new boss lit up a half-smoked cigar.

"I understand from both your résumé and your cousin that you're pretty handy with explosives, Mr. Lafferty. That may indeed be the case, but around here it's caution that rules the day. You may have noticed that not only are we working inside a military base, but a national monument as well. Thus we certainly don't want to cause any unnecessary damage or have any needless accidents. So to ensure this, the charges that you'll be handling will be just powerful enough to get the job done. Do I make myself clear, lad?"

"Why of course you do, sir. And please call me Sean. When we were excavating the extension of the Guinness brewery in downtown Dublin, we had to take similar precautions. And I'm proud to say that while I was in charge there wasn't a single injury or report of external damage."

"That's just what I wanted to hear, lad. If you can work as well as your cousin here, you won't be hearing any complaints from me. Patrick, why don't you show Sean the location of the new cistern and the portion of the old system that we'll be wanting to reroute."

As Patrick led them outside, Sean slyly grinned. "So we're cousins, are we? Funny, but I never saw any family resemblance between us."

"I only make that up to make you more credible," admitted Patrick. "Besides, do you honestly think that I'd publically admit to having you for relative if I didn't have to?"

"Watch it, Callaghan," advised Sean playfully. "Or I'll leave you in that empty vault after I've removed all those royal jewels."

The day went unbelievably quick. The good weather held, and they were actually able to accomplish quite a bit of work before the foreman blew the whistle signaling the end of the shift. It was Patrick who informed him that they were willing to work overtime for regular pay, as long as the light remained. Not about to pass up such a bargain, Angus Ross gave him his blessings, and instructed them to sign themselves out before the guards locked them in for the night.

They worked for an entire hour on their own and recorded their quitting time in the official work log. Yet instead of leaving the castle at this point, they returned to the cistern and crawled inside its narrow, wire-mesh mouth to hide themselves. The interior reservoir was formed of brick and was utilized to store rainwater. It had long since been drained dry, but it still smelled musty, much like an old basement.

Sean and Patrick positioned themselves on a brick ledge to await nightfall. This lip was just wide enough to allow them to sit down. Sean was especially thankful for this perch, since he hadn't worked this hard in months and his back and muscles were sore from the physical effort involved.

To keep from being detected, they kept absolutely quiet. They passed the time by staring off into the black reservoir and breathing its cold, damp air. It was as this blackness seemed to intensify that the shrill distinctive notes of a bagpipe sounded in the distance. Well aware that this traditional salute meant that the sun had set and the castle was now sealed for the night, Patrick stood and beckoned his associate to do likewise. A narrow, recessed set of footholds led them to the cistern's mouth. It was Patrick who cautiously peeked through the wire-mesh screen, and finding the compound clear, furtively crawled out onto the cobblestone courtyard.

With the piper's soulful tune providing an appropriate accompaniment, the two Irishmen took in the rich colors of twilight. A crescent moon could be seen hanging on the western horizon, with the evening star already visible above it. Except for the constantly blinking, battery-powered strobe lights that were mounted on top of the construction barriers, the compound was dark, thus allowing them safe access to the generator where the tools of their other trade were stored.

It was Patrick who removed the generator's metal cover plate and pulled out an elongated wooden crate. Inside this container were an M-1 carbine, three loaded clips of ammunition, and a compact green satchel. A smirk painted Sean Lafferty's face as he gingerly picked up the satchel and checked its contents. Satisfied with what he saw, Sean watched as his associate expertly slid a clip into the M-1, snapped a bullet into its chamber, activated the safety, and looked up to meet his expectant glance.

"We haven't far to go now, Sean. We'll get to the crown room by following along the back wall of the Scottish national war memorial. That will bring us to the Half Moon battery, which adjoins the entrance to the palace yard. We'll be able to get into the royal apartments by way of Queen Mary's room. We did some renovations in there last week, and I made certain to unlock the iron security grate that covers the window. That will put us immediately outside the crown room itself."

"And that's where I'll take over," whispered Sean as he patted the green satchel he held securely at his side.

Patrick managed a nervous smile. "Then, for the cause of one united People's Republic of Ireland, let's do it, comrade."

Sean flashed him a thumbs-up, and Patrick proceeded to once more sweep the compound with his glance. The twilight had all but faded by now, and the sound of bagpipes was absent as the two sprinted across the courtyard and disappeared into the shadows beyond.

"Are you telling me, Sergeant Major, that no one actually saw these two workmen leave the castle?" quizzed Major Colin Stewart, incredulous.

"That I am, sir," replied the regiment's ranking non-commissioned officer.

"Then for all we know, they could still be inside, couldn't they now?" continued Colin Stewart angrily.

The sergeant major appeared uncomfortable as he answered. "I imagine that's very possible, sir."

"That's just wonderful," reflected the major as he pushed his chair back from the dinner table and threw his napkin on his half-full plate. "And wouldn't you know that they just happen to be named Lafferty and Callaghan. Get together a squad, Sergeant Major. I'll lead the search personally."

"Shall I alert the garrison?" asked the red-cheeked NCO.

Colin Stewart stood. "I don't think that's necessary, Sergeant Major. Most likely our sentries merely missed checking off their names as they left the grounds. But just in case, I want you to call the construction foreman and find out all you can about the pair. Also have Mr. Ross give you their local address and a phone number if they have one."

"I'll do so at once, sir."

"Have that squad meet me up at the war memorial on the double, Sergeant Major. And I want each one of them carrying live rounds."

"Yes sir!" shot back the NCO. His back arched straight and his heels clicked together as his commanding officer crisply pivoted to get on with his anticipated duty.

The window allowed them entry into the royal apartments, just as Patrick Callaghan had planned it. The room they soon found themselves had a high ceiling and was decorated in period furniture. It was Patrick who explained its history.

"This apartment once belonged to Queen Mary. It was here that she bore the future King James VI in 1566."

"Are you sure there's no internal security?" Sean asked.

Patrick shook his head. "Absolutely. I worked alongside the electrician who was responsible for pulling out the old alarms and installing a new state-of-the-art system. It won't be completed for another month yet. Meanwhile, we've got nothing to worry about."

"I wouldn't exactly go that far, Patrick," observed Sean, who noticed a portrait of a particularly ugly woman hanging over the fireplace. "I bet this hag over here is Queen Mary herself. One thing that hasn't changed over the years—the English monarchy is just as ugly as ever."

Patrick managed a strained grin and pointed to the door. "It's not much further now, Sean. Follow me."

The door opened with a rusty groan and led to a dark hallway. The wooden-slat floor creaked beneath them as they tiptoed down this corridor and began their way down a flight of stairs. They faced a wall dominated by an enormous stainless-steel door-length vault. Its door was securely sealed, and Sean intently studied its hinges and tumbler-style lock.

"You were right, Patrick, it is a bank vault. I imagine that this too is going to be replaced eventually, because it's certainly seen better days."

"Can you open it?" his associate asked.

"Now what kind of question is that? Of course I can do it. Just give me a minute to get the charges in place, and I'll have us in there in no time flat."

Without wasting another second, Sean opened the green satchel and delicately laid its contents on the floor. He paid particular attention to the white puttylike substance, which he carefully rolled into a half-dozen, golf-ball-sized pellets. He then placed one of these on each of the vault's four jambs, and two over each of its hinges. After connecting them together with a piece of electrical wire, he expertly attached the wire to a compact detonator.

"That should do it, Patrick. I'll give us a minute to get clear before she explodes. And then the Crown of Scotland is ours!"

Major Colin Stewart and his four-man squad were in the process of inspecting the castle's great hall when a thunderous explosion broke the inanimate quiet. The intricate wooden rafters of the hall shook in response to this blast, and the major cried out at the top of his lungs.

"Everyone out into the courtyard! It sounds as if those mick bastards are going for the crown jewels!"

This supposition was given substance as the Highlanders ran outside and viewed the cloud of smoke that was still rising from the roof of the nearby royal apartments.

"Come on, lads!" cried the Major. "For the glory of Scotland, we've got our country's honor to uphold!"

This frenzied shout stirred the souls of the young soldiers who sprinted across the courtyard at breakneck speed. It was Colin Stewart who led the charge into the royal apartments and up the stairway to the crown room. The smoke was still heavy as he spotted the jagged hole in the wall where the vault door had once stood. It was then he heard the sickening sound of breaking glass, and without any thought of his personal safety, he burst into the room where the regalia was stored.

The angry blast of a carbine greeted him as he dived to the ground to dodge the oncoming bullets. Again the crack of glass breaking stirred him into action. He rolled to his left, and using the base of a display case for cover, dared to squat upright. This afforded him the barest glimpse of a long-haired young man reaching into the case that held the crown jewels. Instinct took over as Colin Stewart raised the barrel of his rifle and let loose a burst of 7.62-mm hollow-point bullets. His Heckler and Koch was set on full automatic, and in a matter of seconds twenty-five empty shells littered the floor beside him.

He was in the process of jamming in yet another clip when the members of his squad opened up with their own weapons. Bullets whined overhead, and he was forced to hug the ground to keep from getting hit by the dozens of ricocheting rounds. It seemed to take an eternity for this barrage to cease. The air was thick with the scent of cordite as Colin Stewart cried out.

"Hold your fire, lads!"

Conscious that nothing could have lived through that hail of bullets, he again squatted upright and peeked over the display case. It was when he spotted the blood-soaked wall beyond that he stood fully.

A single bullet-ridden body lay on the floor, covered by broken glass and splinters of wood and plaster. The deceased appeared to be in his mid-twenties and had long brown hair and a fair complexion. He wore blue jeans and a nylon windbreaker. With little time to mourn this stranger's passing, Colin Stewart kicked aside the M-1 carbine that lay at his side and turned to check the integrity of the royal regalia. He breathed a sigh of relief: although the glass of the outer display case had been smashed, the three-inch-thick plexiglass inner case remained intact.

The jeweled crown, sword, and scepter took on a radically new meaning as Colin recognized them for what they were, the symbolic equivalent of the seat of Scottish government. His heart swelled with pride. He found himself feeling ashamed for downgrading his assignment here, when an excited voice cried out behind him.

"Major, it looks like the other one's getting away through Queen Mary's apartment!"

Having completely forgotten that they had been searching for two men, Colin Stewart cursed and went running for the doorway. He reached the queen's room and found his men huddled around the open window.

"I tell you, I saw him climbing over the ramparts of the Half Moon battery," pleaded one of the soldiers.

"Then get after him, lads!" ordered Colin Stewart, who just then heard the distant whining alarm that indicated the rest of the garrison would now be available to join in on the manhunt.

As his men began scrambling out the window, the major sighed heavily. His arm and shoulder hurt where he went smacking into the floor of the crown room. Somehow he had managed to bruise his forehead. But that still didn't account for the puddle of sticky blood that he found staining the ledge of the windowsill. It suddenly dawned on him that if this didn't originate from one of his own men, then at the very least they had been able to injure their quarry. With this hope in mind, the forty-two-year-old veteran agilely climbed out the window to join in on the hunt himself.

Chapter Six

The Pentagon was built as the world's largest office building. Situated on the banks of the Potomac River across from Washington, D.C., the colossal structure housed over 30,000 employees. It was not one building, but about fifty, all interconnected, that formed five complete pentagons placed one inside the other in a series of concentric five-sided rings over two blocks wide. The outermost and largest ring was known as the E-ring. Offices here were the only ones with an outside view and were for the most part reserved for such distinguished personages as the Secretary of Defense, the Secretaries of the various services, the Chairman of the Joint Chiefs of Staff, and the other chiefs. Admiral Allen Long was genuinely flattered when he was offered an office in this coveted part of the building.

From his current vantage point, as he peered out the window behind his desk, he could just make out the rounded dome of the Capitol in the distance. It was mid-morning, and the quick moving storm front that had made his early commute such a nightmare had since passed, leaving a brilliant blue sky in its place. On the banks of the Potomac the trees were green with freshly budded leaves, while tulips and daffodils colored the grassy slopes with spring color.

Allen Long would have much rather preferred to play golf on a glorious morning such as this, but his current workload wouldn't allow it. Lately he had even resorted to taking work home, and the light in his study often burned late into the night.

His wife Nancy argued that the pressures of his job were too much for a man his age. But Allen Long would hear of no such nonsense. He had spent over four decades of his life in the U.S. Navy, and he wasn't going to retire until they tied and bound him, as they had to his old friend Hyman Rickover.

As with Rickover, Allen Long's specialty was submarine development. He had been one of the original project managers of the Trident program and was currently involved with R&D on a new class of nuclear-powered attack submarines that would hopefully go into production soon. Because of his many years of experience with such matters, the navy was using him to act as their main liason with Congress. This was a thankless, often frustrating position. Most of the time he felt more like an accountant than a naval officer as he worked on a seemingly endless collection of appropriations requests.

In an era of monetary constraint and budget deficits, Allen Long was responsible for explaining to the various congressional committees the necessity of each new request for funds. Since much of the technology involved was highly classified, he had to walk a thin line between those with a legitimate need to know and those without. Often it was his decision alone that allowed a senator or congressman detailed information on a project that only a handful of Americans were aware of. Admiral Long took his difficult job most seriously, and often spent many a sleepless night worrying about the consequences of a poor decision.

In addition to his work with Congress, he also oversaw several pet projects with the office of Naval Research and the Naval Ocean Systems Command. His area of special interest was mainly in the field of ROVs, or remotely operated vehicles. Most of these were unmanned submersibles that could reach depths much greater than any manned vessel could. Usually controlled from a mother ship by means of a fiber-optic cable, such ROVs showed great promise, especially in the fields of ASW, oceanographic research, and marine salvage.

It was hoped that the new class of attack sub the navy desired would be able to operate such vehicles. Since this ability would be unique to this class of vessel, the technology involved was expensive. It was up to Allen Long to present a case to Congress detailing the necessity of such equipment.

He would be meeting with the chairman of the Senate Committee on Armed Services in the morning, and was preparing a detailed report on ROVs to present to him. As it turned out, such technology was about to play an important part in a tragedy that had recently befallen the United States off the coast of Ireland. This disaster came to pass when a B-52 Stratofortress collided with a KC-135 tanker during a routine refueling operation. The B-52 had been carrying four nuclear weapons in its bomb bay. All of these devices were believed to have fallen into the sea. The navy was already moving in a variety of ROVs to facilitate the search for these, and he was certain they would soon enough show their worth. Admiral Long was going to make it a point to divulge this information during tomorrow morning's meeting in the Senate office building.

To ensure that he got a detailed, accurate report on the effectiveness of the ROVs as they were deployed in the Irish Sea, the admiral decided to call in one of his experts. Commander Brad Mackenzie, or Mac, as he preferred to be called, was one of the brightest, most loyal junior officers he had ever worked with. Mac's current billet was as a troubleshooter with NOSC, and the admiral had little difficulty convincing the Naval Ocean Systems Command to reassign him temporarily. As Admiral Long's eyes and ears at the crash site, Mac would provide him with almost instantaneous updates on the recovery effort. He would then be able to utilize this information to further convince Congress that the ROV program was well worth the money that would be needed to continue its growth and development.

Mac was still unaware of the reassignment. As Admiral Long checked his watch, he saw that the plane carrying Mac was supposed to have landed at Andrews Air Force base over a half hour ago. He would thus be arriving at the Pentagon any moment now, at which time his new duties would be explained to him.

In a way, the Admiral wasn't looking forward to breaking this news. Mac had been intricately involved with another project for almost a year now. Recently this assignment had taken him to several locations throughout the Pacific basin on the trail of a mysterious submersible that was believed to be Soviet in origin. This elusive vessel supposedly operated on Caterpillar-like treads that guided it over the seafloor. These tracks had been found in such diverse locations as the waters off Karlskrona, Sweden, Sicily, San Francisco, the Marshall Islands, and southern California. In each of these instances, they were located near sensitive military installations.

When a Trident II warhead launched from Vandenberg was lost beneath the waters of Kwajalein Atoll and a DSRV searching for it came across a puzzling set of tracks, Admiral Long recommended that Mac be sent out to identify them positively. At the same time, a hydrophone anchored beneath the seas of the Navy's San Clemente test range picked up the unusual signature of a mini-sub that appeared to be propelled by some sort

111

of tracked drive system. Suspecting that this could be the culprit responsible for the theft of the Trident II warhead, the admiral had Mac sent to southern California. A combination of bad luck and a mysterious mine field kept Mac from participating in the capture of this vessel. Seven American sailors died in that incident, and Mac swore to apply all his efforts in finding the ones responsible. Unfortunately his trail was leading him nowhere, and rather than watch him be eaten up by frustration, the admiral decided to reassign him. Besides which, Mac was the best man available for the all-important job at hand in the Irish Sea.

Allen Long came to the conclusion that a radical change of assignment was just what Brad Mackenzie needed. Though he hated to have to pull him away from his family in Hawaii, Mac was a career officer who had long ago learned either to adjust to such absences or to find a new line of work.

Surely Mac would understand the utter priority of this new assignment. The suspected Soviet mini-sub would probably be around long after the missing bombs were recovered. Mac would have a chance to help his country by assisting in the recovery of these weapons. Then he'd be able to go back to work tracking down his nemesis, this time with a clear and open mind to guide him. Certain Mac would see it his way, the admiral found his thoughts interrupted by the shrill ring of his intercom.

"Yes, bowman," he barked into the transmitter.

"Sir," his secretary reported, "it's Admiral Connors returning your call from Holy Loch, Scotland."

"Excellent," returned Long as he picked up the red telephone handset and activated the secure line.

"Bart, Al Long here. Thanks for getting back to me so quickly. Listen, I understand how crazed you are over there right now with the recovery operation and all, so if you don't mind, I'd like to send someone over the pond to give you a hand. He's a marine salvage expert, Commander Brad Mackenzie, who helped write the book on ROV's . . . yeah, the same one . . . I thought you could use him . . . sure, I'll put him on the next flight. . . . You too, Bart. Stay healthy, and good luck with your mission."

Allen Long hung up and turned his gaze back to the Potomac. He had set the wheels in motion. Now he only needed Mac to arrive so that he could explain to him his new destiny.

The lights of Dundalk harbor were getting increasingly brighter, and Liam Lafferty knew that his long, arduous voyage was finally about to come to an end. For two long days and a night he had been drifting helplessly, the victim of a malfunctioning engine carburetor. Since he had no radio to call for help with, the grizzled fisherman was forced to do the mechanical work himself. Thankful for his time spent at his cousin's garage when he was a lad, Liam had to practically tear down the greasy carburetor and rebuild it, to get the device operating. By the grace of God, his persistent efforts paid off, and with the ancient engine puttering away like its old self, he gratefully turned the wheel toward home.

One stroke of luck was the excellent weather that continued to prevail. His greatest fear was that a gale would strike while the boat was dead in the water. These seas were notorious for such storms, and rarely did two solid days of fair weather pass in a row.

If a storm arrived, he planned to rig a sea anchor and attempt to ride it out. He would also have had to empty out the hold, to make the boat as light as possible. This would have meant returning to the sea the massive elongated cannister he had recently plucked from the waters. Since Liam worked for nearly six hours dragging this weighty object on board, he didn't look favorably upon the idea of having to abandon it so quickly. Besides, he wanted to carry it back to Dundalk and have it properly identified. And then who knew what would follow? For if his suspicions were correct, he'd soon be collecting a fat reward for hauling the charred cannister back to land.

It had apparently floated down from the heavens on a parachute soon after the night sky had lit up like day and the resonant explosion had sounded. Though Liam never saw the cannister hit the water, he arrived in time to find it bobbing on the surface, barely supported by a ring of compressed air floats. Its parachute was still wrapped around it, and it would surely have sunk if Liam hadn't been there to intervene.

With the same block and tackle that he'd used to lift his largest fish-filled nets, Liam brought it on board with the assistance of a straining winch. To keep it from rolling around, he secured it inside the hold. This left him with little room for any additional fish. But the mysterious object would certainly gain him a reward of some sort, and his profit was all but assured.

Liam's initial guess was that it was a piece of a satellite that had exploded in the earth's atmosphere. Most likely it belonged to either the United States of America or the Soviet Union. It didn't matter much to Liam though. Both countries were rich, and would pay him well for returning their property.

With visions of large stacks of cash dancing before his eyes, Liam finished securing his newfound treasure and went to start up the engines for the trip home. They sputtered alive, but only operated for a few fleeting seconds before unceremoniously shutting down on their own. Liam sensed trouble, and sure enough found

114

the engine impossible to restart. After a series of angry curses, he rolled up his sleeves and crawled down into the engine room.

For the better part of two days he worked in this greasy, cramped compartment. He broke only for an occasional meal of salted fish or the briefest of naps. There were several occasions, though, when he rushed topside upon hearing the sound of what he thought was an approaching vessel. But in each instance, the clatter proved to be coming from a grouping of helicopters that must have been in the midst of maneuvers in the area. Since they never got close enough for him to flag them down, Liam could only crawl back to the engine room to get on with his toils.

It was during dusk of the second day that his tireless efforts paid off. The engine coughed alive, and after a brief cry of joy, Liam turned the bow toward the flickering lights of Dunany Point.

Though he wore no watch, he knew it was long after midnight. It had been his father who had taught him how to read the time by checking the location of the stars in the ever-shifting evening sky. Doubting that there'd be anyone down at the main docks in Dundalk to greet him at this hour, Liam decided to tie up at the leisure pier in Dunany. This would put him within walking distance of home. Then after a bath, a nap, and one of his wife's delicious meals, he'd move the boat back into Dundalk and get on with the process of collecting his reward. With this plan settled, he anxiously set a course for the bright white beacon that shone from the Dunany lighthouse.

Liam reached his goal without incident, and after securing the hold with a padlock, climbed off his boat and began the walk homeward. Solid land felt good beneath his feet. His hike took him up a sloping earthen path. Several times he had to momentarily halt to catch his breath. Only a few years ago he could make this climb without stopping to break his stride, and he was well aware of one of the handicaps of his advanced age. Yet he wisely paced himself, and after a period of hiking would halt, wipe his brow, allow his heaving lungs to settle, and only then continue.

He felt a sense of accomplishment upon attaining the summit. Confident that he still had some life left in his old bones after all, the fisherman scanned the darkened bluff. He could just make out the twisted trunks of the grouping of ancient oaks that gripped the rocky soil here, and the outline of several ramshackle cottages that were interspersed among these trees. Strangely enough, the lights nearest to the bluff's edge were still illuminated.

"I wonder what in heaven is keeping Annie up at such an ungodly hour?" he mumbled to the gentle wind.

Guessing that she had either gotten carried away with her knitting or fallen asleep reading, Liam headed for the cottage to find out.

The first inkling he had that something was seriously wrong was when he spotted the blood-soaked doorknob. His pulse quickened in alarm as he noted that there were also drops of blood on the mat.

"Annie!" he screamed as he pushed open the door.

He immediately spotted his wife kneeling beside the couch. Laid out before her with his shirt off was the unconscious body of their son, Sean.

"My heavens, Annie! What in God's name has happened here?"

His wife answered while staunching the flow of blood from Sean's right shoulder. "He stumbled in here about a half hour ago. It appears he's been shot."

"Shot, you say?"

"That's what this wound indicates."

"But who in the world would shoot Sean? I always thought he didn't have an enemy in the world."

Almost in answer to his father's question, Sean began mumbling incoherently. "Patrick . . . Patrick . . . the Crown of Scotland . . . for the glory of the Brotherhood!"

With this, he lapsed back into unconsciousness. While his mother wiped his sweat-stained forehead, Liam pondered out loud.

"Who in the hell is this Patrick? And what does the Crown of Scotland have to do with anything? Surely the lad's delirious."

"He said the same thing earlier," retorted Anne Lafferty. "It's his mention of the Brotherhood that scares me, Liam. Could he be involved with the IRB?"

Liam looked at his wife as if she was crazy. "Our Sean, involved with the likes of the Irish Republican Brotherhood? Surely you're daft, woman. He's much too sensible to be in league with that group of bloodthirsty Marxist terrorists."

"I hope you're right. Because there's no telling what kind of trash he came in contact with in Dublin. And if he *has* gone and gotten himself involved with the IRB, that could account for this gunshot wound."

Liam didn't want to consider this possibility and turned back toward the front door. "All I'm certain of is that our son has lost a lot of blood. And since Sean's going to need some expert tending to if he's going to pull through, I'd better go and fetch Doc Blackwater. Can you handle him until we get back?"

Anne Lafferty nodded. Her husband got on with his urgent mission of mercy. Since neither he nor any of his neighbors had telephone service, he once more proceeded on foot. He didn't even wait for his night vision to return to travel at full stride. This time his route was down a narrow paved roadway that eventually led to

Dundalk's central square. The physician lived on the outskirts of the tiny village of Annagassan, approximately two kilometers from the Lafferty residence. Liam covered this distance quickly. He barely felt the alien tightness in his legs as he climbed up onto the wide wooden porch and anxiously pressed the bell.

The house was dark, and Liam wondered if the doctor had been called away. If this was the case, Liam would be forced to travel into Dundalk to find the next readily available medical assistance. Again he hit the doorbell, this time with panicky impatience. He was all set to bang his fist against the door when a light popped on. This was followed by a hoarse, muffled voice.

"All right out there, hold your horses. I'm coming!"

The door finally opened, revealing a tall, thin, silver-haired man dressed in a robe and slippers. Dr. Tyronne Blackwater was in the process of putting on his wire-rim spectacles. Only when these glasses were in place could he identify the individual who had called him from his warm bed.

"Liam Lafferty, what in the world are you doing on my doorstep at this hour? Is Annie all right?"

"Thanks be to God, she is, Doc. It's my son Sean who's ailing. It appears he's been shot in the shoulder."

"I'll get my bag! Meet me on my driveway beside the garage."

Liam turned to follow the physician's directions and arrived at the garage just as the doctor came out the back door. Somehow in this brief time he had managed to throw on some trousers, shoes, and a jacket, and with his black leather bag in hand, he crossed over to open the garage door. Inside was a dark green Land Rover.

"Get in!" commanded its owner.

Liam complied, and no sooner did he settle himself

into the comfortable leather seat than they roared down the driveway.

"Is he at your place?" asked the physician.

"That he is. Annie's attending to him."

They drove away from the village. Liam had to grip the handrest tightly to keep from tumbling over as the doctor sped down the winding roadway as if he was in the midst of a race.

"How much blood has he lost?" the physician asked. He downshifted to guide them around a tight left-hand turn.

Liam felt his right shoulder press up against the side of the passenger door. "I can't say for certain, Doc. The living room is covered with the stuff, though Annie seemed to have the bleeding under control when I left her."

"Good. If it was indeed a gunshot, and no vital organs were punctured, then blood loss and shock will be our next concern."

A cat suddenly darted out in front of the car, and the alert physician instinctively yanked the steering wheel hard to the right. He hit the brakes, and the Range Rover skidded around the frightened feline. Quick to regain control, Doctor Blackwater shifted into fourth gear and floored the accelerator. Liam's heart was racing as he was thrown back into his seat. The engine was growling away with a deafening roar, and Liam was in the process of making the sign of the cross before him when they rounded another corner and he spotted the lights of his cottage twinkling on the nearby hillside. Liam pointed in this direction, and the physician nodded and turned them onto a pockmarked dirt trail. With the assistance of the vehicle's four-wheel drive capability, they bounded up this pitted pathway and seconds later braked to a halt before the cottage's front door.

Liam didn't know what to think as he climbed out of the Rover and watched as the front door to his house opened and out came Annie.

"My, you two made it here in a jiffy," she calmly observed. "He seems to be sleeping a bit more comfortably now, and the blood has all but stopped flowing from his wound."

"That's just the news I wanted to hear," replied the physician as he quickly made his way to her side. "Annie, my dear, I always said you'd have made me the perfect nurse. Now let's have a closer look at your patient to see precisely what the damages are."

Liam followed them inside and watched as the doctor kneeled down beside the couch and began attending to his son.

"He's a lucky one, all right," observed the physician. "There don't seem to be any arteries severed, and the wound appears confined to muscle tissue. Annie, I'm going to need some boiling water and plenty of clean linen."

"It's on the way," she replied.

While his wife went off to fulfill this request, Liam guardedly peeked over the physician's shoulder. Doctor Blackwater had just given Sean a shot and was in the process of gently probing into the wound with a thin steel instrument.

"Will you be sewing it up, Doc?" asked the fisherman.

"Eventually, Liam. But first I've got to remove the bullet responsible for this mess. In fact, if you look right here behind this mass of flesh, you can just see the devil."

Liam had already seen enough, and fighting back the urge to retch, he politely excused himself. "If you won't be needing me, Doc, would you mind if I wait this out on the back porch? I think I could use some fresh air."

"Not at all, Liam. Hopefully, I'll be able to join you shortly."

The fisherman left the room just as his wife arrived with a pot of scalding water and an armful of towels. Liam gratefully ducked outdoors. As he filled his lungs with the cool night air, his queasiness gradually left him. He realized that it was one thing to peer into the insides of a fish that he had just gutted, and another altogether to view the inner workings of his own son.

He wearily seated himself on the edge of the porch and stared out into the blackness. The stars twinkled in the heavens, while below he could just make out the ever-surging ink-black sea. His body felt heavy and fatigued, yet he couldn't surrender to the call of sleep until he was absolutely certain Sean was out of danger. Confident that Doctor Blackwater could do the job, Liam focused his thoughts on a different concern. For just who could have been responsible for shooting his son in the first place?

Sean's last visit home had been during Christmas. At that time he appeared happy, the picture of a successful city dweller. His job as a construction foreman with Guinness was supposedly going splendidly. He enjoyed living in Dublin, where he had a flat of his own and was saving up for a new car. Surely it sounded as if his future financial security was all but assured. That's why he seriously doubted that Sean would have had anything to do with a Marxist-oriented terrorist group like the IRB.

From what he understood, the Irish Republican Brotherhood recruited its members from the ranks of the economically downtrodden. They were lazy have-nots who were too lazy to work for a living. So they took up arms, and disguising themselves as freedom fighters, stole, maimed, and murdered, all in the name of a united Ireland.

Liam remembered hearing about their latest offensive on the television news only last month. At this time a series of violent incidents wracked the six counties that made up Northern Ireland. Exploding bombs destroyed a number of automobiles, and when one blast went off inside a crowded public bus, over a dozen innocent citizens of Armagh were tragically killed.

Attacks on members of the RUC, Northern Ireland's police force, were also at an all-time high during this so-called early spring offensive. Several cops were taken down by sniper fire, and during one brash attack, the main Belfast police station was hit by a mortar, resulting in horrific casualties.

The British troops subsequently sent in to quell this senseless violence fared no better. They too came under almost constant attack. Liam remembered hearing about one incident that was particularly heinous. Three off-duty British soldiers were invited by a trio of teenaged girls to join them in the outskirts of Londonderry for a party. The soldiers were not much more than teens themselves, and when they arrived, they found themselves accosted by a large group of masked gunmen. The next morning all three of the young Brits were found in a dumpster, each sent to meet his maker by a pistol shot to the back of the head.

It was the IRB who proudly claimed responsibility for this atrocity, and other acts of violence as well. Formed as an alternative to the more moderate IRA, the Brotherhood, as they preferred to be called, publicly declared their desired goal of driving the British out of Northern Ireland, by utilizing whatever force they deemed necessary. And once the English were gone, they would refocus their revolution to the south. The Republic of Ireland would be politically reorganized into a socialist state, and the religious hatred that had ravaged the land for centuries past would be tempered by the establishment of Marxist-inspired agnosticism. And in such a way the "troubles" between the Protestants and the Catholics would be no more.

Liam was all for the cessation of the idiotic violence between the two religious groups. But he certainly didn't want to have to become a godless communist to attain this goal. Freedom of choice was one of the basic rights his forefathers had fought for, and the fisherman was surely not about to surrender this privilege to a bunch of bloodthirsty terrorists who would shoot their own mothers if it would better their cause.

With his gaze locked on the twinkling heavens, Liam prayed that his son hadn't gone and gotten himself mixed up with such a dangerous group. As it turned out, this petition was delivered just as a shooting star soared through the night sky. Liam marveled at this sight, and his thoughts went back in time to the fated night that the entire heavens seemed on fire.

With all the excitement that his homecoming had precipitated, he had completely forgotten about the mysterious object that he had pulled from the seas and stored in the hold of his boat. His son's struggle with death had altered his priorities. Right now, life was the greatest treasure of all, and Liam would easily exchange the reward that would surely be coming to him for the life of his only child.

Liam made the sign of the cross and was in the midst of a reverent Hail Mary when the bass voice of the doctor boomed out behind him.

"Your boy's going to be just fine, Liam. The bullet was intact when I pulled it out. I closed the wound, and since Annie shares his blood type, was even able to do a transfusion."

"Thanks be to God!" said Liam passionately.

"I wouldn't be so quick to give him all the credit," countered the physician, who sat down beside Liam.

"Without Annie"s help, he would surely have bled to death. And if it wasn't for you running over to fetch me as you did, there's no telling what sort of complications would have set in. How about joining me in a wee sip to properly celebrate?"

The physician pulled a compact pewter flask from the pocket of his jacket and added, "What we're about to partake of is some of Martin Kelly's famous sipping whiskey. He gave me a jar when I set his heifer's leg last week. Here's to you and your family, Liam Lafferty."

He swallowed a sip of the powerful potion, winced, and handed the flask to the fisherman.

"And here's to the best doctor in all of County Louth!" toasted Liam as he took a sip of the home brew himself.

They passed the flask between them two more times before the physician looked up into the sky and commented, "It's a glorious Irish night, Liam. Can you believe we've had a whole three days without a drop of rain?"

"It's a welcomed miracle, all right, Doc. Especially after that wet spell. Why, I thought that those gales would never stop blowing."

The physician nodded. "The next front's most likely bearing down on us while we speak. But in the meantime, we've got to make the most of this respite." After swallowing down another sip of whiskey, he added, "If it's okay with you, Liam, I'd like to transfer Sean up to my place in Cootehill as soon as he's a bit stronger. I'll be going up there shortly, and would like to be able to monitor him for infection."

Liam accepted the flask. "Why, that's very nice of you, Doc. But you really don't have to go out of your way like that. You've done enough already."

"Nonsense," returned the physician. "The lad's not

124

out of the woods just yet, and I don't want him to take any chances. Besides, Sean can keep me company while I work the place."

"You're a saint, Doctor Tyronne Blackwater, a blessed, kind-hearted saint."

The physician laughed. "Hey, I wouldn't exactly go that far, Liam. Let's just say since I'm the one who originally brought him into this world twenty-five years ago, I'd like to protect my investment."

"I'll tell you what, Doc . . . I'll accept your gracious offer to take in Sean only if you'll agree to take a load of cod that I just brought in from the sea."

"It's a deal," said the physician. "So your trip was a successful one?"

"More than you would ever dream, Doc. But I'd be telling you a lie if I led you to believe that it was only fish that my hold is filled with."

"What do you mean by that, Liam?"

The fisherman turned and looked the physician straight in the eye. "A wondrous thing happened to me while I was out at sea three nights ago. It was a clear, star-lit evening like this one, and as I was preparing to pull in my lines, the entire heavens exploded in a dazzling fireball of light. I tell you Doc, it was as if the sun had suddenly arisen at midnight. A rumbling blast accompanied this phenomenon, and as the light began to fade, I actually saw something floating down from the heavens above. It took a bit of doing, but I reached this object soon after it hit the sea's surface. What I found was a massive elongated cannister tangled in the shrouds of a parachute. The cannister had a collar of floats around it to keep it from sinking. But they weren't adequate for its great weight, and instead of allowing the sea to eventually swallow it, I decided to take the object on board myself. My guess was that it came from a satellite. And if this is indeed the case, I'd imagine that its owners would probably be willing to pay a pretty substantial amount for its return."

The physician seemed enthralled by this story. "Where's this object now, Liam?"

"Why, locked in the hold of my boat, down at the Dunany leisure pier," answered Liam.

"Would you mind showing it to me?"

"Why of course not, Doc. But you don't mean right now, do you?"

The physician nodded. "I don't see why not. I don't know about you, but I seriously doubt if I'd be able to get back to sleep now even if I tried."

Liam shrugged. "Then I guess we'll go down there and take a look at it, Doc. But is it okay to go and leave Sean?"

"I guarantee you the lad will be out soundly for the next ten hours. And besides, Annie will be close by and knows what to do if any complications should arise."

The fisherman stood and found his legs a little wobbly. Tyronne Blackwater noticed this.

"If you don't mind, I'll do the driving, Liam. It looks like you're showing the effects of the most potent batch of home brew this county's seen in over a decade!"

The drive to the pier took less than ten minutes. Liam had to be awakened when they arrived, and he rather groggily exited the Range Rover and led the way down to the water's edge. Dr. Blackwater was all eyes as the fisherman escorted him to the transom of the battered boat, pulled a key from his pocket, and inserted it into a rusty iron padlock. After a bit of effort, this lock was triggered, and Liam lifted up the wooden door.

The physician had to keep from gasping as he viewed the fire-charred metallic cannister.

"Why, this is incredible, Liam. Are you certain this

was the object that you saw floating down from the skies?"

Fully awake now, the fisherman answered. "Why of course I am, Doc. I would have hauled in the parachute also, but it sank."

Hesitant to get too close to the cannister, the doctor cleared his throat and rather forcefully expressed himself. "It appears that you've indeed managed to pull in a piece of a satellite. It must have broken apart while entering the earth's atmosphere, and you just happened to be at the right place at the right time."

"Then it's worth something?"

"You'd better believe it. This kind of equipment costs a fortune to produce, and its owners will be anxious to show their appreciation when it's returned. So to ensure that they pay you top dollar, here's what I suggest: since it's much too dangerous to leave here unprotected, I'll have several of the lads who do odd jobs for me get down here to transfer it to a safer location. I'd like to do this tonight, before any of the other boat owners arrive. Secrecy is of paramount importance, if I'm to have any success in the negotiation process."

Liam seemed puzzled. "Let me get this straight, Doc—you want me to let you take the cannister, store it away, and then handle all the negotiations with its proper owners?"

"You do want the maximum reward possible, don't you, Liam?"

As the fisherman nodded, Dr. Blackwater continued. "I thought that was the case. So lock it back up, and give me the key. And I'll take care of everything from here on. All you have to do is worry about how you're going to spend that reward money."

Liam hesitated a moment before relocking the hold and handing over the key.

"Good," replied the physician as he pocketed it. "And

one more thing, Liam. You've got to swear to me that you'll keep this whole thing an absolute secret. You're not even to tell Annie about it. Negotiations of this type demand secrecy, and you could spoil everything if word gets out to the wrong person."

Thankful to have the services of the worldly physician, Liam decided to trust his old friend. After all, what did he know about negotiating with the superpowers? He was but a humble fisherman whom the hand of providence just happened to pay a visit to on a night he'd long remember.

Chapter Seven

Captain Mikhail Borisov's gut tightened as his command entered the waters of the Skagerrak. Such tension was always present whenever he prepared to initiate the final phase of a mission. The blond-haired Spetsnaz commando scanned the interior of the mini-sub and saw that his crew were perched before their stations, ready for action. At the *Sea Devil*'s helm, Chief Engineer Yuri Sosnovo gripped the airplane-style steering column that activated both their hydroplane and rudder. The thin, moustached Ukrainian's glance was riveted on the fathometer, and the captain knew that he was very fortunate to have the services of this hard-working, dedicated sailor.

Beside him, the warrant officer held onto the joystick that controlled their trim. Oleg Zagorsk was a Siberian by birth. He had been born deep in the Taiga, and like the frontiersman that he was raised to be, he was tightlipped and liked his privacy. This was fine with Mikhail Borisov, who felt a bit more confident, knowing that he had the services of one of the Rodina's best.

At the stern of the fifteen-meter-long vessel, electronics mate Tanya Olovski was busy wiping the condensation off the diving lock's circuit board. Tanya was their newest crew member, and though she wasn't much to look at, she performed her demanding tasks most efficiently.

Satisfied that the boat was ready to get on with its mission, Mikhail looked over to the gyro compass and spoke firmly. "Comrade Zagorsk, bottom us out. Chief Engineer, prepare to activate crawlers."

The sound of onrushing ballast rose with a roar, and as the tanks filled with seawater, the mini-sub began to sink. At a depth of one-hundred-and-fifty-three meters, there was a noticeable bumping sensation as the rounded hull struck the sandy seafloor. This was the sign for Yuri Sosnovo to trigger the battery-operated motor that ran the vessel's track drive mechanism. Designed much like a tank's, the dual treads bit into the sand and proceeded to propel them along at a speed of three knots.

The captain double-checked the chart that lay wrapped in oilskin before him. Drawn up by a Spetsnaz intelligence team, the map showed a detailed rendering of this portion of Oslo Harbor. Only minutes before, they had ascended to periscope depth to take a final bearing. After a quick course adjustment, Mikhail ordered them back down to the protective depths, calculating that their goal lay on the seafloor only seven and a half kilometers due west of them.

During this brief periscope sweep, he had spotted several Norwegian naval corvettes on patrol topside. Such ships were fast and heavily armed, and could be effective ASW platforms if pursuing the right quarry. But Mikhail knew that the vessel he commanded was not just any ordinary submarine. The mere fact of its condensed size almost guaranteed that the enemy's sonar would never detect them. Even if such sensors *did* manage to chance upon them, the *Sea Devil*'s hull was covered with sonar absorbent, rubberized tiles known as Clusterguard. Since this hull itself was made out of non-magnetic reinforced plexiglass, not even a magnetic anamoly detector would be able to locate the mini-sub.

"Comrade Olovksi, please join me in the bow turret. It's time to ready the articulated manipulator arm," ordered the captain.

A narrow bench spanned the forward-most portion of the vessel's pressure capsule. Mikhail Borisov seated himself on this perch and was soon joined by the boat's electrician.

"I'll begin arming the circuitry, Captain," offered the brawny brunette.

Mikhail watched her efficiently initiate this process. He had to admit that he had been genuinely upset when he first learned from Admiral Starobin that they would be assigned a female crew member. The interior of *Sea Devil* was severely cramped, and privacy was at a minimum. Even the crapper was out in the open, set on the metal plates that covered the battery well.

The white-haired admiral countered Mikhail's protest with an eloquent speech centered around the place of the Motherland's female citizens in the military. Since Socialism meant that all were equal, it would be against the basic tenets of Marxist ideology to bar women from active combat duty if they so desired. Tanya Olovski was duly qualified, and the admiral had no choice but to assign her to the *Sea Devil* when the slot became available.

Mikhail had only to look at the electrician to know that any sexual tension that he might have feared wouldn't be an issue. The big-boned native of Irkutsk was not the type of woman who turned men on. More mannish than feminine, she had a physique that was firm and muscular. And one didn't have to look closely to see the black moustache that covered her upper lip.

This was certainly not the type of girl Mikhail Borisov found attractive. He liked his women soft, fair,

131

and busty. Still a bachelor at forty, Mikhail had his fair share of lady friends. Most were attracted to his thick blond hair, steel-grey eyes, and solid build. A jagged scar that extended the length of his left cheek gave his ruggedly handsome face character. This mark was the by-product of a bar fight in Odessa, and if nothing else, served as an interesting conversation piece.

"We're approaching the final coordinates, captain," observed Yuri Sosnovo from behind.

"Very good, Chief Engineer. Bring us down to loiter speed."

The captain's instructions were instantly carried out, and the soft hum of the tracked drive system lessened noticeably.

"We should be close," reflected Mikhail Borisov. "Comrade Olovski, activate the bow spotlights and open the forward viewing port."

The electrician addressed the console, and in response, a circular metallic curtain slid back, revealing a clear plexiglass porthole. Mikhail leaned forward to look out this opening. A turbid expanse of seawater met his glance.

"Comrade Olovski, angle those spots down toward the sea bed," ordered the captain in a bare whisper.

As this directive was carried out, the floor of the harbor came into view. It primarily comprised ridged sand and an occasional clump of swaying sea grass. As the mini-sub slowly crawled over this flat expanse, Mikhail spotted an empty Pepsi can. Strangely enough, he didn't spot a single fish.

"Perhaps we're searching the wrong quadrant," offered Tanya Olovski. "Do you think we should rise to periscope depth to take another bearing?"

Mikhail smelled her sour breath and curtly responded. "Have faith, Comrade. Just ready that manipulator arm."

Deciding not to press her point, the electrician reached into the rubberized gauntlet that was set into the console. On the other side of the porthole, an elongated steel appendage suddenly came into view. This arm had a single joint in its center and was tipped by a clawlike pincer.

Mikhail looked down at his watch, then readdressed the electrician. "Position the edge of the claw so that it penetrates the uppermost strata of the seafloor, Comrade."

By grasping the manipulator device that was set inside the gauntlet, Tanya guided the claw so that it began carving a U-shaped wedge in the sandy bottom.

"Increase speed to one-half knot," ordered the captain coolly.

"One-half knot it is, Sir," responded the alert helmsman.

The *Sea Devil* gradually picked up speed, and the furrow that its articulated appendage continued digging into the seafloor lengthened.

"I still think another periscope bearing is in order, Captain," dared Tanya Olovski. "Who knows, perhaps we encountered a current that sent us off course."

Again Mikhail looked at his watch. "Patience, Comrade," he whispered. "And where's that faith I spoke of earlier? Don't you trust your captain?"

Before the electrician could answer, the mini-sub shook slightly as the tip of its articulated manipulator arm hit something buried in the sand below.

"All stop!" ordered the captain. "Good, now take us back slowly, Comrade Sosnovo."

The helmsman reversed the direction of the vessel's tracked drive, and the *Sea Devil* backed up over the portion of the seafloor it had just traveled over.

"That's good enough. Hold it right there," instructed

133

the captain.

There was a triumphant sparkle in Mikhail's clear eyes as he looked to his right and grinned. "Well, what are you waiting for, comrade? Dig up that cable and be quick about it. Don't forget, I've got a four week leave waiting for me back at Kronstadt."

The electrician guided the claw into the seabed. She seemed genuinely surprised when her efforts succeeded in snagging a thick black cable. She quickly got over her shock, and delicately clamped the pincers around the cable and carefully lifted it upward. It appeared to extend beneath the sand in both directions, and Mikhail was quick to identify it.

"It's the new communications cable, all right. Even as we hold it before us, top-secret NATO dispatches are being directed through the fiber-optic elements that line the cable's interior. And just think, comrades, soon this vital information will be all ours, without NATO ever being the wiser!

"Go ahead and insert the tap, Comrade Olovski. I'll prepare to release the auxiliary cable that we carry at our side, and then we can get out of here."

The electrician used the controls inside the gauntlet to insert a specially designed probe into the cable. This device was attached to a thin fiber-optic line that the mini-sub carried rolled up in a tight spool stored inside one of its empty torpedo pods.

"The splice is completed, Captain," observed the electrician.

Mikhail Borisov looked her way and winked. "Good job, my friend. Now let's deliver our payload and be off for home. Comrade Sosnovo, come about to course two-three-two. And carefully, if you please. Don't forget that we'll be paying out a cable of our own, and we certainly wouldn't want to cause it to break."

For the next quarter of an hour the *Sea Devil* continued crawling to the southwest. During this time Mikhail Borisov's eyes remained glued to the monitor, which showed that their cable was feeding out smoothly.

"Our depth continues to decrease, Captain. We've just passed the forty-meter mark."

Mikhail injested the helmsman's remarks and merely grunted in response. They were currently following the sloping seabed upward. This brought them ever closer to the rugged coastline that bordered this part of Oslo Harbor.

"We'll continue up the slope until we reach a depth of thirty meters," directed the captain. "That should put us just north of the Norwegian village of Larvik."

"But how will our operative ever find the end of the cable?" Yuri Sosnovo asked from the helm.

His gaze still set on the monitor, Mikhail answered. "When we cut the cable, we'll jettison the spool as well. Attached to this device is an ultrasonic homing beacon that will serve to direct our agent to these waters. Since his cover is that of a fisherman, he shouldn't be noticed as he recovers the spool and unwinds the remaining cable shoreward. Then he merely has to plug it into a transmitter in order for the Kremlin to know NATO's operational schedule at the same time that the Norwegian command is informed of it."

Mikhail had to admit that this was a brilliant operation, that only a genius like Admiral Igor Starobin could conceive of. Proud to be under this officer's command, Mikhail ordered the *Sea Devil* to a halt when they reached a depth of thirty meters. Here the spool holding the rest of the cable was successfully released, and the captain issued the orders that would eventually lead them back home.

To safely reach the deep waters that lay outside Oslo

Harbor, the *Sea Devil* traveled down the Norwegian coastline toward the city of Kristiansand. Once the lights of this town were off their starboard bow, they would change their course to the southeast. Then they would proceed to their rendezvous point with the whiskey-class submarine that would tow them back to the Baltic Sea.

The crew was genuinely relieved that the main part of their mission was over, and to properly celebrate, they passed out the remaining four oranges.

"When I get home I'm going to have my mother cook up a big potful of Ukrainian borscht," said Yuri Sosnovo as he peeled the skin off his precious piece of fresh fruit. "To my taste, there's no finer food in all the motherland."

"All I'm craving is some lean red meat," observed Oleg Zagorsk. "Back home in the Taiga, the men of my village will be preparing for the first elk hunt of the spring. Now there's a meat that never fails to put a smile on even the most finicky youngster's face. Have you tasted a piece of fresh elk liver before, Captain?"

Mikhail Borisov answered from the helm, where he lazily monitored the autopilot. "I can't say that I have, Comrade."

The usually tight-lipped Siberian passionately responded. "That's too bad, Sir. Because to my people, there's no finer delicacy on this planet. Legend says that to partake of the raw liver brings the hunter good fortune."

Tanya Olovski was seated at the trim controls and shook her head disgustedly. "Sounds pretty sickening, if you want my opinion. How can you compare such a revolting thing to a crisp red apple, some sweet grapes, a wheel of tangy cheese, and a loaf of crusty black bread? Now that, comrades, is real eating!"

The Siberian was all set to argue otherwise, when a

136

warbling electronic tone filled the cabin with a piercing noise.

"It's the collision alarm!" screamed the captain, who reached down to halt the mini-sub's forward velocity.

Just as his hand pulled back on the throttle, the vessel shuddered wildly and rolled hard on its right side. The lights blinked off, and the crew went tumbling to the pitching deck.

Mikhail Borisov slammed into the fire-control console with such force that he had the wind knocked out of him. Gasping for air and unable to speak, he looked on as the red emergency lights popped on. Through the dim red haze he saw that the vessel remained tilted precariously on its side. Struggling to scramble over the assortment of tangled bodies was the dexterous figure of Oleg Zagorsk. Somehow the Siberian managed to reach the diving station, and with his hands on the joystick, he began directing water forward to aft via the pump, and vented the forward trim tank straight to the sea.

As trim was regained, the angle of the deck lessened and the rest of *Sea Devil's* complement were able to stand upright once more. This included the boat's captain, who rubbed his bruised shoulder and somehow found the words to express himself.

"Our integrity seems to be intact. But what in the hell did we hit?"

The electrician alertly moved to the forwardmost portion of the compartment, activated the bow spotlights, and opened the viewing port. Greeting her was a puzzling checkered wall that she all too soon identified.

"It's a sub net!" she exclaimed.

The captain joined her. "Well I'll be, it *is* a sub net."

"Do you think we can get around it?" asked the electrician.

"Why waste the effort?" returned Mikhail. "All I have to do is take a little swim with the net clippers, and we can be on our way again in no time at all. Comrade Sosnovo, would you be so good as to prepare the diving chamber for me?"

The captain turned and began his way aft. The air lock was located amidships, beside the battery well. From an adjoining locker he pulled out a black rubber wet suit and a self-contained, closed-circuit oxygen rebreathing apparatus. He wasted no time donning this gear and climbing down into the cramped air lock.

As the hatch was sealed overhead, Mikhail activated the pump lever and a stream of icy cold seawater began flooding into the chamber. The fluid quickly filled the compartment, and though the resulting pressure was most uncomfortable, he opened the valve of his oxygen tank and took several deep breaths. There was little extra room inside the chamber, and he awkwardly reached down to twist open the lower hatch. It was with great relief when his efforts paid off and he was able to slip out into the murky depths.

The net clippers were stowed behind the port torpedo pod. He readily located them and swam forward to begin the task of cutting a hole in the net large enough to allow them safe passage. His extensive training was put to the test as he began the physically demanding job of clipping the wire mesh cable.

The cold water was beginning to numb his bruised limbs, and it took a supreme effort to grasp the handles of the clippers and apply enough pressure to penetrate the wire. Time after time he had to repeat this painful process, until he was all but exhausted and still found himself with three more cable sections to cut away.

Most divers would have long since abandoned their efforts and returned to the boat to get a replacement.

But Mikhail was much too proud to do such a thing. As a Spetsnaz officer, he had a tradition to uphold. For he was representative of the motherland's toughest underwater warrior, and as such, would complete the job to its very end.

It was as he placed the head of the clippers up against the coiled strands of the third section that a distant throbbing whine caught his attention. This sound seemed to intensify, and he knew in an instant that it was the signature of an approaching surface ship. Ever fearful that their collision could have set off a sensor of some sort, Mikhail grasped the handle of the clippers with a renewed intensity.

One strand away from completing the job, the water exploded with a series of resounding blasts. Though these were most likely only weak scare charges designed to frighten an adversary into panicking and giving himself away, Mikhail took them very seriously. And it was fortunate that he did, for just as he snipped through the final link of netting, a deafening blast reverberated from the waters above. The force of this concussion knocked him off the net and threw him into the side of the *Sea Devil* with a dull thud. He found it difficult to breathe, and with the swirling black depths beckoning him to merely let go and surrender to the cold call of eternity, the commando's instincts took over. His limbs were heavy as he pulled his weary body down to the re-entry hatch and gratefully slipped inside the chamber.

The next thing Mikhail remembered was being pulled out of the air lock by the concerned electrician. As the hatch was sealed behind him, he managed to cry out excitedly.

"For the sake of Lenin, get us off the bottom and out of this forsaken spot!"

It was the warrant officer who vented the ballast,

while the chief engineer activated the mini-sub's single propeller and guided the vessel through the hole that Mikhail had just cut for them. There was a loud grating noise as one of the frayed ends of the net scraped up against *Sea Devil*'s hull. But this was nothing compared to the thunderous blasts that awaited them as they passed through the net and entered the deep waters of the Skagerrak.

"Secure for depth charges!" screamed the exhausted captain.

This frantic cry was met by a reverberating concussion that slammed the mini-sub downward and shook it from side to side like a shark tearing apart its prey. Again the crew of four was thrown to the deck as the blast was followed by one of even greater intensity. As the lights faded, a scared female voice shouted out into the blackness, "They've got us for sure! We don't stand a chance!"

"Like hell we don't!" shot back Mikhail Borisov. "Comrade Sosnovo, is our engine still on line?"

With only the red emergency lights illuminating the cabin, the chief engineer picked himself off the deck and limped over to the helm. "The power train is still operating, Captain."

"That's music to my ears!" replied the Captain, who momentarily cringed when another depth charge detonated above them. "Open that throttle up all the way," he added. "And perhaps our Norwegian friends will tire of this senseless game and let us go in peace."

The captain knew that it was very likely that the surface units only had a general idea of where they were located. The standard NATO tactic was for such ships to indiscriminately drop ordnance in the hope that their suspected quarry would panic and take some sort of foolish action that would give them away. In such circumstances, Mikhail was trained to keep under way at all costs. Since shock tests showed that under-water explosions affected a vessel the size of *Sea Devil* far less than a normal-sized submarine, it was to their advantage to get as far away from the barrage as possible.

There was a self-satisfied smirk on the captain's face as the next explosion that greeted them was significantly more distant. Several other similarly weakened blasts followed, and only then did Mikhail stand upright and exhale a full sigh of relief.

"You can relax, Comrades. They've lost us, all right."

With the cabin still bathed in the red emergency lighting, the captain added. "Helmsman, plot the quickest course to the rendezvous point. And keep those throttles wide open. I've got a four-week leave waiting for me back at Kronstadt, and not even the entire Norwegian fleet is going to keep me from using it."

The air route from Prestwick airport to Holy Loch took Commander Brad Mackenzie over a variety of Scottish landscape. From the copilot's seat of a Sikorsky S-70 Seahawk helicopter, he viewed the lush scenery, which included forested hillsides, deep blue lochs, and several quaint villages. It was a gray and overcast afternoon. Mac was weary after his long flight in from Andrews Air Force Base, and as he yawned, the pressure in his ears suddenly equalized. This allowed him to better hear the tape that the pilot had just placed into the cockpit's cassette player. From the intercom blared forth the spirited sound of massed pipers. Mac identified the song that they were currently playing as "Scotland the Brave."

"I hope that you don't mind the music, Commander," said the Seahawk's young female pilot. "I just got transferred here from Norfolk and have really fallen in love with the music of this country."

"Is this your first visit to Scotland?" asked Mac.

She nodded. "To tell you the truth, this is the first time I've ever been out of the States before."

As a medley of familiar pipe tunes emanated from the elevated speakers, Mac began instinctively tapping his foot to the beat. "You know, I practically grew up with this music. My great-grandfather originally came from the Inverness area in the Highlands. Why, I even know how to blow the pipes."

"Now that's something that I've always wanted to learn," reflected the pilot as she smoothly guided the Seahawk over a ridge of rugged hills and into a broad valley. A wide river cut this plain, that was filled with a conglomeration of houses, factories, and highways.

"That's the River Clyde," offered the pilot. "To our right are the outskirts of Glasgow, while beneath us is the city of Greenock. That body up ahead of us is the Firth of Clyde, where Holy Loch is situated."

Mac was somewhat familiar with the landscape, since he had visted the naval base once before. Yet he had never seen it from this lofty vantage point. He took in the bustling docks of Port Glasgow and could just make out Gare Loch, where the English submarine base at Falsane was located.

The Seahawk began losing altitude as they whisked over the town of Gourock and began their way over the sparkling waters of the Firth of Clyde. Here Mac spotted a single submarine headed out to sea. Even though he had seen such a sight many times before, he sat forward excitedly to examine this vessel more closely. It had a sleek black hull and a prominent sail that didn't hold any hydroplanes. As Mac spotted the two sailors who occupied the sail's exposed bridge, the chopper pilot spoke out.

"That submarine is certainly awesome looking. I wonder if it's one of ours."

Mac was quick to reply. "Actually, it appears to be a Brit, most probably one of their new Trafalgar-class nuclear-powered attack vessels. You can tell it's not one of ours because of the absence of hydroplanes on the sail."

"I guess that I should have spotted that right off," returned the pilot. "Though I'm currently just a transport operator, eventually I'd like to get into ASW. From what I hear, that's where all the action is."

Mac would have liked to tell her how right she was, but held his tongue. With his gaze centered on the frothing white turbulence that the sub was leaving behind in its wake, he couldn't help but wonder if the tracked mini-sub had yet to pay these waters a visit. Surely there could be no denying the Firth's strategic importance. Both the United States and the United Kingdom had major submarine bases here. The estuary also was fairly narrow, had plenty of commercial traffic, and had ready access to the open sea. All of these ingredients would act in the mini-sub's favor.

As it turned out, the possibility of such a clandestine operation was no longer Mac's primary concern. This had all come to pass a little more than eight hours ago, when he arrived in the Pentagon office of Admiral Allen Long. With a minimum of small talk, the admiral explained to Mac his new assignment. And when this intensive briefing was over, Mac clearly understood the reasoning behind this abrupt switch in duty.

Sure, he had given the search for the mysterious mini-sub a whole year of his life, and as events off the coast of southern California had proved, his tireless efforts were bound to pay off soon. Yet when the B-52 went crashing into the Irish Sea with a payload of four nuclear weapons on board, his continued search for the tracked vessel no longer had the vital priority that it once held.

In all of American history, never before had the country permanently lost one of its nuclear weapons. Such devices of mass destruction were among the most closely monitored elements of the U.S. military arsenal. To ensure that such a nightmarish scenario didn't come to pass off the coast of Ireland, the President was demanding that the Navy give the recovery effort its total attention.

Admiral Long explained that Mac's reassignment was only one small piece of this effort. All over the world, ships were being diverted and specialists recruited to assist in this all-important task. Certainly the search for the mysterious tracked mini-sub could be temporarily put on hold while Mac applied his expertise in a new direction.

"There's Holy Loch," remarked the pilot as she swung the Seahawk over the town of Dunoon and pointed its blunt nose to the north. "That place is sure busy these days. Why, I've been bringing up passengers almost non-stop for the last thirty-six hours. We sure never got a workout like this back in Norfolk."

Mac peered out the plexiglass cockpit window and viewed the rectangularly shaped inlet of water where the U.S. naval installation was located. Barely two miles long and a mile wide, the loch had received its distinctive name several centuries before when a ship ran aground carrying a load of earth from Jerusalem that was destined for the foundation of a Glasgow cathedral. The marine salvage expert had always thought this name ironic, for today the loch's use was far more hellish than holy.

As they initiated their descent on the helipad, Mac

got a glimpse of the conglomeration of vessels currently docked at the base's pier. He spotted a massive tender, approximately eight submarines, a fleet oiler, and several large ocean-going tugs. The docks themselves seemed to be unusually active, with both men and equipment visible in great number.

The Seahawk landed with a jolt, and as the rotors whined to a halt the pilot commented. "I hope you enjoy your stay, Commander. Maybe I'll have you on the way back."

Mac released his harness and replied, "I'd enjoy that, Lieutenant. Thanks for the lift. And don't be afraid to pick up a set of pipes and give them a try. It's not as hard as it looks."

The soulful strains of "My Home in the Green Hills" accompanied him as he exited the cockpit and climbed out the fuselage door. Waiting for him on the tarmac was a short, wiry individual dressed in officer's whites. He wore aviator-type sunglasses and had an unlit corn cob pipe in his mouth. Mac was somewhat surprised to find him wearing the rank of admiral.

"Commander Mackenzie, I presume," greeted the senior officer with a slight Southern drawl. "I'm Admiral Connors, the base CO. Welcome to Holy Loch."

Mac accepted his handshake. "Why thank you, sir. Admiral Long sends his regards."

A fond look flashed in the admiral's eyes as he responded. "We go back a long way, Commander. They don't come any finer than Allen Long, who, incidentally, speaks most highly of your abilities, young man."

As Mac nodded humbly, the CO added, "I don't want you to think that I come out and personally greet everyone arriving at Holy Loch this way. In this instance, time is of the essence, and I want to start tapping your expertise as soon as possible. That's why I thought I'd present my initial briefing to you right

145

here at the airfield in the officers' ready room. If you'll just follow me, we'll head on over to that hangar and get things rolling.

"Now what's this I hear about you coming into Scotland by way of Kwajalein Atoll? I had duty in the Marshalls during the initial A-bomb tests, and no one has to tell me how damned remote those islands are."

As Mac filled his host in on the roundabout route that had taken him almost halfway around the world in the last forty-eight hours, they entered the hangar. It was a cavernous structure filled with seven dark-blue Sikorsky Sea Stallions and dozens of scurrying mechanics. To the din of pounding sheet metal and the machine-gun-like report of a riveter, they headed to a stairwell and climbed up a single flight. This put them in a carpeted hallway, far removed from the racket of the machine shop. They proceeded down this corridor, whose left side was lined with huge plate glass windows that allowed one a clear view of the hurried activity going on in the hangar bay below.

"Those Sikorskys down there are being fitted with towed sonar sleds," commented the admiral without breaking his crisp stride. "They've been brought in from all over the U.K. where their primary mission has been search-and-rescue. As we learned in the Persian Gulf during mine-sweeping operations there, the Sea Stallion is one hell of a versatile whirlybird. It's one of the toughest vehicles in the air, and we're planning to utilize them day and night until we get the job done."

They entered a doorway marked "Wardroom," and found themselves in the private confines of the pilots. The room was currently empty and contained several comfortable-looking leather couches, a buffet snack bar, and a big-screen television.

"Would you like a sandwich or a cup of coffee?" asked the CO.

Shaking his head that he was fine, Mac followed the Admiral into an adjoining room. This one looked as if it belonged in a school. Several rows of desks faced a wall-length blackboard on which a detailed map of the northern part of the United Kingdom had been taped. Standing beside this map, in the process of inserting a small, red, pennant-shaped stickpin into it, was a man in a green flight suit. He appeared to be a bit younger than Mac and sported a bruised face and a cast on his right arm.

"Commander Mackenzie, I'd like you to meet Captain Lawrence Stockton, the pilot of the B-52 that we lost the other night."

Mac had trouble hiding his amazement as he politely nodded towards the airman.

"What's the matter, Commander, haven't you ever seen a ghost before?" asked the pilot bitterly.

Admiral Connors was quick to interject. "Actually, four other members of Captain Stockton's crew managed to escape from the Stratofortress. Unfortunately, the crew of the KC-135 tanker wasn't so lucky."

The two newcomers joined the pilot beside the map. Mac could see in a glance that all the red stickpins were confined to the Irish Sea, at a point halfway between the eastern coast of Ireland and the Isle of Man.

Quick to note Mac's interest in this map, the pilot voiced himself. "Those red flags show the known extent of the debris field. As you can see, most of the wreckage seems to be confined to a single, rectangularly-shaped grid approximately forty-five miles long and twenty miles wide."

"What's the meaning of those two black stickpins and the one in yellow?" asked Mac.

Captain Stockton looked up to catch the Admiral's glance. Only when the CO gave him his nod of ap-

147

proval did the pilot answer Mac.

"The two black pins show the original locations of the pair of bombs that have already been recovered. The yellow pin indicates the finding of a floatation collar device only."

"Floatation collar device?" questioned Mac.

The pilot's previously aggressive tone softened. "Each of the four weapons that we were carrying were fitted with a heavy plastic collar, designed to fill with compressed air in the event of a disaster like the one we were part of. Their purpose is to keep the bombs afloat long enough to get a rescue team to them."

"Two of the devices worked just perfectly," added Admiral Connors "The first SAR choppers on the scene tagged their homing beacons immediately, and secured them with a more permanent collar until the recovery ship arrived on the scene."

"We're still not certain what went wrong with the third device," offered the pilot. "All we do know is that its collar properly inflated, and when the SAR chopper got to it, the bomb was nowhere to be seen."

"The consensus is that it somehow slipped out of its harness during impact," explained the admiral. "If that's the case, we have a pretty good idea where we'll find it. All we have to do is to take into consideration the going current and the speed and direction of the wind, and we can approximate the point where the bomb originally hit the water. Now as to the location of the fourth weapon, that's still up for grabs."

Mac's attention was focused on the grid of stickpins. "What kind of bathymetrics are we talking about down there?"

This time it was the admiral who provided the answer. "The average depth in that part of the Irish Sea is about seven hundred and fifty feet. The terrain of the seafloor is for the most part a gently sloping gradient, though some canyons up to one-thousand feet could be encountered. I've got a hydrographic ship presently coming in from the Norwegian Sea. It will be at the site early tomorrow morning, and then we'll know exactly what we're dealing with."

Mac seemed a bit uncomfortable with his next concern. "Is there any possibility that either of those two missing bombs could have split apart on impact with the sea? And if we do manage to locate them, could they detonate on us?"

"The Air Force had already informed us that it's highly unlikely that either device's integrity has been compromised," retorted the admiral firmly. "The bombs are welded together in a casing of solid steel, and not even a collision with the sea could wrench them apart. As to your second question, you can rest assured that when we do find the two bombs, you needn't worry about an atomic explosion. There's no way in hell that such a thing could happen."

"I beg to differ, Admiral," countered Captain Stockton. "Though under normal circumstances we'd have absolutely nothing to worry about in that respect, I'm afraid that one of the missing bombs could be a problem."

"Don't start that doomsday crap with me again," spat the redfaced admiral angrily. "I'm warning you, Captain, I could have you thrown into the brig for this!"

Lawrence Stockton seemed to ignore this outburst as he looked Mac in the eye and calmly continued. "You see, Commander Mackenzie, I was in the bomb bay at the time of the accident. We were experiencing difficulties in the arming circuitry of one our bombs. It happens from time to time, and the unofficial procedure to correct this condition is to open the trigger mechanism and bypass the permissive action links by shooting a full charge of electricity into the system. At this point the overload usually corrects itself and we can get on with our business. Yet it was just as my bombardier was about to fry the circuit that our whole world came apart. And that's the last I saw of either my bombardier or that damned A-bomb."

Without giving the pilot a second to regain his composure, Mac retorted. "Exactly what are you trying to say, Captain?"

"As I've been trying to tell them from the moment that they pulled me out of the drink, one of those bombs is cocked and ready to go!"

Having heard enough of the pilot's hysterical ranting, Admiral Connor's interceded. "The Pentagon assures me that it's impossible to arm an atomic device without receiving the proper PAL code from the National Command Authority, which in most instances is the President. With that said, I'll have no more of your outbursts, Captain Stockton! Our job is going to be difficult enough without you going and putting such nonsense into my people's ears. Now if you'll excuse us, I'd like to talk to Commander Mackenzie alone."

Lawrence Stockton took this cue, and as he turned to leave the briefing room, his gaze momentarily locked onto Mac. No words were spoken; he seemed to silently implore Mac to remain objective. The marine salvage expert expressed his open-mindedness with a slight nod of his head, as the pilot pivoted and slowly limped back into the wardroom.

"You can rest assured that Captain Stockton is talking hogwash, Commander. The Defense Department guarantees me that there's not the slightest chance of either one of those missing A-bombs detonating. So that leaves us with one concern and one concern only, and that's finding the cursed things before anyone else does.

"Now in that respect we have several things going for us, not the least of which is that the crash happened late at night, in an isolated quadrant of the sea, far from any major population centers. There's been no mention in the Irish news media of any peculiar sightings on the night of the tragedy, so it appears that they still don't realize what's occurred off their coast. This anonymity is most important, as this entire matter's being handled on a need-to-know basis only. Only top Pentagon and government figures have been told the complete details of the crash. Because of logistics and security concerns, it was decided to inform the Brits of the incident. We've agreed to allow their First Sea Lord to share the news with a select handful of military officers with a ranking of Major or above, on a top-secret basis. The majority of these individuals have operational command duties in the northern portion of the U.K. and since this whole thing happened in their backyard, their cooperation is essential.

"So I guess that brings us back to square one. How do we go about finding the frigging thing?"

Admiral Connors used the scarred bit of his corncob pipe as a pointer as he directed Mac's attention back to the map.

"Though this entire operation is being run under the auspices of the U.S. Air Force, the Navy has been asked to lend a hand to our sister service. And that's where you come in, Commander. Given what we know about the debris field, what do you think our chances are of finding those two bombs?"

Mac took his time formulating an answer. "I'd say that with the technology available to us in this day and age, the chances are excellent, Admiral. The depth of the operation doesn't sound excessive, and once we've got that detailed bathymetric chart of the quadrant to study, we'll know precisely what we're up against.

151

What kind of salvage equipment do you have to draw upon?"

"Just name it and it's yours, Commander. We've got carte blanche on this one. All the Defense Department wants in return is results."

Mac thoughtfully stroked his chin. "That hydrographic ship that you mentioned was on the way is a great start. Those Sea Stallions out in the hangar bay will be helpful too. They can initiate a preliminary sonar scan of the seafloor while we assemble a proper salvage flotilla. What other surface vessels are at our immediate disposal?"

"We've got a pair of Avenger-class mine warfare ships coming in from the Bay of Biscay. Traveling with them is a Cimarron-class oiler and a Oliver Hazard Perry-class frigate. Right here at Holy Loch are several oceangoing tugs and the sub rescue ship the *Pigeon*."

"Is a DSRV deployed aboard her?" asked Mac, hopefully.

The Admiral nodded. "She's carrying the *Mystic*. Though both vessels were undergoing minor overhauls when news of the crash arrived, I've got the dockyards working overtime getting them seaworthy once again. They'll be ready to go in another twelve hours."

"Admiral, the *Mystic* is sure going to make our job a lot easier. Now if only we could get a hold of some ROV's."

There was a devilish gleam in Admiral Bart Connor's eyes as he responded to this. "I've taken the liberty of setting you up an office right down the hallway from this room. There's a phone in it and an exact duplicate of this map. And by the way, when you're ready to go to the site, I'd like you to use the USS *Bowfin* as your base of operations. She's a nuclear-powered fast-attack sub that's got one of the best crews in the Loch operating her."

Barely hearing this, Mac absentmindedly thought out loud. "I wonder if K-1 is available from Woods Hole. . . . Then I'd better get on the horn with the guys at NOSC and get CURV sent out here from San Diego on the double."

Admiral Connor noted his guest's preoccupation and struggled to stifle a satisfied smirk. His old friend Allen Long had been so right when he called recommending Brad Mackenzie for the job. Now if only his luck held, and the young commander was able to help them locate the two missing A-bombs before the unyielding pressure that he continued getting from Washington drove him to an early retirement!

Chapter Eight

The rain came down in a fine, cold mist. But that didn't deter Major Colin Stewart from walking the drafty ramparts of the castle, his afternoon ritual. With his hands cocked behind the protective confines of his rain slicker, Stewart briefly halted when the distinctive booming blast of an artillery piece sounded a single time nearby. He didn't have to look at his wristwatch to know that it was one P.M. As he glanced over the stone wall beside him, he could just make out Princess Street through the mist. The wide paved thoroughfare was crowded with buses, trucks, and automobiles. On the sidewalks scurrying pedestrians continued on their ways, oblivious to the inclement weather. Modern buildings lined this walkway, and the major knew that he was looking at the dynamic new face of the ancient city of Edinburgh.

A wet gust hit him square in the face, and he turned his back on it to continue his introspective stroll. The outside world took on a radically new perspective when viewed from the walls of the castle. It was almost as if time halted here, allowing one to see it as a continuous flowing stream, with the tides of history providing the current.

The major's current concern was centered on the daring robbery attempt that had recently occurred here.

He had only just learned the identity of the young intruder who was shot to death during this attempt. Army intelligence, with the help of Scotland Yard, was able to match the deceased's fingerprints with those of one Patrick Callaghan of Belfast. The twenty-four-year-old had a long record of criminal activity, starting at the age of fifteen, when he was convicted of petty larceny. After a brief stay in a detention home, he was again arrested, this time at the age of seventeen, for car theft. This brought him a two-year prison term.

Callaghan served only eighteen months of this sentence. Following his early parole, he began working as a lorry driver and stayed relatively free from trouble, except for a minor conviction for public drunkenness. Yet it was most likely at this time that he joined the Irish Republican Army.

It was on the eve of his twenty-first birthday that he was arrested outside of Armagh with a truckload of stolen Armalite rifles and ammunition. An IRA informer revealed that Callaghan had been very active in the organization and had smuggled many more than one load of weapons over the border in the trucks he drove. Though this fact could never be proved, Patrick Callaghan was convicted of gun-running and sent to Long Kesh for a five-year term without the possibility of parole. While in prison, he met Bernard Loughlin, the founder of the Irish Republican Brotherhood. Originally formed as a militant offshoot of the IRA, the IRB was philosophically a Marxist organization with close ties to terrorist groups in Libya and the Middle East. When Loughlin escaped from Long Kesh, Patrick Callaghan was at his side; a helicopter swooped down and carried them off to safety. Both men had since been at large and were believed to have participated in a number of snipings, car bomb attacks, and robberies in both the Republic of Ireland and the north.

There was no doubt in Colin Stewart's mind that

Callaghan was a bad seed from the very beginning. He was just the type that terrorist organizations such as the IRB loved to recruit, and his premature demise was certainly no great loss. Yet what really bothered Stewart was the fact that such a renowned terrorist was currently doing his dirty deeds on Scottish soil. Except for a few minor incidents in the past, the Irish "troubles" hadn't paid their country a visit.

Scotland was primarily populated by a conservative Protestant element. To the average Scot, the religious war that had been plaguing Northern Ireland for centuries was a wasteful, foolish mess, one they wanted no part of. Colin remembered well an incident that occurred in Edinburgh several years ago, when a trio of IRA sympathizers were loose in the city, trying to stir up public support for their cause. Spray-painted revolutionary slogans soon covered almost every vacant wall in the city. Yet when a young Welsh soldier was shot to death while hiking Arthur's Seat and a car bomb was found inside a car parked outside the castle, the people had had enough. With a minimum of commotion, a committee was formed to deal with the problem. And the very next morning, all three IRA agents were found hung by their necks from light standards behind Usher Hall. That was the supposed end of the troubles in Edinburgh.

Was Patrick Callaghan's presence inside the walls of the castle the other night indicative of a change of terrorist policy? Colin Stewart shuddered to think of the consequences for Scotland if this was true. Until more intelligence information was received, he could only pray that this was an isolated incident. Perpetually short of money to fund their revolution, the IRB most probably thought they could get away with carrying off the Scottish crown jewels. But now one of their ranks lay cold in the morgue, the royal regalia still secure as ever in their resting place as they had been for hun-

156

dreds of years past. Surely they got the message that such a fantastic operation was ill-conceived from the very start.

Sincerely hoping that this was the case, Colin Stewart climbed down to the rampants that graced the western walls of the castle. The mist had all but stopped now, and he could just make out the harbor area and the gray waters of the Firth of Forth in the distance.

When he was active in the SAS, anti-terrorist operations had been his specialty. He had been at the Iranian embassy in London on May 6, 1980, when the SAS interceded to save the lives of twenty-one frightened hostages. As a devout student of religious fanaticism, he understood the warped sense of values that such groups based their actions upon. The only way to control such an organization was to root it out at its very base. That's why Stewart's next great concern was tracking down Patrick Callaghan's accomplice.

Somehow this individual had succeeded in escaping from the heretofore all but impregnable confines of Edinburgh Castle. He was last seen scurrying over the walls of the Half Moon battery, where a blood trail led them as far as the gatehouse. The sentries there reported sighting no trespassers. But unless he just disappeared into thin air, he managed to elude them and vanish into the surrounding city.

Stewart immediately notified the metropolitan police. He then personally called the local hospitals and clinics, who spread the word to every doctor in the city to report the treatment of any suspicious gunshot wounds to the castle at once. When twenty-four hours passed and these efforts failed to show results, Stewart feared the worst.

Still not ready to throw in the towel just yet, he received permission from headquarters to expand the search. To determine his next move, Stewart tried to think like his prey. Since he now knew that the man was most probably Irish, there could be only one place where he would be attempting to flee to, and that was home. Now the Highlander had only to figure out how the wounded terrorist would manage such a feat.

The only way he'd be able to return to Ireland was by sea or air. If he chose to travel by sea, there could be any number of places where he could depart from. Stewart would begin by asking army intelligence to initiate a sweep of every port on the western shore of Scotland, with most of their effort to be centered on Glasgow. Certainly a wounded young Irishman was bound to draw some attention, especially if he utilized public transportation.

Plane travel would be a bit easier to monitor. Since there were only so many airfields in the vicinity, they could be intensively covered. Again they would concentrate their efforts at the major public airports in Glasgow, Prestwick, and Edinburgh. Here passenger manifests could be scrutinized and all flights to Ireland carefully screened.

Since there was always the possibility that he'd attempt chartering a small plane from a private field, Colin Stewart would ask assistance from the RAF. One of their Nimrod AWACS platforms was on continuous patrol over the Irish Sea and would have a taped record of every single flight headed westward. In this way they could track down any unauthorized aircraft that left Scotland without filing an official flight plan.

Though the possibilities were still very good that he would manage to escape their dragnet, Colin Stewart felt that it was absolutely necessary that they at least made the effort. A serious wrong had been done when one of the most hallowed shrines in all of Scotland had been violated. One of the perpetrators had already paid the ultimate price for this folly. And if Major Colin Stewart had anything to say about it, his accomplice would soon feel the iron hand of Scot justice also.

A little over two hundred miles to the southwest of Edinburgh castle lay the green rolling hills of County Caven in the northern portion of the Republic of Ireland. Primarily made up of small farms, County Caven was a relatively poor district, where potatoes and lamb provided basic subsistence.

It was sixty-two years ago that a Belfast-based surgeon moved his new wife and infant son out of the city and into County Caven. He chose a two-hundred-and-fifty-acre plot of land outside the village of Cootehill on which to build his new home. No expense was spared on this estate, which included a magnificent manor house, barn, and several cottages for the help. Here he planned to raise his newborn boy as a country gentleman, far away from the pollution and sectarian violence that had made Belfast all but uninhabitable.

No sooner was the last brick of the estate laid when the Great Depression hit Ireland with a vengeance. The surgeon had been planning to augment his medical practice by raising sheep and produce. But the new economic climate made such a dream impossible. After his savings were drained, he was forced to return in earnest to his old trade. He became a traveling country physician, going from village to village treating the sick, who most often could only pay him in trade goods, the setting of a broken leg costing a chicken and so forth. Meanwhile, his wife was charged with the vast responsibility of attempting to wring some sort of nominal existence from the land they had settled upon. As the years passed, she succeeded in this challenging endeavor, though the cost of this triumph drained her energy and ultimately broke her resolute spirit.

It was in such a world that their son Tyronne grew up. Far from being a pampered physician's son, Tyronne spent his childhood working the farm. Though both his parents died when he was only a teenager, they left him a legacy that went far beyond the estate and its land. For his parents had managed to instill in him a probing intellect and an awareness of the social inequalities that threatened to tear Ireland apart some day.

To heed the call of destiny, Tyronne leased the estate and went to Dublin to become a university student. Like his father he was drawn to medicine. After graduation he worked out of a cottage in Dunany, where he administered to a vast practice that extended all the way from Dublin to the south to Dundalk in the north. Often he gave away his services to the poor for free, as a way of expressing the social idealism that his parents had taught him.

Yet charity work was far from fulfilling, and as the years passed he became increasingly frustrated with the social injustice that continued to plague his country. This abuse was especially prevalent in Northern Ireland, where the same poverty and sectarian violence that originally sent his parents fleeing from Belfast continued to exist. Realizing that something very drastic would have to occur to change this situation, he joined the Irish Republican Brotherhood.

To aid the cause, he offered the IRB free use of his family estate, known to the locals as Cootehill House. The presence of strangers here was explained away when the physician announced the opening of a clinic on the grounds. In this manner his comrades in the IRB could journey here without arousing the suspicions of the local Garda outpost.

Tyronne Blackwater genuinely loved Cootehill House. He visited it every chance he got. Merely setting his eyes on the emerald pastures and the distinctive arched manor house never failed to fill him with memories of his parents and a childhood spent unlocking the secrets of the land.

Of all his favorite times to visit was spring, when the budding flowers and lush green growth were at their splendid best. Though he was well into his sixties now, Tyronne still felt the same excitement and wonder that he had experienced as a child. This was especially apparent on this glorious day in May, as he emerged from the pine woods he had been hiking in all morning and directed his glance toward the manor house.

The light rains that had accompanied him earlier had long since moved to the east. A thin strata of high-flying clouds colored the sky with a powdery blue, and the sun felt warm and comforting. From his vantage point at the edge of the forest he could see Marie Barrett attending to the vegetable garden that she had planted herself along the manor's south wall. The young woman from Londonderry had long red hair, smooth white skin, pale green eyes, and a figure that caused his elderly heart to flutter every time he laid his eyes on her. If he didn't know any better, he could have easily mistaken her for a simple country girl who would make some lucky man a wonderful wife. But though Marie loved to work in the garden and tend the animals, she was definitely not cut out for the life of a farmer. Guiding her existence was a firm political philosophy that had its roots in Marx and Lenin. Tyronne knew that this same delicate creature that he watched tending the tomato plants was equally at home with an assault rifle in her hands.

Visible behind her beside the barn, in the process of stacking squares of sod, was another one of Cootehill House's current tenants. Bernard Loughlin had been living on the estate for almost a year now. He too was a city boy, having grown up in Belfast, who readily adjusted to an agrarian lifestyle. Tall and lean, Bernard

161

was well into his forties, though no one knew his exact age for certain. One only had to take a close look at his face to know that he had seen much of life in his years. There were deep character lines etched on his cheeks, and with a black eye patch that covered his right eye and a long, brown ponytail, he almost resembled a modern-day pirate.

Bernard Loughlin was one of the original founders of the IRB, and one of the most ruthless men that the physician had ever met. Car bombs and snipings were his specialty. He had a callous disregard for human life, as long as it wore a British uniform. Yet he was a fair man in his own way, and a genius of strategy. He also knew how to judge a man's character instantly and determine his worth to the cause. Together with Marie Barrett, who helped dictate political strategy, Bernard commanded a virtually invisible army of guerrilla warfare specialists, who yearly displayed their loyalty to the Brotherhood with a blood oath.

Though some of their methods were a bit distasteful, especially when the loss of innocent lives was concerned, Tyronne knew that this crudeness was but a temporary evil. The IRB was an army of change that wouldn't lift its offensive until the goal was reached. And since in any war loss of life was inevitable, they had to look beyond the bloody present to the day when all Ireland was one socialist state, united by the bonds of equality and brotherhood.

Proud to be a part of this movement, the physician followed the narrow earthen trail to the edge of the vegetable garden.

"Good morning to you, Marie Barrett. And what a lovely morning it truly is."

The redhead looked up from the plant she was tending and returned the physician's greeting. "And a pleasant good morning to you, Doctor. Have you been out long?"

Tyronne leaned his wooden walking stick up against the white stone wall that surrounded the vegetable patch. "Since sunrise, my dear. Even though I've been here almost three days, I don't feel really at one with the place until I've properly walked the grounds. How are those tomatoes of yours coming along?"

Marie delicately picked off a stunted limb. "I'll be getting ready to tie them up to their sticks shortly. They're really growing, and this year we should have an excellent crop."

"It's that new variety that we imported from the States that's done it my dear. That and your tender loving care of course."

Marie smiled, then stood up straight and looked toward the house. "I guess I should be checking on Sean. He was sound asleep when I poked my head in there earlier."

"Good," returned the physician. "The lad needs his rest. Yet if we're going to get any strength into him, we're going to have to get him out of that bed eventually. So come on, nurse, let's see what we can do about it."

Hand in hand the two innocently walked into the manor house. In the anteroom Tyronne removed his mud-stained boots and hung up his raincoat. Then he followed the redhead through the large kitchen and into the living room. This part of the house was decorated just like his mother had left it. The furniture here was a bit shabby with age, but still comfortable and functional. A twisting stairway took them to the second floor. Sean's bedroom had been Tyronne's as a child, and was set into the front portion of the house facing the meadow. They entered and found their patient propped up in bed with his vacant stare focused out the open window.

"Good morning, Sean. It's a glorious morning out there," greeted the physician.

Sean's voice was hoarse and heavy. "I was just thinking about Patrick again. He knew all the time that he didn't have a chance of getting out of there. Yet he stood his ground all the same, and sprayed those damn Brits with bullets so that I could make good my own escape. If our situations had been reversed, I wonder if I could have met death so boldly."

"Of course you would have, lad," offered the physician. "But as it turned out, fate had other plans for you. Patrick Callaghan was a good boy, and it's a damn shame that he had to be taken from us. But he's not the first and he won't be the last to give up his life for the Brotherhood. So quit your selfish brooding, and start thinking about how you're going to use this second chance at life to best advantage."

This compassionate speech hit home, and Sean turned his glance away from the window. "You're right, Doc. I guess I should be grateful just to be here."

"Damn right," retorted the physician firmly. "And one other thing, lad—if I were you, I'd be saying a little prayer of thanks for those wonderful parents of yours. Why, you've got your own mother's blood pumping through your body, and if it wasn't for your father, I would have never been there in time to save you."

The mere mention of his father caused an introspective grin to crease Sean's face. "So the old fool finally came through."

Tyronne Blackwater shook his head in disagreement. "Liam Lafferty may be simple in his ways, but he's a fine man in his own right. You should be very proud of him, lad, especially when you see with your own eyes the great gift he fished from the seas for us."

Puzzled by this statement, Sean looked to Marie for clarification. "What do you mean by that?"

The redhead teasingly smiled. "Why don't you come out to the barn and see for yourself. Do you think he can make it, Doc?"

"I don't see why not," answered the physician. "It wasn't one of his legs that was almost shot off."

Determined to find out what they were talking about, Sean struggled to sit up straight. His heavily bandaged shoulder made this simple movement an effort, and Marie was quickly at his side to lend him a hand.

"Come on, Sean. It will do you good to stretch your legs and get some fresh air," prompted the redhead.

Sean removed his legs from beneath the covers, then remembered he was wearing only a t-shirt. Marie caught a quick glimpse of his naked torso and turned to get his pants for him.

"Come on, soldier. Since when are you the shy type? After all, it's nothing I haven't seen before."

Sean managed to get into his sweatpants on his own, and after slipping into some thongs, attempted to stand. It was at this point that he was overcome by a wave of dizziness. Alertly his escorts scrambled to his side to steady him.

"Breathe deeply, lad. This spell is only natural. It's nothing to worry about," offered the physician.

Sean filled his lungs with air, and just as quickly as it arrived, the spell passed. He nodded that he was fine, and even took a few tentative steps on his own to prove it.

"There'll be no keeping you down now, Sean Lafferty," observed Marie playfully.

By the time they descended the stairway and crossed through the living room, Sean's stride had a new sense of confidence to it. It was as they began their way through the kitchen that his old personality began to show.

"You don't suppose that there'd be a nice ice cold bottle of Guinness in the fridge, would you now?"

Tyronne Blackwater gave the redhead a sly wink as

he answered. "It's a wee early for that, lad. Perhaps we'll talk about that a bit later. But once we return from the barn, Marie will be happy to make you a hearty breakfast. Won't you, my dear?"

The redhead nodded. "Just name it and it's yours, Sean."

Sean seductively eyed the redhead's curvaceous body. "Well, since you're offering, it has been a pretty long time."

Not certain if he was joking or not, the physician interceded. "I don't know what's worse for you, Sean Lafferty, a Guinness, or what naughtiness you have on your mind."

"Well, Doc, you have been saying all along that I have to start thinking about getting back to my normal self once more," offered Sean, who followed Marie out into the courtyard.

"Oh, to be young once again," mumbled the physician as he continued outdoors himself.

A brick pathway took them past a large fish pond that was covered with lily pads. As they approached the entrance to the barn, Dr. Blackwater sped up to lead the way inside. He reached into his pocket, pulled out a key, and inserted it into the padlock recessed in the barn's front door. It triggered with a click, and the old-timer proceeded to pull the door open.

Sean Lafferty really didn't know what to expect as he followed his two escorts inside. As the lights were switched on, he spotted a large stack of peat. Stored behind these squared segments that would be used as fuel were dozens of wooden crates. Upon closer examination, Sean could see that each container had the official RUC seal on it. The Royal Ulster Constabulary were the local police force of Northern Ireland, and as Sean spotted the inventory list stenciled on the sides of each crate, he couldn't help but shake his head in wonder. Crates of M-16 rifles lay on top of a container

166

holding Browning M-60 machine guns and endless rounds of ammunition. An even larger storage container held a 90-mm recoilless rifle.

"Ah, our spoils from the Newry raid," observed the wounded terrorist. "This is the first time I've seen it all together like this, and it certainly is a sight to behold."

"It's more than that," broke a deep voice from behind. "It's the future destiny of Ireland."

Sean pivoted in time to see the tall, gaunt individual from whose lips these words were uttered enter the barn. Bernard Loughlin had a red bandana tied around his forehead, and wore a stained sweatshirt with the seal of the University of California at Berkeley embossed on it. With fluid strides he walked to Sean's side, looked him over with his good eye, and then reached out to hug him.

"Comrade, it's good to see you up like this," welcomed the IRB's co-founder. "When I last saw you, you were in such a weakened state that you didn't even recognize me as I carried you up to your bed. And now just look at you, well on your way to a full recovery."

"Thanks to all of you," Sean added humbly.

"I believe it was a Japanese philosopher who once said, You only live twice. Once when you're born, and once when you look death in the face. I, too, have come back from a serious combat wound like yours, Sean, and understand how confusing it is for you right now. Why I bet you've been up there tormenting yourself, trying to figure out why it was Patrick who was taken and not you."

"How did you know?" Sean asked, astonished.

Bernard Loughlin grinned slyly. "You're forgetting that you're talking to someone who has already looked death in the face, Comrade. So enough of your soul-searching. Your mere presence here is reason enough to celebrate, even if your mission wasn't a successful one."

"I still say that it was a daft idea from the very start," reflected the physician.

"Let's not get into that again!" countered Bernard Loughlin firmly. "We tried and we failed, it's as simple as that."

"At least our goal was clear," offered Marie. "If we were able to acquire the crown jewels, the enemy would be on their knees right now, begging to get them back."

"How very ironic it is that soon they'll be in this very same position, even without those jewels," said the one-eyed terrorist.

Noting that Sean didn't seem to know what he was talking about, Bernard turned to address the physician. "Has he been told about our find yet?"

"We were just about to show him when you arrived," answered Dr. Blackwater.

"Good," retorted Bernard. "I'm eager to see his face when he sees the object his own father was responsible for bringing to us."

The ponytailed terrorist beckoned Sean to join him beside the crate containing the recoilless rifle. There was a large object covered by a green tarp on a pallet. Not until all three members of his audience were gathered around him did Bernard pull off the tarp. Exposed for all to see was a seven-foot-long cylindrical canister that had a set of stubby iron fins mounted on its tail.

"Is that a bomb?" Sean asked.

Bernard's good eye sparkled as he breathlessly answered. "That it is, Sean. But don't mistake it for just an ordinary piece of ordnance. For the device that you see before you has just made the Irish Republican Brotherhood into a nuclear superpower!"

"Are you saying it's an atomic bomb?" queried Sean. "Why, that's impossible. Come off it. This is a practical joke, isn't it?"

Bernard's expression was deadly serious as he responded to this. "No, it isn't a joke, Comrade. Doctor, why don't you explain how this device came into our possession."

The physician cleared his throat and proceeded to relate to Sean the story of Liam Lafferty's incredible discovery in the waters of the Irish Sea. As Dr. Blackwater concluded this tale, Bernard added, "I've got to admit I didn't believe it myself when the Doc first called me. But then I did a little checking around with our contact at Royal Navy headquarters at Northwood, and this is what I learned. On the very night that your father witnessed the flash in the sky that he reported and then pulled this device on board, an American B-52 Stratofortress collided with another aircraft while initiating an in-flight refueling. Both planes went down in the Irish Sea, and as best as we can learn, the B-52 was carrying a load of four atomic bombs at the time. Two of these weapons were subsequently found by the Yanks, while Liam Lafferty pulled in the one you see before us. Now, I know this tale sounds incredible, Sean, but you have my word that it's God's honest truth."

With his gaze still locked on the shiny steel canister, Sean stuttered, "I still can't believe it. My own father pulled an atomic bomb from the sea without anyone but us knowing about it? Why, its absolutely amazing!"

"Don't forget that he's still under the impression that it's a piece of a satellite," said Dr. Blackwater. "And he's relying on me to negotiate a suitable reward."

"We'll pay him handsomely for his efforts, sure enough," offered Bernard.

As the reality of this extraordinary tale began to sink in, Sean dared to vent his curiosity completely. "Taking it for granted that what you say is true, may I ask what in the hell the Brotherhood plans to do with this thing? If it really is an A-bomb, it could kill millions!"

"We realize that," said the doctor. "And before we go and rush into anything drastic, we're taking a long, hard look at our alternatives."

"Alternatives?" repeated Bernard. "I thought I made myself absolutely clear in this matter, Doctor. Because as far as I'm concerned, there are no alternatives. This bomb is a blessing from above, and it will be used where it can inflict the greatest amount of injury on our sworn enemy, that being English soil!"

"I beg to differ with you," countered Tyronne Blackwater. "What you're talking about using here is the most powerful explosive device ever created by man. If it was to detonate right now, half of County Caven would be incinerated, with the resulting radioactive fallout poisoning the land for a thousand years to come. To set it off in a city the site of London would cause untold havoc. There's no telling how many innocents, and how many IRB supporters, would die from the resulting blast, firestorm, and fallout. And don't forget, this same radiation will be borne on the winds and will settle down in Europe, the Soviet Union, and even in Ireland itself. That alone will be enough to quickly turn the world community against our cause for all time to come."

"I'm not talking about setting it off in London," returned Bernard. "What I had in mind was an isolated military installation."

"Why do we have to detonate it at all?" asked Marie. "If you ask me, the mere fact that we possess the bomb is enough to blackmail the Brits into meeting our demands and then some."

Bernard thought about this for a moment. "That's an interesting plan, comrade, but any blackmail attempt involves some degree of trust between the parties involved. And when the Brits and the Yanks learn that we have the bomb, they'll come down on us so fast that we'll never know what hit us."

"If we're not going to blackmail them with it, and it won't be exploded in London, just what do you plan to do with the bomb, Bernard?"

The one-eyed terrorist intently scanned the faces of his audience as he answered. "Actually, I've been pondering that same question ever since I learned the exact nature of this device, and so far this is what I've come up with. It was released in the papers last week that the Brits will be christening their first Trident-missile-carrying submarine six days from now. This celebration will be taking place in Scotland, at the Falsane naval installation on Gare Loch. As befitting such a christening, the Queen and the Royal Family will be attending the launching. What I propose is to spoil their little party by sneaking the bomb into Gare Loch and having it detonate just as the Queen smashes that bottle of champagne over the sub's bow."

Briefly halting at this point to allow his shocked audience a moment to digest this, Bernard continued, this time with a hint of passion in his tone. "Just think of it, Comrades. With one mighty blast, we'll rid the earth of not only one of the deadliest armadas of nuclear submarines to ever sail the seas, but the Royal Family as well!"

"Good heavens, Bernard!" managed Dr. Blackwater, who shook his head in amazement.

Marie Barrett was shocked into speechlessness. Beside her, Sean's brow narrowed in deep thought.

"I must admit, that's an incredible plan, Bernard," said Sean. "And though it all sounds amazingly simple, I have two questions for you. How do you plan to sneak the device into Gare Loch, and just how does one go about detonating a bomb such as this one? Surely there's a protective lock on it of some type to keep it from going off either by accident or by unauthorized hands such as our own."

"Sean's got a good point there," added the doctor. "I believe the lock he's talking about is called a PAL, or Permissive Action Link. Supposedly the only way for a nuclear bomb to be armed is by a special code relayed by the United States President in times of crisis."

Bernard wasted no time with his reply. "That may very well be, Doctor. But as Sean here so astutely observed, first we have to get the device into Gare Loch, which just so happens to be across the Firth of Clyde from Glasgow Harbor. If I remember correctly, isn't that oceangoing tug that we recently purchased to assist us in our gun-running operations still being kept for us at the docks there?"

"That it is, Bernard," answered the physician. "As you know, I handled the transaction myself. The vessel is registered in my name, and it will be kept in Glasgow Harbor until a more suitable location is found for it."

"Then can any of you think of a more suitable platform on which to bring the bomb into Gare Loch?" offered Bernard with a sly grin. "Since the tug still carries Scottish papers and is home-ported nearby, no one should question its presence in the Firth of Clyde on the day of the christening. And who could blame its skipper for wanting to get as close as possible to Falsane to see all the festivities? Surely other surface craft will have similar ideas, and the authorities will have their hands full keeping all of them at a proper distance.

"Now, as to getting the bomb to explode once we get it there . . . since it's obvious that we just can't connect a fuse to the device and detonate it that way, we're going to need the services of an expert. You all know about the new nuclear power station that the Republic is building outside of Dublin. Last year, when the ecologists were raising such a fuss about it, I remember hearing the project's director speak regarding the nuclear industries safety record. The chap was bright and incredibly persuasive, and it was his dynamic personality more than anything else that helped save the project from certain defeat. I was so impressed that I did a little background check on him.

"His name's Dr. John Maguire. He was originally born in Shannon, yet he was schooled almost exclusively in the States. He got his undergraduate degree at MIT and his doctorate in nuclear physics at Cal Tech. After graduation, he went to work for the Sandia Corporation. This company is one of the world's major designers of nuclear weapons, and I was somewhat surprised at the time that the Americans would allow an Irish citizen to be employed in such a sensitive position. Supposedly Maguire was disillusioned with the weapons business and took the position in Dublin as soon as it was offered to him.

"Though I doubt we can count on the good doctor merely to volunteer his services, I believe we'll be able to convince him that it will be in his best interests to do so. They say he's quite the family man, and practically lives for his wife and two young daughters. Now do you suppose he'd be willing to share the secret of the bomb in exchange for his dear family's safety?"

"It sounds as if you have this entire operation pretty well thought out," commented Sean.

"I still don't like it," offered Tyronne Blackwater. "Nuclear weapons always have scared the death out of me. With the radiation and all, there are just too many unknown factors, and I say the risks outweigh the benefits."

Disappointed with this response, Bernard turned his attention to the only female present. "And what about you, Marie?"

The redhead hesitated a moment before offering her opinion. "I must admit that it does sound tempting.

With the Royal Family out of the way and the submarine base obliterated, the Brits will be devastated. And then it will be the IRB that will be negotiating from a position of power."

"I agree," said Sean. "Even if we don't come right out and take responsibility for the blast, we merely have to follow it with our planned summer offensive. With all the new weapons at our disposal, we'll attack every single British military installation in Northern Ireland. Those poor Brits will be numbed by the loss of their beloved Royal Family, and I doubt they'll be in much of a mood for fighting. In fact, I bet public sentiment will just say the hell with it, and Parliament will give in to our demands just to get us out of their hair."

Bernard nodded. "My sentiments exactly, Sean. This gift your father fished from the sea for us will soon enough take the fight out of them. That I can guarantee you. So if there's no further discussion, I say let's get on with it. Six days isn't a hell of a lot of time to get an operation of this magnitude underway, and I'm going to need the full cooperation of each one of you to pull it off.

"Marie, I want you to take off for Dublin at once. Find out all you can about Dr. John Maguire's family life. I've got a feeling that some of the lads will soon be paying the good doctor a little visit.

"And you're going to have to carry your weight also, Sean—wound or no wound. I'd like you to be responsible for intelligence on the Falsane naval installation. We're going to need to know its exact layout, and just where the Trident christening is going to take place. If you'll just follow me over to the house, I'll show you the charts of the area that I've already managed to lay my hands on."

"Come on, I'll go with you," offered Marie. "Besides, I'd better get some food into that stomach of yours, Sean, or you'll be of no use to us whatsoever. Are you coming, Doctor?"

The physician heavily sighed. "I'll be joining you in a moment. You go ahead while I lock up the place."

The three terrorists left the barn, leaving the owner of Cootehill House alone before the steel-encased, torpedo-like cylinder. With his eyes locked on the bomb, the weary physician mumbled softly to himself.

"Liam Lafferty, my friend, now I'm not so certain that what you pulled from the sea was such a blessing after all."

Chapter Nine

It was on a cold, windy night that Captain Mikhail Borisov and the crew of his *Sea Devil* arrived back in Kronstadt. No sooner did the mini-sub dock inside the moonpool of its specially designed support ship than a crisply uniformed junior officer presented himself at the gangplank.

"Captain Borisov, let me be the first to welcome you home. If it's convenient, Admiral Starobin would like you to be his guest at the Komsomol dining hall this evening."

Mikhail had been on the top deck of his vessel supervising the final docking procedures as this surprise invitation was delivered. Though he had been looking forward to a shower, a quick meal, and a long nap on his own, one couldn't take such an invite lightly. He cleared his throat.

"I'd be honored to accept, Lieutenant. But could you please ask the admiral to give me at the very least forty-five minutes to clean myself up in the officer's club and get into a fresh uniform?"

"Why of course, Captain. The admiral understands that you have only just come back from a long mission, and you have an hour to prepare yourself. Shall I send a car for you?"

"I'll walk," returned Mikhail curtly.

With this the junior officer saluted smartly, clicked

his heels together, and pivoted to return to headquarters. Mikhail looked on as he disappeared up the ladder that led from the moonpool.

"What's the matter, Captain? Is there some sort of trouble?" queried a voice from behind.

Mikhail turned his head and spotted the source of this query, his moustached chief engineer, who had just climbed up onto the deck via the mini-sub's forward accessway.

"No, Comrade Sosnovo, it's nothing you need to be concerned with. It looks like I'll be at the Komsomol dining hall, if you need me."

"So you couldn't wait to get a fresh meal, huh Captain?" said the Ukrainian with a wink. "Don't forget, if they're offering the Ukrainian borscht tonight, don't pass it up, sir."

"I won't, comrade. Now I'd better get up to the locker room at the officers' club and make myself presentable. Right now, I stink so bad that every diner in the whole restaurant would lose his appetite the second I walked into the place."

Well aware that he was leaving his *Sea Devil* in good hands, Mikhail left the vessel by way of the gangplank. Their current floating dock was a large rectangular pool that had been cut into the lower hull of an Ugra-class support ship. This same opening could be closed to the sea and drained, and the *Sea Devil* could thus be transferred, giving the versatile mini-sub yet another deployment possibility.

A steep ladder took him to the main deck of the support vessel. Here an alert sentry snapped him a crisp salute and escorted him off the ship and onto the concrete pier. It was good to be back on solid footing after his long voyage. Oblivious to the icy gusts, he pulled tight the collar of his cotton tunic and began his way towards the officers' club.

The area around the docks was bustling with activity. A battalion of tough-looking Marines were in the process of boarding an Ivan Rogov-class landing ship. Mikhail had spent a fair amount of time on one of these impressive vessels himself. In addition to troops, they were designed to carry up to forty battle tanks and a variety of support vehicles. The landing ships also had a docking bay in which hovercraft were stored, and two helicopter landing spots both fore and aft.

While wondering what far corner of the earth these troops might be off to, he passed the main embarkation area and followed the railroad tracks that ran parallel to the docks as far as the base power plant. Here he turned inland, utilizing a sidewalk to cross into the administrative and living areas.

The officers' club was situated beside the base commissary. It occupied a fairly new three-story brick structure built in the late 1970s. Mikhail headed for this building's basement, where a fully equipped gymnasium, complete with an Olympic-sized swimming pool, was located. He kept a locker here for just such occasions.

Because of the fairly late hour, the locker room was deserted as he entered. Thankful to have the place to himself, he stripped off his stained coveralls and headed straight for the showers. Under a torrent of steaming hot water he washed away the accumulated grime of two weeks spent locked up within the cramped confines of his *Sea Devil*. He had to wash his hair three times to get it squeaky clean, and he used the better part of a bar of soap to get the rest of his body completely clean. He finished up this soaking by turning off the hot tap and crying out as a flood of icy cold water shot out from the showerhead. Not until he covered his entire body with this invigorating spray did he turn off the tap altogether.

He felt like a new man as he sauntered over to his locker and got his toilet kit. At the sink he brushed his teeth and shaved. The familiar face that stared back at him from the steam-covered mirror looked weary and strained. His steel-gray eyes were bloodshot, and fatigue lines marked his highly etched cheeks and brow. Taking a moment to trace the scar that lined his face, Mikhail turned to dress himself.

The Komsomol dining hall was located on the third floor of the officers' club. It was plushly decorated, with red, royal blue, and gold predominating. Lit only by candlelight, the spacious room featured a strolling violinist, who was in the midst of a spirited piece by Khachaturian as Mikhail entered.

"Captain Borisov, it's good to see you again," greeted the smiling maitre d'.

"Hello, Vitaly," returned Mikhail warmly. "It's been much too long. How's the wife and that new baby of yours?"

"She's still running me ragged, Captain. But the baby, he makes it all worth it. Did you know that little Viktor is already crawling? My mother sewed him a sailor suit, and you should just see how he looks in a uniform. So when are you finally going to settle down and start a family of your own?"

Mikhail shrugged his muscular shoulders. "Find me the right girl and I'll start on that family right after dessert," he said with a wide grin.

"Oh, to live the life of a sailor with a beautiful, exotic woman in every port," reflected the maitre d', who sighed and looked down at his clipboard. "Admiral Starobin is waiting for you in the main dining room, Captain. If you'll just follow me, I'll take you right over to him."

Every table in the candlelit dining room was taken,

but because of the lack of direct light and the great amount of space between each station, one could dine here in almost complete privacy. Mikhail was led to a spot beside a full-length picture window. Here a white-haired senior officer sat alone sipping a cocktail, staring out the window.

"Excuse me, Admiral, but Captain Borisov has arrived," greeted the maitre d'.

Quickly turning his head at this, Admiral Igor Starobin smiled broadly. "So he didn't stand me up after all, Vitaly. Ah, it's good to see you, Captain."

Taking this as his cue to leave, the maitre d' quietly backed away and left the two officers to themselves. As he did, Mikhail accepted the admiral's handshake and seated himself.

"I hope that I didn't keep you too long, Admiral."

"Not at all, comrade. In fact, you're right on time. I realized that you only just returned from sea, but I couldn't wait to personally convey to you our appreciation for a job well done. Your little trip to Norway was a complete success. Why, we're already benefiting from your efforts. But enough of such shop talk . . . how about joining me for a drink? And then we'll get some fresh food into you."

The admiral lifted up his right hand and snapped his fingers. Seconds later a waiter arrived. Without asking his guest, Igor Starobin ordered a chilled bottle of Caspian vodka and an assortment of appetizers. In no time at all this request was fulfilled, and as they held up their glasses, the white-haired senior officer initiated the first toast.

"To my esteemed guest! Welcome back from the sea, Captain. Your motherland is proud of you."

Mikhail humbly nodded and took a sip of his drink. The vodka went down smoothly, and the blond commando reached out to try some of the caviar. Quick to join him was his host, who covered a flat whole wheat cracker with caviar and hungrily gulped it down.

"Now this is decent caviar, comrade . . . not like that crap they sell us at the commissary."

"From what I hear, all the good stuff gets sold for export," offered Mikhail.

"I believe you're right, my friend. But it just doesn't seem to make any sense. I know we need the trade, but why barter away one of the Rodina's finest natural resources, and leave none for its own citizens? Why, decent Russian caviar is easier to buy in New York City than it is in Moscow!"

Before Mikhail could reply, the waiter appeared tableside. "Excuse me, comrades, but the kitchen will be closing shortly and I'd like to get your orders in. May I recommend either the fresh baked sturgeon, or the house specialty, Ukrainian borscht."

"I'll take the sturgeon," said the Admiral.

"Make mine the borscht," said Mikhail. "My senior electrician is from Kiev, and all I've been hearing these last two weeks is how damn tasty the dish can be when it's prepared properly."

"I'll tell the chef to stir the pot for you, comrade," offered the waiter as he ambled off to the kitchen to put in their orders.

The admiral sipped his vodka and looked his guest in the eye. "So tell me, comrade, other than your successful tap of the NATO communications cable, did your *Sea Devil* function properly?"

"Other than a backed-up crapper and a couple of minor shorts, she operated splendidly, Admiral. We gave her watertight integrity a real workout when a couple of Norwegian corvettes depth-charged us off the coast of Larvik."

"How in the world did they ever tag you?" asked the concerned senior officer.

181

"Don't worry, Admiral. It wasn't a signature deficiency on our part that gave us away. You see, we hit an unmarked sub net that triggered our presence to their ASW forces."

"Off the coast of Larvik, you say?" repeated the Admiral thoughtfully. "I want you to leave me that net's exact coordinates. I've got Korsakov and his team going into those same waters next week, and there's no sense risking their mission on something we already know about."

"You'll have those coordinates on your desk tomorrow morning," returned Mikhail, who added with a grin, "I'll drop them off to you on my way out of the base as I begin my leave. I'm booked on a ten A.M. Aeroflot flight to Odessa, where I've got a whole four weeks to work on my tan."

Admiral Starobin feared just such a thing and was all set to deliver the bad news when the waiter arrived with dinner. Deciding to let his guest eat this last meal in peace, Igor held his tongue and dug into his sturgeon.

Across the table from him, Mikhail Borisov breathed in the rich collection of scents that were emanating from his steaming hot bowl of borscht. Using a large spoon, he sipped a mouthful of the beet-red broth and found it tasty and perfectly seasoned. He needed a knife and fork to get at the assortment of delicacies that filled the rest of the bowl. They included tangy sausage, potatoes, cabbage, carrots, onions, celery, and several tender chunks of meat. He used a heel of crusty rye bread to sop up the remaining broth, which he extended with a dollop of sour cream.

"My chief engineer was correct, this dish is one of the finest I've ever tasted. How was your fish, Admiral?"

"Adequate," replied his host. "Though I would have

preferred a bowl of that borscht, at my age a plain piece of broiled fish makes more sense for the old heart. Now what do you say to dessert?"

No sooner did these words leave the Admiral's lips than the waiter arrived with two platters of sliced pineapple spears.

"Well, look what we have here," observed Igor Starobin. "I guess a cargo ship arrived here from Cuba recently. Though it's going to take a lot more than pineapples to pay off the huge debt Castro and his gang of thugs owe us."

"At least this is a commodity that we can't grow in the motherland," added Mikhail as he cut into the luscious yellow fruit and began devouring it.

The admiral waited for their snifters of brandy to arrive before managing to bring up the sensitive subject that had necessitated this dinner in the first place.

"I hope you enjoyed your meal, Captain. I just wanted to tell you once again how very proud I am of you. Without your tireless effort, the motherland would be a less secure place to live. All of us can rest more easily just knowing that vessels like *Sea Devil* are at our disposal, to thwart the imperialistic ambitions of our sworn enemy.

"You have helped make a dream that was conceived over forty years ago become a reality. As you very well know, it was during the closing days of the Great War that I first laid my eyes on *Sea Devil*. Though this crude Nazi prototype was far from the sophisticated vessel that we have today, the mere idea of combining amphibious tracked drive and submarine propulsion was a unique, ingenious concept whose possibilities seemed endless to me. The designers at the Red Banner Shipyards agreed, and as a result, the craft that we today call *Sea Devil* was born.

"Through the years there have been many doubtors

in the defense ministry who were skeptical of *Sea Devil's* operational effectiveness. True, we have had our failures, just as we've had our triumphant successes. Yet to win these unbelievers over to our side once and for all, I recently submitted the plans for an unprecedented covert operation to both Admiral of the Fleet Markov and the Premier's closest aide, Deputy Secretary Stanislav Krasino. And much to my utter delight, only yesterday I received the go-ahead from the Politburo itself.

"As I prepared to set the operation in motion, I could think of no better qualified officer than you to lead my strike team into action. For what I propose is a mission whose successful outcome will change the very balance of power between East and West unalterably in our favor!"

With this rousing statement, Igor Starobin briefly halted to take a sip of his brandy and catch his breath. Certain that he had the undivided attention of his rapt dinner companion, he continued.

"What I propose is to have you take *Sea Devil* up Scotland's Firth of Clyde to the American naval installation at Holy Loch. There you will place a specially designed series of limpet mines beneath the hull of a yet-to-be-named imperialist nuclear submarine. These explosives will be placed in such a manner that their activation will split the vessel's hull apart and cause the sub's still-critical reactor to go plummeting to the seafloor below. The result will be an ecological disaster of unprecedented scope, as raw plutonium is released into the pristine waters of the loch, poisoning them for a thousand years to come.

"Just think of the international outrage that will follow such a disaster, comrade! Without being able to point a finger at the actual perpetrator, the Americans will be assailed by every nation on this planet. Why, the Europeans will be absolutely furious, and demand that the United States withdraw its nuclear weapons from their soil before such a calamity can reoccur. And in such a way not only will we succeed in permanently shutting down the naval installation that poses the most direct threat to our shores, but also cause the removal of American cruise missiles and shorter range tactical nuclear weapons from Europe as well!

"I had hoped to initiate this mission upon your return from leave, for I know the hectic schedule that you've been on these past few months. But one of the preconditions that the Politburo insisted upon when they gave me the go-ahead was that it take place to coincide with the Queen of England's visit to the Falsane Naval Base at nearby Gare Loch. Here she will christen the first English submarine to be equipped with Trident missiles."

"And when will that take place?" Mikhail asked calmly.

"In five and a half days," answered the admiral, who noted that Mikhail took this news without flinching. "I feel the timing is most appropriate. The presence of the Royal Family will be a welcome addition, as the tragedy unfolds and the eyes of all the planet center on the waters of Scotland's Firth of Clyde."

"I agree," replied Mikhail. "Are these specially designed limpet mines that you spoke of ready to go?"

Igor Starobin nodded. "Even as we speak, they are being flown up to Kronstadt from the test facility at Baku."

"Then all I need are some charts and a schematic on where the charges are to be placed," said the blond-haired commando.

"Then you'll accept the mission?"

"Of course I will, Admiral. Just like yourself, I have dedicated the better years of my life to *Sea Devil,* and this operation will be the pinnacle of my efforts. In my humble opinion it's a brilliant plan that only one vessel in the world can successfully pull off. Since time is critical, is it okay if I undergo the mission with my current crew?"

Surprised with the young captain's cool acceptance of this perilous assignment, Igor answered him. "I see no reason why not, comrade, though you must make it perfectly clear to your crew that *Sea Devil*'s capture will not be tolerated. You will travel in civilian clothes, taking nothing on board that can be traced back to the motherland. In addition to the standard cyanide pills, the vessel will be rigged with a explosive charge that is to be detonated if capture appears imminent. I don't have to remind you that these are some of the most closely monitored waters on the planet. We both are well aware of your vessel's capabilities, but even *Sea Devil* is going to need a little additional luck on this mission."

"My people will understand, Admiral. After all, we are Spetsnaz, and no challenge or risk is too great for us."

"If only I had a few more like you, comrade," reflected the white-haired veteran. "I am putting all my hopes in your capable hands. If I was only a little younger, I'd be going on the mission myself. But those adventurous days are long past for me. Soon I'll be forced to retire, and at the very least I can meet this inevitable day with my head held high, knowing that my life's work has been worthwhile. For this operation will signal the fruition of a long career that began in another era, almost five decades ago."

"I'll do my best not to let you down, sir," offered Mikhail sincerely.

"I know you will, Captain. And just to let you know how appreciative we are of your effort, upon your return I've been authorized to give you an entire three months leave, plus the exclusive use of the defense minister's own Black Sea dacha."

A wide grin painted the captain's rugged face as he lifted his brandy snifter. "Three months and the use of the defense minister's dacha, you say? I think that I can handle that, Admiral. I really think I can."

Of all the inquiries Major Colin Stewart initiated in an attempt to locate the escaped terrorist, only one proved promising. Several hours after the shoot-out at Edinburgh Castle, an RAF Nimrod AWACS platform recorded monitoring a light plane crossing over the Scottish border west of Glasgow and headed toward the Irish Sea by way of the North Channel. This aircraft eventually landed at a private airstrip located northeast of the two of Dundalk in the Republic of Ireland. It was only later, when RAF intelligence could find no official flight plan for this unusual late night transit, that Major Stewart was notified.

With no other leads to follow, Stewart asked command for permission to investigate this suspicious flight more closely. Not the type who asked favors often, the commander of the 75th Highlanders received the okay to take a four-man squad into the Republic and attempt to locate this aircraft and determine its purpose.

It was with the highest expectations that Colin Stewart assembled his handpicked squad and loaded them into a Land Rover. Their immediate destination was Prestwick Airport, where the 819th Helicopter Squadron was based. Here they left the confines of the Rover and boarded a Royal Navy Sea King helicopter.

"I see that you're headed for our base in Northern Ireland at Armagh," greeted the Sea King's pilot as Colin Stewart strapped himself into the observer's seat.

"You fellows wouldn't be going to bandit country, would you?"

The Highlander met this innocent query with a sly grin. "Let's just say that me and the lads are on a little fishing expedition. Now if you'll be so good as to get this whirlybird skyward, I'll save a part of our catch for you."

The nuclear-powered attack sub USS *Bowfin* put to sea at daybreak. The mirrorlike waters of Holy Loch were veiled by a thick shroud of swirling fog as the 292-foot-long Sturgeon-class vessel guardedly entered the waters of the Firth of Clyde. A foghorn sounded mournfully in the distance, yet the *Bowfin* carried no such device itself. To see through the blinding mist and keep from colliding with an oncoming ship, it relied on its sensitive BPS-15 surveillance radar.

From the sub's exposed bridge, cut into the top part of its sail, Captain William Foard monitored their progress. The forty-two-year-old Naval Academy graduate had been stationed at Holy Loch for over a year now, and was well acquainted with these waters. He knew the narrow estuary to be tricky even on those rare occasions when the weather was good. The morning fog only made his difficult job that much more of a challenge, and he scanned that portion of the Firth visible beyond the sub's rounded bow with a vigilant intensity. Behind him, two alert seamen did likewise.

"Sir, Commander Mackenzie would like permission to join you on the bridge," broke the voice of the quartermaster from the intercom.

"Send him up," replied Foard.

Soon after, a blond-haired, khaki-clad officer climbed out of the hatchway that was recessed into the floor of the exposed bridge.

"It's damn chilly up here," observed Mac as he zipped up his jacket.

"A typical spring morning in Scotland," returned the *Bowfin*'s CO. "Were you able to get settled in okay?"

"No problems, Captain," answered Mac, whose gaze attempted to penetrate the thick mist. "The XO was most gracious to offer me half of his stateroom as he did."

"Though there's a few on board that feel Lieutenant Commander Bauer is a bit cold and distant, he's a pretty decent guy once you get to know him. I understand that you two have worked together before."

"That we have, Captain. I was stationed at the Barking Sands Underwater Test Range on Kauai, and Lieutenant Commander Bauer was the XO of one of the subs we were working with."

"I've worked Barking Sands. That's some facility that we have out there."

Any response on Mac's part was interrupted by the activation of the intercom. "Sir, we have a surface contact on radar bearing one-six-three, range one-zero nautical miles and closing. Looks to be a tug or a fishing trawler of some type."

"Very good, Mr. Murray," returned the captain. "Most likely they're headed towards Port Glasgow and should stay on their side of the channel. Let me know otherwise."

"Will do, Captain," retorted the ship's navigator as the intercom was silent.

"The weather's sure a bit different in Hawaii," reflected Mac.

The CO grunted. "Once we get to the fifty-fathom curve and go under, we could be cruising off the tropical shores of Barking Sands, for all I know. In another half hour or so, the weather topside will be the least of our concerns. That's one of the benefits of traveling by submarine."

"How do you like being stationed in Holy Loch?" questioned Mac.

"So far, I don't have any serious complaints, Commander. My wife's of Scottish ancestry, and when I got my transfer orders, she couldn't wait to get over here. We've got a small cottage in Dunoon that's got all the comforts of the States. Personally, when I'm not driving the *Bowfin*, I like to spend my free time playing golf and fishing. And in both activities, Scotland excels."

"I'm a golfer myself," returned Mac. "Have you gotten up to St. Andrews yet?"

The mere mention of his favorite pastime put a boyish gleam in the captain's eyes. "No, I haven't, though I have played Gleneagles. The little lady and myself took the train up there and had a marvelous time. Can't say much for my score, but the course itself is gorgeous, and the scenery even better. It's located right at the southern part of the Highlands and abounds with heather-filled meadows, crystal-clear lochs, and plenty of fast-moving streams. Luckily I brought along my fishing gear, and caught the biggest salmon of my life on the nearby Devon River."

"Sounds like Scotland's been good to you, Captain. For the last couple of years, I've been living on the north shore of Oahu. We've got a few pretty good golf courses of our own, though the scenery's a bit different."

"That's awful lovely country in its own right," said the CO with a sigh. "I'd be a liar if I didn't tell you that this fickle Scottish weather can get a bit nerve-wracking sometimes. During the winter just passed, we had three weeks straight of nothing but solid rain. Naturally it came just as we returned from a 45-day cruise. By the end of the first week, we were dreaming of palm trees, blue skies, and white sand beaches. By the end of the third week, even New London, Connecticut, was starting to sound good."

"I didn't think that submariners got cabin fever," Mac said with a grin.

The CO shook his head. "At least when I'm aboard the *Bowfin,* my wife's not around to constantly pester me about painting the interior of the house and fixing the plumbing. That can get old real fast."

Again the intercom crackled alive to report a nearby surface contact, and as the captain responded to this call, Mac looked out to the *Bowfin*'s teardrop-shaped bow. Through the roiling mist he could just see the waters of the Firth as they smoothly cascaded up over the sub's rounded hull. Nearly half the forward portion of the deck was covered by this frothing seawater that left behind a characteristic splashing surge in its wake.

"Seems we're just about to pass a slow-moving trawler that lies to our starboard some five hundred yards away. They shouldn't be any problem as long as they remain on course."

Mac looked to his right, but failed to spot the vessel.

"The Firth can get awfully crowded with civilian vessels sometimes," added the CO. "It's not the best place to locate a submarine base, but I shouldn't complain. It's a hell of a lot more convenient than having to steam in from the United States mainland. Because a short northward jog of only a few hundred miles puts up right on Ivan's doorstep."

"I understand that the Brits have a sub base here as well," said Mac.

"That's right, Commander. It's located a few miles east of us in Gare Loch. Falsane is where they keep a good majority of their boomers, and where their new Trident vessels will be operating out of."

"Sort of puts us smack at ground zero in the event of a war, doesn't it, Captain?"

The *Bowfin*'s CO looked at Mac as he replied to this. "As far as I'm concerned, if such a horrific thing were going to come down, that's right where I'd like to be. It's the survivors of such a conflict that I'd pity. I'd much rather go up in a flash, though as a submariner there's a good chance that I'd be directly participating in such a conflict at sea, rather than merely just getting fried at port."

"If the unthinkable ever occurs and the nuclear genie *is* released, Oahu won't last long either," added Mac. "The Reds will hit the island with a barrage of submarine-launched warheads that will make December 7, 1941, look like a turkey shoot."

"But don't forget, Commander, our job's to ensure that such a tragic turn of events never happens. That's why it's so damned important that America remain strong. One thing I'm absolutely certain of is that the Russkies respect strength above all. They're not about to launch a nuclear strike if they know Uncle Sam will be able to retaliate effectively. Right now, our triad of nuclear delivery systems ensures our continued security. But for how much longer, I just don't know. Ivan's continually improving his ASW skills, which means that soon our Trident submarine fleet won't be so invulnerable. Congress still can't decide on an updated ICBM basing mode to replace Minuteman, and I'm afraid that our fixed-wing capabilities are a bit questionable."

"I hear you, Captain," returned Mac. "It's hard to believe that the first flight of a B-52 took place way back in 1952. Hell, that's two whole years before I was even born, and those planes are still up there flying deterrent patrols. SAC and the Air Force have done one hell of a fine job maintaining such platforms. But the questions remains, can they still do the job that they were designed to do almost four decades ago?"

"Let's hope to God we never have to learn the answer to that question, Commander. And speaking of the B-52, what do you think our chances are of finding those two bombs that are still missing?"

Mac thoughtfully stared out into the fog. "We should be able to do it, sir. Our current level of technology is certainly advanced enough to handle the operation. Unfortunately, our resources are limited, and the logistical concerns of such a mission are extremely challenging.

"Washington's in a hurry for us to recover the missing ordnance, and rightly so. Yet without the proper equipment, our job's going to take only that much longer to accomplish. Our oceanographic ship, the USS *Lynch*, arrived at the site only yesterday. There are but a dozen such vessels in the fleet, and we were lucky they were in the Norwegian Sea when the crash occurred. The *Lynch*'s job will be to make an intensive bathymetric scan of the seafloor beneath the debris field. This profile will be of invaluable assistance once the bombs are located and it becomes time for their actual recovery.

"We've currently got Sea Stallion helicopters at the site pulling sonar sleds over the area. Soon a pair of Avenger-class minesweeping ships will be arriving to give the choppers a hand. The sonar capabilities of these vessels are excellent, and with them we'll be able to scan every square inch of the sea bottom. Also on hand is the sub rescue tender *Pigeon*, along with the DSRV *Mystic*. The *Mystic* will be utilized to eyeball suspicious contacts along with a variety of ROV's that have already arrived."

"It certainly sounds as if you've got a handle on it, Commander. Yet since this whole operation has been working under a need-to-know basis only, how are you explaining to the outside world what all these platforms are doing out there? Surely the Irish are going to be curious, and I wouldn't be surprised if Ivan's eye in the sky has already beamed photos of the crash site back to the Kremlin."

Mac hesitated before responding. "This whole operation is being explained away as a submarine rescue drill. Yet the longer it takes to find the two missing bombs, the shakier this story is going to get. In order to help speed things up, I've already begun circulating a flier among the fishermen in the area, asking if they happened to see anything out of the ordinary on the night of the accident. Because either one of the bombs could have fallen in an altogether different part of the Irish Sea, I felt that such an inquiry was necessary."

"It sure won't hurt," said the captain as he looked at his watch. "We'll have you out to the site soon enough, Commander. Meanwhile, how about joining me down below for some breakfast? The chow's pretty decent on this pig boat, and I know you won't be disappointed."

"I'd enjoy that, Captain," replied Mac, who watched as the *Bowfin*'s CO barked into the intercom to send up a replacement.

As Mac climbed down the narrow steel ladder that led below deck, the distinctive scent of machine oil replaced that of the sea. The accessway led directly into the control room. Here the current OOD stood watch beside the periscope well. Mac took in the two seated helmsmen perched before their airplane-style steering columns awaiting the order that would take the *Bowfin* down into its natural element.

When there was enough water beneath them to safely allow this dive, the chief petty officer positioned behind the helm would be called upon to change the state of their buoyancy by triggering the valves at the tops of the ballast tanks. In this way the air inside these tanks would be vented, allowing seawater to flood in from below and cause the vessel to lose its positive buoyancy and sink. This process would then be reversed when they wished to surface.

Close by, the radar operator anxiously stood facing his pulsating green scope, quick to call out each new surface contact that lay before them. Alertly plotting these sightings on a chart was the *Bowfin*'s navigator. It was to this sandy-haired, bespectacled officer that the captain addressed his remarks.

"Mr. Murray, I'll be in the wardroom. Let me know as soon as we pass Little Cumbrae Island. The sooner we dive and get out of this pea soup, the better it will be for all of us."

"Yes, sir."

Confident in his crew's ability to safely see the *Bowfin* through these fog-enshrouded waters, Captain Foard beckoned Mac to follow him aft. A narrow cable-lined passageway took them by the sonar and radio rooms. Mac would be utilizing the powerful transmitter of this latter compartment to contact Admiral Long at the Pentagon once the ROVs were deployed and he was able to gauge their effectiveness.

They passed by the ship's office, ducked through an open hatchway, and entered a fairly spacious compartment dominated by a large table. Seated alone here, sipping a mug of coffee and immersed in a pile of paperwork, was a middle-aged officer sporting a crew cut. The captain had to clear his throat loudly to get the man's attention.

"Excuse us, XO. Commander Mackenzie and myself were just going to have a little breakfast. Would you like to join us?"

Lieutenant Commander Ted Bauer put down his pen.

"No thanks, Captain. I've got a couple of extra pounds I'd like to lose, and I'd better stay as far away from Cooky's hotcakes as possible."

As the CO seated himself at the head of the table and Mac sat down beside him, an alert orderly appeared with two mugs of coffee.

"We'll be having two Scottish breakfasts, Mr. Warren," instructed the captain.

As the order was sent down to the galley on the deck below, the XO pushed aside the stack of reports that he had been working on.

"I understand that we've still got the fog topside, Skipper. Do you want me up on the bridge?"

"Lieutenant Murray can handle it. How are the crew's competency reports coming?"

The XO shrugged his shoulders. "I keep working on them, but I don't see any progress. It doesn't seem like I'll ever finish."

"You'll manage like you always do," said the Captain, as the orderly arrived with two bowls of oatmeal.

As the two officer's dug into these servings, the XO asked, "How do you like the *Bowfin* so far, Mac?"

Mac gulped down a spoonful of the thick cereal and answered. "She seems like an efficient, proud boat, Ted. I'm still kind of flabbergasted that Admiral Connors gave me the use of her."

"We're happy to be of service," replied the XO. "She's a bit different than my last command, though. You remember the *Blueback,* don't you, Mac?"

Mac grinned. "How can I ever forget her? I think I spent more time in her torpedo room than I did at Barking Sands."

"You never *did* say what you two were working on back on Kauai," observed the captain.

Mac looked at the XO before replying. "Though it was classified top secret at the time, I guess we can

196

tell you about it. Hell, we're all going to be working with CURV soon enough, as soon as it gets here from San Diego.'

"CURV?" repeated the captain.

"That stands for cable-controlled underwater research vehicle," explained Mac. "We originally designed it at NOSC to recover test-fired torpedoes. It's primarily comprised of ballast tanks, lights, and a claw, and has a 3,000-foot depth limit."

"We sure pushed it to its threshold back at Barking Sands," observed the XO.

"Actually, the *Blueback* was almost responsible for us losing the first CURV prototype," revealed Mac. "It was originally designed only to go down to 2,000 feet. But it seemed that everytime you fired a torpedo, it ended up at a depth greater than that. So to show command that CURV was worth all the time and effort that we had been putting into her, we made some quick adjustments and sent her down to recover the *Blueback*'s torpedoes. At a depth of 2,600 feet, the port ballast tank ruptured. It's a miracle that the starboard tank remained intact and we were able to nurse it to the surface."

"I still say that it wasn't our fault that the guys at Barking Sands gave us the wrong firing coordinates," justified the XO.

"I'm just glad that we were able to save the prototype," added Mac. "Without it, the test would have been a complete failure, and there's no telling if we'd ever get the funding to build another test unit."

"So I gather that CURV is now a working element of the United States Navy," concluded the captain.

"It most certainly is," answered Mac. "The new models work with fiber optics and are equipped with a camera that can send back remarkably clear photos at depth. This facilitates recovery and allows the unit to

197

work on its own."

"Let's just hope that all of us will get a chance to see CURV do its thing in the Irish Sea," offered the captain, who looked on as the orderly arrived with a platter heaped with blueberry hotcakes, scrambled eggs, sausage, kippered herring, and crusty scones.

"Dig in," ordered William Foard without ceremony. "And don't be afraid to eat hearty, Commander. Because it sounds to me like you're certainly going to have your work cut out for you these next couple of days."

Chapter Ten

Dr. John Maguire had just arrived at his office at Dublin's Shamrock Nuclear Power Station on the banks of the River Liffey when a call arrived for him on his private line. In a very serious, calm tone of voice, a woman explained to him that his wife and two daughters had just been kidnapped.

The physicist's first reaction was that this was all some sort of sick practical joke, and he was tempted to hang up the receiver and call plant security. It was at that moment that his oldest child's voice emanated from the telephone. There could be no denying the six-year-old's frightened tone as she begged her father to take this call very seriously or they would hurt her mommy. Sobered by this plea, Maguire listened anxiously as the kidnapper directed him to leave at once for the Central Dublin postal exchange. He was ordered to drive alone, and above all, not to inform the authorities of this call. For if he did, he would never see his family alive again.

Maguire's brow was soaked in sweat, his hand trembling, as he hung up the telephone and contemplated his next move. His position as director of the Shamrock plant gave him instant access to the Republic's highest ranking political and military figures. But he was no stranger to the assortment of terrorist groups active in his country. And knowing full well that the lives of his family would mean absolutely nothing to such ruthless individuals, he decided against notifying the police. He tried to appear as composed as possible as he informed his secretary that he would have to cancel his morning appointments and leave the office. His secretary was caught totally off guard by this revelation, and was unable to get her boss to explain his reasoning behind this abrupt change of plans.

The drive to the postal exchange seemed to take forever. When he finally arrived, he remained in his car, as instructed. At one point during his wait, a pair of uniformed gardia patrolmen strolled by his automobile, and Maguire fought the temptation to appeal for their assistance. Soon afterward, there was a loud knock on the passenger window, and a woman dressed in a hat and sunglasses beckoned him to allow her entry. He quickly did so and breathlessly listened as she spoke to him with a dreaded familiar voice.

"I want you to head for the N3 by way of Phoenix Park. And for the sake of your adoring family, drive carefully, Doctor."

It wasn't until they were well north of the city limits that Maguire found the nerve to voice himself. "Who are you? Where are we going, and where are you keeping my family?"

"My heavens, Doctor Maguire, aren't you the curious one. But if you want to see those babies of yours grow up to take husbands, you'll keep that mouth of yours shut and do like I tell you!"

The physicist forced himself to hold his tongue as they continued traveling north on the two-lane highway. Outside the town of Navan the clear sky darkened, and soon they were in the midst of a driving rainstorm. The lush green estates of Meath county was known for could hardly be seen as Maguire struggled to keep his car on the road.

It was as they passed through the village of Virginia that the rains abated. A rainbow formed on the northern horizon, and his escort ordered him to turn off the main highway near the town of Stradone.

"We'll be taking the back roads from here on, Doctor. So watch your speed and keep your eyes peeled for oncoming traffic."

Maguire wisely heeded this warning in time to steer clear of an approaching lorry that had no intention of sharing the narrow road with anyone else. Doing his best to miss the assortment of potholes that abounded here, he noted the parched appearance of the passing countryside. The hilly landscape here was dotted with ramshackle cottages and rock-strewn fields marked by winding stone hedges. A tinker's caravan passed on their right, and the physicist got a brief view of its gypsies seated on the side of the road playing cards. Certain that they were in County Caven at this point, he learned this fact for certain when he spotted a tilted road sign that indicated that the village of Cootehill was three kilometers away.

At one point they had considered building a nuclear power plant in this part of the Republic. It was hoped that the jobs and abundant energy the plant would create would help this perpetually backward area develop. One of the sites they were considering was south of Cootehill, on the banks of the Annalee River. John Maguire was flown out here by helicopter and found the location most promising. Yet it was the Republic that finally decided that the site's relative proximity to the border with Northern Ireland made such a location undesirable. For the further north they now went, the closer they came to that infamous portion of Ireland known as "bandit country," the virtually untamed home of the political terrorist.

Was such an organization responsible for his current

abduction? The physicist could only guess that this was the case as they drove through the sleepy village of Cootehill and turned off onto a winding country lane. The roadway here was all but impassable. Its asphalt was cracked and pitted, and in many places virtually nonexistent. Trying his best to ignore the rough ride and his vainly protesting shock absorbers, Maguire was ordered to turn left at a sign that read *Cootehill House*. A partially flooded lane took them through a forest of stately pines. A large lake was visible to the left. As the road twisted and they began their way up a rather steep rise, Maguire spotted the rounded arches of an estate house at the summit of this hillside. An ominous, heavy feeling formed in his gut with the realization that this gothic-looking habitation signaled the end of their long trip.

"You'll park by the barn at the back of the house," instructed his abductor.

Maguire did as he was ordered, receiving his next instructions as he put the transmission into park and turned off the ignition.

"You may exit now, Doctor. And by the way, let me be the first to welcome you to Cootehill House."

His escort displayed an unusual degree of civility with this remark, and with the hope that things might not be as bad as they seemed, he opened the door and stepped outside.

The air was cool and crisp, the ground wet, as if it had just rained. Maguire guessed that the estate house that he stood beside had to be at the least fifty years old. Even then, it was in an amazingly good state of repair. The grounds were also well kept. This included the large vegetable garden adjacent to the estate's southern wall.

"Damn!" cursed his escort as she left the car and took off for this plot.

The physicist was surprised to find his abductor drawn to a tomato plant that seemed recently to have been trampled on. She had also removed the hat, sunglasses, and raincoat she'd been wearing, revealing herself to be an attractive young girl in her mid-twenties, with straight red hair and a curvaceous figure.

"So this must be the esteemed Dr. John Maguire," came a deep voice from behind him.

The physicist pivoted and set his eyes on a tall, swarthy-looking character with an eyepatch over his right eye. Only as he approached did Maguire note that he wore his long hair pulled back in a ponytail. Dressed in ragged blue jeans and a Berkeley sweatshirt, he looked much like a middle-aged version of a 1960s hippie. Yet there was something sinister about his appearance, and the scientist's gut tightened as he again spoke.

"It really is an honor to meet you, Doctor. I heard you speak some time ago, when the Republic was considering whether or not to invest in its first nuclear power plant. Though I myself sided with the ecologists who resisted this plant, I couldn't help but admire the clarity of your thought as you delivered your very persuasive presentation."

"And to whom, may I ask, am I speaking?"

"Names are not really important at this stage of the game, Doctor. Just know that I hold convictions equally as strong as your own, though I'm certain you and I could have some very spirited debates on a variety of subjects if the opportunity presented itself."

Frustrated by the deliberate vagueness of this answer, Maguire emotionally exploded. "Well, how in the hell am I supposed to know what's going on here if you won't even tell me your name? What do you want with me, and what have you done with my family?"

"So the good doctor has a temper after all," returned his one-eyed host. "Go ahead and shout all you want. Relieve the tension that's bottled up inside of you, but be assured that *I'm* the one who'll be asking all the questions around here. Otherwise, you'll never see that family of yours again!"

Certain that he meant this, Maguire softened. "What you do to me is not important. Just don't hurt my family. Please, I implore you!"

The cofounder of the Irish Republican Brotherhood seemed to deliberate a moment before verbally reacting to this plea. "That's the kind of attitude that will show results around here, Doctor. Your family is being held outside of Dublin by a group of my associates. I give you my word of honor that no harm will come to them as long as you cooperate with us."

"Can I at least speak to them?" asked the physicist.

"I believe that can be arranged," replied Bernard Loughlin thoughtfully. "But first I have a little task for you to perform. Do it to my satisfaction, and you'll earn both your family's release and your own as well."

"Anything you say," implored the scientist. "Just don't harm them . . . that's all that I ask."

"Your loyalty is very touching, Doctor. I like that in a man. A person should passionately believe in something, whether it be another person or an ideal. I myself am involved with the latter. But that's irrelevant. It's time to get on with the task that necessitated your presence here. Marie, forget about those damn plants of yours, and get over here where you belong!"

This invective served to redirect the attention of the redhead Maguire had driven up with from Dublin.

"I'm sorry, Bernard. I guess I should have staked those tomatoes before I left."

"You and your damn tomatoes!" shouted the one-eyed terrorist. "Forget about your damn veggies for a moment and concentrate on more important things, like finding the good doctor so that we can get on with this thing."

"Where is he?" questioned the redhead defiantly.

"How the hell should I know?" screamed Bernard. "Try his study. If I know the old man he'll be in there, sipping poteen and engrossed in his father's diary."

While she hurried into the manor house to carry out his directive, Bernard Loughlin escorted his guest to the locked doors of the barn.

"Damn women!" muttered the terrorist angrily. "No matter how tough they say they might be, they're all satin and bows on the inside."

Not knowing how to respond to this, John Maguire nodded timidly, and discreetly turned his head to examine the grounds more closely. Beyond the green meadow that surrounded the house was a thick pine forest. Such tracts were planted with governmental assistance several decades ago to counter the severe deforestation that had plagued Ireland through the centuries. A partially worked peat bog could be seen at the edge of these woods. In place of wood and coal, such a substance was the native fuel of poor regions such as this one.

The nuclear physicist had hoped his reactors would make such a time-consuming practice obsolete. Only then would new industry be attracted to areas such as County Caven. And as its population began to be trained to work in these new jobs, its rural populace would be given an abrupt introduction to the modern wonders of the high-tech era that they lived in.

Such was John Maguire's vision of what he had hoped his homeland would be someday. Yet as he was all too soon to learn, the Irish people just weren't ready to make such a drastic jump forward. His carefully laid plans had met with nothing but distrust and skepticism. Endless bureaucratic red tape made the obtaining of a simple construction permit an ordeal, and it was only after a superhuman effort on his part that he was able to convince his countrymen finally to go ahead and build Dublin's Shamrock reactor. Soon to go on line, the plant would be a clean, cheap source of electricity, and one hoped it would calm the suspicions of the doubters who had constantly opposed him every long step of the way.

His ponderings on Ireland's future were all too soon diverted by concerns of a much more immediate nature when two figures emerged from the manor house. One of them was the redhead named Marie. The other was an older gentleman with silver hair, a stooped posture, and a kindly, almost grandfatherly demeanor.

"So this is our respected guest from Dublin," greeted the elder. "I've heard a lot about you, sir. Too bad we couldn't have met under different circumstances, but such is life. Shall we get on with it, then? I'm certain you're eager to return home and be reunited with your family."

Instantly liking this fellow, John Maguire felt as if a great weight had been lifted from him, and his face broke into a relieved smile. "You don't know how true that is, my friend. Now, how can I be of service to you?"

Dr. Tyronne Blackwater answered while pulling a key from his coat pocket and inserting it into the barn door's recessed lock. "You might say that we have a little technical problem with a piece of equipment inside and we'd like you to take a look at it."

The lock triggered with a loud click as the puzzled physicist replied. "If it's within my know-how, I'd be glad to assist you."

Bernard Loughlin had to stifle a chuckle as he pulled back the rusty doors of the barn and switched on its interior lights.

206

"Our little gadget's over here," said the elder. "If you'll just follow me, we'll see what you can make of it."

Maguire entered the barn and first spotted a stack of dried peat squares. Behind this mound were dozens of wooden crates with official RUC seals stenciled on them. On the floor immediately beside the largest of these crates was a large pallet. Displayed here was a curiously shaped steel cylinder that looked disturbingly familiar to the nuclear physicist. It was only as he bent over to take a closer look at the object's rounded nose that he gasped in horror.

"My God! Where did you get this?"

Bernard smirked. "Let's just say it was a little gift to us from the sea. Now, how do we go about detonating it?"

Hardly believing what he was hearing, John Maguire countered, "You can't be serious! Do you have any idea the amount of death and destruction this device is capable of producing?"

"Look, we didn't drag you all the way up from Dublin to hear you mouth off," retorted Bernard. "Show us how to explode this damn thing, or that family of yours dies!"

Quick to intercede at this point was the calm voice of the silver-haired elder. "Can you at the very least have a look at it, Dr. Maguire? You'd sure save a lot of hurt and sorrow by doing so."

The physicist looked up to the old man and stuttered. "But . . . this is a hydrogen bomb! Do you realize how many locks and fail-safe measures are incorporated into this device to keep it from going off? I couldn't bypass them even if I wanted to without the authorized code of the day, which only the President of the United States knows. He keeps it constantly at his side in a briefcase called the football."

"I told you it would be impossible," said the red-head. "It looks like we're going to have to use it for blackmail purposes after all."

"Like hell we are!" shouted Bernard, who looked at the physicist with a wrath-filled glance. "I know that you worked for the company that designed this bomb while you lived in the United States, so quit playing games with me, Doctor. Open it up, and do whatever it takes to get it operational, or you can kiss that family of yours good-bye."

"But I can't!" implored Maguire, whose frustration nearly brought tears to his eyes.

Without paying this passionate outburst the least bit of attention, the one-eyed terrorist coolly addressed Marie Barrett. "Comrade, call the lads and have them kill the youngest child. Make sure her sister and mother are there to watch as her brains are blown from her skull."

The redhead nodded and turned for the doorway.

"You wouldn't dare!" yelled the sobbing physicist."

"I'm afraid he would, lad," observed the elder calmly. He turned and watched as Marie was about to leave the barn.

Just as the redhead was about to pass through the doors, John Maguire cried out: "Hold on! Oh God, forgive me for this! I'll need some tools."

Bernard grinned triumphantly. "You've got them, Doctor."

He then snapped his fingers and beckoned the red-head to fetch the tool kit. She obediently proceeded into an adjoining room and came out with a good-sized galvanized steel container, which she then set on the floor beside the bomb. It was Bernard who opened it, revealing a wide assortment of tools.

"I believe this should suit your needs, Doctor," observed the one-eyed terrorist.

John Maguire looked down at the kit's contents and picked up a screwdriver. His hands were trembling as he inserted the head of this tool into one of the four screws that anchored the bomb's trigger plate. Sweat flowed off his soaked forehead and splattered onto the metallic skin of the device as he removed the final bolt and pulled the plate off. Displayed inside was a complex grid of circuit boards and wiring. His practiced eye went to the arming switch that would have to be manually triggered by the B-52's flight crew to open the firing circuit. He did a double take upon finding the switch unlocked, which meant that somehow the fail-safe mechanism had already been bypassed.

"Sweet Mother Mary, it's already been cocked!" he exclaimed in wonder.

"What the hell does that mean?" returned Bernard.

The physicist's expression was clouded with puzzlement as he explained. "Somehow, whether intentionally or by mechanical error, the arming circuit of this bomb has been unlocked. This process was apparently done without the use of an authorized PAL code, which leads me to believe that the flight crew responsible for this weapon had been working on it when it was lost."

"That's all fine and dandy, Doctor. But how do we explode the damn thing?" asked a very impatient Bernard.

John Maguire answered him directly. "All you have to do is hook up an electrode to the copper clip on this final circuit board. To initiate the arming sequence, you merely have to zap it with a 12-volt charge. You'll then have about two minutes before the final detonation takes place."

"That's it?" Bernard asked, incredulous.

"I'm afraid so," returned the physicist. "Because the way it looks to me, someone's been in here already, doing all the work for you."

Bernard fought to hold back his excitement as he looked up to address his two associates. "Did you hear that, comrades? All it takes is a simple automotive battery charger for us to hit our enemy with the most painful blow of all time. We've done it, comrades! And soon the Brotherhood will reign victorious!"

With his glance locked on the silver-haired elder, John Maguire dared to express himself once again. "Are you still serious about using this device? We're not talking about any ordinary bomb blast here. This weapon is seventy-five times as powerful as the bomb dropped on Hiroshima, and it is capable of killing millions."

"Get him out of here!" cried Bernard in disgust.

"Would you like me to drive him back to Dublin?" asked Tyronne Blackwater.

Bernard thought about this for a moment and answered, "I'll be taking care of the good doctor, comrade. Why don't you go back to the house and find out the exact whereabouts of our tug. It should be docking in Dundalk shortly, and I want to know the second it arrives there."

"As you wish, Bernard," replied the current owner of Cootehill House, who briefly met the scientist's concerned gaze before leaving the barn altogether.

"Why don't you go and have a seat over by the peat stack, Dr. Maguire," instructed Bernard. "I'll be taking care of you shortly."

"But you said I could speak to my family once I finished helping you," reminded the physicist.

"I said go over there and sit, Doctor!" directed the terrorist angrily.

Daring not to incur Bernard's full wrath, John Maguire did as instructed. This left Bernard and Marie alone beside the pallet.

"Well, Bernard, should I return him to the city?" whispered the redhead.

"Are you kidding?" returned Bernard. "The good doctor knows too much already. I think it's best for all concerned if I take him for a little walk in the bog."

Knowing full well what he meant by this, Marie again queried. "And his family?"

"Tell the lads to eliminate the pigs!" spat the terrorist icily.

Without batting an eye, the redhead turned to convey this directive. As she passed the seated scientist, she flashed him the briefest of pitiful stares before ducking out into the sunlight beyond.

Captain Mikhail Borisov had only one day to himself before his unexpected duty was to call him back to his command. With no family or friends to speak of, the blond-haired Spetsnaz officer was free to spend this brief leave as he liked. The island of Kronstadt was not the most scenic place, and since he had no time to travel into nearby Leningrad, Mikhail decided to spend his time holed up in the best hotel in town. To keep him company, the muscular commando invited Tanya Brusovo to join him.

He had met Tanya at a party at the officers' club three months ago and was immediately attracted to her dark eyes, long black hair, huge breasts, and shapely legs. As he found out over drinks, she was a delightful conversationalist whose stories about growing up on the shores of Lake Baikal were genuinely interesting. And as he was soon to learn that very evening, she was also a wild woman in bed.

Only recently divorced from a submariner, Tanya worked in Admiral Starobin's office as a secretary. Mikhail didn't feel the least bit uneasy as he intervened

211

on her behalf and asked the admiral if she could miss a day of work to spend time with him. With a grin and a wink, the senior officer approved this request and even provided three bottles of Ukrainian champagne in the event that either of them got thirsty.

A fierce storm was in the process of blowing in from the Baltic as the taxi carrying Mikhail and Tanya arrived at the canopied entrance to the Hotel Piskar. The Spetsnaz commando shoved some rubles into the driver's hand and roughly pulled his date from back-seat of the Lada.

"It looks like we're going to be in for quite a storm," observed Tanya, who tried vainly to keep her new hairdo from being blown apart by the gale-force winds.

"As long as the roof stays on, let it blow!" returned Mikhail as he led the way inside.

The desk clerk was an elderly babushka whose eyes lit up upon spotting Mikhail's uniform. "Ah, I see I have the honor of serving one of our naval heroes this morning. My late husband was in the Red Banner fleet for twenty of our forty years together. Those were wonderful days, though now that he's gone, I do wish we'd been able to spend more time together. My dearest Pasha loved the sea and was presented an Order of Lenin second class for seeing action against the Nazis while headed for Murmansk. Why do you know that once he even had the honor of seeing Stalin himself? His ship was docked here in Kronstadt when our beloved leader emerged on the deck of the cruiser beside him. Pasha's eyes never failed to light up whenever he described that special day."

"He sounds like quite a man," offered Mikhail quickly as the babushka halted to catch her breath. "I'd love to hear more of his wartime experiences, but my leave is short and we haven't seen each other in over a month."

There was a sparkle in the old lady's gray eyes as she turned toward Tanya and smiled. "There's no need to explain, comrade. Just sign the register here, and I'll give you the best room in the house for the standard tourist rate. You'll even have your own bathroom and a lovely view of the harbor . . . though I doubt there's much to see on a stormy day like this."

Mikhail signed the ledger and took the key.

"Can I get you anything before you go up?" offered the clerk. "I could make up some breakfast, if you'd like. Or how about a nice piping hot pot of tea?"

"You're most gracious, comrade, but we'll be just fine with the room," returned Mikhail, who took Tanya's warm hand in his and led her up the staircase.

"What a delightful old lady," reflected Tanya as they reached the second floor landing and searched for their room.

Mikhail spotted it at the very end of the corridor and anxiously led them toward it. "She sounds a bit lonely," he added. "Why don't I go back downstairs and invite her up for a drink? Why I bet she'd love a glass of champagne. And then she could tell us the story of her life."

A disappointed look crossed Tanya's face, though Mikhail was quick to change her mood when he grabbed her by the buttocks and pulled her close. It was after giving her a deep, wet kiss on the lips that he seductively whispered, "Don't worry, my little sex kitten. I'm yours alone for this entire glorious day."

With his free hand he managed to open the door to their room and then kick it shut with his foot. They went straight to the king-sized bed without even bothering to open the champagne. Mikhail couldn't wait to get at Tanya's luscious breasts and nearly ripped off her blouse as he reached in to fondle them. By the

213

time he got her bra off, her massive nipples were red and hard, and Mikhail bent over to suckle them. As his tongue went to work on her erect nipples, Tanya began breathlessly panting. Inflamed by his touch, she reached down to fondle Mikhail's swollen crotch. She seemed to like what she found down there as she unzipped his pants and tenderly stroked his throbbing, thick erection.

"I've got to have you inside of me," cooed Tanya passionately.

Quick to satisfy this request, Mikhail pulled off the rest of his clothes, and did the same to Tanya's. He laid her out on the rumpled white sheets and took a second to lustfully examine her shapely body before climbing on top of her.

Their lips met hungrily, and while their probing tongues intertwined, Mikhail guided the head of his rock-hard phallus up against the moist lips of his lover's vagina. Well aware of the abnormally large size of his manhood, he carefully pushed his hips downward. Tanya's kisses became more frantic as he continued pushing himself forward, until after what seemed like a blissful eternity, his all was given.

All so slowly now, he reversed the direction of his thrust until his phallus was just about to be pulled free. Yet before it did so, he slid it downwards once again, this time plunging it into the hot, sticky depths with a smooth, quick stroke. Tanya ahhed in delight, her pleasure further heightened as he began thrusting into her with a spirited rhythm. In order to take his all, she kicked up her legs overhead and attempted to merge her trembling body into that of her lover.

Oblivious to the crackle of lightning, the booming thunder, and the howling wind outside that constantly rattled the only window, they made love in this position for a good quarter of an hour before the grinding motion of Tanya's hips began to further intensify. Mikhail noted this change, accompanied by the deep probings of her tongue. Instinctively quickening the pace of his thrusts, he felt his own climax began to rise.

Suddenly Tanya's body began quivering, and her soft, white skin filled with goose bumps. Grunting in ecstasy, she shoved her hips upward as her womb erupted in sheer bliss. Mikhail felt a surge of molten-hot fluid fill her depths, and let loose with his own eruption. Seed that had been stored inside of him for weeks on end rose upward in a spine-tingling orgasm, and not until Tanya had milked him dry did their hips stop grinding.

For the rest of the day, they continued their love-making, with only the champagne and their passion to nourish them. The sun had long since set, the storm no longer audible outside, when Mikhail reluctantly informed his lover that it was time for him to return to duty. After a long hot shower, he crawled back onto the bed where Tanya awaited him. They kissed, and Tanya pulled her head back and softly whispered, "You are truly the lion of the Spetsnaz, Mikhail dearest. Go in peace, and may it not be long until the sea sends you back to my lips."

Mikhail left the hotel alone. Tanya's scent was still with him as he crisply walked down a deserted side street whose narrow length was partially flooded by the day's storm. He had to display his identification card to be allowed entry through the barbed-wire topped gates that surrounded the pier. Here a tough-looking Uzbekian sentry approached him with a German shepard on a short steel leash. The dog proceeded to sniff Mikhail's clothing, and after determining that he wasn't carrying any illicit drugs onto the base, meekly backed away.

215

The Spetsnaz commando knew that for the most part, these dogs were merely for show. The drug problem that infected the Red Banner fleet was a very serious one. Hashish and opium smuggled up from the south were the most abused substances. Utilized to fill those long, lonely hours that a sailor was faced with while at sea, the drugs slowed reaction time and dulled mental alertness. Such conditions could mean disaster in times of crisis, and the fleet was attempting to deal with the crisis by stricter security measures and a variety of drug education programs.

Ever thankful for his limited vices, Mikhail approached the pier where his current command was hidden away in the moonpool of the Ugra-class support ship. Immediately beside the gantryway of this vessel, a shiny black Chaika limousine was parked. Mikhail briefly stopped to admire this automobile that flew the crimson red pennants of the Admiral of the Fleet from its chrome grill.

"Captain Borisov!" shouted a voice from the gangplank.

Looking up to see who was calling him, Mikhail was soon facing the same eager aide who had initially invited him to join Admiral Starobin for dinner at the officers' club a mere twenty-four hours ago.

"I'm glad you got here, sir," added the breathless junior officer. "Admiral of the Fleet Markov and Admiral Starobin have been waiting for you for a good ten minutes now. They instructed me to escort you to the Ugra's wardroom as soon as you arrived."

"Well then, lead on," said Mikhail.

As he climbed onto the support ship and began his way through a maze of twisting corridors, Mikhail couldn't help but be impressed by the identities of the two officers currently waiting for his presence. It was awkward enough to keep an important figure such as

216

Igor Starobin waiting. Yet if he had known that the Admiral of the Fleet himself would be down here like this, Mikhail would have curtailed his delightful love-making session and left for the pier a bit earlier.

Konstantin Markov was a naval legend. Mikhail had only met him face to face once before, when he received his advanced commission after graduating from Leningrad's prestigious A. A. Grechko Naval Academy. Responsible for the current state of the motherland's fleet, Admiral Markov was a man of vision who rose to power in those dark, confusing days that followed the conclusion of the Great War. As an advocate of a strong submarine force, he fought off those in the Defense Ministry who desired to channel the Rodina's limited funds into the surface fleet. He eventually succeeded in this endeavor, and today the Soviet Union had the most powerful armada of submersibles the world had ever known. Proud that his *Sea Devil* was part of this program, Mikhail crossed through officer's country and gratefully ducked into the wardroom.

He found the two admirals seated at the circular table drinking tea, along with the Ugra's captain and its *zampolit*.

"Well there you are, Captain Borisov," greeted Igor Starobin. "Look who's come down here to wish you a fond farewell."

Taking this as their cue to leave, the Ugra's senior officers excused themselves, along with the aide who had acted as Mikhail's escort.

"It's a pleasure to see you again, Admiral Markov," offered the Spetsnaz commando smartly.

The Admiral of the Fleet stood and embraced Mikhail. "The pleasure's all mine, comrade. Though it's been over a decade since we last talked face to face, don't think that you've been out of my thoughts. I've followed your illustrious career with great interest,

217

and it's with pride and admiration that I stand before you."

"I hope your leave went well," Igor said with a wink.

"I had a delightful time, Sir. In fact, I'm afraid I got a bit carried away. Please excuse my tardiness."

"Nonsense," retorted the Admiral of the Fleet. "It's we who are early this evening. And besides, we passed the time talking with Captain Yuriatan and his political officer. They seem to run an efficient operation here, one that should have no trouble getting your *Sea Devil* out into the North Sea."

"I thought that we were going to be traveling by submarine," observed Mikhail.

"When we first spoke, that had been the intention," explained Admiral Starobin. "But because of our severe time constraints, it was decided to have the Ugra offer you transit on the first leg of your mission. They'll be carrying your *Sea Devil* as far as the Orkney Islands. Here you'll rendezvous with the India-class submarine *Lagoda*. This vessel will then convey you all the way to the entrance to the Firth of Clyde. The *Lagoda* will also remain on picket duty while you proceed with your mission, and will provide your transport back to Murmansk once the mission is completed."

"And what a glorious mission it will be!" exclaimed the wide-eyed Admiral of the Fleet. "When I first heard Admiral Starobin present it, I remember thinking that it hadn't been since the Great War that such an ingenious plan had been attempted. To tell you the truth, I was as surprised as the Admiral here when the Premier gave us the go-ahead. And all along we thought that our leaders in the Kremlin were spineless!"

"There's hope for the future of the motherland yet," added Igor Starobin. "This will be especially apparent once the Americans are forced out of Holy Loch. And by the way, we've determined the identity of the submarine that your charges will be attached to. For security reasons, we picked one of their older Permit-class attack subs. Its precise anchorage and a detailed diagram of its hull are included in your sailing packet."

"Do you really think that *Sea Devil* can do it, Captain?" asked the Admiral of the Fleet.

Without hesitation, Mikhail answered, "Why of course she can, Admiral. Although it's true that I'm an officer in the Spetsnaz, I love life too much to volunteer for a mission that I thought would be suicidal."

"That's all I wanted to hear, comrade," returned Konstantin Markov with a relieved sigh.

Admiral Starobin looked down at his watch and stood. "The tide will be changing shortly, and that means that the *Ugra* will soon be setting sail. Shall we go down into the moonpool to take one last look at *Sea Devil* before we're forced to leave, Admiral Markov?"

"By all means," answered the Admiral of the Fleet.

"I believe I can lead us down there without getting us lost," offered Mikhail Borisov.

"If you can sneak a tracked mini-sub deep into uncharted enemy waters, surely finding the moonpool should be the least of your worries," joked Konstantin Markov, who followed the young captain out of the wardroom.

A series of ladders led them down a succession of decks. The constant, muted drone of the Ugra's steam plant was readily noticeable in this portion of the ship, and the air was heavy and warm.

It was with great relief when Mikhail ducked through a familiar hatchway and halted on a latticed-steel catwalk. Before him now was the massive rectangular reservoir around which the ship had been designed. At the bottom of this pool, since been drained of water, was *Sea Devil*. The tracked mini-sub seemed unnatural out of its intended medium. Looking more like a tank than an undersea vessel, it was anchored directly to the steep plates that formed the *Ugra*'s lower hull.

"So that's the vessel that's going to change the world's balance of power," reflected the Admiral of the Fleet, who had taken up a position beside Mikhail.

Mikhail nodded. "I know she doesn't look like much, but *Sea Devil* contains everything I need to complete my mission. That is, as long as those specially designed limpet mines were placed inside her, as promised."

"They're down there, all right," revealed Igor Starobin. "I had my aide deliver them to the ship himself. I believe he transferred them to your warrant officer."

"That would be Oleg Zagorsk," explained Mikhail. "He's Siberian by birth, and grew up in the taiga. Though he's not much of a talker, he knows how to follow an order, and he's proficient with every single one of the *Sea Devil*'s operating systems."

"How's your female crew member working out?" asked Igor Starobin.

"Not as bad as I had first feared," admitted Mikhail. "Comrade Olovski is a competent electrician who's willing to learn, and so far she hasn't let us down."

"I'm glad to hear that," replied Admiral Starobin.

Konstantin Markov thoughtfully reflected. "I would have thought that having a woman on a platform as confining as *Sea Devil* would be a distraction. Haven't you experienced any sexual tension among your other crew members, Captain?"

Mikhail grinned. "Sir, it's apparent that you've never laid your eyes upon Tanya Olovski. Why, I've seen more attractive men in my time."

220

A shared laugh was cut short by the shrill cry of a steam whistle.

"Sounds like the *Ugra* is ready to go," observed the Admiral of the Fleet. "Unless we're going to accompany you all the way into the North Sea, we'd better get going. May good fortune be your constant companion, Captain."

After accepting Markov's firm handshake, Mikhail turned to face Admiral Starobin.

"I, too, wish you nothing but good fortune, comrade. Remember that I'd be going along in your place if I could, and that you'll be responsible for displaying the capabilities of my life's work for me. May your voyage be a smooth one, and your return a time for joyous celebration. And don't forget about that three-month leave on the shores of the Black Sea that's awaiting you. If you'd like, I'm even willing to throw in Tanya Brusovo."

"I'd like that very much," replied the blond-haired Spetsnaz commando, who returned Igor Starobin's playful wink with one of his own.

Chapter Eleven

Major Colin Stewart and his four-man squad arrived in Armagh by helicopter dressed in green combat fatigues. They left the British army post soon after the Sea King touched down, yet this time they traveled by automobile, and one would have had to look closely to see that they were soldiers. A quick change into civilian garb at the barracks made this transformation possible. The addition of various fishing gear supported their cover of being a group of Scottish Highlanders on leave, who were spending their vacation time seeking out the elusive Irish salmon.

It was outside of Newry, as they approached the border with the Republic, that they were forced to halt at a roadblock. A column of black smoke could be seen clearly spiraling up into the heavens beyond the next rise, where a Lynx helicopter was hovering protectively. Colin Stewart could sense trouble as a burly, sour-faced sergeant major wearing the insignia of the First Battalion of the Parachute Regiment on his tunic came over to the driver's side of their car and greeted them gruffly.

"You'll be getting no further until I see those ID cards."

Colin Stewart held up the plastic laminated card that showed his picture and rank. The sergeant major instantly stiffened to attention.

"I'm sorry, Major. I didn't realize you were one of us."

"What's going on here, Sergeant Major?" asked Stewart.

"It's bandits, sir . . . they ambushed one of our recon squads about an hour ago. When our lads ducked behind a nearby bunker to return fire, a mine went off, killing three of them instantly. Why, those Mick bastards had it set up all the time!"

Colin Stewart sighed heavily. "Were you able to arrest any of the ones responsible?"

The sergeant major shook his head. "They disappeared back into the fields before our reinforcements arrived. We'll get the heathens eventually, because this has all the markings of an IRA hit."

"What makes you believe that?" asked the Highlander. "From what I understand, the IRB has been increasingly active in this area."

"It's not the Brotherhood this time, Major. This is my sixth tour here, and it never fails that every May fifth, the IRA carries out one of these ambushes to remind us that today is the anniversary of the day Bobby Sands died from his hunger strike. If you ask me, that's a pretty morbid way to be remembered."

"That it is, Sergeant Major. Is it safe for me and my lads to continue on to the border?"

The burly Para looked inside the car and replied, "They just completed sweeping the road for mines, so I guess it is, sir, but if I were you, I'd seriously consider doing your fishing somewhere else. Bandit country is no place to be spending a leave."

"We'll remember that, Sergeant Major," answered Colin Stewart, who returned the Para's salute and beckoned their driver to continue.

They carefully passed over the rise and spotted an assortment of military personnel scouring the countryside looking for evidence. The Lynx was in the process of evacuating the last of the wounded, and Colin Stewart noted the bloodied earth that stained the still smoking bunker.

"Kind of makes you want to get out there and kick some ass!" bitterly observed one of the young Highlanders from the backseat.

"Just hang in there a little bit longer, lads" advised the grizzled veteran. "I've got a feeling that we're going to get a chance to get even soon enough."

A drive of another three and a half kilometers brought them to the Garda outpost that signaled the border. The vertical green, white, and orange flag of the Irish Republic flew from the flagpole here, and Stewart prepared to greet the uniformed customs officer who ambled over to intercept them.

"Good day to you, gents. Do you have some kind of identification?"

Stewart gathered together the squad's ID cards and handed them over. The customs officer glanced at them with interest and handed them back.

"So you're all Scot Highlanders. I understand you've got some magnificent countryside up there. May I ask what you'll be doing inside the Republic?"

"Not at all," replied Colin Stewart with an amiable smile. "Me and the lads have heard that the Irish salmon are even bigger and tastier than our own variety, and we mean to find out ourselves if this is the God's truth or not."

"So you're fishermen," reflected the Garda official, who proceeded to scour the car's interior. "I see you're going to be fly casting. As a fellow angler myself, I feel it makes the sport more challenging. Now would you mind opening up the boot and letting me have a little look around?"

Ever thankful that they had their armaments stashed

away in a specially designed compartment set beneath the undercarriage, Colin Stewart got out of the car and opened the trunk himself. After a brief search, the customs officer looked up to meet the Highlander's firm stare.

"I suppose that you heard all about the ambush that just took place up the road a piece. It's a senseless waste of life, it is, and I'll leave you to your fishing with one word of advice: keep a low profile, and don't go probing into affairs that aren't your concern. That's the surest way of any for you lads to get yourselves in trouble."

"I'll remember that," said Stewart as he closed the trunk and returned to the car.

Only when they were moving south once again did he turn to address his men. "Welcome to the Republic of Ireland, lads. As of this moment, we're all on our own here. Technically, since we're out of uniform and carrying concealed weapons, we could be shot as spies if the Republic so desired. But if we play our cards right, we shouldn't have to worry about such a thing."

A sign passed on their left that indicated that Dundalk was ten kilometers away. Seeing this, the major added, "The first airfield we'll be checking out is less than four kilometers from here. There's only one other field in the general vicinity. And since the *Nimrod* monitored the suspect aircraft landing in this quadrant, it's got to be in either of them."

With the help of a detailed map, they turned off the main road and began their way down a narrow country lane. This route wound its way past a collection of picturesque stone cottages and emerald green pastures filled with sheep and ripening hay. Coming to an unmarked crossroads that wasn't on their map, Stewart instructed the driver to bear to the left. This gamble soon paid off as they spotted a weather-beaten sign marked, *Drumbilla Airdrome — 1 kilometer.*

Another sign led them down an even narrower roadway whose asphalt was cracked and in many places choked with weeds and brush. It was obvious that this poorly maintained thoroughfare hadn't seen traffic for some time now, and they learned this for certain upon viewing a weed-choked Quonset hut in the distance. A cracked concrete runway lay before this dilapidated structure, which had long ago sheltered it's last aircraft.

They drove up to the Quonset hut anyway and parked before the hangar entrance. Colin Stewart volunteered to peek inside and found the corrugated steel shell empty except for dust, garbage, and cobwebs. Someone had spray painted *Brotherhood Forever* on the rusted side of the building, yet the Highlander doubted that this airstrip could have accepted an aircraft under any circumstances.

"Let's hope we have better luck at the other field, lads," said Stewart as he climbed back in and signaled the driver to continue to their alternative destination.

They found this second airport located right off the main road. Also built around a Quonset-type service hangar, this field was in much better shape and had a variety of light aircraft parked along the tarmac. They halted alongside a sign advertising Patrick Rayburn's Flying School. There was a single ancient lorry parked here, and Colin Stewart explained his plan.

"I'll take Private Campbell with me and see if we can find whoever belongs to that lorry. Meanwhile, you lads can stretch your legs, if you'd like. But don't wander too far."

Colin and his sandy-haired associate began their way over to the hangar. The sound of pounding sheet metal greeted them as they rounded the structure's curved corner and approached its open entranceway. Here a single grease-stained mechanic was visible, beating away with a hammer on the engine cowling of a rust-eaten Piper Cherokee. Their crisp footsteps echoed off the hangar's metallic floor as they entered, and Colin Stewart loudly cleared his throat.

"Excuse me!" shouted the Highlander.

The startled mechanic turned around suddenly, and in the process his hammer went clattering to the floor. "Good heavens, where on earth did you two come from?" he anxiously questioned.

"Actually, from Edinburgh," answered Colin in his best Scottish brogue. "We've been in your beautiful country fishing, and were wondering if it's possible to find someone to fly us back home."

Eyeing them suspiciously, the mechanic replied. "You'll be wanting the charter airport at Dundalk, then. . . it's about seven kilometers south of here."

"We were hoping we wouldn't have to go that far," returned Stewart with a forced smile. "Are you certain we can't hire a plane here? We'd be willing to pay top dollar."

This last statement seemed to get the mechanic's attention as he thoughtfully scratched his grease-stained forehead. "So you'd be wanting to fly all the way over to Edinburgh. That's quite a long flight, especially for the likes of the small planes kept here. Why, the only aircraft with that range would be Patrick Rayburn's twin-engine Cessna."

Colin Stewart briefly eyed his sandy-haired associate before answering. "Is that Patrick Rayburn the flight instructor?"

"The same," shot back the mechanic. "If you'd like, why don't you give him a call at home. And don't forget to tell him that Paddy Murphy sent you."

While the mechanic unsuccessfully searched his stained coveralls for something to write with, Private

Robert Campbell alertly stepped forward with a pen and pad.

"Why thank you, lad," said the mechanic as he scribbled down the pilot's telephone number.

"Can we see his plane?" asked Colin Stewart.

"I don't see why not. It's parked on the other side of the flight line, beside the gasoline pumps. She's a first class piece of equipment, with radar, a multi-frequency radio, and auxiliary fuel tanks."

"Thank you, Mr. Murphy," said Stewart as he pocketed the pilot's phone number.

"Not at all, sir," replied the mechanic as he bent down to pick up his hammer. "And don't forget to tell him that Paddy sent you!"

Quick to exit the hanger, Colin headed straight back to the car.

"Corporal Duncan, bring along the tool kit," whispered Stewart. "And the rest of you, follow me to the other side of the flight line."

By way of the hangar's rear, they quickly proceeded to the line of planes parked on the other side. All of these were small, single-engine models except for the last, which sported dual engines and an elongated white-and-green steel fuselage.

After stationing lookouts, Stewart climbed up to the cockpit. Peering through the plexiglass windows, he found it littered with empty cups, cigarette butts, and other assorted trash. To examine the interior closely, he signaled Corporal Angus Duncan to join him. The brawny native of Inverness deftly climbed up beside his commanding officer and utilized a pick to force open the Cessna's door lock.

The scent of sour milk was overpowering as Stewart climbed inside the messy cockpit. Holding his breath to keep from choking on this nauseating smell, he rummaged through the assortment of items stored here.

He found several charts on the copilot's seat, beneath a partially eaten cheese sandwich. Hurriedly he flipped through this stack, halting on that which lay on the bottom. A substance that looked much like dried blood stained the edges of this chart, and Colin Stewart's pulse quickened as he unfolded it and found a course drawn in red pencil, extending from Dumbarton, Scotland, to their current location north of Dundalk, Ireland.

"We've got it, lads!" revealed the rugged Highlander as he gratefully scrambled out of the smelly cockpit with the chart in hand.

As his men excitedly gathered around him, he added, "Not only is the exact course drawn out for us, but it appears our suspect's blood stains the map as well."

"What do we do next?" asked one of the enlisted men.

Stewart grinned. "That's easy enough, lads. Now it's time to pay pilot Patrick Rayburn a little visit. Shall we?"

A quick telephone call found the pilot at home. Having nearly to scream to be heard over the assortment of children bawling in the background, Rayburn somewhat reluctantly gave Colin Stewart directions to his house. This stone cottage turned out to be less than ten minutes from the airfield. It was situated on an isolated rural lane, with a thick stand of evergreens set behind it.

"I believe I can handle this alone, lads," offered Stewart. "Why don't you deploy in the forest, in case I need you."

The bricks of the walk were cracked and out of place as Colin proceeded to the front door. A television set could be heard blasting away inside, along with the incessant cries of a wailing infant. The Highlander had to knock loudly on the wooden door several times to produce a response.

"Who's there?" screamed a man.

"Mr. Rayburn, it's the chap who called earlier from the airfield. Paddy Murphy gave me your number."

The door opened with a squeal, revealing a slightly built, beard-stubbled man in his mid-twenties. He wore a dirty t-shirt and shorts, and talked without taking the cigarette out of his mouth.

"So you're the fellow who wants to fly to Scotland. I don't know why Paddy even gave you my number in the first place. I'm merely a flight instructor. For commercial flights you should go down to Dundalk or Dublin."

"But I don't want to fly from either of those locations, Mr. Rayburn," replied Stewart coolly.

Taking a moment to size up the solidly built Scotsman, Patrick Rayburn shrugged his skinny shoulders. "Well, then, it's going to cost you, my friend."

A young boy dressed in a cowboy hat suddenly came running into the living room, chased by two screaming girls dressed as Indians. Their high-pitched cries of mock warfare were almost deafening, and the pilot disgustedly turned and shouted at them.

"Please, kids, Daddy's talking business here!"

Completely ignoring this, the children continued their battle, while in the background the infant's wails intensified.

"I'm sorry," offered the shaggy-haired pilot. "The wife just started a new job down at the linen mill, and I'm a little new at babysitting."

The Highlander smiled. "There's no need to explain, Mr. Rayburn. I've got some youngsters back home myself. Why don't we talk out in the backyard, if that's okay with you."

"That would be fine," said Patrick Rayburn, who stepped outside and squinted at the bright sun shining forth from the heavens. "Looks like the good weather's still holding," he matter-of-factly observed as he led the way around the cottage.

The tree line extended to the very edge of the backyard, which was filled with broken furniture, partially burnt trash, and a rusted-out Ford. Well aware that his men were hidden close by, Colin Stewart inhaled a deep breath and turned to face the pilot directly, his forced smile suddenly absent.

"Mr. Rayburn, I'd like to know the identity of the passenger whom you flew back from Dumbarton, Scotland, several nights ago."

"Whatever are you talking about?" asked the puzzled pilot.

The Highlander's glance turned deadly serious. "Oh, come off it, Rayburn! I'm in no mood for games!"

The red-faced pilot gathered himself and exploded in rage. "I don't know what the *hell* you're talking about, mister. But I *do* know that I want you off my property *this instant!*"

"It's not going to be that easy to get rid of me," said Stewart as he reached into his jacket and pulled out the bloodstained map.

"Where did you get that?" snapped the flight instructor.

"You know damn where, Rayburn . . . from your smelly cockpit. So quit the b.s. and tell me whose blood it is that stains this chart."

"I don't have to say one word to you," retorted the Irishman. "In fact, I think I'm going to call the police."

As Rayburn turned for the house, Colin Stewart spoke up firmly. "Do you really think that's wise, Mr. Rayburn? After all, abetting a known IRB operation is a felony in this country that will earn you a minimum three-year stay at the Long Kesh Prison."

Halted by this revelation, the pilot pivoted abruptly. "I'm not associated in any way with the IRB, mister," he said, his voice quivering.

"That may be so," Stewart replied. "But the individual you flew back from Scotland most definitely is. So unless you start talking right now, I don't have any choice but to go to the Republic authorities."

With any anger on his part long vented, Patrick Rayburn emotionally collapsed, on the verge of tears. "I'm nothing but a hardworking family man, mister. Do you have any idea what organizations like the Brotherhood do to squealers?"

"Just tell me the name of this fellow you flew back from Scotland," urged Stewart. "And the IRB never has to be any the wiser."

Knowing full well that he had been caught red-handed, the pilot began whimpering. "I never thought I was doing anything wrong, I swear to you. So I didn't file an official flight plan. Big deal. With all that cash he was waving in my face, I really didn't think it would matter."

"Who was waving that cash, Mr. Rayburn?" continued Colin Stewart resolutely.

"He told me that he got shot in a hunting accident," reflected the pilot. "I should have known that the bastard's cash was tainted."

"For God's sake, man, what was his name?"

"It's Sean Lafferty," offered the emotionally drained pilot. "Though I had never laid eyes on him before, he said that he grew up nearby and could produce some local references, if needed."

With the great tension of the moment finally dissipated, Stewart felt his tone soften. "Did you get any of these references?"

"Are you kidding?" returned the pilot. "The only references he needed was that wad of punts he was soon

232

shoving into my hand."

With the name of the suspected terrorist now firmly embedded in his mind, Colin Stewart nodded appreciatively. "Thank you, Mr. Rayburn. You've been most helpful. And I realize it's not much, but you can rest assured that neither Sean Lafferty nor any other member of the IRB will ever learn what you shared with me this afternoon."

There was an expression of defeat in the pilot's dark eyes as he looked up and sighed. "Mister, it really doesn't matter. I was a marked man the moment I put that cash in my pocket."

The last Colin Stewart saw of the dejected pilot was as he somberly made his way back into the cottage. It took only a single snap of the Highlander's fingers to cause his men to suddenly materialize out of the surrounding forest. Flashing them a thumbs-up, he beckoned them to join him beside their automobile.

"We've got the bastard, all right," revealed the relieved senior officer. "His name's Sean Lafferty, and since he supposedly grew up in this area, he shouldn't be too hard to track down. Angus, how about driving us into Dundalk, and seeing if the local postal exchange office has a listing for Mr. Lafferty in their directory?"

"You've got it Major," replied the brawny corporal, who slid into the driver's seat while his coworkers climbed in behind him.

The Rose-and-Thistle Pub, on the shores of Dundalk, was on the southern outskirts of the city. Because it was so close to the docks, it was frequented mainly by fishermen and longshoremen, though an occasional tour bus stopped by from time to time to give its passengers an authentic taste of the real Ireland.

Liam Lafferty had originally stopped by the pub to get a quick pint before dinner. He was halfway through his third Guinness of the evening when Billy Kelly and Henry Morrison entered the bar and sat down beside him. Like Liam, both individuals were weather-faced fishermen who had been plying their ancient trades for too many decades to count.

They were in the midst of a spirited argument regarding the wisdom of purchasing one of the new LO-RAN directional finders when a late-breaking television news story caused the grizzled bartender to signal them to be quiet. All three fishermen looked up to the set in time to see the photograph of an attractive middle-aged women and two young girls flash up on the screen. It was accompanied by the voice of the newscaster.

"The Maguire's bullet-ridden bodies were found on the banks of the Royal Canal near Ashtown. Dr. John Maguire, the noted nuclear physicist and director of Dublin's Shamrock nuclear power station, is still missing. Yet there is no reason to believe he was in any way responsible for the tragic deaths of his family, though the gardia have still not ruled out that such a link exists.

"In other news, three English soldiers lay dead in Armagh this evening, the victims of an exploding mine. The incident took place on the anniversary of . . ."

As the bartender turned down the volume, Liam Lafferty somberly shook his head. "Can you imagine such a horrible thing? Why, those two little girls never even had a chance to make it out of preschool."

"It certainly is a tragic waste," observed Billy Kelly. "Who could be so twisted as to do such a thing?"

"I say it was the father," offered Henry Morrison, as he sipped off the creamy head of his stout.

"Now what leads you to say such a ridiculous thing,

Henry Morrison?" countered Liam.

The bald-headed fisherman retorted, "It's the radiation that did it. Dr. Maguire was so overloaded with the stuff from working at that power plant that he went crazy and did away with his family just for spite's sake. They'll be finding his body next, all glowing and green with decay, floating in a bog. You'll see."

Liam grimaced. "Henry Morrison, I always thought you were a wee bit daft, but now I'm certain."

"It's all that sun that did it to him," explained Billy Kelly.

"I say it's from drinking too much poteen," suggested the grinning bartender.

Henry Morrison would have no part of this kidding as he continued. "You guys, might laugh at me, but I'm serious. That radiation's bad stuff. They don't know half of its side effects, and who knows how much of the world's current insanity is caused by it?

"You'd better listen closely, gents, because this world's too full of toxic chemicals and radioactive pollutants. Who knows what that flier that they tacked up by the pierside this afternoon was referring to. If you ask me, the Yanks most probably lost some kind of dangerous chemical that for all we know could have fallen right over our heads."

Puzzled by this statement, Liam interrupted him. "What flier are you talking about, Henry?"

Billy Kelly provided an answer. "That's right, Liam, you had already left when those two soldiers tacked it up. Seems the Americans want to know if any of us saw anything suspicious in the night skies last week. They're even willing to offer a cash reward for any information that they deem relevant."

Shocked by this revelation, Liam fought to hold his tongue. "A reward, you say? That's incredible!"

"Lord only knows what they lost out there," reflected

235

Henry Morrison. "Probably next, we'll be pulling in fish with two heads on them. Though speaking of the devil, did I ever tell you gents about the time I came across a cod that had no dorsal fin on it? Why, it was unbelievable. I had just anchored off Carlingford Lough when I . . ."

Barely paying this story any notice, Liam pondered the content of the flier that his co-workers had just mentioned. Per his promise to Dr. Blackwater, he had yet to tell anyone about the mysterious object that he had fished from the seas and the fantastic light in the heavens that had accompanied it. Surely this same incident was what the flier was referring to. To see it with his own eyes, he hurriedly finished off his stout and excused himself.

By the muted light of dusk, Liam hurried down to the main pier. Sure enough, tacked to the bulletin board there was an official-looking flier. With the sea gulls crying in the distance, he read the poster and was somewhat surprised to find it signed by the United States Navy. So *they* were the owners of the elongated capsule that had floated down from the heavens, thought Liam, whose next step was quite obvious . . . he would have to inform Dr. Blackwater of this at once!

He needed to get change from a stranger in order to use one of the dockside telephones. Yet much to his frustration, all that he got when he dialed the physician's number was one of those infernal answering machines. Supposing that he was still up at his clinic in Cootehill with Sean, Liam decided to return home, where Dr. Blackwater had left his County Caven telephone number on the back of one of his business cards.

Liam splurged on a taxi. This got him back to his cottage in a little under fifteen minutes. It was almost pitch dark outside as he paid off the driver and began the long hike up his walk. A brisk wind howled in from the northwest. The stars had long since been blotted out by a low mantle of fast-moving clouds, and Liam was expecting the rain to begin falling any minute. He was grateful as he climbed up the last step and breathlessly made his way onto the porch. It was at that moment that he first heard the male voices inside and realized that his wife wasn't alone.

He entered anxiously and found Annie seated on the couch, with five burly young men surrounding her. Though they were all dressed in civilian garb, there was no doubt in the fisherman's mind that they were military, as a sandy-haired, square-jawed individual stood and flashed Liam an official looking ID card.

"Mr. Lafferty, we're with the authorities, and we wish to know . . ."

Before the stranger could continue, Liam interrupted him. "I know what you're here for, young man. And I'm sorry to say that it's no longer in my possession."

Confused by this response, Major Colin Stewart looked vainly to Mrs. Lafferty, and was prepared to question anew, when Liam spoke again.

"I feel truly horrible about it. I really do. I should have reported fishing it from the sea the minute I got back. I still don't know why I ever listened to the doc like I did."

Though the Highlander still didn't know what Liam was going on about, he couldn't help but express his curiosity. "Just what exactly are you referring to, sir?"

"Why, the piece of satellite, of course," retorted Liam. "What else would I have fished from the sea on that fated night when the heavens caught fire?"

Fearful that her husband had either had too much to drink or had gone completely insane, Annie Lafferty interceded. "Liam, these men are here inquiring about Sean. They say that his life could be in danger, and they want to speak to him *at once.*"

The confused fisherman scratched his stubbled chin. "Then you're not with the United States Navy?"

Colin Stewart shook his head. "Most definitely not, Mr. Lafferty. We're here solely concerning your son. So if you value his life at all, you'll tell us where we can find him."

"Of course I value his life. And though I don't know what all this fuss is about, you can find him at Dr. Blackwater's clinic at Cootehill House," returned Liam matter-of-factly. Suddenly realizing how close he had come to breaking his promise to the physician, Liam added, "In fact, I was just about to call up there and talk to the doc. Shall I tell him that you're going up there?"

"Most definitely not," returned Colin Stewart emphatically. "Come on, lads, we've got some traveling to do."

The five strangers stood up and hurriedly exited. This left the confused fisherman alone in the living room with his wife. His thoughts dulled by the alcohol he had consumed earlier and by his mind-boggling discovery down at the docks, Liam scratched his chin.

"Well, don't just sit there with that worried look on your face, Annie. Sean will be just fine. He's in Doc's care now, and these lads who just paid us a visit will soon see that for themselves. So since that's settled, what's for supper?"

"How can you even think about food at a time like this, Liam Lafferty? I think those men were holding something back. I bet it concerns how Sean got that gunshot wound. Who knows, maybe they're the ones who did it to him."

With the realization that he wasn't going to be getting any peace of mind this evening until he got to the bottom of this mystery, he decided to get on with his call to Cootehill. Then he'd tell Dr. Blackwater about the flier he had seen down at the pier, and the visit of the five brawny strangers, with or without their blessings. One thing that he could be sure of was that the doc would know what to make of these intruders.

Chapter Twelve

Mac found himself spending most of his time aboard the submarine with the *Bowfin*'s navigator. Together they charted the rapidly expanding debris field that was being conveyed to them via underwater telephone from the hydrographic ship. They also constantly updated the positions of the search fleet topside. This conglomeration of sonar platforms was recently augmented by the arrival of the two minesweepers. Their high-density sensors swept every inch of the sea bottom with a probing sonic beacon, and they had already located a large part of the B-52's fuselage that had previously eluded them. Currently searching adjoining sectors were the Sea Stallion helicopters with their towed sonar sleds, and the powerful sensors of the sub rescue ship USS *Pigeon*. A welcome addition were two frigates that took up positions at the edge of the debris field to keep out unwanted trespassers, such as the Russian intelligence trawler that briefly brushed by them earlier.

It was the *Bowfin*'s navigator who had the idea of trying to figure out the basic trajectories of the survivors of the crash in order to pin down the likely path of the missing bombs. Mac was impressed with the bespectacled lieutenant, who had recently graduated from the University of Michigan with a degree in advanced mathematics. After receiving the exact coordinates where the crew were plucked from the seas and making an adjustment for drift due to the current, Tim Murray constructed an intricate formula of drag coefficients and wind speeds.

Since the two bombs that had already been located were found miles apart, it was determined that they were ripped out of the plane's fuselage one by one, not pulled out together, as was originally supposed. This could make their difficult job even harder, since there was no telling if the parachutes of the missing devices even deployed correctly.

Mac realized that their job could take weeks. That's why it was so important to organize the initial search efficiently. Otherwise they'd end up wasting valuable hours backtracking over quadrants that had already been scanned. Consigned to just such a time-consuming operation, Mac was pleasantly surprised when word was passed down to them that one of the minesweepers had made a promising discovery in the debris field's southernmost sector.

Quick to mark the coordinates of this find on the chart, the sub's navigator calmly observed, "Taking into consideration the location of the two bombs that have already been found, this sector was one of the more interesting ones. Yet the object they've spotted could be any number of things."

"It looks like we're just going to have to go down there and eyeball it for ourselves," said Mac. "Thank goodness K-1 arrived from Woods Hole last night."

"And don't forget, we've always got the DSRV *Mystic*," added the navigator, who looked up from the chart as his CO entered the control room from the aft hatchway.

"I just got word that we've tagged something topside," greeted Captain Foard. "What do you make of it, gentlemen?"

"It's certainly worth checking out more closely, sir," answered the navigator. "Though I wouldn't get my hopes up just yet."

"Who knows, maybe we got lucky," offered Mac.

"Keep the good thought, Commander. Because I was also informed that the *Mystic* is going down to take a look at it, and that Command would like you to ride shotgun as its official observer."

"I should have guessed as much," replied Mac, who was getting to be a regular on such an unorthodox means of transportation.

Stepping back from the chart table, Captain Foard turned to address the control room team gathered around their stations around him. "Helmsman, take us up to sixty-five feet. Chief Bates, prepare to surface."

With this, the captain made his way over to the periscope well. Mac felt the angle of the deck beneath him gradually tilt upwards as the *Bowfin* emerged from the cold, black depths.

"Sixty-five feet, sir," observed the alert diving officer.

"Up scope!" ordered the captain crisply.

There was the characteristic hiss of hydraulic oil as the periscope raised up from below. The captain hunched over the scope, pulled down its two tubular steel handles, and peered through the rubberized viewing coupling. Only when he had made a complete circle did he step back and call out.

"Down scope. Bring us up, Chief."

The control room filled with the roar of venting ballast as the now lightened submarine floated to the surface.

"The *Pigeon*'s going to be sending a launch for you, Commander," instructed the CO from the periscope well. "You might want to throw some personal things together in case you're unable to get transit back to the *Bowfin* later. You never know with the weather

242

around here. You'll be getting up on deck by way of the forward accessway. Can you find it all right?"

"I believe so, Captain," answered Mac. "I'll be right there."

Mac quickly proceeded aft, to his stateroom. Here he packed a small seabag with a change of underwear and socks, and made certain to include his toiletry kit.

He was met at the forward accessway by a seaman. "Sir, I'll be escorting you out onto the outer deck. It's a bit rough up there, and the Captain wanted to be sure that we are wearing our life vests."

Almost as if to emphasize this statement, a swell crashed into the *Bowfin*'s keelless hull and the vessel heeled hard to starboard. Forced to reach out to the bulkhead to keep from falling over, Mac readily accepted the orange life vest that the seaman handed him.

As the hatch of the accessway was opened, a gust of cool, fresh, salt-scented air entered the corridor where they stood. Mac found this draft refreshing, and anxiously followed the seaman outside.

An officer and two other seamen waited for them besides the sub's sail. Making certain to grasp tightly onto the steel-cable handrail, Mac joined them.

It was the officer who pointed out the approaching whaleboat. This craft was still several hundred yards off their port bow, its progress seemingly slowed by the pounding swells that dotted the surrounding sea with whitecaps.

"This transfer could be a bit tricky, Commander," said the red-cheeked ensign. "The trick is to time it so that it occurs between swells. Don't be in any hurry, and feel it out before you go for it."

Mac flashed him a thumbs-up and did his best not to worry as the ensign beckoned Mac to join him on the side of the hull. It was a bit more difficult to stand here, though the taut steel cable rigged for the occasion certainly helped. Mac could clearly see the three-man crew of the launch now as they cautiously inched their way toward the *Bowfin*. Waiting while a set of swells rolled in from the northwest, the helmsman of the whaleboat made his final approach just as the last of these passed.

"This is it, Commander," offered the ensign as he supported Mac while he edged his way to the very edge of the rounded deck and leaped out onto the gunwale of the launch. A pair of sturdy hands caught him here and guided him down onto the wooden plank deck.

"Welcome aboard, Commander Mackenzie," said the helmsman, whom Mac was somewhat shocked to find was a woman. "We'll have you back on the *Pigeon* in no time. Just sit back and enjoy the ride."

She opened up the throttle and pulled away from the USS *Bowfin* with a throaty roar. Mac watched as the sub gradually began to fade in the distance, its sleek black hull looking lethal in the glistening sun.

The lines of the ship they were soon approaching were in vast contrast to the *Bowfin*. The 251-foot submarine rescue tender sported a pair of side-by-side twin stacks and had an assortment of catwalks and rigging on its equipment-cluttered deck. Mac knew that the *Pigeon* was the first catamaran-hulled ship built for the United States Navy since Robert Fulton's *Demologos* in 1812. Because its primary mission was to support the two DSRVs it was capable of carrying on its deck, such a unique hull design was ideal.

As it turned out, the transfer onto the tender was achieved with the least bit of difficulty. Built for stability, the *Pigeon* was hardly affected at all by the rough seas, thus facilitating Mac's efforts as he climbed up onto the deck. Waiting for him was a short, moustached officer.

"Commander Mackenzie, I'm Ensign Blanco. Welcome aboard the *Pigeon*. We're currently getting into position to release the *Mystic*, and you'll find Lieutenant Crowley on the fantail. Shall I escort you to him, sir?"

"I don't think that will be necessary, Ensign. I've been aboard her sister ship, the *Ortolan*, and should be able to find the lieutenant on my own."

"Very good, Commander. Just ask any of the crew if you get lost."

Leaving the junior officer with a salute, Mac began his way aft. An exterior catwalk took him down the ship's length and past the dual hangars where the DSRVs were stored. Shaped like a fat black cigar, the *Mystic* was visible inside one of these hangars. Several deckhands were busy getting the deep submergence rescue vehicle ready for sea, and Mac left them to their work and continued on to the stern.

Mac found Lieutenant Matt Crowley seated at the edge of the fantail, with a fishing rod in hand. The bearded DSRV pilot wore a straw hat, a bright Hawaiian shirt, and matching shorts, and was shoeless. He seemed completely captivated by the music on his cassette player headphones. He was thus unaware of Mac's presence as the marine salvage expert sauntered up beside him.

"So this is how you're planning on finding those missing A-bombs."

Matt Crowley looked up and returned the wide grin that his newly arrived visitor was in the process of flashing him.

"Well hello, Mac. Long time no see. Would you like some pretzels or a Coke? I'd offer you a cool frosty one, but duty calls."

"I'm fine, Lieutenant. But I see that you're still play-

245

ing it loose and casual. Any bites yet?"

"Shit, Mac . . . I don't even have any bait on my hook. I'm just using this fishing pole as an excuse to unwind. Besides, they called me in just as I was about to start a week's leave, and if I know the Navy, I'd better be taking full advantage of every free second that I can get."

Looking out to the pair of swirling white wakes left behind by the *Pigeon's* dual propeller shafts, Mac shook his head. "It sure isn't Kauai."

"Tell me about it, partner. You still living the good life out there?"

"I certainly am. Since I saw you last, we finally moved into our new place on Turtle Bay."

"How do those twins of yours like it?"

Mac grinned. "They love it! You should just see them take to the water. Why, they already have matching surfboards! But I've got to admit that their latest passion is baseball."

"I'm glad to hear everything is going good for you, Mac. I'm still the perennial bachelor, bunking wherever the Navy sends me. Though I did meet this Thai babe in Bangkok while I was on R&R there. She could make an honest man out of me yet."

"I seriously doubt that," said Mac, who suddenly remembered that he had met one of Crowley's associates recently. "By the way, Richard Sullivan sends his regards."

"No kidding," returned Crowley. "You must have been down under, then."

"Almost. I met up with the *Avalon* in the Marshalls."

"Did ole' Dick get your feet wet, Mac?"

Unwilling to go into the operation in any detail, Mac merely nodded that he did, and was somewhat thankful when Crowley pointed to the horizon and abruptly changed the subject.

"There's the *Lynch*. We should be getting close now. What do you know about this K-1 that we'll be rendezvousing with?"

Mac eyed the clean lines of the Conrad-class oceanographic ship in the distance. "She's one of the newest deep-diving submersibles that we've got. She was built for the Office of Naval Research and is operated by Woods Hole. K-1 is the prototype of an entire fleet of such vessels, and is 22 feet long, 8 feet wide, weighs 13 tons, and has room for a pilot and two observers."

"What kind of range does it have?"

"About 15 to 20 miles. And that's at a top speed of 4 knots and a maximum submergence time of 24 hours. I had a bit of say when it came down to outfitting her, and made certain that she carried scanning sonar, a closed-circuit television system, an articulated manipulator arm, and a fully operational underwater telephone.

"Right now, we're extremely fortunate to have K-1 with us. She was having her electrical system overhauled when the B-52 went down. Somehow they got it pieced back together in time to load the vessel into a C5-A and fly it out here."

"It sounds like a potent little package," observed the veteran DSRV pilot. "But for my money, I'll still go with the *Mystic* any day of the week. We might not be so high-tech, but we get the job done all the same."

A nearby telephone began ringing, and Crowley picked up the handset and crisply spoke into its transmitter. "Mystic Fishing Club . . . Yes, Captain. In fact, we can see the *Lynch* right now . . . We'll be there, sir."

As he hung up the handset, Crowley pushed back his hat and yawned. "Duty calls, partner. Shall we?"

With fishing rod and cooler in hand, the *Mystic*'s pilot looked more like a beach bum than a naval officer as he led the way. They stowed their gear in the hangar, where both of them slipped into matching dark-blue coveralls. Sewn on the chests of these jumpsuits were golden embossed patches showing a pair of dolphins surrounding a DSRV, crowned with a trident.

They entered the *Mystic* by way of a hatch set beneath the humped casing on the DSRV upper deck. A ladder brought them down into the central pressure capsule. Mac needed no guidance as he squeezed his way feet first into the copilot's chair. The tight confines of such a vessel was getting most familiar to him as he buckled his harness and clamped on his miniature headphones.

Matt Crowley was in the process of activating the *Mystic*'s electrical system when a tinny voice emanated from the headset. "We're over the target and preparing to put you in the water. How do you read me? Over."

"Loud and clear, mother hen," returned the gruff voice of Matt Crowley. "We're ready whenever you are."

A series of green lights mounted into the console showed that all systems were primed and operational, and Crowley initiated a quick test of the vessel's hydraulics. He smoothly pulled the steering yoke back into his lap, and satisfied with what he felt, pushed it forward once again.

"This little lady's ready to go to work," said Crowley as he donned a Los Angeles Dodgers baseball cap.

There was a slight dropping sensation as the DSRV was lowered into the water. The *Mystic* began to roll slightly, and the pilot's face lit up when the voice on the other end of the intercom curtly announced, "Release complete."

"Hit those port ballast tank switches for me, will you, partner?" asked the pilot.

Mac reached forward and depressed two toggle switches. As the pilot activated the pair of switches set on his side of the console, the DSRV command capsule filled with a loud hissing sound. This was followed by a muted gurgling roar as the now empty ballast tanks began filling with seawater.

His glance riveted on the depth gauge, Mac monitored their descent. At fifty feet, his body pitched forward as Crowley pushed down on the steering column and pointed the *Mystic*'s rounded bow straight down into the awaiting depths. This dive was in drastic contrast to the gentle descent he experienced off the Kwajalein Atoll, and Mac grinned as he remembered that he was now being driven by the infamous "Angles and Dangles" Crowley.

The depth gauge had just passed five hundred feet, when their headphones next activated. The voice that broke from the miniature speakers was coming from the the USS *Lynch*. Much like an air traffic controller, this individual proceeded to guide the *Mystic* to its rendezvous with the K-1, aided by the oceanographic ship's three-dimensional sonar capability.

At seven hundred feet, Crowley snapped on the DSRV's powerful spotlights. Mac stared out the viewing port, fascinated by the glowing plankton, beady-eyed shrimp, and luminescent fish. It was soon after an immense skate passed by them that Mac saw a trio of soft white lights glowing ethereally in the distance. Seconds later, their controller called down from the *Lynch*, notifying them that they should be getting a visual sighting of K-1 shortly.

It was at this point that Crowley switched radio frequencies and spoke into his chin-mounted microphone. "Did someone down here order a large pepperoni pizza to go?"

The steady voice of a woman answered back. "That

was supposed to be anchovy-and-onion. Would you mind returning it and bringing what we ordered?"

"Angel," retorted Crowley. "You couldn't tip me enough to make it worth my while."

"I don't know about that," purred the female seductively.

"Would you please clear this channel and keep your chatter limited to the job at hand?" interrupted the cold voice of the controller.

"Oh, lighten up, for God's sake," mumbled Matt Crowley as he looked over to his copilot disgustedly.

"K-1, we want you to follow *Mystic* on the final approach. And please, both of you, proceed cautiously. Our bathymetric model shows the contact to be situated on a subterranean ledge that overlooks a trench 900 feet deep in some spots. If the contact is our broken arrow, we certainly wouldn't want to make it any harder to retrieve than it already is. Do you copy that? Over."

"We read you loud and clear," replied Crowley, who pushed his microphone aside and addressed his copilot. "Jesus, does this guy think he's dealing with a bunch of amateurs here?"

Shaking his head in renewed disgust, Crowley guided *Mystic* to the seafloor. As the sandy bottom came into focus, Mac momentarily slipped back in time. In a flash he was inside yet another DSRV, sweeping over the clear waters of the South Pacific. Yet the track he soon spotted on the floor of the Irish Sea was vastly different than that he located off of Kwajalein. It was much wider, and didn't leave behind the characteristic treadlike marks that the other did.

Quick to spot this trail was the *Mystic*'s pilot. "Well, I'll be. There *is* something down here. But I wouldn't go and bet the farm just yet. I've seen similar marks left behind by trawler's nets, large fish, and underwater avalanches."

Mac doubted that this distinctive trail was caused by any such outside phenomena, but kept quiet. Almost two feet across, the track was much larger than that caused by a trawler. It was also much deeper than a fish impression, and reminded him of the marking that a barrel sliding down a muddy hill would leave behind.

A strained silence followed as *Mystic* glided over the rutted seafloor, its spotlights illuminating the black depths like an alien sun.

"DSRV *Mystic*, we're on your tail and have the tracks in sight," broke the excited voice of K-1's pilot. "And by the way, this is Dr. Judy Brilliant at the helm."

"We copy that, Dr. Brilliant," replied the *Mystic*'s pilot. "This is Lieutenant Mathew Crowley at your service, ma'am. I believe we should be coming to the end of this trail shortly. Just stick close, and keep praying that we hit pay dirt."

Mac was anxiously hunched forward now and focusing his attention solely on the passing seafloor. So deep was his level of concentration that he failed to immediately spot the immense, billowing object just visible before them. This was not the case for Matt Crowley, who shouted out triumphantly.

"Holy Mother Mary, it's a parachute!"

Having never seen a parachute in such an alien medium before, Mac realized that the *Mystic*'s pilot was correct. "My God, it *is* a parachute! And what a great big son-of-a-bitch it is!"

"Let's get some pictures," said Crowley, as he reached up to activate the DSRV's bow-mounted video camera.

"Mac, could you hit that right rudder a bit, and back down on the throttle. I don't want to lose this baby."

Mac gingerly hit the controls as ordered, while Crowley continued his frantic picture-taking. As the current lifted the silken chute upward, he got a brief glimpse of an elongated metallic capsule that had a fin on one end. Startled by this unexpected sighting, Mac stuttered, "Je . . . Jesus, Crowley. It's the bomb!"

It only took a second for the *Mystic*'s pilot to concur, and both officers celebrated with cramped but spirited high-fives.

As news of their discovery was relayed topside, the controller's previously staid tone of voice was noticeably shaken. "Well done, *Mystic*. Let K-1 in so that they can zap it with their fiber optic camera and let us have a look up here."

"Will do, Command," returned Crowley, who steered the *Mystic* around the billowing parachute and initiated a wide, lazy turn.

There could be no missing the excitement that tinged the voice of Dr. Judy Brilliant as she spotted the chute. "We've got it as well, Command. Have activated our bow turret camera. Are you copying our photo transmission?"

A long pause was followed by a passionate response. "We see it, K-1, and it's a glorious sight to behold! Can you move in closer so that we can get a definite on Broken Arrow?"

"Roger, Command," returned Dr. Brilliant.

Mac knew that Broken Arrow was the code name for the missing atomic device, and that the officials topside wouldn't rest until they saw the bomb with their own eyes.

"I hope she doesn't try moving in too close," warned Crowley. "That current could change any second, and if K-1 was to get fouled in that chute, they might never be able to get free."

"Just a little bit closer, K-1," directed the controller.

"And increase the lense magnification to maximum intensity. What we'd like to see is the serial number that's printed beside Broken Arrow's fin."

Matt Crowley seemed unusually tense as he turned *Mystic* back towards the ledge where they had made their discovery. Just as they were able to spot K-1's muted lights in the distince, a concerned female voice broke from the intercom.

"Command, the helm seems to be completely unresponsive. No matter how much thrust I apply, we remain static. I'm afraid that we're hung up on something."

"Damn!" cursed Crowley, whose prophetic remark suddenly seemed to have come true. "Try your reverse thrusters, Doctor Brilliant!" he ordered into his microphone.

It seemed to take an eternity for K-1 to respond. "It's no use! Our thruster pods are caught in the parachute, allowing us zero maneuverability."

This disturbing fact was visually corroborated as *Mystic* closed in on the static mini-sub.

"Damn it to hell! They'll never be able to get out of that mess on their own," observed Crowley to his passenger.

Mac looked down at his watch. "Well, we'd sure better come up with something quick. Because in another twenty hours or so, K-1's power pack is going to run dry, and then that crew's going to suffocate to death."

Peering out at the foundering mini-sub, Crowley could only think of a single drastic course of action. "There's only one way that we're going to get them out of there in time, partner. And that's to use *Mystic* to shove 'em out."

"But the bomb?" countered Mac. "You heard what kind of bathymetrics that we're dealing with here. If we go barreling into that chute, there's a very good chance the bomb's going to end up tumbling off the ledge and falling into the trench that lies below."

"To hell with that frigging bomb!" screamed Crowley. "Come on, partner. We're dealing with three human lives out there. And they're civilians to boot."

With the realization that there was no other way to cut them loose in time, Mac softened. "Then what are we waiting for?"

Without even sharing their plan with Command, Crowley flashed his copilot a thumbs-up and opened up the *Mystic*'s throttle. "Hold on, Doc," he said into his microphone. "Because the United States Navy is coming to the rescue."

"Lieutenant Crowley, this is Control. Please refrain from any rash moves until we've had some time to toss this thing around up here."

"I'm afraid I didn't copy that, Control," responded Crowley, who flashed his partner the briefest of winks before turning his total attention back to the difficult job at hand.

At a distance of twenty yards, Crowley cut the *Mystic*'s engines and allowed their momentum to carry them forward. They struck the mini-sub a glancing blow amidships, hitting them with just enough force to send K-1 hurtling free of the chute's grasp. Fearful that this collision might have cracked K-1's hull, Crowley followed in the mini-sub's baffles until its dual propellers activated with a bubbling white vortex.

"All right!" exclaimed the *Mystic*'s jubilant pilot.

"Thanks for the assistance, Lieutenant," cried the shaken voice of Dr. Brilliant. "If you don't mind, we're going to head topside to see what the damages are. And don't forget, the next pizza's on me!"

After flashing the *Mystic*'s lights in response to this offer, Crowley turned the DSRV around. Yet as they returned to the subterranean ledge where the bomb had been perched, all they found in its place was a whirling cloud of sediment.

"Damn it!" swore Crowley, as he pounded his clenched fist against the bulkhead.

"That's not going to bring it back," said Mac. "We gambled and we lost. At least we saved three lives in the process."

"Let's go into that trench and track it down. I'm not going to rest until we tag it again."

"We'll find it eventually. But I think it would be a wasted effort on our part if we just went down there blindly like this. In this instance, it's best to surface, recharge *Mystic*'s batteries, and let the sonar topside do the work for us. Then we merely have to go down there and pull it up."

Having had time to cool off, Crowley nodded. "I hear you, Mac. No use rushing into that trench without some idea where that bomb's hiding. And the one thing we can be sure of is that it's not going anyplace in the meantime."

Crowley yanked back on the control yoke, and in almost instant response, the *Mystic* began the long trip back to the surface.

Their reception topside was not as grim as they had expected. Command was genuinely relieved to have the three civilians from Woods Hole safely back aboard the *Lynch*. Yet they were still upset with Matt Crowley's rash decision to effect their rescue on his own.

It was the powerful three-dimensional sonar of the oceanographic ship that indeed located the bomb once again. This time it was found at a depth of 997 feet, lying on its side on a flat expanse of sandy sediment. Though Crowley immediately volunteered the *Mystic*'s services, the arrival of the remotely operated vehicle known as CURV at the site allowed Command to turn down this offer.

255

Because he was part of the team that originally developed the cable-controlled underwater research vehicle, Mac was invited over to the *Lynch* to watch it in action. One of CURV's great advantages was that it could be controlled from the surface without jeopardizing human life down below. Capable of attaining depths of up to 3,000 feet, the ROV had no trouble reaching the subterranean trench where the bomb had lodged.

From the control room of the *Lynch,* Mac watched the two-man team that had flown out from San Diego expertly manipulate the joystick that determined CURV's speed and course. At a depth of 900 feet, they activated its powerful bow spotlights and fiber-optic camera. A detailed picture of the surging sea filled the monitor, and Mac could have sworn that he was back on the *Mystic* once more, watching the the scene unfold from one of the DSRV portholes.

A familiar scooped-out trail on the sandy seafloor led them once again to the billowing parachute. Fifteen feet above it, the ROV's three electrical motors were stopped. Illuminated by two high-power mercury vapor lights, the nose of the bomb could be clearly seen, wrapped in the chute's harness. This sighting caused a relieved shout of joy to fill the previously tense control room.

Mac joined in this brief celebration, yet knew that the most critical part of the operation was yet to come. Since it was apparent that the parachute harness was firmly connected to the bomb itself, CURV's hydraulically operated articulated manipulator arm proceeded to hook the grapnel end of an inch-thick nylon line into the apex of the chute's canopy. Another line followed, each having the strength to lift over 10,000 pounds. The best guess was that the bomb and the water-logged parachute would put this estimate to the test, and there was a shared feeling of apprehension as the winch set on the *Lynch*'s stern began to slowly pull in the dual lines. Almost an hour later, the tip of the parachute broke the surface. Skin divers were sent into the water at this point to wrap wire straps around the dangling weapon. These straps were attached to an iron chain lifting line that pulled the device up out of the water and lifted it safely onto the deck of the ship.

Another chorus of relieved cheers sounded in the control room. Mac accepted a hearty handshake from one of CURV's operators, and found himself already mentally formulating the dispatch that he'd soon be sending off to the Pentagon. He knew that Admiral Long would be especially thrilled that it had been an ROV that was responsible for recovering the bomb. Surely this would give him the additional support he needed to successfully argue his case for continued funding in this field before Congress.

Mac made his way topside to get some fresh air. Low-lying gray clouds veiled the sky, adding an almost menacing touch to the seas that surrounded them. With one half of their demanding task now completed, all that they needed to do was recover the other bomb for their mission to be a total success. With the hope that Lady Luck would remain with them and that it would be spotted shortly, Mac plodded off for the radio room, to convey news of their find to Washington.

Approximately 450 miles north of the oceanographic ship USS *Lynch*, Captain Mikhail Borisov and his crew crawled into the *Sea Devil* as it lay anchored to the moonpool of their support tender. The three-day surface voyage from Kronstadt had taken place without incident, and now they were about to begin the next leg of their mission, this time strapped to the deck of the attack sub *Ladoga*.

The spacious tender had been a most comfortable home, and the grim reality of their precarious duty set in as they took their positions inside the cramped confines of the tracked mini-sub.

"The pressure capsule is sealed, Captain," instructed the moustached chief engineer, Yuri Sosnovo. "I show containment at one hundred percent."

Satisfied that *Sea Devil* was now ready to go on its own way, Mikhail Borisov spoke firmly into the underwater telephone. "We are ready for release, Comrades. And thank you again for your gracious hospitality."

"You are most welcome," came a voice from the speaker. "And may all of us aboard the *Ugra* take this opportunity to wish you a safe return."

There was a loud clicking noise as the restraints that held *Sea Devil* down onto the steel decking released, and the moonpool began flooding. They kept their positive buoyancy until the reservoir was almost completely filled.

"You may begin taking on ballast, Comrade Zagorsk," ordered Mikhail, who had just been informed that the steel plates that formed the bottom of the moonpool had been opened to the sea.

They descended to a depth of ten meters, and Borisov ordered the helmsman to activate the throttle. Powered by the massive batteries beneath the aft deckplate, *Sea Devil*'s single propeller began madly spinning, and the vessel moved forward at a speed of four knots.

The condensation had already began dripping off the collection of snaking pipes and cables that formed the control room roof, and electrician Tanya Olovski soon had her first minor short to contend with. With his charts safely covered in oilskin, the captain expertly guided them towards the rendezvous coordinates where their next mode of transportation was hopefully awaiting them.

"I wonder if Captain Zinyagin is still in command of the *Ladoga,*" reflected the chief engineer as he fine-tuned the vessel's trim. "Last year, when the *Ladoga* gave us a lift into the Mediterranean, I'll never forget that lecture he gave us about the meaning of duty and honor in the Red Banner fleet. I honestly didn't think that the Rodina's Navy still had officers like that in positions of command."

"He's from the old school, all right," returned Mikhail. "But his conservative command policies shouldn't distract you from the fact that Captain Zinyagin is a qualified submariner, who was going in harm's way when you were still suckling at your mother's breasts. Now the fellow I'll never forget was the *Ladoga*'s *zampolit*. That fat little bastard got on my nerves from the very start. Why, the nerve of that pig even to talk to us about the important part our suicide pills play in the event a covert operation goes sour. As if that beady-eyed fool knew what it was really like to constantly lay one's life on the line."

"I've never seen someone sweat so much in my entire life," added Yuri Sosnovo. "I swear, by the time that political officer finished his briefing, that handkerchief of his was dripping wet, along with the entire collar of his shirt. I remember thinking at the time that what I'd like to do with my cyanide pill was to shove it up his fat ass."

This observation produced a loud snicker from the mouth of Tanya Olovski, who had been in the midst of replacing a circuit board.

"Go ahead and laugh all you want, comrade," replied the chief engineer with a smirk. "But if that *zampolit*'s still on board the *Ladoga,* you'll be sharing my sentiments soon enough."

This statement was punctuated by the deep voice of

Oleg Zagorsk. "We've got a submerged sonar contact, Captain. Range three thousand meters, bearing three-zero-zero."

Mikhail looked down at his chart, his glance centered on the small red star he had drawn halfway between the Orkney and Shetland Islands.

"I'll bet my pension that's the *Ladoga,*" he said as he reached for the underwater telephone.

A quick call confirmed this fact, and the crew scrambled to prepare *Sea Devil* for the intricate docking procedure that would now follow. With a minimum of trouble the *Sea Devil* was guided into the forward-most of the two semi-recessed deck wells set abaft the *Ladoga*'s sail. After securing the minisub's operational systems, the diving lock was utilized to transfer the crew down into the attack sub's interior.

Waiting for them at the bottom of the ladder was a tall, bald-headed officer whose immaculate uniform was bedecked with an assortment of colorful campaign ribbons. At this smooth-faced veteran's side was a corpulent individual with deep brown eyes and dark bushy eyebrows. Constantly kept busy mopping his forehead and jowls with a sweat-stained handkerchief, the *Ladoga*'s *zampolit* stiffly projected his scratchy voice in greeting.

"On behalf of the entire crew, welcome aboard the *Ladoga,* comrades."

"Yes indeed," added the attack sub's Captain, who directed his next remark to *Sea Devil*'s CO. "And a special welcome home to you, Captain Borisov. It's good to be of service to you once again."

"Thank you, Captain Zinyagin," replied Mikhail. "It's hard to believe how much time has passed since our last meeting. Why it seems that we were just cruising past the straits of Gilbraltar together."

"That it does," returned Captain Dmitri Zinyagin

with a sigh. "Yet I'm certain that all of us have traveled far and wide in the meantime. Would you like to join us in the wardroom? I was just about to join our *zampolit* here in convening the boat's bi-weekly Komsomol meeting."

"I'm certain that you would find our discussion today most inspiring, Captain Borisov," added the portly political officer. "During this meeting both the captain and myself will be offering our ten rules for effective naval leadership. Perhaps you'd like to share with the members of the *Ladoga*'s young communist club your own philosophies on this matter?"

Briefly meeting his chief engineer's brooding gaze, Mikhail replied. "Though this offer sounds most tempting, I must humbly refuse. As you well know, we are in the midst of a challenging operation, and since our stay on the *Ladoga* will be brief, I think it's best if we spend our time getting settled in our quarters and resting."

"That's only understandable, comrade," retorted Captain Zinyagin. "There'll be time enough for us to share our command philosophies upon your return. And surely at that time your crew will join in as well. It's always refreshing to hear what the Spetsnaz has on its mind in regard to the principles of leadership.

"Now enough of this chatter. Captain Borisov, if you'll just follow us, we'll guide you down to the quarters we've chosen for you. I hope you don't mind, but on this cruise we're a bit cramped, and you'll be sharing a stateroom with our senior lieutenant. The rest of your crew has been allotted berthing space in the forward torpedo compartment."

Mikhail was quick to speak up. "If it's okay with you, Captain, I'd rather bunk with my shipmates."

Astounded by this, Dmitri Zinyagin protested. "Surely you can't be serious, Captain. I'm certain you'll

261

be much more comfortable sharing the senior lieutenant's cabin."

"It's not a matter of comfort," replied the blond-
haired Spetsnaz officer firmly. "Aboard *Sea Devil* we
have learned to function as a tight-knit team, and
since any disruption of this unit weakens the bonds of
trust that weld us together, I'd prefer remaining with
my shipmates during the duration of our transit."

"As you wish comrade," said the *Ladoga*'s CO
coldly. "I'll have our Michman show you and your
crew down to your quarters."

Conscious of the *zampolit*'s intense, beady-eyed stare,
Mikhail nodded and gratefully followed the sub's warrant officer, who efficiently materialized to escort them
to the torpedo room. Their living quarters turned out
to be nothing but mattresslike pallets that had been
laid directly on top of the torpedo storage racks. With
not even a curtain for privacy, *Sea Devil*'s crew made
the best of the circumstances.

"I'll tell you one thing," offered the moustached
chief engineer. "I'd much rather have these torpedoes
for company than this vessel's senior officer complement. Those two were as impertinent as they were during our last visit here."

Tanya Olovski sat cross-legged on her spongy mattress and offered her own observations. "I see what
you mean about the *zampolit*. During the whole time
he visited with us, not once did his sweat break. That
poor fellow must go through one uniform after the
other."

"I once knew a fellow with the same problem back
in the taiga," reflected Oleg Zagorsk. "Not only did he
sweat like a mule, but he had horrible body odor as
well. Our village elder said that he was possessed by a
fiery demon, and he gave him a potion to drink to
drive out the spirits."

"Did it work?" quizzed Tanya.

"He died horribly two days later," returned the serious Siberian.

"I bet the enlisted crew of the *Ladoga* wish they had some of that potion to give to their present captain and *zampolit*," said Yuri with a grin. "I can just imagine what it would be like serving under those two."

"You'd better behave, Comrade Sosnovo, or during your next fitness report, I'll recommend a transfer for you to this ship."

"Oh, please, Captain, not that!" pleaded the chief engineer as he knelt down in front of his CO and raised his hands in mock supplication.

As his shipmates roared in laughter at the Ukrainian's antics, a young seaman guardedly poked his head up over the torpedo rack and shyly cleared his throat. "Excuse me, comrades, but is it true that you are really Spetsnaz?"

Mikhail Borisov sat up straight and answered in his deepest, authoritative tone. "As a matter of fact, it is, lad. And just whom do we have the honor of addressing?"

The red-cheeked enlisted man sheepishly replied, "I am torpedo-mate third class Vasili Buchara, sir."

"Seaman Buchara, I am Captain Borisov of the 3rd Spetsnaz brigade, and these are my shipmates. You know, I once knew a fellow by the name of Buchara. I met him in basic training, and if I'm not mistaken, I believe he was an Uzbek."

"So am I!" eagerly volunteered the seaman. "Why, I was born on the shores of the Aral Sea."

Pretending to be impressed with this revelation, Mikhail replied, "The Aral Sea, you say? That's certainly beautiful country. Now how can we be of service to you, lad?"

Calmed by the officer's caring demeanor, the wide-eyed Uzbek continued. "Though I've been in the service only a little over ten months now, I was hoping to join the Spetsnaz someday, and I was wondering if service in the special forces was really as difficult as they say it is."

"Take whatever you hear and multiply it a hundredfold," returned Mikhail. "And then you'll come close to understanding the degree of difficulty involved in the training of a Spetsnaz operative. Sure, our basic training is painful. But you'll emerge from it a real man—able to swim, run, and hike distances you never dreamed of attaining on your own. You'll also learn how to properly operate every weapon from a crossbow to a howitzer, and learn one hundred ways to kill a man with your bare hands. If you train hard and make certain to master each level as it's presented to you, you too can be a part of the Rodina's finest."

"You don't think that my small size will hold me back?"

"Can't a small man be just as brave as a tall one?" asked Mikhail. "Size doesn't matter when it comes to training a killer, lad. In fact, in some instances, having a small stature can even be an advantage.

"I remember a time once in Afghanistan when we were ordered to infiltrate a rebel stronghold that overlooked an important crossroads. As we climbed in over the stone walls, we made our first contact with the enemy and a violent firefight ensued in which we endured. Yet as we tallied up the rebel fatalities, it was noted that several of the wounded Mujahidden had seemed to have disapppeared. Shortly thereafter, we found the first tunnel. Apparently the fortress was honeycombed by such passages, which were too narrow to accept a big man such as myself. And that's when Corporal Litvak stepped forward.

"Litvak was our newest squad member and had a

build much like yours. He also was one of the bravest men I have ever met. He single-handedly crawled into that tunnel with nothing but a knife and a couple of grenades to protect himself with."

"And what ever happened to him?" asked the breathless Uzbek.

Mikhail purposely hesitated a second to build up the suspense. "Ten minutes after he had disappeared into that tunnel, Litvak reappeared with his jacket pocket filled with the bloody ears of the half-dozen rebels he personally killed down there. For that act of heroism he received the Order of Lenin, though I'm afraid poor Litvak died several weeks later after getting hit by a runaway truck while crossing the street in downtown Kiev. But it all goes to show that physical stature doesn't make the man. It's heart and courage that the Spetsnaz is continually looking for."

Awed by this narrative, the young seaman smiled. "Thank you for that, Captain. My dream has always been to join the special forces and to serve the motherland to the best of my abilities. I'm genuinely relieved to know that such a goal is reachable in my case, and I'll do everything within my power to attain it."

"You do that, lad," said Mikhail forcefully. "And always remember that service to the Rodina comes first."

Responding to this advice with a crisp salute, the wide-eyed Uzbek excused himself to return to his duty.

"You've inspired not only that boy, but us as well," offered *Sea Devil*'s chief engineer.

"And here I thought I was beginning to sound more like the *Ladoga*'s long-winded *zampolit*," returned Mikhail, who lay back on his mattress. "Now our goal is less than twenty-four hours away, and before you know it, it will be time for action. Get some rest, comrades. Then we'll see about getting some fresh food into our bellies. Because I can assure you that once we leave this submarine, we won't have the time for even a nap until this all important mission is successfully completed."

Chapter Thirteen

Marie Barrett waited until the lorry carrying Bernard, Dr. Blackwater, Sean, and the bomb was well on its way to Dundalk before heading off for the garden to properly stake up her tomatoes. As it turned out, only one plant of the twelve in the ground was a total loss. Yanking it up by its withered roots, she proceeded to pound a series of thin waist-high wooden stakes into the soil behind each of the remaining plants. Once this time-consuming job was completed, she delicately tied the stalks onto the poles with strips of cloth torn from a worn-out sheet.

She was halfway done with this task when two fatigue-wearing young men passed by the plot. Both sported rather longish brown hair and had Armalite rifles slung over their shoulders.

"Good day to you, Marie," greeted the taller of the two. "It looks like you're going to have quite a crop there."

Briefly looking up to brush a loose strand of red hair out of her eyes, Marie answered politely, "I sure hope so, Tommy Carlin. I started these plants from seeds sent to me from America, and I'd sure hate to lose them."

"Make certain to pinch off those suckers growing between the vines," advised the other soldier. "That way the buds will get plenty of nourishment."

"Since when did you take up farming, Micky Corrigan?" asked Marie.

"You'd be surprised what me and my mum grew in the tiny plot of open land we had in between our Belfast tenement. Though tomatoes did poorly there because of the lack of direct sunlight."

"You city kids never fail to amaze me," remarked the redhead as she turned her attention back to her gardening.

"See you later, Marie," said the Belfast native, who had to hurry his stride to catch up with his country-bred partner.

Sending the squad of soldiers up to Cootehill House had been Bernard's idea. The IRB's cofounder decided to take this rather drastic action when he received a call from Dundalk warning him that some strangers were in town asking about Sean Lafferty's whereabouts. Because there was a chance that they could be headed up to County Caven, Bernard sent for the troops, who were currently deployed throughout the estate grounds.

It was very reassuring for Marie to know that she wouldn't be left here all alone while the others were headed for the pier at Dundalk. The manor house was immense, and sometimes at night when she was staying there by herself, she could have sworn that she heard footsteps and people talking. The only one to take her reports seriously was Dr. Blackwater, who one night beside the fireplace admitted that he too had heard the ghostly noises. Strangely enough, he attributed them to his parents, whom he believed still walked the grounds of the estate searching for the peace of mind that had escaped them in their rather short, tragic lives.

Marie had a genuine liking for the silver-haired physician. He was a kind, sensitive individual who

268

sincerely cared about people. Through the years he had been an avid supporter of their movement. His medical expertise was invaluable. More than once his skills as a doctor saved the life of a wounded IRB patriot. Just recently he had displayed this proficiency on the shoulder of Sean Lafferty. And only a few short days after being on the brink of death, Sean was up and about, his gunshot wound all but forgotten.

Of course, one of the greatest gifts the physician had given them was the use of his beloved Cootehill House. The estate was more than just a place to hide from the authorities or heal from a wound; it was a home away from home where an individual could put down roots and learn from the land.

During her stay at the manor, Marie rediscovered the glories of life all over again. The mere act of working with the soil taught her an invaluable lesson about mankind's fragile hold on the planet. She now realized that cities had corrupted the human soul, and that their only salvation would be when people realized this and went back to the land.

Capitalism served to veil this primal fact from the masses. Driven by the insatiable greed for material objects, the majority of the world's population didn't know what effort went into the food they so hurriedly threw into their baskets at the supermarket. Better they should grow their own vegetables and raise their own cattle than lust after that bigger diamond or fancier automobile.

After a hard day's work in the fields, Marie felt more complete, both physically and spiritually. And she contributed this coming together of mind and body directly to the positive influence of Cootehill House. This was Dr. Tyronne Blackwater's greatest gift to the Brotherhood, and as far as Marie was concerned, she would always be indebted to him for it.

Satisfied that her tomatoes now had a better chance to grow to maturity, the redhead tied up the last plant and stood to examine the rest of her garden briefly. Beside the row of tomatoes that already had several yellow buds on it were a line of sprouting carrots, radishes, and cabbage. Yet another part of the garden was reserved for canteloupe melons. By far the largest patch held that Irish staple the potato. If all went well, she'd be in the midst of her first harvest shortly, when her hard labor would really bear fruit.

Already looking forward to this day, Marie stepped over the low stone wall that kept the rabbits and squirrels away, and began her way toward the manor house to wash up. After leaving her mud-stained boots in the anteroom, she crossed through the kitchen. The pot of mutton stew that she had started earlier in the day was cooking away on the stove. It filled the room with a tangy aroma, and she knew the lads would eat their fair share come suppertime.

She used the large restroom on the ground floor to wash up in. It took a bit of scrubbing to get the caked dirt out from under her chipped nails, which hadn't seen a proper manicure in years.

Before returning to the kitchen to check on dinner, she decided to stop by the doctor's study and read the newspaper one of the lads had just brought up from Dundalk. This room was on the other side of the parlor, and it was one of Marie's favorites. It had been Dr. Blackwater's parents' bedroom long ago, and it had a cathedral ceiling, a fireplace, and a splendid view of the meadow. The doctor had his desk set up in front of the window, to take advantage of the direct light.

As she sat down in his favorite red leather chair, Marie picked up the newspaper that lay before her on the desk. She couldn't miss the bold type headline that graced the front page, nor the photo of the attractive middle-aged woman and two young girls. By now all of Ireland was talking about the deaths of Mrs. John Maguire and her daughters. As Marie skimmed the article, she noted that a good part of it centered around the fact that Dr. Maguire was still missing, and that the police hadn't ruled out any implication on his part in the homicides.

Marie couldn't help but snicker at this groundless innuendo. She knew that it was just like the decadent capitalistic press to make such a sensational insinuation for the purpose of selling more newspapers.

"If the fools only knew the truth," mumbled the redhead to herself.

It was at that moment that she noted an article at the bottom of the page circled with red ink. The headline read, *Queen to Christen Trident*. It went on to give the sketchy details of the English monarch's visit to Scotland's Gare Loch the next afternoon to dedicate the U.K.'s first Trident-missile-carrying submarine.

Chills ran up her spine. For she could just picture the headlines two days from now, when news of a tragedy of epic proportions hit the stands for all to see.

Sitting back in the chair, she gloried in the fact that solely because of the IRB's efforts, an empire that had ruled for centuries would soon crumble as its supreme leader was incinerated in a nuclear firestorm. Surely this was all that was needed to arouse the oppressed from their slumbers. With the realization that their age-old tyrant was gone for all time, the Celts would unite in a single socialist movement that would replace imperialism with the voice of the worker and strip all senseless borders from their maps.

Though many innocents would die to make this dream come true, that was the price they had to pay for decades of blind servitude. By its very definition revolution meant a radical, sudden change involving the overthrow of one government and the substitution of another by the governed. One had only to look at the chaos that had taken place in America in 1776, in France in 1789, and of course the greatest popular uprising of all, the Russian Revolution of 1917, to know that the blood had to stain the streets red in order for the people to speak.

In a way, the overthrow that the Brotherhood was about to trigger would be antiseptic compared to the past struggles that had divided nations for decades on end. With the detonation of a single blast, a corrupt, decadent way of life would pass, to be replaced by a movement whose bywords would be freedom and equality for all. No bloody battles would accompany this drastic change of social orders, and brother wouldn't be forced to take up arms against brother to make it come true. All this would be ensured when the fireball rose above Gare Loch and the Royal Family was removed from the face of the earth in one blindingly bright blast.

Conscious that the weapon that would alter the course of history was on its way to Scotland, Marie anxiously sat forward and noticed there was a flier of some sort placed on the desk beside the newspaper. This poster looked as if it had been ripped off a bulletin board. Ignoring its torn edges, she read the fine print and a wide grin soon painted her freckled face. For here was an official notice from the United States Navy practically begging the local fishermen for information regarding any unusual aerial phenomena they might have experienced at sea recently. Surely this was a bomb that they were referring to, the very same weapon that would be transported over the sea to change the course of destiny!

Marie broke out in an ironic fit of laughter at this and was forced to gain control of herself when the desk-mounted intercom began ringing. Breathlessly she picked up the handset.

"Hello, this is Marie."

"Marie, it's Seamus at the gatehouse. Spread the word, comrade. They're here!"

Major Colin Stewart ordered the car in which they traveled up from Dundalk to a halt about an eighth of a kilometer away from a gray stone gatehouse. At this point the squad exited the vehicle and opened its trunk. From a concealed locker, they removed their equipment.

With hardly a word spoken, they hurriedly changed into matching green and brown camouflage fatigues. To hide the exposed skin of their faces and hands, a specially formulated burnt cork compound was utilized. Only when their lightweight Kevlar bulletproof vests were in place did Stewart hand out the weapons. All five commandos carried Hechler and Koch 7.62-mm assault rifles with twenty-five bullet clips. They also were outfitted with Beretta 9-mm pistols, razor-sharp combat knives, and an assortment of gas, stun, and shrapnel grenades. Two of the soldiers carried ropes with grappling hooks.

"We'll follow the road that leads beyond the gatehouse by way of that copse of pines," instructed Stewart in a whisper. "Stay alert, and keep an eye out for mines and booby traps. There's no telling what we may be walking into here."

As his men signaled that they understood, the major ordered Private Robert Campbell to take the point, and off they went into the thick woods. The ground was soggy and littered with broken tree limbs, yet the commandos pushed onward, oblivious to the obstacles.

Colin Stewart was grateful when the pothole-ridden road began a wide turn leading uphill. As they began their ascent, the footing improved and their forward pace quickened.

They halted at a small circular clearing, and their pointman beckoned for the major to join him beside a fallen evergreen trunk. Colin Stewart did so, and set his eyes on a good-sized arched manor house sitting at the crest of the hill. There was a large barn behind it.

"That's it," whispered Stewart. "Yet it doesn't look like there's anyone home."

"They're there, all right, Major. I can smell 'em," returned the sandy-haired private.

As the squad gathered together, their CO presented his plan of attack. "If Sean Lafferty's up there, chances are he's inside the manor. Since he's our primary objective and there's no telling what kind of security is present up there, we'll initiate a two-pronged attack. Private Campbell and I will approach the house by way of the south wall. We'll use one of the ropes to enter the structure by way of its second-floor window. Meanwhile, Corporal Duncan will lead the rest of you around the manor by way of the barn. If no opposition is encountered, you'll then take up positions beside the south wall while we finish our sweep of the manor's interior.

"Now, Private Campbell seems to think that we're not alone out here. I've certainly seen no signs that would indicate this, but that only means that we've got to proceed only that much more cautiously. So remember your training, and if we should get into a scuffle, use whatever force is needed to protect yourselves. With that said, I can only wish you good hunting. Go get 'em, lads!"

With a coil of rope wrapped around his shoulder, Stewart led the way through the forest to the hill's summit. At this point, the squad split up. While three of his men began a wide, circular route around the back of the estate, Stewart and Private Campbell darted across the meadow in front of the manor. They were nearly halfway across this wide expanse when the first gunshots sounded. Both commandos immediately dived to the turf-covered ground as they heard the sickening whine of bullets whizzing overhead.

Semi-protected by a shallow gully, Stewart spotted the muzzle flash of a rifle from one of the upper windows. After pointing this out to his young associate, the veteran deactivated the safety of his rifle and shouted out.

"I'll keep you covered, Private, while you scramble up to the south wall. If the firing from the second floor continues, see if you can lob a grenade up there."

"Will do, Major," returned the enlisted man.

As Stewart angled the barrel of his assault rifle up toward his target, he hit the trigger and cried out, "Go for it, lad!"

A deafening barrage of semi-automatic gunfire followed. As the second-story window shattered, the private stood and went sprinting over the remaining meadow, dodging and weaving like a professional football player. He didn't stop until he reached his goal and waved that he was all right.

Colin Stewart emptied his clip and cursed angrily when the sound of gunfire once more exploded from the window. While he reached for another clip, a bullet smashed into the turf only a few inches from his right shoulder. Instinctively he pressed his body deeper into the ground in order to make the smallest possible target.

He had just put a fresh round of his own in the chamber and was preparing to answer the sniper with another volley when there was a single deep crackling blast. He cautiously peeked over the lip of the depression and saw a thick column of black smoke streaming from the same window where the sniper had been. Knowing full well that this smoke was the by-product of one of Private Campbell's grenades, Stewart stiffly stood and scrambled to the manor's south wall.

"Nice going, Private," remarked the out-of-breath veteran as he climbed over a low stone fence and crossed over a vegetable garden to get to the wall itself.

"It looks like we can get the grapnel into that wood siding that lines the window ledge, sir."

"How are you at climbing?" asked Stewart.

"I'm like a squirrel, Sir," boasted the enlisted man.

"Well, we're soon enough going to see if that's the case." Stewart slid the coil of rope off his shoulder.

Just as he prepared to loft the hooked grapnel upward, an assortment of exploding gunshots sounded in the distance.

"Looks like the rest of the lads are getting a taste of some action themselves," said Stewart, who needed two tosses to get the grapnel set properly.

Private Campbell took the nylon rope in hand and wasted no time beginning his climb. It was a bit awkward as he reached the ledge where the grapnel was set, and he had to lift his leg up to pull his body over the sill. As he tumbled into the open window, Colin Stewart grasped the rope and began pulling his own way upward. Though it took just a bit longer for him to complete his climb, he succeeded in reaching the sill, where his associate waited to help him the rest of the way.

Inside, they found themselves in a bedroom dominated by a large canopied bed. A poster of Che Guevara was tacked to the wall behind it. Though his hands still stung from the climb, Stewart readied his rifle at his side and whispered, "We'll search this floor first. And don't take any chances. I've got a feeling that this place is just crawling with surprises."

Noting that the sound of gunshots continued outside, Stewart led the way out into the hall. One by one they proceeded to check each upstairs room. They found only one of them occupied, by a long-haired, fatigue-wearing young man who had apparently taken Private Campbell's grenade blast full in the chest.

"It's never a pretty sight," reflected the veteran as he kicked the body aside and spotted the Armalite rifle that the terrorist had been using to keep them pinned down with.

"I doubt if he's carrying any ID. We won't know if he was our man until we can run a fingerprint check on him. Meanwhile, it looks like we've got a whole nest of rats to root out here. Shall we try downstairs?" offered Stewart.

The veteran commando led the way down a spiral staircase. As he prepared to step out onto the landing, a sudden movement on his left side caught his practiced eye, and he raised up the barrel of his rifle, swiveled, and fired. A single return shot ricocheted overhead, causing Stewart to hunch down and look on as another fatigue wearing terrorist stumbled into view in an adjoining corridor. There was a pained look in his face as his Armalite clattered to the floor and his blood-soaked torso followed soon afterwards.

Without stopping to check his condition, Stewart signaled Private Campbell to follow him into the nearby parlor. Two doorways bisected this comfortably furnished room, and beckoning Campbell to check out the one on the left, Stewart turned to the right. A short, dark corridor brought him to a closed wooden door. He pressed his back up against the wall and gingerly reached out to try the iron doorknob. The door was locked, and Stewart slung his rifle over his shoulder and pulled out his pistol. He clipped a 9-mm round into its short barrel and took a deep breath. Then, with a swift, lightning-like movement, he stood back and barreled into the door with the side of his body. As the latch tore out of its flimsy frame, the door swung open with a blistering crack and Stewart's forward momentum sent him tumbling inside.

The deafening sound of exploding bullets greeted him as he smacked into the carpeted floor hard on his right shoulder. A thick leather sofa provided his only cover, and he listened as a dozen rounds smacked into it with a heart-stopping thud.

Slowly the numbing pain that had temporarily paralyzed his entire right side lessened and he was able to firmly grasp his pistol. It was then that the strained voice of a woman cried out to him.

"You're just a bit too late, comrade. This skirmish signals the beginning of a revolution that will soon have the entire planet in its grasp!"

"Just hand over the individual known as Sean Lafferty, and this senseless bloodletting can be done with," countered Colin Stewart.

"Comrade, this *bloodletting,* as you call it, hasn't even *begun* yet!" cried the female terrorist, who expressed her vehemence with a volley of automatic rifle fire.

Several of these bullets whined overhead, and the commando decided that he had had enough. He pulled out a smooth-skinned stun grenade, pulled its pin, and lofted it with a high arc toward the voice's source. Seconds later, the room reverberated with a thunderous concussion that prompted Stewart to re-grasp his pistol and cautiously stand upright. A cloud of swirling gray smoke veiled his view. Yet as it began to dissipate, he gasped in horror upon spotting a red-headed young woman standing behind a desk, her Armalite assault rifle pointed right at him.

"I just wanted to see the face of the imperialistic order that will soon be obsolete," spat the green-eyed terrorist. "Your time has come, comrade. And ours has just began!"

Unwilling to let her prophetic words come true, Colin Stewart desperately leaped sideways, all the while lifting up the barrel of his pistol and firing blindly. The Armalite responded, its explosive report deep and resounding.

Stewart rolled off the side of the sofa, and before he could lift himself upright and finish emptying his clip, noted that the Armalite had suddenly gone silent. The scent of gunpowder was thick in the air as he brought himself to his knees and discreetly looked in the direction of the gunfire.

Veiled in a thin whitish haze, the redheaded terrorist's body could be seen seated in a high-backed red leather chair behind a large desk. Her green eyes vacantly stared out to the room beyond, and Stewart spotted a single gunshot wound located in the exact center of her forehead.

A solemn silence prevailed as he stood and made his way over to the desk. Displayed here was the front page of the latest Irish newspaper. Stewart had skimmed this very same edition earlier in Dundalk,

279

and knew that its lead story described the grisly murders of Mrs. John Maguire and her two daughters. What he had previously missed, though, was an article on the lower part of the page, in this instance one circled in red ink. *Queen to Christen Trident* was the headline.

In all the excitement Colin had almost forgotten about the Royal Family's visit to Gare Loch tomorrow afternoon. When he had first learned that the Queen would be traveling to the Falsane Naval Installation to launch the new submarine, he had genuinely hoped that he could be there to witness this historic event. Yet the attempted robbery at Edinburgh Castle had abruptly changed all this.

As he finished reading the article, his eye spotted a flier on the desk beside the newspaper. It appeared to have been ripped from a bulletin board, and upon closer study, he saw it had apparently been written by the United States Navy. This immediately aroused his curiosity, and he read the flier thoroughly.

At the mere mention of aerial phenomena he knew the paper was referring to the crash of the American B-52. It appeared that the Yanks were subtly asking for the assistance of the local fishermen in a somewhat desperate effort to help them locate the missing atomic bomb. Having been previously notified of this tragic event, Stewart found his attention diverted by the sudden arrival of Private Campbell.

"I've completed my sweep of the house, sir. Though the other side of the floor was empty, I got a chance to speak with Corporal Duncan in the kitchen. We've lost Peter MacLeod, Major. He was killed during the firefight that ensued as they broke into the barn. Before he went down, they say he took out two of the bloody terrorists all on his own. Two others were shot dead as they attempted to flee, and a third is still on the loose in the bog. Angus is out there right now with Private Mckay, trying to hunt 'em down."

Just then noticing the corpse seated in the chair beside his CO, Campbell added, "Who in the hell was that redheaded bird?"

"From the way she was preaching to me before she died, probably the ideological leader of this bunch of Red scum," retorted the major bitterly. "Did Corporal Duncan mention what it was that the terrorists were trying to defend inside the barn?"

"Why, I almost forgot the good news, Major. It appears that we stumbled upon a major arms cache.

"Angus says there's a virtual arsenal in there, with everything but an atomic bomb stashed away in crates marked with the official RUC seal."

Colin Stewart listened intently to this report, his glance still on the flier that he had just been studying. The private's coincidental mention of the A-bomb suddenly triggered something in Stewart, and his thoughts went back in time to Dundalk, when they had first learned where Sean Lafferty was supposedly hiding.

Seconds before the suspect's father told them about Cootehill House, he had been babbling on about some sort of satellite he had fished from the sea. He had even mentioned that this event had occurred on the night the sky caught fire. Though at the time Colin ignored this confused disclosure, it suddenly dawned on him what the old fisherman may have recovered.

"Jesus Christ!" the shocked veteran whispered to himself.

Unaware that this invective was overheard by his puzzled subordinate, Stewart managed to focus his thoughts, and a bevy of concerns rose in his consciousness. Had it been an atomic bomb that Liam

Lafferty had pulled from the sea on the night the sky had caught fire? And if it was, was this device currently in the hands of the terrorist organization his son belonged to? Even more frightening, did they intend to use it, and if so, where?

Colin Stewart's glance strayed to the newspaper article circled in red ink, and in a terrifying flash of awareness, the commando knew the answers to his questions. So deep was his level of concentration that he didn't even notice it when two more members of his squad entered the study.

"Major, you'll never believe what we found in the bog while we were chasing after that escaped terrorist," said Corporal Angus Duncan breathlessly.

Stewart looked up and accepted a mud-stained laminated plastic ID. The picture of a middle-aged bespectacled man was displayed here, along with the following information—*Property of Dr. John Maguire, Director, Shamrock Nuclear Facility.*

"It's him, Major!" added the corporal. "We found the body of the missing nuclear scientist that everyone's talking about—minus the back of his skull, which was blown apart by a bullet."

Barely aware of the significance of this gruesome discovery, Colin Stewart had an entirely different concern as he responded. "Lads, it's extremely important that we get back to Dundalk as soon as possible."

"Won't we be taking some fingerprints first to see if one of the men we killed was our suspect?" asked Robert Campbell.

"And what about that arms cache we found?" added Angus Duncan. "We can't just leave it here for those rascals to do with as they please."

Stewart replied to these questions while heading for the study's sole doorway. "We'll call the Republic authorities along the way and let them take care of it.

Right now, only one thing really matters. And that's getting me to Liam Lafferty's house in Dundalk, on the double!"

Liam arrived at the docks just as the dawn was breaking over the eastern horizon. His first priority was to give his trawler a good cleaning. He did so with a bucket of soap suds and an old scrub brush that he mounted on a broom handle. It was well into morning when he finished this tiring chore. The pier was bustling with activity by this time, and he tossed the bucketful of soapy water that he was finished with into the harbor and sat down on the transom to have a smoke.

He had just finished his second bowl of tobacco and was in the process of debating whether or not to load another when a familiar-looking lorry backed onto the docks and pulled over to the slips by the commercial tugs. Doing his best to ignore the arthritic pains that throbbed in his joints, the grizzled fisherman climbed off his boat and proceeded over to the parked lorry.

Much to his utter surprise and delight, he spotted Sean sitting in the truck's passenger seat. Before he could call out to his son, Dr. Blackwater greeted Liam. Pulling him off to one side, the physician explained what they were doing down here.

Ever mindful of the interest of the United States Navy, Dr. Blackwater was preparing to convey Liam's treasure over to Port Glasgow. Needless to say, Liam was thrilled with this news, for soon he'd have his anticipated reward.

Just as exciting was the fact that Sean was already on his feet. Though his shoulder was still bandaged, the lad didn't seem any worse for wear as he supervised the unloading of the pallet the piece of the satellite was chained to. Tightly covered by a full-length black tarp, the pallet was lifted onto the deck of an oceangoing tug. Throughout this entire process, Dr. Blackwater, Sean, and a funny-looking stranger with an eyepatch and a ponytail were extremely attentive. Once, when the winch they were using slipped, Dr. Blackwater ran out to steady the rocking pallet, which was eventually loaded into the tug without further incident.

Liam watched this operation intently. Sean was so busy that he only had time to give his father a curt hello before returning to work. Hopeful that they'd get to spend some time together once the satellite was returned to its proper owners, Liam looked on as Sean, Dr. Blackwater, and the one-eyed stranger climbed onto the tug. This stranger must have been the vessel's pilot, for he proceeded to climb up into the wheelhouse and start its diesel engine.

"Are you sure you don't want me to go along?" Liam shouted from the pier.

"I'm certain you can keep plenty busy thinking up ways to spend your reward money, Liam," replied the physician. "See you soon!"

With this, the lines holding the tug to the pier were released, and the boat steamed out into the harbor with a resonant blast of its air horn.

Liam was torn between returning home to inform Annie of how splendidly Sean was getting along, and going to the Rose-and-Thistle to celebrate. After the briefest of deliberations, he chose the latter.

Eamon McGilligan, the bearded owner of the pub, was outside, taping the afternoon's lunch selection to the window, when Liam came sauntering down the sidewalk.

"Eamon, old friend . . . how are you doing on this

splendid spring morning?" asked the fisherman.

The potbellied bartender had to do a double-take to properly identify the speaker of these upbeat words. "My heavens, Liam, you've been hitting the Guinness already at my competitor's, and it's not even noon yet."

"Whatever makes you say such a thing, Eamon? Why, I'm as sober as a judge. Though I intend to change that as soon as humanly possible."

"I haven't seen you this cheerful so early in the day since your long shot came in first in the Derby. And that was three years ago. Don't tell me that you've gone and won the lottery!"

"In a matter of speaking, Eamon. Now, is there anyone inside to serve me a pint, or am I going to have to perish from thirst?"

"I'll be in shortly, Liam. Meanwhile, Billy Kelly and Henry Morrison are inside, and I'm sure they'll be able to keep you occupied until I get my menus taped up. Kitty's gone and cooked up a fresh pot of corned beef and cabbage. And I can personally attest to its excellence."

"Perhaps in a wee bit, Eamon," replied the jolly fisherman as he strode through the pub's double doors.

It was dark inside, and the room smelled of cabbage and cigarettes. Perched at their usual places at the bar were his two weathered associates. Liam climbed onto a stool beside them as Henry Morrison was in the midst of one of his infamous stories.

". . . Why, I heard it from the lips of Roddy O'Neill himself. He saw it come out of the water with his very own eyes. And then he looked on in amazement as a group of seaman climbed out of a hatch and scurried over to the propeller shaft to cut them free. Before Roddy could go and call the Coast

Guard, they succeeded in their efforts, and the thing sank back down into the black depths from which it had come. And there was old Roddy, awestruck at his helm, and out his best net to boot.

"I tell you, it's an insult to the Republic to have such a thing happen in our own territorial waters. And it's not only the Brits who are responsible, but the Yanks and the commies as well. What do you think about those damned submarines that have been fouling our nets recently, Liam?"

Liam waited until he was finished packing his pipe with tobacco before voicing himself. "Personally, Henry, I think it's all balderdash. What in the world would a submarine be doing in Ireland's waters? We don't have any sensitive military installations to speak of, and there's plenty of places more important for them to go poking their noses in. If you ask me, old Roddy just made up the story to explain to his wife how he went and lost his new net. We all know the real reason was because he drank too much of that poteen that he's so famous for."

"I beg to differ with you, Liam Lafferty," countered the storyteller with a shake of his bald head. "I say it's submarines, and if we don't do something about them soon, none of us will be able to make a decent living anymore. Why, even as we speak, there's those supposed American naval exercises going on off our coast. And now they say we'll be arrested just for fishing there."

"First it's chemicals falling out of the heavens, and now it's submarines coming up out of the depths, and naval exercises. If it's getting so dangerous out there, why do you even bother going out to sea anymore, Henry?" queried Liam as he put a match to his pipe.

The bald fisherman finished off his pint before answering. "Liam Lafferty, I'm ashamed at you for even asking such a question. You know that danger doesn't mean a thing to me. I love the sea, just like you and Billy do, and I'll keep working her till my dying day."

Billy Kelly could sense an argument brewing, and he did his best to change the subject. "Whatever are you doing gracing us with your presence this early in the afternoon, Liam? I thought you were going to properly overhaul that carburetor of yours today."

Tempted to tell his friends the real reason behind his decision to stop at the pub, Liam decided to wait until the Doc was back with the reward. "My bones were hurting something fierce, Billy, and I thought that a little Guinness would be just the tonic to take away the pain. But now I'm beginning to wonder if they even serve the stuff in here anymore."

Just then Eamon McGilligan slipped behind the bar and got to work preparing three pints.

"And make sure to make 'em good ones, Eamon," warned Liam, who supervised the bartender's efforts as carefully as if Eamon was a bank teller counting out his change.

It took several minutes for the creamy head of the stout to settle so that the bartender was able to fill the pint glasses as full as possible. Satisfied that Eamon did his job properly, Liam held up his glass before him.

"Here's to old friends and full pints," he toasted. He appreciatively sipped the rich Guinness and added, "You know I was just wondering, gents, if you fellows were really to hit it big, like a lottery jackpot or something of the sort, how would you go about spending the money?"

Billy Kelly was the first to respond. "That's a very interesting question, Liam. If such a godsend were to come my way, I'd buy me a big estate down south in County Cork, and raise thoroughbreds for suckers like you fellows to bet on. And then I'd travel to Kentucky each and every spring to replenish my stock, and stop off at Broadway and Hollywood along the way."

"How about you, Henry?" continued Liam.

The bald-headed fisherman took a sip of stout and answered. "That's easy, mate. Since I'd spend my time in one even if I had a fortune, I'd buy me a nice quiet little pub."

"I'd be willing to sell mine real cheap," returned Eamon McGilligan. "Because if I had the dough, I'd get a sleek yacht and sail off for Tahiti to marry one of those topless native girls. Now that would be living like a real king!"

"Since you asked the question, what would you spend it on, Liam?" queried Billy Kelly.

Liam thoughtfully tamped down the tobacco in his pipe. Yet before he could express himself, the double doors to the pub swung open, and in walked a tall, sandy-haired stranger. Finding something about this man disturbingly familiar, Liam racked his brain in an effort to place him. And then it came to him: this was the fellow who had been over at his house the other night asking questions about Sean's whereabouts.

Immediately sensing trouble, Liam slouched down on his stool and tried to look as inconspicuous as possible. Even then the stranger carefully scanned the room and headed his way. In a last-ditch effort at anonymity, Liam purposely dropped his pipe tool on the floor and went to his knees to search for it. This only served to inflame his arthritic joints as he located the tool beside a pair of mud-stained combat boots.

"Liam Lafferty?" quizzed an icy voice from above.

Sheepishly Liam looked up and as defiantly as possible answered, "Who wants to know?"

"We met the other night when I stopped by your cottage to ask about your son," returned the stranger. "I just talked to your wife, and she said that I'd find you either here or on your boat. Is it possible that I could have a few more minutes of your time, in private?"

Not willing to make a scene in front of his friends, Liam stood stiffly and forced a cordial reply. "Why, of course, my friend. If you'd like, we can take one of the booths in the back."

Conscious of the curious stares of his drinking companions, Liam followed the stranger over to the booth. Only when they were well out of hearing distance did Liam speak out angrily.

"What is it this time? As it turns out, my son is just fine. And here you went and scared me and my wife to death for absolutely nothing!"

Colin Stewart studied the heavily lined face of the old fisherman. "Right now I'm not interested in Sean. What I want to know is more about that object you mentioned fishing out of the sea on the night you saw the mysterious fire light up the sky."

Shocked that the stranger remembered his misguided revelation, Liam tried to play ignorant. "I don't know what in the world you're talking about, sir."

"Oh yes you do," rejoined the Highlander forcefully. "When we first met, you apparently thought we were there on another matter, and babbled away about a piece of satellite that you pulled from the sea. You even thought that we were sent by the United States Navy to retrieve it. Now I realize you don't understand the real significance of this matter. But all I can tell you is that your son will be in big trouble if that object you found doesn't get back to its rightful owner."

"But it will!" sputtered Liam excitedly. "In fact, its on its way right now!"

"What do you mean by that?" shot back Colin Stewart.

Well aware that his interrogator wasn't the type of man he could easily fool, Liam decided to be truthful. "The satellite's on its way to Port Glasgow even as we speak. I saw Dr. Blackwater and Sean load it onto a tug with my very own eyes this morning. So if you have any idea of trying to take the reward for yourself, you can forget all about it."

"Believe me, it's not the reward that I'm concerned with. Could you describe this so-called satellite that you recovered, Mr. Lafferty?"

His mind set at ease by the way in which the Scotsman's tone of voice had suddenly lightened, Liam did his best to describe his treasure in words. As he did so, the stranger's probing eyes never left his face, and the fisherman could tell just how important this description was to his interrogator.

While Liam went on to explain each detail of the recovery effort, Colin Stewart intently listened, appalled by what he was hearing. His first instinct was to immediately notify the commander of the Royal Navy headquarters unit at Northwood. With his assistance, the tug could perhaps be apprehended. And if that couldn't be achieved, at the very least the Royal Family could be kept as far away from Gare Loch as possible.

Though this would have been the prudent course of action, the Highlander knew that his case was still pitifully weak. Command would want solid evidence to begin a search of this scope. And this was particularly the case if the Queen's plans were to be altered. Right now, all he had was the word of a drunken old fisherman, and a few bits of circumstantial evidence that made great sense to him, but would appear inconsequential as far as Command was concerned.

It was with this circumspect realization that Stewart decided to take a vastly different tack. The fisherman was in the process of explaining the engine problems that he'd had on the night of the find when the Scotsman interrupted.

"Excuse me, Mr. Lafferty, but would it be possible for you to take me out to the spot where you found the object in your boat right now? I'd be willing to pay you for a full day's charter."

"I don't think that I'd have any trouble finding it," replied Liam. "But you do realize that there's some sort of naval exercise going on out there, and that we'll most likely get stopped by the authorities along the way."

Praying that just such a thing would happen, Colin Stewart anxiously stood and instructed the fisherman to lead the way down to the docks.

Chapter Fourteen

The utter enormity of the job at hand was finally beginning to register in Mac's consciousness. They had been unbelievably lucky to find the first of the two missing bombs when they had. Now, as the search went on in earnest for the final weapon, he realized that it could be almost anywhere in a fifty-mile radius of water. This was the current extent of the debris field as determined by the latest information relayed to him by the various platforms of the ever-expanding search fleet.

To better coordinate this effort, Mac decided to remain on the oceanographic ship. Its communications systems were a bit more flexible than the attack sub's. Staying on the *Lynch* also meant that he could become more closely involved with CURV, and the other ROV's currently hard at work scanning the seafloor for any sign of their elusive quarry.

Just recently one of the minesweepers had relayed to them a promising contact. The object in question was located at a depth of 636 feet, lying on its side on a base of sandy sediment. Ever hopeful that this would signal the end of their search, Mac ordered the *Lynch* in to investigate.

He sat at the controls as CURV was dispatched down into the depths. It was with the greatest of expectations that he triggered the device's mercury-vapor floodlights and activated its fiber-optic camera. A hushed tension prevailed in the control room as Mac maneuvered CURV down to the coordinates given to them by the minesweeper.

His eyes glued to the monitor screen, Mac watched as the seafloor came into focus. Soon afterward, a cylindrical object could be seen in the distance, and with his pulse ever quickening, Mac opened up the ROV's throttle. Already looking forward to the triumphant dispatch he'd soon be sending to Admiral Long, he reached forward to fine-tune the camera's focus. It was then that he noticed that the object was not the missing nuclear device at all, but a rusted-out water heater that someone had unceremoniously dumped here.

With his high hopes dashed, Mac guided CURV back to the surface. He couldn't hide his disappointment as he made his way to the chart table to cross off one more promising contact.

He was in the process of recording the current location of the K-1 mini-sub when an ensign informed him that he was wanted down in the radio room. Supposing that he had a call coming in from Washington, Mac went to see what it was all about.

The radio room was situated on the deck below. Being no stranger to this portion of the *Lynch*, he found it on his own, and expecting next to hear Admiral Long's voice at the end of the line, picked up the handset.

"Commander Mackenzie here."

The voice on the other end was a bit scratchy, but otherwise clear. "Commander, this is Lieutenant Newton aboard the frigate USS *Hawes*. We're out here on picket duty, and have just intercepted a fishing trawler. There are two individuals on board this vessel, and they're insisting that they speak to the person in charge of the nuclear bomb recovery."

293

This hadn't been the first trespasser that they'd had to contend with, though one element of the lieutenant's report immediately caught Mac's attention. "Did they explicitly say *nuclear* bomb recovery, Lieutenant Newton?"

"Yes they did, Commander. That's why I decided to inform you personally, because I didn't think that our real purpose out here was public knowledge."

"It most definitely is not, Lieutenant. You have my permission to escort them over to the *Lynch* at once."

Not having the vaguest idea how these outsiders had learned about the true nature of their search, Mac hung up the handset. He arrived up on the *Lynch*'s bridge in time to see the frigate approaching from the west. He needed binoculars to spot the small wooden trawler that followed in the sleek warship's wake. Supposing that this could all be nothing but a wild guess on the part of these fishermen, Mac waited until the trawler was only a few hundred yards away before climbing down to the main deck and making his way to the gangway.

The *Lynch*'s deck crew alertly deployed several thick rubberized fenders as the trawler moved in to complete its rendezvous. As the two bobbing ships got closer together, a tall, sandy-haired man called out from the trawler's transom.

"Is Commander Mackenzie there?"

"I'm Mackenzie," answered Mac, who stood amidships, at the deck's edge.

"I'm Major Colin Stewart, commanding officer of Her Majesty's 75th Highlanders, and I've got some rather distressing news about your efforts out here. You see, I believe I know where one of those missing bombs that you're searching for can be located."

This was all that Mac had to hear to signal the Scotsman to join him on the *Lynch*. With a bit of effort the battered trawler tied up to the oceanographic ship's side, and its two occupants climbed aboard using a portable rope ladder.

The Scotsman proved to be about Mac's height. Mac guessed that he was in his early forties, though his build was solid and muscular.

"I realize that this whole meeting is a bit unusual, Commander. But I'm certain that you'll soon enough understand the unique circumstances surrounding it. I'd like you to meet Liam Lafferty. Mr. Lafferty is a fisherman from Dundalk. It was his trawler that brought us out here."

"I suppose you'd be the fellow responsible for putting those fliers down at the docks," remarked Liam as he studied the blond-haired Yank naval officer. "I guess I should have contacted you when I first found the blasted thing. From what it looks out here, it would have sure saved you a lot of time and trouble."

Mac had to look to the Scotsman for an explanation of Liam's puzzling confession.

"What Mr. Lafferty's trying to say is that he was out at sea on the night that your B-52 went down here."

"May I ask how it is that you know about the crash, Major?" asked a perplexed Mac.

"Not at all, Commander. You see, I'm the C.O. of one of the units that the First Sea Lord informed of the accident soon after it occurred. And it's a good thing that I was included in this group, because otherwise I might have never been able to figure it all out as I have. Is there somewhere a bit more private where we can hash this whole thing out?"

His curiosity fully piqued, Mac nodded and led them inside. An empty compartment that had been set up for use as a classroom served their purposes perfectly. And with the hatch secured, Colin Stewart continued.

"Though a lot of the details are unnecessary at this point, for expedience' sake, let's just say that my personal involvement with this whole thing began when I arrived in Ireland on the trail of a suspected terrorist. It was while I was in the midst of this search that I met Mr. Lafferty here, and first heard about the object that he fished from these waters. Liam, why don't you share with the Commander the story you told me earlier?"

Liam proceeded to repeat his account of the fated night when the sky caught fire. The blond-haired Yank seemed genuinely fascinated with his tale, and was particularly eager to know more about the exact shape of the object.

"Would you mind drawing it on the blackboard for me?" asked the likable American.

A bit shyly, Liam walked up to the portable blackboard at the head of the classroom. Never known for his drawing skills, he did his best to convey the object's cylindrical shape. He even went so far as to include the narrow fins that were attached to one end of it.

"Why, that's incredible!" remarked the Yank as he studied Liam's rendering. "You say that you actually brought it aboard all by yourself and then took it back to Dundalk with you?"

"That I did," returned the fisherman. "It's just too bad that the Doc's already left for Port Glasgow, because it seems he could have saved a lot of trouble merely by bringing it directly to you."

Confused by this remark, Mac turned to Colin Stewart for clarification. "Dr. Blackwater is Liam's friend who agreed to handle the object's return to its proper owners."

A look of sudden relief crossed Mac's face. "Thank God for that."

"Don't be so quick giving your thanks, Commander," retorted the Scotsman. "It appears that Dr. Blackwater is involved with the terrorist organization whose antics originally brought me to Ireland. I also have reason to believe that he knows the exact nature of the object he's currently ferrying across the Irish Sea." Looking at Liam at this point, Colin Stewart added, "Mr. Lafferty, would you mind waiting outside for a moment?"

Liam shrugged his narrow shoulders, and not really knowing what he was doing here in the first place, did as he was instructed. Only when the fisherman slammed the cabin door shut behind him did the Highlander continue.

"Pardon my circumspection, Commander, but the old-timer still thinks that it was a piece of a satellite that he pulled from the sea that night. And that terrorist who brought me to Ireland in the first place was his own son. He appears to be a member of the Irish Republican Brotherhood. The IRB is a violent Marxist organization whose goal is the removal of all British influence from Northern Ireland, and the creation of a single Socialist Irish Republic.

"This Dr. Blackwater that currently has the bomb is also a member of the IRB. He knows full well that the bomb is not a satellite, and he intends to use it to further their twisted cause. Why, I've only just returned from his estate in County Caven, where I lost one of my men during a violent clash with some of his cronies. They fought to the death and were protecting a massive arms cache that was recently stolen from the RUC armory at Newry. It was during my own search of the manor house that I came across circumstantial evidence which leads me to believe that the IRB plans to utilize the bomb to disrupt the Queen's visit to our Falsane Naval Base on Gare Loch, less than twenty-four hours from now."

"Wow, that's a mouthful," reflected Mac, who believed the Scot, but still had trouble grasping the scope of the incident that he was alluding to. "So what you're saying, then, is that even as we speak, an IRB hit squad is on its way to Gare Loch with our bomb in tow, with every intention of using it to blow up the Queen of England? That's incredible!"

"It's much more than that," said Colin Stewart. "It's absolutely frightening. Those damn fools could kill millions!"

"Calm down, Major," advised Mac. "If your story proves to be true, and they indeed have our device, that still doesn't say that they'll be able to detonate it. Uncle Sam has incorporated a little gizmo called the PAL into all of its nuclear weapons that makes an accidental or unauthorized use of the bomb all but impossible."

Mac had just about forgotten his brief meeting with the B-52 pilot whose plane had been carrying the bomb, and whose rantings warned that the device was unintentionally cocked at the time of the accident. Instead his thoughts were focused entirely on the Highlander as he replied.

"In ordinary circumstances, I'd agree with you, Commander. We also incorporate permissive action links into our nuclear weapons. But what scares the daylights out of me is the fact that while my soldiers were searching the IRB compound, they came across the recently killed corpse of one Dr. John Maguire. All you'd have to do is read the local paper to know that Maguire has been missing these last couple of days. During this time, his wife and two young daughters were also found executed. What makes these gruesome deaths so compelling is the fact that Dr. Maguire was the director of Dublin's Shamrock nuclear facility. His résumé includes a stint with your Sandia Corporation, the firm that designed the nuclear bomb your B-52 was carrying. In other words, Commander, if there was anyone on this planet who would know how to circumvent those PALs, it would be Dr. John Maguire!"

Chilled by this revelation, Mac gasped. "Dear God! Who else knows about this, Major?"

"As of this moment, you're it, Commander. The chaps I work for would want a lot more solid evidence before giving me any serious consideration. One doesn't go altering the Queen of England's schedule on the ramblings of a drunken Irish fisherman."

"I guess it all comes down to us figuring out a way to stop the IRB from carrying out their demented scheme," said Mac. "What kind of vessel did you say was being used to carry the bomb?"

Colin Stewart answered, "It's a tug, Commander. And I'm afraid that only makes our job that more difficult, for on any given day there's literally dozens of tugs frequenting the waters of the Firth of Clyde."

Mac was already contemplating his next move. "Fortunately, I've got a friend back in the Pentagon who should give us the clearances we need without asking too many questions. And if I do get his blessings, would you mind coming along on a little submarine ride with me to check this thing out firsthand?"

As he accepted the Scot's affirmative nod, Mac added, "Perhaps we'd better ask Mr. Lafferty to join us. If we're going to stop the right tug, he's going to have to be the one to eyeball it for us."

"That's a most astute observation, Commander. Since his own son's currently on that tug, he shouldn't be too hard to convince. Now, how can I ever thank you for supporting me like this? I came into your life from out of the blue. And for all you know, I could be a complete lunatic."

Mac stifled a grin. "In a manner of speaking, I

299

hope that's the way it turns out, Major. Because if this story of yours is true, my country could be indirectly responsible for one of the worst peacetime disasters ever to hit the planet. Let's get moving, and nip this madness in the bud before it gets totally out of hand."

As he flashed the personable Yank a hearty thumbs-up, Colin Stewart could only thank his lucky star this man had been brought to him. Trust was a rare enough commodity these days, even among old acquaintances. And to find this virtual stranger so open to his speculations reaffirmed Colin Stewart's belief in a humanity that was worth fighting for after all.

The crew's mess of the *Ladoga* was in the stern of the attack sub's lower deck. It was a fairly good-sized compartment, filled with a half dozen six-man tables. In an effort to give this space some character, red-checkered plastic cloths covered each table. The bulkhead walls were covered with various realistically painted pastoral scenes whose subjects included sparkling Lake Baikal, a sunset over the Ural mountains, and a forest near the great river from which the sub derived its name.

Seated at one of these tables in the midst of supper was the crew of *Sea Devil*. True to his character, Mikhail Borisov turned down an offer to eat with the *Ladoga*'s captain and chose instead to remain with his team. The Spetsnaz officer's presence in this part of the ship, normally reserved for enlisted ranks, was most unusual and would likely be the topic of conversation for weeks to come.

Oblivious to the whims of stuffy protocol, Mikhail enjoyed this chance to see how the average sailor on the sub faired. And so far he had to admit that he was impressed. His meal was the same that was being served in the officers' wardroom, though instead of china and silverware, it was dished straight onto compartmentalized heavy plastic trays.

This evening they were served boiled beef, potatoes. carrots, and cabbage. Freshly baked poppy-seed rolls accompanied this repast, whose dessert proved to be a tasty pear tart. Sorry that he couldn't have anything stronger than heavily sweetened black tea to wash it down with, *Sea Devil*'s CO contentedly munched away on his cabbage, while his engineer finished up the remark he was in the midst of.

". . . and that's why I still think it's fundamentally wrong for warships of this size to have segregated mess facilities. What's wrong with the enlisted and commissioned ranks eating together in the same room? Not only would it save precious space, but it would give the officers a better chance to know what's on the average seaman's mind."

"But I thought that's what the biweekly Komsomol meetings were for," countered Tanya Olovski.

"That might be the case on other ships in the Red Banner fleet, but certainly not this one," returned Yuri Sosnovo. "Why, you heard the *Ladoga*'s pretentious senior officers. How much thought do you think that they give the average sailor's plight on this ship? They're much too busy expounding their own lofty theoretical viewpoints to allow the Komsomol to become the open forum it was intended to be."

"I'd say it's fortunate for Captain Zinyagin that you're not a permanent member of his crew," offered Mikhail between bites of beef. "Otherwise he could have a serious mutiny on his hands."

The chief engineer shook his head. "I'm not espousing violence in this instance, Captain . . . only a sailor's state-given right to have an open environment. And that's why I feel that by having only a single mess on ships of this size, the officers would be obligated to take into consideration such concerns."

"I doubt if Captain Zinyagin would agree," observed Oleg Zagorsk. "He reminds me of a village chief that I once heard of, who had his subjects wait on him as if he were the Czar. He never did care a damn about the average worker, until one of them snuck into his cabin one day and decapitated him."

Tanya Olovski remarked while mopping up her gravy with a poppy-seed roll. "I think that Yuri has a good point, especially when applied to the *Ladoga*. Never have I felt a boat with so much inner tension on it. Have you noticed how the officers order around the enlisted personnel as if they were cattle? I feel it's true that a captain is the one who's responsible for establishing a vessel's morale. And on this ship, there's something seriously amiss. A first step to reestablishing normality is for Captain Zinyagin to recognize that he has a serious problem and then to address it by opening himself up to the feelings of his subordinates."

"One good thing that I can say about the *Ladoga* is the quality of this food," said Mikhail, who thought it well to change the subject. "I've seen the boat's limited storage and preparation facilities, and that cook of theirs must be a real magician. Why, this beef is as tender as a loving mother's heart."

"If only we had a decent-sized mess on *Sea Devil*. Then I'd cook you up a potful of Ukrainian borscht that would quickly put this meal to shame," offered Yuri Sosnovo.

"Speaking of *Sea Devil*, I think it's wise for all of us to eat hearty this evening. We will be deploying shortly, and this could be our last full meal in some time," said Mikhail.

A period of introspective silence followed as the mini-sub's crew dug into their food with renewed vigor.

302

They were well into their desserts when the young Uzbekian seaman who had introduced himself in the torpedo room earlier shyly left his table and approached them.

"Excuse me, comrades, I couldn't help but notice you over here, and I wanted to take this opportunity to say hello once again."

"That's most cordial of you, sailor," replied Mikhail. "Pull up a chair and join us."

Torpedo mate third class Vasili Buchara humbly shook his head that he couldn't. "I'm afraid that I have to get back to my watch, sir. But thanks for the offer. I just wanted to let all of you know what an inspiration it's been meeting you. I have greatly admired the Spetsnaz from afar since I was a little boy, and talking with you has given me a new goal to work for. No matter how long it takes, I'm not going to rest until I too can join the proud ranks of the motherland's special forces."

Mikhail caught the glances of his crewmates and smiled warmly. "That's excellent news, comrade. The Spetsnaz is always looking for new blood, and from what I've seen of you, I'd say that your chances were excellent of gaining entrance to our training program. Have you brought up your interest to the *Ladoga*'s political officer as yet?"

"Oh no, sir. I wouldn't dare bother the ship's *zampolit* with such an insignificant concern."

"Nonsense," retorted Mikhail. "As political officer, it's his duty to assist you with your military future. So if you don't want to be in that stuffy torpedo room for the rest of your life, speak up, lad! A candidate for the Spetsnaz has to have a mind of his own, and not be afraid to show some initiative."

"I'll do so at the first opportunity, sir. And perhaps the next time our paths cross, I too will be wearing

303

the fabled striped tunic and red beret."

"Good luck to you, lad," offered the veteran, who watched the young sailor leave the mess with an expectant grin turning the corners of his mouth.

"I just hope that the *zampolit* doesn't hang him from the yardarm for asking for that admissions application," reflected Yuri Sosnovo.

"If he does, he'll have to answer to me upon our return," shot back *Sea Devil*'s CO. "Now the hour's getting late, and all too soon we'll be deploying. So get some rest while you can. I'll join you as soon as I finish going over our final launch coordinates with Captain Zinyagin."

While leaving the mess deck, Mikhail noticed the almost reverential stares he drew from the other enlisted men who had been eating there. He imagined that the young Uzbek had already told his shipmates all about the fabled Spetsnaz warriors who shared this voyage with them. With a polite nod, the blond commando acknowledged their interest and slipped through the forward hatchway.

A ladder took him up two decks to where the command spaces were situated. The corridors here were packed with snaking cables and pipes. It was as he passed by the closed doors of the radio room that a young seaman intercepted Mikhail with his right index finger pressed to his lips.

"Please be absolutely certain to proceed as quietly as possible, sir," he whispered. "The captain has just ordered a state of ultra quiet."

As this seaman hurriedly made his way aft to spread the message to the rest of the crew, Mikhail continued traveling in the opposite direction. When he finally made it to the *Ladoga*'s attack center, he found the ship's captain and *zampolit* huddled over the seated sonar operator. Illuminated as it was by red lights to protect the crew's night vision, the compartment had an atmosphere that was noticeably tense. Mikhail reached the sonar station just in time to hear the sub's captain.

"Is it still approaching, Comrade Zitomir?"

The sonar operator wore bulky headphones and had his stare locked on the repeater screen as he answered. "Affirmative, Captain. They'll be almost directly on top of us any moment now."

His flabby jowls glistening with sweat, the concerned zampolit voiced himself. "Perhaps we should reverse course and wait for a more opportune moment to transit the channel."

The captain, who noticed that Mikhail Borisov had just joined them, responded to his political officer's suggestion with a disgusted shake of his head. "If only we had that luxury, Comrade Zampolit. It's imperative that we get our esteemed passengers to their drop-off point by six P.M. And that leaves us little time for tarrying. Surely a British Leander-class frigate shouldn't be much of a match for a vessel the likes of the *Ladoga*. What do you think, Captain Borisov?"

"Under normal circumstances, the *Ladoga*'s stealth capabilities should effectively mask us from such a platform," returned Mikhail. "Thus we should be fine as long as our ultraquiet state is not compromised."

"And as long as I'm at this helm, it won't be!" retorted Dmitri Zinyagin.

"I still think we should take a more cautious approach to this transit," countered the perspiration-soaked political officer. "Of all the choke points we have to pass through, this channel is the narrowest."

Mikhail knew that the zampolit was referring to the North Channel. Less than 20 kilometers wide, it separated the northeastern tip of Ireland from Scotland's Mull of Kintyre.

"Comrade Tartarov, I've heard enough out of you!" spat Captain Zinyagin. "You will refrain from further comment regarding my tactical decisions, or I will have you removed from this attack center!"

Fear momentarily clouded the bloodshot eyes of the political officer as he humbly nodded in obedience to this command. Seconds later, a distant, high-pitched whine could be heard in the hushed compartment. The sonar chief identified it.

"I'm picking up strong surface cavitation topside, Captain. It's the Leander, all right, and it's going to pass right over us!"

Mikhail listened breathlessly as the signature of the frigate's propellers rose to an almost ear-splitting whine. This was accompanined by a distinctive hollow pinging sound that every submariner learned both to respect and fear.

"We've been scanned with active sonar," observed the sensor operator unnecessarily.

Mikhail instinctively looked upward, and could picture the sleek frigate as it cut a frothing white swath through the shallow waters of the channel. Deep in its combat information center its Royal Navy crew would be hunched over their sonar repeaters, ever vigilant for the moment when their sonic scan would reflect off of a solid underwater contact. Hopefully, the thick anechoic tiles that lined the *Ladoga*'s hull would do their job and by absorbing the scan keep it from reflecting upward. Otherwise the all-important element of surprise that their mission depended upon would no longer be theirs.

Like a charging freight train, the frigate passed directly overhead. Mikhail found himself taking a series of deep, calming breaths. As he angled his gaze back downward, he noted how cool and collected the attack sub's captain seemed to be as he intently watched the

Leander's sonic signature express itself on the repeater screen. Beside the veteran senior officer, the ship's political officer looked like he would drop to the deck with a coronary any moment now. While doing his best to wipe his soaked forehead dry with a handkerchief, he was in the process of nervously biting to the quick the fingernails of the other hand. His agitated stare was almost comical to the Spetsnaz commando, who had long ago learned that anxiety could kill a man just as surely as a bullet could.

Mikhail was in the midst of wondering why such a high-strung individual would choose to serve in submarines when the throbbing whine of the frigate's turbines reached their crescendo. Ever so gradually, the resonant sound began to lessen until it was all but indistinguishable. This brought a relieved sigh from the captain's lips. "So much for the ASW capabilities of the British Leander-class frigate. Admiral Markov is right, the Royal Navy is far from the great fleet it once was. Instead of wasting their money with such ridiculous, costly programs as Trident, they should invest in some new surface ships. Why, during the Falklands conflict, even an insignificant naval power such as Argentina was a challenge for the Brits. I'd love to see what the Red Banner fleet would do to them. We'd annihilate them before they'd even be able to leave port."

"Shouldn't we be attaining those deployment coordinates shortly, Captain Zinyagin?" interrupted Mikhail.

Called back to thoughts of his current duty, Dmitri Zinyagin answered, "As originally planned, we'll be releasing *Sea Devil* as soon as we reach the waters south of Sanda Island. Then you'll be faced with a fourteen-hour voyage up the Firth of Clyde to your final destination. I imagine that you're anxious to get it over with, aren't you, Captain?"

"I've been looking forward to this operation ever

since Admiral Starobin told me about it back in Kronstadt," returned Mikhail. "My entire crew is ready for action, and I foresee no serious obstacles that should hinder us along the way."

Dmitri Zinyagin looked directly into his colleague's steel-gray eyes and replied. "Though my briefing did not include the exact purpose of your mission, I presume it has something to do with the imperialist naval installations at Holy Loch and Falsane. I envy you, Captain Borisov. These are waters every submariner in the Red Banner fleet dreams of penetrating one day."

Sensing that the veteran was hoping that Mikhail would take him into his confidence and reveal his mission, the Spetsnaz commando grinned. "As commander of *Sea Devil,* I've visited places on this planet that would truly astound you, Captain. If only the Defense Ministry would allow me to write my memoirs!"

"I'm certain that it would be an instant best-seller both in the motherland and in the West," offered the *Ladoga*'s CO. "Now if you'd like, this vessel is more than capable of conveying *Sea Devil* a good deal closer than Sanda Island. I've been studying the charts, and it appears there's open water all the way to Little Cumbrae Island, which would put you right at the mouth of the Firth of Clyde."

"That offer's most inviting, Captain Zinyagin. But there's no need to risk the *Ladoga* for the sake of a few additional kilometers. We've got plenty of time to attain our goal. Besides, by utilizing our tracked-drive system, we'll be traveling to the Firth by way of Kilbrannan Sound. This poorly monitored waterway will lead us directly into the Sound of Bute, where we'll gain entrance to the Firth."

"As you wish, Captain Borisov. You can rest assured that the *Ladoga* will be waiting for you at the drop-off point when you're ready to return home."

"We're counting on that, comrade. Now I'd better get down to the torpedo room and assemble my crew."

"You do that, Captain Borisov," returned Dmitri Zinyagin, who watched the Spetsnaz officer pivot and head for the aft hatchway.

"That one's a cocky bastard," observed the *Ladoga*'s political officer.

"That's the nature of the beast," reflected Captain Zinyagin. You go and give a hotshot like that a twenty-meter-long, three-crew command, and he thinks he's a regular naval hero. He should only know what it's like to sacrifice forty years of one's life in service to the motherland. And as for that mini-sub of his, I guarantee you that the *Ladoga* could outperform *Sea Devil* any day of the week. I only wish that Command had seen fit to send us up the Firth of Clyde. Yet as it now stands, all we are is a damned underwater taxi-cab."

Well aware of his captain's bitterness, the *zampolit* guardedly responded. "My sources tell me that we'll be getting rid of our Spetsnaz comrades just in the nick of time. It seems there's an element in the crew who have turned to emulating our brave commandos. All they talk of is becoming Spetsnaz themselves, and needless to say, their work is starting to suffer from this foolishness."

"That is most distressing news, Comrade Zampolit. These shirkers are just looking for an excuse to be negligent in their duties. And as for them wanting to become Spetsnaz themselves, that's certainly a joke. Most of the spineless wimps aboard this ship couldn't even pass the physical. And they'd dirty their shorts the first time danger presented itself. It looks like we'll have to further tighten discipline aboard this vessel."

"Perhaps a special meeting of the Komsomol is in order," offered the political officer. "At this time you

309

could restate your command policies, and I'll put together a lecture on the dangers of striving for the unattainable."

"I think that's an excellent idea, comrade. We'll wait until *Sea Devil* is deployed before informing the crew of this get-together. And then it will be solely up to us to reinstill some pride in this vessel."

Already mentally planning the contents of his speech, Captain Dmitri Zinyagin sauntered over to the periscope well. Ever suspicious of anything that might weaken his command, he anxiously looked to his watch to calculate how much time was left until they could ascend to take a final bearing, to prepare for *Sea Devil*'s final deployment.

Chapter Fifteen

The tug was well out in the Irish Sea when a brisk northwesterly began blowing. The previous calm seas turned almost instantly treacherous, and Bernard was forced to pull back on the throttles to keep the tug from capsizing. Perched beside him in the enclosed wheelhouse, Dr. Tyronne Blackwater held on for dear life as the massive swells smashed into their blunt bow. Any less seaworthy a craft would long since have had to return to port, and the physician was a bit more confident knowing that their vessel was extremely stable.

It seemed that each time a swell struck them, Bernard Loughlin would angrily mumble a curse, and Dr. Blackwater did his best to calm him down. "Easy now, Bernard. You can't fight weather like this, so you just might as well go with it."

The one-eyed terrorist was positioned behind the tug's wheel and responded to this advice while once more easing back on the throttle. "Damn it, Doc. We're barely doing ten knots as it is. At this rate, we won't get to the Firth until daybreak."

"And what's wrong with that, my friend? That still gives up plenty of time to get up to Gare Loch and do our dirty deed just as the christening is about to take place."

A particularly massive wave hit the tug's hull at an

angle, and the deck canted hard to starboard. A sturdy iron handhold kept Dr. Blackwater upright, while Bernard momentarily lost his balance and crashed into the side of the wheelhouse with his right shoulder. Quick to recover, he grabbed for the helm to keep the tug on course.

"I was just hoping that we could get past the Sound of Bute before sunrise," added Bernard. "I've got a feeling that's where we're going to encounter the first Brit blockade."

"What makes you think that they'll be going to such an extreme?" asked the physician.

Bernard answered passionately. "Oh come on, Doc! You know how paranoid the Brits are! Just knowing that their beloved Queen will be passing over those same waters will be reason enough to stop every single vessel headed up the Firth."

"And so what if they do, Bernard? Don't forget that this tug is duly registered in the Port of Glasgow. Why we have just as much right to be on the Clyde than anyone else."

"I'd still feel more comfortable penetrating the sound under the cover of night," continued Bernard.

Again the tug rolled hard to the right, and this time it was the physician who lost his footing. Forced to reach out for the deck-mounted compass to keep from tumbling over, Dr. Blackwater just managed to remain standing.

Outside the glassed-in wheelhouse a murky twilight prevailed. The gray, ever-darkening dusk sky seemed to merge with the surging gray sea, and it was impossible to determine where the two met at the horizon. Oblivious to the poor visibility, Bernard steered on the bearing given to him by the compass. For the majority of their voyage, this course would take them almost due north.

312

They were in between swells when the door to the cabin opened and in walked Sean. His presence caused a sour expression to cross Bernard's face.

"Phew! You smell like a dead fish, Sean Lafferty," observed the IRB's cofounder disgustedly.

"What do you expect after being down in the bilge for the last half hour with a couple hundred smelly cod for company?"

"How does it look down there, Sean?" asked Dr. Blackwater.

"You'll have to see it with your own eyes to believe it, Doc. You can't even see the bomb anymore."

"Bernard, that was a stroke of genius when you suggested that we stop that trawler and purchase its load," offered the physician.

"I just hope we won't be forced to test my theory," replied Bernard.

Sean smelled his shirtsleeve and wrinkled his nose in disgust. "Well, I can personally vouch for its effectiveness. Those cod are only just starting to thaw out. And since there's no refrigeration in the bilge, they're going to really be stinking to high heaven in a couple more hours."

As a wave tossed the bow of the tug upward, and gravity pulled it abruptly back down into the sea again, Sean's knees buckled. Reaching out to support him, Dr. Blackwater shook his head.

"I'd still feel better if you were down in the hold resting, Sean. That wound of yours has a good way to go until it's healed, and one fall could rip it right open."

"Then I just won't fall, Doc. I hardly feel the pain anymore."

"You young bucks are remarkable," reflected the silver-haired physician. "If it was anyone my age who suffered a gunshot like that, they'd still be in the hospital."

"Me being laid up in Cootehill House was hard enough," admitted Sean. "Although I was lucky to have one of the prettiest nurses in all of Ireland attending to me. I wonder how Marie's getting along?"

"As long as she has those blasted veggies of hers to take care of, she'll be just fine," said Bernard.

The mere mention of the precocious redhead caused a smile to turn the corners of the physician's mouth. "She has done a remarkable job with that vegetable garden of hers. I haven't seen anything quite like it since my mother's time."

"Did your mother have a garden at Cootehill House too, Doc?" queried Sean.

"You don't know the half of it, lad. Not only did she have a small plot for her personal use, but she was responsible for the upkeep of the rest of the estate as well. With my father perpetually out on house calls, she supervised the raising of sheep, cows, chickens, and pigs, and saw to it that over eighty prime acres of potatoes were properly cared for. She was sure something for a city girl, and now Marie's just sort of moved in and taken her place. I can't tell you how it does my heart good to see her enjoying the place like she does. I still say she'd make a hell of a wife, if one of you would get up the nerve to ask her."

"I beg to differ with you," said Bernard. "Marie's too independent to settle down permanently. Besides, I can just see her now, with a baby in one hand and an Armalite in the other."

The three men shared a brief laugh as the deck beneath them rolled to and fro like a carnival ride.

"Speaking of marriage, how about you, Sean?" asked the grinning physician.

"You've got to be kidding, Doc. When would I ever find time for a wife and kids? And since it's a struggle

314

merely to take care of myself, how would I ever support her?"

"Were you ever married, Doc?" asked Bernard.

The physician responded with a fond smile. "That I was, lads. And she was a lovely girl at that. Her name was Patricia. She was a local gal from Dundalk. Her father was a surgeon, and it was when I inherited his practice that I decided to put down roots on the coast. Though she couldn't have children, she kept a warm, clean, happy house. And if it wasn't for the cancer that eventually ate her up, we would have been married for forty-five years come this June."

A moment of reflective silence followed, only to be broken by the cool voice of Bernard Loughlin. "You know, I lost a wife myself. I took Katherine as my bride when we were both nothing but wide-eyed teenagers. We even had two children, a boy and a girl."

Amazed by this revelation, Sean interrupted. "I didn't know that about you, Bernard. Where are they now?"

"In a cemetery outside of Derry," answered the terrorist bluntly. "I lost the whole bunch of 'em to a car bomb most likely meant for myself. I never did learn for certain who the bastards were that were responsible for this slaughter. Some say it was the RUC, others the Brits. And I even heard tell that the explosives were placed there by the IRA. But regardless of who did it, that was enough to show me that revolution and marriage just don't mix."

With no dark secrets of his own to confess, Sean excused himself to bring up some supper. It was pitch black outside by the time he returned with a large wicker basket filled with loaves of shepherd's bread, a wheel of goat cheese, and a half dozen green apples. Though the pitching seas did little for their appetites, they forced themselves to eat to keep up their strength.

315

Bernard volunteered to take the first evening watch, leaving Dr. Blackwater and Sean free to go below and get some rest. Two bunk beds filled the vessel's single stateroom. It was while he lay on the bottom mattress of one of these bunks that Sean got the nerve to ask a question that had been on his mind since they'd left Dundalk.

"Doc, I've been meaning to ask you—how are we going to manage detonating that bomb, and at the same time get far enough away to survive its blast?"

The elderly physician, reclining on the adjoining bunk, exhaled a deep breath before answering. "I was hoping you'd bring that up, Sean. Me and Bernard talked it over while you were down in the bilges, and we came to the conclusion that to ensure that the device detonates properly, someone's going to have to stay with it until it goes off. And we thought that it was only fitting that both Bernard and myself should be the ones to do this deed."

"But that would be sheer suicide!" countered Sean. "And what's the Brotherhood to do afterward, when both of you are blown to a million pieces?"

"Hopefully, go on just like they are right now," returned the physician calmly, "the only difference being that two of its senior officers will be martyred, and the enemy dealt an antagonizing blow that they'll never be able to recover from."

"But I thought we could hook up a remote control device with the timer from the VCR. That way the bomb will receive the charge it needs to explode, and all of us can be miles away on our way back home to celebrate."

"The thought is tempting, lad. But this whole thing is just too important to trust to a mere timing mechanism. Me and Bernard also agreed that it would be a waste of life to sacrifice all three of us. So we decided

316

to stop at Ardrossan and drop you off."

"I won't hear of any such thing! If both of you are willing to see this thing out to the end, I am too. And I'll be hearing no arguments otherwise!"

"You're as pig-headed as that stubborn father of yours, Sean Lafferty. And it appears that the Brotherhood is about to have a trio of martyrs to venerate."

Suddenly grasping the fact that his life would all too soon be over, Sean sat up in his bunk and gazed out into the blackness. "I guess that will leave Marie as the IRB's commander," he observed thoughtfully.

"It appears so, lad. I have full confidence in her ability to handle the movement on her own. And she'll certainly not have to worry about having a base of operations to mold the new shape of Ireland from. Because before we left County Caven, I drew up a codicil to my will bequeathing my beloved Cootehill House to her."

"That was kind of you, Doc. Now if I only had something of value to leave for my parents."

The physician responded passionately to this statement. "But you have, lad! Don't you see? You're about to be giving them the greatest gift of all — a united Ireland!"

"You mean to say that all this food I'm eating comes from that little kitchen you showed me, and that you serve such meals even while underwater? That's simply amazing!"

Liam Lafferty made this observation while seated in the wardroom of the USS *Bowfin*. Before him was a full-course fried chicken dinner. Though he had been more frightened than hungry when the sailors initially led him down into the submarine, the Yanks' pleasant companionship and the tempting aroma of food changed all this.

"This chicken is delicious!" raved the grizzled fisherman as he bit into a steaming hot, juicy breast. "And what's that sweet red jelly made out of?"

"Cranberries," explained Lieutenant Commander Ted Bauer, the *Bowfin's* XO. "In America, we like to serve it with poultry dishes, and it's a staple of our Thanksgiving dinner."

Liam spooned a mouthful of the tasty jelly and followed it with some gravy-laden mashed potatoes. On his second helping of biscuits and honey, he stopped eating long enough to comment, "If the lads back at the Rose-and-Thistle could only see me now! Here I am, cruising beneath the Irish Sea and eating like a king at the same time. Henry Morrison's going to be beside himself with envy! I'll have some more of that iced tea, if you please."

The XO was getting a kick out of watching the Irishman indulge himself. Yet he prayed that the fisherman wouldn't eat so much that he'd go and get himself sick.

"How would you like to go on that tour of the ship now, Mr. Lafferty?" asked the XO in an attempt to entice him away from the dinner table.

"But what about that pumpkin pie you mentioned?" returned Liam.

"I'll make certain Cooky locks up a piece with your name on it," promised the *Bowfin's* second-in-command.

On that conciliatory note, Liam plucked the last piece of white meat off the breast and mopped up the remaining gravy with a biscuit. "I guess I could do with a little stretching of the old legs," he added as he wiped his face and pushed his chair back from the table. "Would you mind if I light up the old pipe while we take our stroll?"

"I don't think that would be a problem, sir. Though you'll have to extinguish it once we reach the reactor room."

Hearing this, Liam's eyes opened wide. "Is that a nuclear-powered reactor you're referring to, my friend?"

The XO nodded, and Liam vehemently shook his head. "If you don't mind, I'd rather skip that part of the tour. From what I understand, that nuclear radiation is awfully nasty stuff."

"You needn't worry about any radiation danger aboard the *Bowfin,* Mr. Lafferty. The ship's reactor is encased in a lead vessel that makes it practically leak free. Besides, I was only going to show you its control console. But if you want to skip it altogether, how about if we go and take a look at the torpedo room? We've got some fish up there that are really something to see."

"You're carrying fish on this vessel?" Liam asked.

The XO had to summon every ounce of self-control to keep from bursting into laughter as he responded. "Mr. Lafferty, I guarantee that these fish are unlike any species you've ever laid eyes on before. In fact, in my book, they're even deadlier than the great white shark."

With his eyes open wide, Liam threw down his napkin and stood. "Lead the way, Yank. This I've got to see!"

While the XO went about initiating the Irishman into the intricacies of underwater weaponry, the *Bowfin's* CO hosted his own two guests in the ship's control room. Captain William Foard was somewhat surprised when the orders came in from COMSUBLANT authorizing him to take the two foreign nationals on board. He also found his current mission somewhat puzzling. For all purposes, Commander Brad Mackenzie now had the authority to utilize the *Bowfin* as he saw fit. This was most unusual, and Foard could only suppose that the NOSC officer had some high-placed friends in the Pentagon.

Captain Foard was currently gathered around the ship's chart table with Commander Mackenzie, or Mac, as he preferred to be called, and the Scotsman, Major Colin Stewart. They had a detailed bathymetric chart of the waters immediately outside the Firth of Clyde before them, and Foard was in the process of giving them the current status update.

"At this pace, we should be approaching the entrance to the Firth toward daybreak. Of course, all you have to do is say the word, Commander, and I can pull us off our present course and get us into the Clyde much sooner."

Mac answered while studying the zigzagging blue line that showed their course northward since leaving the search site. "I don't think that's necessary right now, Captain. Considering the agitated sea and the limited speed of the tug, I don't really think they're that far ahead of us. What do you think, Major?"

Colin Stewart pointed to the waters just east of Arran Island. "Even at half speed, they shouldn't be much further than here. Yet since it's their course that's still the point, I feel our current time-consuming search pattern is more than justified."

"Then if that's settled, I'll start edging the *Bowfin* up toward periscope depth," said the captain. "We're about due for our next visual sweep, and maybe this time we'll have something for our other passenger to take a look at."

"I wonder how the old guy is making out?" Mac asked.

The captain grinned. "The last I heard from the XO, he was over his case of stage fright and stuffing his mouth with a fried chicken dinner with all the trimmings. And Mr. Lafferty seems to have gotten over his shyness as well. At last report, he was talking away with such a vengeance that Lieutenant Commander Bauer could hardly get a word in edgewise."

"The old-timer's a character, all right," added Mac. "Now let's just pray that this whole story of his isn't some sort of fantastic fabrication. Because if it is, and we were to take out a tugload of innocent civilians, then I might as well kiss my career good-bye."

This last statement was directed toward Colin Stewart, who returned Mac's probing stare without flinching. "You don't have to worry about that, Commander. Those IRB terrorists are out there with your bomb, all right. And I just pray to God that we can find them before it's too late for all of us!"

Chapter Sixteen

The eastern horizon was just beginning to glow with the first tentative light of dawn when *Sea Devil* separated from its semirecessed storage well that was set abaft the *Ladoga*'s sail. Silently propelled by its single battery-powered propeller, the mini-sub proceeded to the north, up Kilbrannan Sound to the still waters of the Sound of Bute. All systems were operating perfectly as Mikhail Borisov ordered the helmsman to guide the vessel cautiously to periscope depth at this point.

"Watch your trim," cautioned the *Sea Devil*'s CO as he watched Yuri Sosnovo begin lightening the boat by venting seawater from its ballast tanks. "We certainly wouldn't want to accidentally breach the surface in these unfriendly waters."

The chief engineer responded with the barest of nods, his entire concentration focused on the delicate task of altering the sub's buoyancy just enough to allow its periscope to break the water's surface. It was with great relief that he looked to the depth gauge and calmly called out, "We're at periscope depth, Captain."

"Good work, Yuri," complimented Mikhail as he made his way over to the periscope well. "Now we should be able to get that precise bearing."

With the assistance of warrant officer Oleg Zagorsk, the periscope was guided up from its well. Practically hunching down on his knees to guarantee that too much of the lens didn't penetrate the surface, Mikhail initiated a quick sweep of the water's topside. Though the sun had yet to break the horizon, there was enough light for him to hurriedly triangulate their position.

"Down scope!" he ordered firmly, as he backed away from the well and stood upright. "I was able to get three different bearings. So give me my charts, Comrade Zagorsk, and I'll determine our exact coordinates."

Without bothering to remove the oilskin covers that protected the charts from the constantly dripping condensation, the Siberian alertly handed them to his commanding officer. Mikhail used a ruler and a pencil to plot the three bearings he had just seen with his own eyes.

"We're currently halfway between the Isle of Arran to our southwest and Bute Island, which lies four kilometers to the north of us. I was able to just make out a directional beacon further east that I believe to be emanating from Little Cumbrae Island. Since it's through the channel that lies immediately to the west of this island that we'll be entering the Firth of Clyde, shall we proceed in that direction?"

Hearing not a word of dissent, Mikhail ordered *Sea Devil* back to the seafloor, where its unique tracked propulsion system took over. A little over a quarter of an hour passed when he once more directed them to periscope depth.

"Now I should have a better view of the channel

we'll be transiting to get to our destination," offered Mikhail as he anxiously hunched over and put the rubberized viewing coupling to his forehead.

The sun had broken the horizon by now, and clearly illuminated was a frightening scene that caused Mikhail to cry out.

"Down scope! Bring us back to the seafloor, Yuri, and waste no time about it."

As the roaring sound of the ballast tanks taking on water filled the cramped control space, Mikhail backed away from the well. It wasn't until they gently hit bottom that he explained what he had sighted topside.

"I'm afraid it's not going to be as easy to penetrate the Firth as we had hoped. Blocking the channel up ahead is a line of three anchored Brit frigates. They appear to be Cornwall-class type 22 vessels, which means that they're equipped with a comprehensive set of ASW sensors. Most likely they're sitting out there anticipating just such a covert intrusion as we had in mind."

"I bet it's prompted by the visit of their Queen," supposed Yuri Sosnovo.

"From what I understand, the Brits are every bit as cautious when it comes to security matters as our own KGB," added Tanya Olovski.

"I say that we should proceed as if we didn't even know they were there," offered *Sea Devil*'s Warrant Officer. "With our stealth capabilities, they'll never spot us, even with a dozen frigates."

Mikhail Borisov thoughtfully rubbed his scarred cheek. "That might be so, Comrade Zagorsk. But this mission is much too important to find out differently. Thus, for circumspection's sake, I feel it's best if we silently loiter at this position and wait for another vessel to come along. Then as this vessel proceeds to penetrate the blockade, all we have to do is follow in its baffles. When we're veiled by its propeller wash, they'll never know we're even down here."

From an adjoining portion of the same Sound, Captain Dmitri Zinyagin also viewed the line of anchored Cornwall-class frigates from the powerful lens of the *Ladoga*'s attack scope. Taking in the line of sleek ships, the veteran officer grunted and stepped back from the scope.

"Have a look yourself, Comrade Zampolit. For this is an obstacle that even our brave Spetsnaz colleagues wouldn't dare take on by themselves."

Petyr Tartarov moved his corpulent torso over to the periscope well, hunched over, and put his sweat-stained forehead up against the eyepiece.

"My, that's indeed a formidable barrier. Does this mean their mission is over?"

"Heavens no," returned Dmitri Zinyagin. "Though there's always the chance that *Sea Devil* would try running the blockade, I'd say that Captain Borisov wouldn't take the risk. If I were in his place, I'd wait for the approach of another ship, preferably a nice noisy surface vessel. Then all he'd have to do is follow in this craft's wake all the way into the Firth."

The political officer responded to this while backing away from the scope. "That's a brilliant tactic, Captain. But I wonder if Captain Borisov will think of it."

"From what I understand, the Spetsnaz takes a good amount of time training their naval officers in just such basic strategy. He'll have thought of it, all right. And I guarantee you that he's sitting out there right now, waiting for this vessel's approach."

As Dmitri Zinyagin instructed his senior lieutenant

to take his place at the scope, the *Ladoga*'s CO followed the *zampolit* over to the vacant weapons console.

"I've notified the crew about this afternoon's special Komsomol meeting, Captain," revealed the political officer. "I'm assuming that you have your speech in order.

"That I have, comrade. But I just wish that I could back up my concepts with more than mere words. If only there were some way that I could show the men that an ordinary member of the Red Banner fleet was just as good a soldier as the Spetsnaz. I'm still of the impression that they think of themselves merely as glorified taxi drivers. What they need is a taste of real action. It's just too bad that Command didn't send the *Ladoga* in *Sea Devil*'s place."

A bit uncomfortable with this line of reasoning, Petyr Tartarov nodded. "That's an interesting concept, Comrade. But don't give up on the power of ideological conditioning just yet. I learned long ago that the only way to get into some of these stubborn sailors' heads is to constantly pound a point into them. By increasing the frequency and intensity of our Komsomol meetings, we can do just that."

"I hope you're right," said the captain with a sigh. "Because the morale on this ship seems to be worsening with each hour's passing."

"I know I am, Captain. And I hope to prove it to you during today's Komsomol meeting. So if you'll excuse me, I'd better get down to my cabin and finish my preparations."

Petyr Tartarov gratefully left the tense confines of the attack center. Never feeling truly at home in this part of the ship, he proceeded aft to that part of the *Ladoga* reserved for its officers. He crossed through the deserted wardroom and was surprised to find a

326

single lanky enlisted man waiting in the hallway opposite his stateroom.

"Comrade Zampolit, I was wondering if I could have a word with you?" the sailor nervously called out.

Though Tartarov had seen this individual before only in passing, he could see by his insignia that he held the lowly rank of torpedo mate third class.

"What is it, sailor? I'm a busy man with many things to do," he said as he fumbled for his key.

The enlisted man held back his response until the political officer managed to open the door to his cabin, and he tentatively followed him inside.

"Sir, I am torpedo mate third class Vasili Buchara," he revealed after clearing his dry throat. "And I would like an application to the Special Forces Academy."

Not believing what he was hearing, Tartarov looked up astounded. "What's this you say, sailor? You want to apply to become a Spetsnaz? Why, that's the funniest thing I've heard all day."

Expecting just such a response from the *zampolit,* Vasili dared to hold his ground. "I'm sorry you feel that way, sir. But this is no joke, and I would still like that application."

"So you would, huh?" retorted the red-faced Zampolit. "I'll give you this piece of advice, Comrade Buchara. The Spetsnaz is not about to be interested in a scrawny little sailor like yourself. Why, you're not even a Great Russian, are you?"

"No sir, I'm an Uzbek," said the blushing enlisted man, who was beginning to wonder if this was such a good idea after all.

"Well then, I hope that your family has some political clout, because even if you were physically up to it, the Special Forces is also socially elite. So quit

327

wasting my time, and more important, yours as well with this foolish fantasy. Make the best of your current service, and be proud that you've been given the privilege of wearing the uniform of the Red Banner fleet. If that is all, Seaman Buchara, you're excused. And don't forget to come to this afternoon's Komsomol meeting. There's certainly a lot that you'll learn by attending."

Having lost what little courage he had by now, the seaman responded with a weak salute and submissively backed out into the corridor

"So now even the Uzbeks want to join the Spetsnaz," disgustedly mumbled the *zampolit* to himself. Tempted to immediately inform the captain of this ridiculous confrontation, Petyr Tartarov sat down heavily on the edge of his bunk. There could be no doubting the degree to which the influence of the *Sea Devil*'s crew had poisoned the morale of the *Ladoga*. With the hope that it wasn't already too late to apply an antidote, the *zampolit* reached out for his legal pad to work anew on this afternoon's all-important speech.

Meanwhile, back in the *Ladoga*'s attack center, Captain Zinyagin found himself called to the periscope by the excited voice of his senior lieutenant.

"Sir, it appears that there's another vessel approaching the line of frigates. I believe it's a tug of some sort."

Quick to replace his subordinate at the scope, the captain took his time responding. "So it is comrade. This ship should provide just the sort of cover that *Sea Devil*'s been waiting for. And if Captain Borisov is wise, he'll follow in this tug's wake all the way up the Firth, to the sensitive naval installations that I just know in my gut he's being ordered to survey."

It was while wishing that their commands were

switched that a sudden inspiration came to the veteran. With or without Command's blessings, he'd at long last take the initiative and order the *Ladoga* to follow *Sea Devil* up into the Firth of Clyde as soon as the first opportunity presented itself. Then they could ride shotgun over the vulnerable tracked mini-sub while its crew of Spetsnaz operatives got on with its mission.

Inspired by this impromptu idea, Dmitri knew that it would serve yet another vitally important function. With the realization that they were going in harm's way, just like the *Sea Devil,* the crew would unite. No longer would they think of themselves as mere taxi drivers, but rather underwater warriors, who would earn the motherland's respect, just as the Special Forces had!

Completely oblivious to the machinations going on in the seas beneath them, Bernard Loughlin pulled back on the throttle of the tug as he spotted the line of frigates that blocked the channel up ahead.

"Doc, I think you had better get up here!" he shouted into the intercom.

With his good eye, Bernard scanned the blockade with binoculars. He was in the process of studying the missile launcher visible on the bow of the ship nearest to them when both Dr. Blackwater and Sean joined him in the wheelhouse.

"What's the matter, Bernard?" asked the physician.

Bernard pointed to the north. "Looks like the Brits decided to blockade the entrance to the Firth after all. I believe those are Leander-class frigates."

As Dr. Blackwater accepted the binoculars, he raised them to his eyes and corrected his colleague. "Actually, they're Cornwall-class Type 22's. But that makes little difference. They're still not going to bother us in the least."

"I wish I could agree with you, Doc," returned Bernard. "The Royal Navy are a fastidious bunch, and if they really want to look for trouble, they usually find it."

The physician handed the binoculars to Sean and retorted, "Have you no faith in your own plan, comrade? Even if they do board us, one sniff of that bilge will be enough to convince even the most detail-oriented petty officer to abandon any further search effort."

"Those frigates sure don't appear to be heavily armed," observed Sean. "I don't even see a single deck gun."

Dr. Blackwater was quick to reply. "Don't let that fact fool you, lad. Naval warship designers today have replaced the guns of old with missile launchers. They might not appear as intimidating, but they get the job done much more effectively."

"Which frigate should I head for?" asked Bernard.

"Just keep your present course," advised Dr. Blackwater. "We'll let them tell us what to do. And if they do board us, let me do all the talking, if possible. I've been doing my bloody best to perfect a Scot brogue, and I always did like amateur theatrics."

The tug was several hundred meters closer to the blockade when its radio-telephone activated. Dr. Blackwater picked up the handset and accepted the greetings of a Royal Navy lieutenant, who then ordered them to approach the ship nearest to Little Cumbrae Island and prepare to be boarded. Calmly accepting this inevitable fact, the physician once more shared his knowledge of human nature with his shipmates.

"Sean, you stay up in the wheelhouse with Bernard,

330

and both of you, just look natural. Don't make any threatening moves, and take this all in stride as the minor inconvenience that it is. And if you are asked a question, answer it directly, with as few words as possible. I've got the registration papers on me, and will try to get this whole thing over with as soon as possible."

The boarding party arrived via a whaleboat. It was led by a fair-haired officer in a white tunic and matching shorts. Four enlisted men accompanied him, and each one wore a holstered handgun.

With a forced smile, Dr. Blackwater accepted their line and called out to them. "Good morning, gentlemen. What's with the reception committee?"

"It's just a routine check," replied the officer, who climbed on board the tug with two of his men. "Could I see your papers, please?"

The physician reached into his pocket and pulled out the tug's registration form. Before studying it, the officers ordered his men to take a look around.

"Is there anything wrong?" asked Dr. Blackwater politely. "I certainly hope you don't think we're guilty of some infraction. An admiralty fine now is all we need. This entire trip has been nothing but a financial disaster from the start."

Barely paying this any mind, the officer intently studied the tug's papers. "I see that you're home ported in Glasgow. Are you headed there now?"

Tyronne Blackwater nodded that they were, and the officer continued. "And where are you coming from?"

"I'm sorry to say, Dublin," returned the physician with a smirk. "No offense to the Irish people as a whole, but as long as I live, I hope never to return to that place again. Do you realize that we pulled a barge all the way over there from Ardrossan, and when we went to collect our fee as agreed, the bastards told me that they didn't have the cash, and asked if they could owe it to us? I could tell right then and there that they didn't have any intention of paying us. And before we were forced to leave without any compensation whatsoever, I was able to talk them into a barter arrangement. In place of the money they owed us, I took on a mixed load of smelt and cod. Yet how was I to know that our refrigeration plant would give up the ghost halfway across the Irish Sea? And now all we've got to show for our efforts is a bilgeful of spoiled fish. Why, they're so rotten that I doubt if even the fertilizer works will have them!"

Seconds later, one of the enlisted men seemingly corroborated this story when he reported finding a foul-smelling load of spoiled fish in the tug's hold. When his shipmate returned from his search of the vessel's forward compartments and had nothing out of the ordinary to report, the fair-haired Royal Navy lieutenant handed the registration papers back to the tug's owner.

"Sorry for the inconvenience, Sir. And I'm also sorry for your bad luck. Do have a safe trip back to port, and please be patient as you reach the upper reaches of the Clyde. The Queen is visiting the Gare Loch naval installation this afternoon, and I'm afraid there's a bit of a crowd congregating up there already. Seems that everybody who has a boat wants a chance to see Her Highness as she christens our first Trident submarine. Do have a look yourself. You should get there just in time for the festivities."

"Perhaps there's a pot of gold at the end of this long voyage after all," reflected Dr. Blackwater as he led the sailors over to the rail and helped them as they climbed back into the whaleboat.

The physician waved good-bye and casually turned

for the tug's wheelhouse. With his best poker face he then proceeded to address his shipmates.

"Well, don't just stand there, comrades. Open up that throttle. And let's get on with that date with history that's waiting for us at the other end of the Firth of Clyde!"

As the tug's engines rumbled alive, all three members of its crew failed to spot the oblong, rectangular lens that just broke the water only a few meters aft of the tug's transom. On the other end of this viewing device, Captain Mikhail Borisov watched as the frothing white wake of the tug's propeller colored the gray seas. Only when he was satisfied that the vessel was headed up the channel did the blond-haired commando step back from the periscope.

"You may lower the scope, Comrade Warrant Officer," he ordered. "Helmsman, all ahead full. It's absolutely necessary that we stick as close to the tug as possible. I'll man sonar myself."

As *Sea Devil's* single-bladed propeller whirred alive, its CO hurried over to the sonar console. He sat down on a narrow bench and clipped on a set of miniature headphones. This allowed him to monitor the series of sensitive hydrophones mounted throughout the mini-sub's hull. As he isolated those microphones set into the bow, the throaty rumble of the tug's engines was clearly audible, as was the cavitational hiss caused when millions of tiny bubbles collapsed on its propeller.

"Bring us up another meter, Oleg," instructed the captain. "And be ever cautious of water density changes as we initiate our passage into the fresh water of the Firth."

The trick now was to get as close to the bottom of

the tug's hull as possible without striking it. In this manner, the enemy sensors would pick up only a single entity on their monitor screens.

The deafening ping of an active sonar unit caused Mikhail to reach out and turn down the volume of his hydrophone receivers. This same distinctive hollow noise was heard throughout *Sea Devil*, even by those without headphones.

"We should be passing by the line of frigates just about now," offered the helmsman, Yuri Sosnovo.

"This is the moment of truth," added Oleg Zagorsk, who was perched beside the diving station.

At her post at the main circuit board, Tanya Olovski looked up at the snaking cables that lined the ceiling of the mini-sub, as if she could see the surface platforms responsible for the monotonous pinging sound. Her upward glance was shortlived, though, when a well-placed drop of condensation hit her smack in the left eye.

Though it seemed to the crew to take hours to dissipate, in reality only a few minutes passed before the British sonar scan began to noticeably fade. A joint sigh of relief filled the cramped compartment as the nerve-racking pinging dispersed altogether. It was their captain who spoke for all of them as he pushed back his headphones.

"It appears that we have successfully passed the first major obstacle, comrades. Yet we mustn't celebrate prematurely. We still have a good distance to go yet until our goal is attained. If our luck holds, perhaps we'll have this tug to run interference for us most of the way. So keep ever vigilant, and if the fates so will it, we shall prevail."

Sliding back his headphones, Mikhail urgently added, "We must have more power, Yuri! Full ahead emergency, if you must. This tug is a godsend, and I don't want to lose its cover. And besides, to hell with conserving our battery power! Only one thing matters, and that's getting us to Holy Loch!"

Chapter Seventeen

Liam's tour of the *Bowfin*'s torpedo room was cut short by an urgent call from the sub's captain.

"Get our guest up to the bridge on the double, XO. It's time he earned his keep around here."

They hurried back to the control room and joined the captain, Commander Mackenzie, and Major Stewart around the periscope.

"Mr. Lafferty, I've got a tug up there that I want you to take a look at," said Captain Foard.

Liam had already peered through the periscope several previous times, and was getting accustomed to it, as he calmly ambled over to the viewing coupling. "Just point the way, captain. I'll be giving it my best effort."

William Foard briefly checked the direction in which the lens was pointed and then beckoned the fisherman to have a look. While Liam did so, the captain briefed his XO.

"We were on our way to the channel leading into the Clyde when we spotted an oceangoing tug off Farland Head. They seem to be merely anchored up there, and if we're lucky, it's our boys."

Any hopes that Foard might have had were dashed by Liam's matter-of-fact observation. "Nope, it's not them."

"Are you absolutely certain?" asked the Captain.

Liam backed away from the scope and looked directly at the *Bowfin*'s CO. "These eyes of mine are still pretty good for an old man, Captain. And when I tell you it's not them, I mean it."

Not wanting to push the point any further, the XO diplomatically intervened. "How about returning to the wardroom and trying some of that pumpkin pie that Cooky's saving for you down there?"

Liam smiled. "I've been waiting for you to ask, my friend. You know, you Yanks don't eat so bad. What are you serving for breakfast?"

The XO briefly caught his captain's eye and winked before escorting Liam back out of the control room.

"Now what, gentlemen?" asked Foard.

Mac looked to his watch. "I say it's time to start heading up the Clyde, Captain. If they plan to make that christening, then that's where we're going to find them."

"I agree," said Colin Stewart. "At least the Firth is the only sea route that leads into Gare Loch."

"Thank goodness we have that going for us," returned the captain as he conveyed the orders that would send them towards Little Cumbrae Island and the channel that led directly into the Firth of Clyde.

Mac and Colin were in the process of following the captain over to navigation when the sonar operator spoke out.

"Captain, I'm picking up a strong active sonar scan in the waters directly ahead of us, bearing three-four-zero, range three miles. It seems to be coming from more than one surface platform."

Curious as to the source of this disturbance, Foard returned to the periscope well with his two guests close on his heels. Only when he turned the scope to the bearing just conveyed to him and increased the magnification of the lense tenfold did he comment.

337

"Well, I'll be . . . there's a line of frigates out there blocking the channel. As I speak, they're in the process of boarding a fishing trawler, that was headed in our direction."

"That must all be part of the security precautions for the Queen's visit," ventured Colin Stewart.

Mac was quick to add, "If that's the case, if our tug has already passed through the channel, they'll have a record of it."

"Quartermaster, have communications patch me through to the squadron leader of the group of Brit frigates that lie immediately north of us," ordered the captain.

Less than a minute later, this directive was carried out and Foard was instructed to pick up the nearest telephone handset. Both Mac and Colin anxiously watched the captain as he began his brief conversation. There was a concerned look on the C.O.'s face as he hung up the handset and addressed his guests.

"Well gentlemen, it seems nine tugs have entered the channel since midnight. All checked out, and were ultimately headed to Port Glasgow, with the latest one passing less than a half hour ago."

"At least that narrows down the odds a little," observed Mac, who looked on as the captain called out.

"Helmsman, take us down to eighty feet. All ahead full! Next stop, the Firth of Clyde."

Silently loitering off the coast of Little Cumbrae Island, the India-class attack sub *Ladoga* monitored the approach of the the *Bowfin* long before the American sub contacted the commander of the British surface ship squadron. Captain Dmitri Zinyagin excitedly seated himself before his vessel's auxiliary sonar console as soon as the first contact was established. Here he breathlessly listened as the distinctive signature of this bogey was positively identified as being an American Sturgeon-class submarine. Zinyagin had been praying that such a vessel would come this way. And now, with the Sturgeon's presence, his inspirational plan of action could at long last be implemented.

There was an expectant gleam in Zinyagin's eyes when the American sub turned toward the line of frigates and activated its underwater telephone. Though he wasn't able to monitor this conversation, he guessed that the Yanks were asking permission to pass under the blockade. This supposition was confirmed when the Sturgeon continued on toward the channel, propelled by the full power of its engines

"All ahead, emergency speed!" ordered Zinyagin passionately. "Helmsman, prepare to interface autopilot with the primary underwater sonar contact that we're currently monitoring."

The attack center briefly trembled as the *Ladoga*'s propulsion system went on-line. Though they would never be able to catch up with the nuclear-powered *Sturgeon*, all that they were attempting to do was follow in the American sub's baffles, that sound-absorbent cone of water that all such vessels leave in their wake.

As he monitored this chase on the hydrophones, Zinyagin's voice cried out once again.

"Senior Lieutenant, open those throttles all the way. I must have speed, and have it now! Helmsman, interface the autopilot."

Though Zinyagin never took his eyes off the repeater screen, he knew this last directive was carried out when a green light began blinking on the right side of his console. This meant that the *Ladoga* was now being steered solely by the data being relayed to the helm by the ship's sensors. In effect, the American vessel was now controlling their course, and the helmsmen were able to release their steering yokes and let the computers take over their jobs for them.

A quick glance at the knot indicator showed that they had just enough speed to reach the *Sturgeon*'s baffles. Aligned right behind the American sub's tail at this point, they should be able to follow it beneath the blockade without either the frigates or the Sturgeon ever being the wiser.

Though the theory was solid, this tactic was put to the test when the sound of an active sonar scan filled his headphones. Would the frigates monitor only a single return beneath them? Or were his calculations flawed? Well aware that the moment of truth had arrived, Zinyagin sat forward tensely as the volume of the hollow pings reached their crescendo. Only when they began to gradually fade did he exhale a long sigh of relief.

"What in the world is going on here, Captain?" broke a scratchy voice from behind.

Having anticipated this confrontation, Dmitri Zinyagin pulled off his headphones and turned to face the puzzled *zampolit*.

"What does it look like, Comrade Tartarov? We're proceeding into the waters of the Firth of Clyde, where we belong in the first place."

"What are you talking about, Captain?" returned the red-faced political officer. "I have a duplicate set of our orders locked up in my safe, and they say absolutely nothing about us entering the Firth. Why, because of this rash move you're needlessly endangering all of us!"

Conscious that their harsh words were starting to draw the attention of the attack center's complement, Zinyagin stood and beckoned the *zampolit* to follow him over to the vacant weapon's console. Only when

340

the door to this cork-lined cubicle was shut behind them did the captain continue.

"Don't you understand what's occurring here, Comrade Tartarov? Not only am I protecting *Sea Devil*'s vulnerable flank, but I'm also winning back the confidence of my crew."

"It sounds more to me like the only thing that you've won for yourself is a court martial, Captain. Your actions are inexcusable, and if we live to survive this unauthorized intrusion, I'll personally see to it that the only vessel that you'll ever command again will be a garbage scow on Lake Baikal!"

The captain stood firm. "That might be your opinion, Comrade Zampolit. But I'm certain that my fellow naval officers will see things in a different light. Every CO knows that sometimes one is forced to deviate from the standing order of the day when faced with circumstances that threaten the security of one's command. An individual would have to be blind not to see the dangerously low level of the *Ladoga*'s morale. Was I just supposed to sit back and watch this condition worsen? It was getting so bad that I actually feared a mutiny!"

"Surely you're overreacting, Captain. I'll admit that there are several members of the crew whose esprit de corps is lacking. But these handful of individuals don't threaten your command. They are only a small bunch of confused malcontents, whose loyalty I was hoping to win over during this afternoon's Komsomol meeting."

"To hell with another of your damned meetings!" spat the frustrated captain. "The time of useless talk is over! As far as I'm concerned, the only way to get this crew back solidly behind me is to lead them into battle. This way they'll all too soon realize that as valued members of the Red Banner fleet, they are just as good as any Spetsnaz operative. It's no wonder they've been looking at themselves as mere taxi drivers, because that's all we've been until now. I'm as sick as they are of constantly playing second fiddle to our esteemed comrades in the special forces while they earn all the glory. It's time to show the Defense Ministry that we too are worthy of their trust. The *Ladoga* is a proud ship, and we're more than capable of assisting *Sea Devil* as it penetrates these highly sensitive waters."

Hardly believing what he was hearing, Petyr Tartarov shook his head. "I am indeed sorry that you feel this way, Captain. Regardless of your personal opinions, you are still guilty of breaking a direct operational order. I implore you to come to your senses and reverse our course before it's too late. Otherwise the consequences to your long career will be most detrimental."

"There will be no turning back, Comrade Zampolit! And as far as my career is concerned, the moment my crew lost trust in me was the moment it ended. I only pray that it's not too late to win them back. Now if you'll excuse me, I'd better get back to the attack center."

Only when the captain had left the weapons console altogether did the sweat start pouring down Petyr Tartarov's forehead. Doing his best to staunch it with a handkerchief, the political officer reluctantly contemplated his next course of action. There was no doubt in his mind that the captain had suffered some sort of serious mental breakdown that would necessitate an immediate change of the *Ladoga*'s command. Yet he couldn't merely stroll into the attack center and order the captain's replacement. He would need support. And for this he would have to appeal to the members of the Komsomol. As loyal Communists, surely their vision would be clear, and they'd understand that a change of command was a vital necessity in this instance. With this hope in mind, the political officer left the cork-lined cubicle to begin the unpleasant task of organizing a mutiny.

Above the cold, dark-green waters of the Firth of Clyde, the morning sun strengthened, gradually burning off the mist that had previously enshrouded the estuary in a swirling white veil. From the wheelhouse of the tug, Bernard Loughlin watched as the rolling green hills came into focus. Even the cold-hearted Irishman had to admit that this sight was an inspirational one.

The scenery was especially majestic on the left side of the channel. Here the tree-covered hills extended all the way to the water's edge. An occasional cottage and small covered dock was the extent of man's presence here, and the one-eyed terrorist supposed that it would be good to live in such a beautiful place.

From what little he had read about Scotland, he knew that it was primarily a pastoral country, with vast tracts of undeveloped wilderness. The Scots themselves were a proud, independent people, who had a cultural identity separate from their British occupiers. Yet unlike the Irish, they were apparently content to allow their ancestral land to be absorbed permanently into the United Kingdom.

Bernard knew of several Scottish separatist groups whose goals were much like their own. The IRB had hoped to stir these individuals to action by daring to break into Edinburgh Castle and make off with the country's symbolic royal regalia. Such a heist would have generated an intense wave of nationalism that would have spread throughout the countryside. And for at least one disturbing moment the peoples of this land would remember what it was like to be a true Scot once again, independent of the imperialistic yoke that had long ago stripped them of their identities.

Though the robbery went sour, the hand of fate had given the Brotherhood one more chance to kindle the fires of Scottish separatism. Bernard still had trouble believing that in only a couple of hours the despised monarchy that had enslaved this land and his own as well would be no more. Erased from the earth in a nuclear fireball, the Queen and all she stood for would be gone for all eternity. Like slaves who had been shackled for generations past, the people would rush in to fill this sudden void. And as a result, a single Celtic state made up of the countries once known as England, Wales, Scotland, and Ireland would come into existence, united by the bonds of non-sectarian Socialism.

When Bernard first founded the IRB, never in his wildest dreams did he think that because of his efforts alone, such a state would come into existence. Their possession of the nuclear device made this day possible, and his only regret was that he wouldn't live to see his sacrifice bear fruit. Yet in its own way, his martyrdom would cement the movement and make possible the great social revolution that was about to engulf the land.

The sound of someone approaching broke his deep pondering.

"Hello, Bernard. Doc says it's time to spell you."

Barely aware of the passage of time, Bernard nevertheless stepped back from the wheel and allowed Sean Lafferty to take the helm.

"Keep an eye out for those marker buoys, and keep out in the center of the channel whenever possible, Sean. Don't hesitate to call down the minute something doesn't look right to you."

As Sean answered these instructions with a mock salute, Bernard affectionately patted his comrade on the back. "How's your shoulder holding out, lad?"

"It's still throbbing, but I'll be able to carry my weight, Bernard."

"You're an inspiration to all of us, Sean Lafferty. Your country will soon be very proud of you."

With this curt comment, Bernard left the wheelhouse and climbed down the short ladder that led directly onto the tug's stern deck. Before going below and having some tea, he walked over to the transom. Stored in the locker here was the battery and cable that they would use to detonate the bomb. Though he had already checked its condition several times since leaving Dundalk, he couldn't resist giving this gear another look.

"We have that surface contact, sir. Bearing three-five-six, range two miles."

The sonar operator's revelation reached Captain William Foard as he was gathered around the chart table with Mac and Colin Stewart.

"That should be close enough for us to have a proper look," observed the *Bowfin*'s Captain. "Quartermaster, have the XO escort Mr. Lafferty up here on the double."

"Yes, sir," shot back the seaman responsible for all interdeck communications aboard the sub.

"Shall we see if Dame Fortune is smiling on us this time, gentlemen?" offered the captain as he beckoned them to join him at the periscope well.

"Helmsman, make our depth sixty feet. Up scope," ordered William Foard.

In response to this, the periscope hissed upward, with the Captain quick to hunch over it and locate the vessel responsible for their sonar contact.

"It's a tug all right. And from its draft lines, I'd say

345

that she was carrying a substantial amount of weight."

As he increased the magnification of the lens, Foard added, "Get a load of this character on the transom. He certainly looks the part."

Mac replaced him at the scope and nodded. "With that eyepatch and ponytail of his, he looks like a regular pirate. Do you think this is one of your men, Major?"

Before Colin Stewart could look for himself, the sound of Liam Lafferty's voice rose throughout the control room, his thick accent unmistakable. "And here I was just lying down for a wee nap. You fellows keep me busier than my wife."

"This shouldn't take long, Mr. Lafferty," remarked the captain.

Liam ambled over to the scope and nonchalantly gazed through the lens.

"It's him!" cried the fisherman. "I could never forget a puss like that."

"All right!" shouted Mac, who watched as Colin Stewart took a look through the scope.

"I hate to ask you this, Mr. Lafferty, but are you positive that this is the tug you saw being loaded back in Dundalk?" quizzed the Scotsman.

"One hundred percent positive," said Liam. "There's no doubt in my mind whatsoever. And if you just be patient, my own son will show up on that fancy-looking device of yours shortly."

Captain Foard briefly met the stares of Mac and Colin before turning his attention back to the Irishman. "Thank you, Mr. Lafferty. You can go back to your nap now."

"But don't you want me to point out Sean?" asked Liam.

"That's not necessary, sir," replied the Captain. "We believe you when you say this is the tug. So your job is over now. I'll have Ensign Pollard escort you back to your quarters."

"You'll be getting no further argument from me," said Liam, as he slipped his pipe in his mouth and followed his escort back below deck.

Colin Stewart took another look through the scope. "Now that we've found them, what do we do with them?"

"I don't think we have much of a choice," returned Mac. "We can't just ascend to the surface and place them in custody. One look at this sub and they'll go and blow that device for sure. Yet if we hit them with a torpedo, the resulting explosion could rip that bomb apart and cause the very same ecological disaster that we're trying to prevent."

"Not if that torpedo wasn't carrying a warhead and was being utilized just to punch a hole through their hull," offered the grinning captain.

"Is such a thing possible?" asked the Scotsman.

The captain answered, "Mister, this is a United States Naval vessel, and the word *impossible* isn't in our vocabulary. Shall I inform the torpedo room to ready such a fish?"

"I say go for it," said Mac. "Though while your men are readying that torpedo, I'd like to notify the *Lynch* and have them chopper in a ROV for the subsequent recovery. I don't think it would be a bad idea to call in the DSRV *Mystic* as well."

"If you really think you could sink them without spewing plutonium all through the Clyde, I'm with you also, Captain," remarked Colin Stewart.

William Foard looked the Scotsman right in the eye. "I can't guarantee anything but death and taxes, but I believe I can punch a nice neat hole in their bow just below the waterline. That means that the initial impact will be well away from the stern bilge. And since that's

347

where a weapon the size of an A-bomb would have to be stored, the shot should be a clean one."

"Then you've got my vote," returned the Highlander. "Just make certain that first shot's a good one, Captain. Because I seriously doubt if we'll have the time to attempt a second one."

The *Bowfin*'s CO nodded. "I'll try my best, Major. Now if that's settled, let's go and get Uncle Sam's property back to its rightful owner."

"Are you absolutely certain they've taken up a position right in *Sea Devil*'s baffles?" questioned Dmitri Zinyagin.

"I am, sir," answered the *Ladoga*'s senior sonar operator. "My last scan showed *Sea Devil* located immediately below the tug, which puts the *Sturgeon* in the waters directly behind them."

Zinyagin thoughtfully stroked his jaw. "I don't like this, comrade . . . I don't like it at all. Most likely they were spotted while penetrating that line of frigates. And now this sub has been sent in to do the dirty work. Thank the fates that I decided to follow them up the Firth. Otherwise, *Sea Devil* would never stand a chance.

"Comrade Zitomir, feed the acoustic signature of the *Sturgeon* into the fire control computer. Are tubes one, two, and three still showing a green light?"

"Yes they are, sir," answered the sonar chief. "I still show a red on number four, though."

The captain grunted. "It's that damned compression leak again. Most likely it will be out for the rest of our cruise. But that makes no difference. Three wire-guided acoustic homing torpedoes should be more than adequate to rid the seas of the imperialist threat."

Dmitri Zinyagin watched as the senior technician efficiently addressed his digital console. Only when he was certain that the three torpedoes were armed and ready to fire did he allow his thoughts to wander.

The *zampolit* had had the nerve to question Dmitri's authority to run the *Ladoga* as he wished. As commanding officer, that was his prerogative. Over four decades of selfless duty had given him the instinct to know when to take the initiative. And now his daring gamble was about to pay off in a way he never really expected.

How the men would flock to support him when they learned that because of Dmitri's dauntless gambit, the *Sea Devil* had been spared certain destruction. They would emulate him just as they had Captain Mikhail Borisov, the infamous lion of the Spetsnaz! Already looking forward to their adoration, Zinyagin was abruptly called back to the present by the agitated voice of his chief sonar operator.

"Our target has just opened its torpedo doors, Captain!"

Without a second's hesitation, Dmitri Zinyagin forcefully commanded, "Fire one! Fire two! Fire three!"

Mac was in the process of studying a detailed bathymetric chart of this portion of the Firth of Clyde in an effort to determine the difficulty of the salvage effort that would soon be facing them when the control room filled with the frantic cries of the *Bowfin*'s sonar operator.

"Incoming torpedo salvo! I count three separate torpedoes, bearing one-five-five, range two miles and rapidly closing!"

With the hope that all of this was some kind of horribly realistic drill, Mac watched as the sub's captain stepped forward to orchestrate a response to this surprise threat.

"Chief Langsford, I didn't authorize any practice drills today."

"This is no drill, sir!" returned the sonar technician. "We've got three torpedoes continuing to close in on us."

This was all the captain had to hear to snap into action. "I pray to God that our Mk-70 MOSS that we just got out of refit is on line. If so, fire tube number one."

"I show a green light on MOSS availability, Captain," replied the weapon's officer coolly. "Proceeding to fire."

Mac looked on with amazement as the deck shook and the compartment filled with the hissing sound of compressed air.

"I show a clean launch, Captain," reported the weapon's officer.

"All ahead emergency! Come to course two-five-zero," instructed William Foard.

Mac had to tightly grip the side of the chart table to keep from tumbling over as the helmsman turned his steering yoke and the *Bowfin* rolled hard on its left side.

"How much water do we have beneath us, Lieutenant Murray?" asked Foard, who kept his balance by holding onto a steel handrail.

The sub's bespectacled navigator was standing beside Mac and alertly answered. "Not more than one hundred and twenty five feet, sir."

"Damn!" cursed the captain. "What's the status of those fish, Chief Langsford? And do you have our Mk-70 as yet?"

The sonar operator replied while pressing his headphones to his ears. "The torpedoes haven't responded to our change of course yet, Captain. MOSS is headed off on bearing zero-six-six, and is really churning up a storm."

Mac was most familiar with the weapon known as the Mk-70 MOSS. This device was an ROV of sorts, designed to simulate the *Bowfin's* sound signature for the purpose of leading an attacking acoustic homing torpedo astray. It apparently proved its worth when the sonar operator excitedly reported.

"One of the fish has taken the bait, sir. It's going after MOSS with a bone in its teeth!"

"And the others?" asked Foard.

The chief held back his response until the racket that was being channeled into his headphones temporarily sorted itself out. "They're coming this way, Captain. They just completed their course change, range now down to one and a half miles."

Finding himself with one less threat to worry about, Foard tensely beat the side of his thigh with his right fist and proceeded to think out loud. "Since it's obvious that we can't outrun or outdive them, we can either prepare ourselves to take a hit, or gamble that we can shake them some other way. Yet if we can't go deep to put a knuckle in the water, how about if we try it going the opposite direction?"

Satisfied with this plan of attack, the captain instructed the planesman to send the sub shooting toward the surface. Not even stopping to consider what would happen if they were to encounter another vessel up here, Foard directed the crew to hang on.

"Torpedo range is down to one mile and still closing, sir," reported the sonar operator.

With his eyes glued to the depth gauge and the knot indicator mounted above the seated planesmen, the captain verbally willed his command onward. "Come on baby, you can make it. Come on!"

"Depth is down to forty-five feet, Captain. If we

don't pull out soon, we're going to breach!"

Ignoring this warning from the frantic diving officer, Foard cringed when the sonar operator added, "Range is down to three-quarters of a mile. Both torpedoes are following us up."

"Hold tight, men!" ordered the captain, who directed his next instructions to the diving officer. "We're going to breach like a frigging whale, Lieutenant Lawrence. And as soon as we hit the water, I need you to put on emergency ballast and get us wet again real quick. I'm counting on the racket that we're going to leave topside to give those two fish a fit, and that's when we're going to try to sneak off back into the depths."

Mac braced himself for this unorthodox maneuver to take effect. The angle of the deck beneath him was extreme, and he had to grip the edge of the chart table so tightly that it was digging into the palms of his hands. Yet he didn't dare let go, or he would end up sliding backward into the aft bulkhead along with the broken coffee cups, ashtrays, and other assorted implements that had already tumbled in this direction.

"We just passed twenty-five feet," observed the helmsman.

"Torpedo range is down to one-half mile," added the chief tensely.

"Here we go!" shouted William Foard, who wisely braced himself for the powerful concussion that followed.

Mac wasn't so prepared, and was thrown to the deck as the submarine went shooting through the Firth's previously calm surface bow first, and then went crashing back down into the water. As he blindly grabbed the leg of the radar console, Mac heard the roar of onrushing ballast. And before he could pick himself up, the angle of the deck reversed itself and he went sliding in the opposite direction.

It wasn't until they were at a depth of thirty feet that Mac was able to stand upright. He found himself perched against the weapons console. Beside him, his Scot colleague was likewise holding on for dear life. They traded a long, concerned glance as the voice of the sonar operator broke the tense silence.

"I've lost the torpedoes in the knuckle that we left behind up there, Captain. The water's still sizzling topside!"

A hopeful grin turned the corners of Colin Stewart's mouth, and just as Mac was about to exhale a relieved sigh of his own, the sonarman added, "Damn it, one of them is following us down! Somehow it's still on its wire. Range is a quarter of a mile and closing."

With this, the mood in the compartment turned instantly dark once again. Mac could now see fear reflected in the eyes of the Scotsman. For the first time since the alert, Mac had the feeling that they weren't going to make it after all. This heaviness stayed with him even as the captain optimistically cried out.

"This old lady's not licked just yet. Open those throttles wide, Chief, and bring us around hard on course zero-eight-zero. That fish is going to have to really prove itself to catch the USS *Bowfin!*"

And from the weapons room of the *Ladoga,* Seaman Third Class Vasili Buchara watched the madly spinning spool from which their sole remaining wire guided torpedo derived its target's location. Even though a great victory was about to be theirs, the Uzbek felt no joy. Instead his feelings still smarted from his humiliating confrontation earlier with the sub's *zampolit.*

Shamed and hurt by this encounter, only one thing mattered to Vasili, and that was to avenge his dishonor. And the only way he knew how to properly retaliate was to hurt the object that meant the most to the obese political officer. He'd shame Tartarov's command!

Vasili could picture the sweating *zampolit,* and the rest of the ship's officers, in the *Ladoga*'s attack center right now, basking in the glory of the victory that would soon be theirs. As if these buffoons knew what the real meaning of heroism was! As far as Vasili was concerned, they were all cowardly fools who could never hope to stand up to a man like Mikhail Borisov. It had been this same brave commando who had told Vasili that a candidate for the Spetsnaz had to have a mind of his own and not be afraid to show some initiative. And this was exactly what the young Uzbek would display as he reached forward and severed the torpedoes' fiber-optic wire with a single push of the disconnect button.

Mac had been in the process of bracing himself for the inevitable explosion that was bound to engulf them any second when the *Bowfin*'s sonar operator cried out in astonishment.

"It's gone! One moment it was right on our tail, and then in the blink of an eye, the darn thing just disappeared. Its wire must have broken."

A moment of stunned silence followed as this unexpected news was digested. Yet this was all too soon followed by a chorus of relieved cheers. Not prepared to celebrate just yet, Captain Foard raised his hands overhead to quiet his men and then forcefully addressed them.

"We've only won the first round, gentlemen. Now it's time to hurt the bastards responsible for this cheap shot and score a knockout punch. Chief Langford, hit 'em with active and cycle their signature through the computer. Then once we know who they are, interface this signature into the Mark 48s in tubes one and two."

"Aye, aye, sir," returned the sonar operator.

As the *Bowfin* prepared to take the offensive, the weapons officer took up his position at the console where Mac was standing. Mac watched him at work and was soon joined by the Scotsman.

"Who do you think is responsible for this attack, Major?" asked Mac. "And do you think they're in league with the group on the tug?"

Colin Stewart also watched the weapons officer at work. "Though I seriously doubt the IRB has an attack sub in their inventory, it sure appears that way. Who knows, maybe Ivan's giving them support with this one."

This supposition was apparently given substance when the chief sonar operator revealed the results of his scan. "We've got that signature ID. Captain. Big Brother shows an eighty-seven-percent probability that we're dealing with a Soviet India-class submarine. They're currently loitering beneath the waters south of us, at a relative rough range of three miles."

As the captain prepared the *Bowfin* to do battle, Mac absorbed this astonishing news, for he had very recently encountered this same class of vessel almost halfway around the world, off the coast of San Clemente Island! He knew that the India-class wasn't your average run-of-the-mill attack sub. It was specially designed with a purpose in mind, that being to transport the Russian equivalent of the DSRV. And though there was still no solid evidence, Mac was positive that the semirecessed wells that were cut into its aft deck could also carry vehicles such as the tracked mini-sub that had been his arch nemesis for almost a year now.

Mac shivered in awareness when a sudden thought

came to mind. Did the India's presence here mean that the tracked mini-sub was also currently deployed beneath the waters of the Firth? And if it was, was their mission in any way related to that of the tug? Well aware that if they found such a relationship to exist it would lead to a major East-West confrontation, Mac barely flinched when the powerful voice of the *Bowfin*'s captain called out commandingly.

"Fire one! Fire two!"

As the *Ladoga*'s senior sonar technician, warrant officer Pavl Zitomir was heartsick when he had to relay news of their attack's failure to the captain. He was positively terrified when a signature of even greater consequence streamed through his headphones minutes after their last torpedo mysteriously parted from its guidance wire.

"Captain, we are under attack!" he cried at the top of his lungs. "Our bow hydrophones show a salvo of two torpedoes headed our way on bearing zero-eight-zero, range 3,000 meters."

Stunned by this unexpected report, Dmitri Zinyagin reacted instinctively. "Get those throttles opened up, Chief Engineer. All ahead emergency! Helmsman, bring us around crisply to course two-two-zero. And if you value your life, Comrade Weapons Officer, you'll prepare two decoys for an immediate launch."

The captain watched how efficiently his men carried out these orders. There was no hesitation on their part, no signs of cowardice or reluctance to follow his command. Rather they were like a well-oiled machine whose thousands of hours of rote practice drills were at long last about to be tested for real.

The *Ladoga* began to pick up speed, and its deck canted hard on its right side as the vessel's massive rudder bit into the cold water of the Firth's black depths.

"Torpedo range is down to 2,500 meters, Captain. And they're continuing to close quickly."

"Where's that speed, Chief Engineer?" urged Dmitri Zinyagin. "If you want to see that family of yours again, you're going to have to do better than this pathetic pace."

It seemed to take forever for them to break twenty knots, and since the American torpedoes were advancing at twice this velocity, speed alone wasn't going to save them.

"Lieutenant Primorsk, are those decoys ready yet?" asked Zinyagin impatiently.

The *Ladoga*'s weapons officer seemed perplexed as he pushed back his headphones. "My men are trying, sir, but it seems that one of them is in the midst of some kind of fit. He's climbed up onto the torpedo racks and is threatening to smash the loading rail mechanism."

"You've got to be kidding me, Lieutenant," cried the disbelieving CO. "Make your men get this ridiculous situation under control before it causes the deaths of all of us!"

"Torpedo range is down to 2,000 meters," reported the tense voice of Pavl Zitomir.

Still not satisfied with the figure on the knot indicator, Dmitri was all set to vent his rage when the *zampolit* came strutting into the attack center. Surprisingly enough, a half dozen brawny seamen accompanied him. Puzzled by this unauthorized appearance, the captain turned to them.

"What in the hell is this all about, Comrade Tartarov?"

As the seamen proceeded to take up positions throughout the compartment, the political officer re-

357

plied, "Captain Zinyagin, in the name of the Komsomol, I hereby order you to relinquish your command immediately. You have been charged with dereliction of duty, and will have an opportunity to present your case before a full naval tribunal once we return to Kronstadt."

"Are you insane, Tartarov?" screamed the captain. "We've got two Yankee torpedoes headed straight for us, and you pick this time for a mutiny."

To this the *zampolit* shamefully shook his head. "Your theatrics might work on the impressionable minds of the attack center's crew, but they fall on deaf ears as far as I'm concerned." Then, looking up to the seamen who accompanied him, he added, "Comrades, you may go ahead and take our disturbed captain into custody."

As three of the largest sailors moved in to carry out this directive, Dmitri Zinyagin furiously shouted, "You fools! Don't you realize that you're signing your own death warrants by this groundless act of stupidity?"

Almost to emphasize this statement, the ship's chief sonar technician frantically called out. "The torpedoes have just broken the 1,000-meter threshold, Captain!"

For the first time since he entered the attack center Petyr Tartarov sensed the legitimacy of the crisis that he had unintentionally stumbled into. Still wary that this was but a clever trick by the captain to gain the confidence of his command team, the *zampolit* waddled over to Sonar. Without asking permission, he proceeded to rip the headphones off Pavl Zitomir and put the padded speakers up to his own ears. Though he was far from a qualified sonar operator, he knew enough to identify the distinctive grinding racket for what it was. This realization immediately expressed itself on his shocked, sweat-stained face.

"My heavens, we're under attack! Captain Zinyagin,

how did you ever allow such an unthinkable thing to happen?"

The *Ladoga*'s CO couldn't help but smile as he watched the cowardly political officer's flabby limbs begin shaking with fear.

"In a few more minutes, the answer to such a question will be irrelevant, Comrade Tartarov," returned the captain. "More important is the fact that your ill-timed mutiny has cost us valuable seconds that could have been much better spent attempting to escape this threat. Because as it looks now, the *Ladoga* is doomed!"

"But that can't be, Captain! Please, forget about the charges that I made against you. Just do whatever you can to save our lives!"

Relishing the *zampolit*'s discomfort and ignoring his frightened plea, Dmitri Zinyagin coolly told him, "If I were a follower of the old faith like my beloved mother, I'd get down on my knees and pray. Because the way it looks to me now, that's about the only thing that's going to save us."

Chapter Eighteen

Warrant Officer Oleg Zagorsk was monitoring *Sea Devil's* hydrophones when a pair of distant, muted explosions sounded from the waters behind them. Even without the benefit of headphones his shipmates could hear these blasts, and it was their CO who attempted to identify them.

"I bet there's a British underwater demolition team working beneath the waters of the Clyde this morning, Comrades. Most likely they're removing some sort of obstacle from the channel, or blasting out a foundation for a new pier. Whatever it may be, as long as they stay out of our way, they're of no concern to *Sea Devil*."

"Shouldn't we be ascending soon to take a bearing?" asked Tanya Olovski as she wiped the condensation from the glass face of their compass.

"Do I hear just a hint of impatience in your tone, comrade?" observed the Captain. "Relax, and rest assured that I will get us to our destination without getting *Sea Devil* lost."

Quick to check his own watch, Yuri Sosnovo got into the act. "As I figure it, we should be approaching Gourock shortly."

"You figure correctly," said Mikhail firmly. "And since Holy Loch lies directly across from Gourock, this is where we'll be making our turn to the west."

"But what if we were to overshoot it?" asked Tanya. "Who knows what kind of current we might have picked up when we entered the Firth."

Mikhail tapped the oilskin-covered charts that lay rolled up on his lap. "I guarantee you that we won't pass it by, Comrade Olovski. And to allay your fears, I plan to surface in five more minutes to take a bearing. Hopefully all this can be accomplished without us having to lose our escort topside. I can tell you one thing for certain . . . that tug has been a godsend."

Sean Lafferty stood alone in the wheelhouse, his gaze locked on that portion of the channel visible before them. Since relieving Bernard, Sean had remained at the helm, totally responsible for the tug's course and speed. The Dundalk native enjoyed this time to himself. It gave him an opportunity to appreciate the passing scenery and more important, to think.

The past couple of days had seemed to fly by with an incredible swiftness. It seemed that only yesterday he and Patrick Callaghan were on their way to Edinburgh Castle to steal the crown jewels. But a virtual lifetime had passed since then. Patrick was dead, and he was in the midst of an incredible new operation that would soon alter the course of history. To think that it was because of his father that this mission had come into being made it that much more astonishing.

Shaking his head in wonder, Sean briefly looked down at the chart and identified the beacon ahead as Cloch Point. To his right lay Lunderston Bay, while the heavily forested hills that overlooked Dunoon passed on the left.

There was an assortment of surface traffic visible on this part of the Firth. A variety of fishing boats, barges, tugs, and pleasure craft plied these waters. He had also recently passed an oceangoing cargo ship that was headed out to sea. He guessed that this traffic would be getting more congested as they rounded Gourock and turned east toward Gare Loch, the site of the royal christening.

Just thinking about the earth-shattering events their efforts would soon trigger caused a heavy lump to form in Sean's throat. Until Patrick Callaghan's tragic passing, he had never really given much thought to death. Even during all the dangerous operations that he'd previously participated in, the idea of his own mortality never really crossed his mind. It was almost as if all the ambushes and bombings had been merely child's games. And though people did die during these undertakings, Sean felt magically protected.

It was hard to believe that in less than an hour's time he would disappear off the face of the earth. At the very least, his end would be quick. But did he really have to die? This was the question that had been eating at him ever since Dr. Blackwater had explained his fate.

It had seemed so noble at the time to volunteer his services to the very end. But perhaps he had been too hasty to condemn himself as he had. What was wrong with him being dropped off at a safe distance like his colleagues had offered? At least then he could get involved in the new Celtic Brotherhood that would sweep this land once the Royal Family was gotten rid of.

A blinking channel marker flashed up ahead, and as Sean positioned the tug so that it would pass well to the right of it, he consigned himself to the course destiny had picked for him. He would see this operation to its end, and bravely meet death, as his good friend Patrick Callaghan had.

The intercom rang and Sean fumbled for the handset. It was Dr. Blackwater.

"How's it going up there, lad?"

"I'm doing just fine, Doc," returned Sean.

"That's good. It seems you're finally putting to use all those boating lessons your father passed on when you were a youngster. Bernard and I are planning to go down into the bilge and get to work on preparing the bomb for detonation. So that means I won't be able to spell you at the helm for at least another quarter of an hour."

Sean's throat was dry as he responded. "That's no problem, Doc. As long as you get up here before we reach Gourock and hit all the traffic, I'll be fine."

"I thought you would, lad. Keep her steady now. It's going to be hard enough standing upright in that stinking hold as it is."

Sean hung up the handset and reached down for the wheel with his good hand to alter their course slightly. Only when he was satisfied that they were well within the confines of the main channel did he allow his memories to stray to the innocent days of childhood, the blessed warm summers that he would never again experience.

Mac had been standing beside the Scotsman when their torpedoes hit home, and the two traded a relieved grin as the resonant explosion reverberated throughout the *Bowfin's* control room. What he hadn't been prepared for was the gut-wrenching groaning sounds that followed as the India-class attack sub broke apart and sank to the seafloor of the estuary.

With no time to spare to gloat over this victory, Captain Foard redirected their thoughts back to the mission that had brought them into these waters in the first place. "Helmsman, make your new course zero-two-zero. Hopefully we won't have any more surprises, and we can finish the job that we came out here to do. Chief Langsford, let me know the second you pick up that tug's signature on the hydrophones. Lieutenant Higgins, is that specially fitted non-detonating torpedo ready to roll?"

"That it is, Captain," answered the weapons officer. "We've got it tucked away and ready to fire in tube number one."

"Then let's get on with it, gentlemen. All ahead full!"

The deck tilted slightly as the *Bowfin* turned on its new course. But other than that there was no sensation that would point to the fact that they were presently surging through the depths at a speed of over twenty-five knots. This fact impressed Mac, who looked to his right when Colin Stewart addressed him.

"Well, Commander, let's pray that we can end this business once and for all. Any more thoughts as to what that Red sub was doing out here?"

Though Mac would have loved to share his theory about the tracked mini-sub with the Scotsman, for security sake he didn't. "I don't know. Maybe they are in league with the IRB. But more likely, this could all just be some sort of strange coincidence."

"I find that a bit hard to swallow," returned Stewart. "After all, we had that tug practically in our sights when they attacked us. It looks more and more to me like they were working together."

Mac could only shrug his shoulders and wonder if the India was indeed on a totally unrelated mission. And if it was, was their unique cargo still on board when the *Bowfin's* torpedo struck, or had it already been deployed? For if this was the case, their search wouldn't end with the retrieval of the bomb. At that point, it would only just be beginning once again.

"Watch your trim, Comrade Sosnovo," cautioned

Mikhail Borisov as *Sea Devil* rose from the depths and approached periscope depth. "To breach now could be disastrous."

The chief engineer barely paid these words any attention as he confidently went about his job like the true professional that he was. Like a magician, he went about the delicate task of ridding the mini-sub of just enough ballast to accommodate their needs and keep them from breaking the water's surface.

The only moisture on Yuri Sosnovo's forehead was from the constantly falling condensation as he initiated a final adjustment and matter-of-factly commented, "Periscope depth, Captain."

Mikhail immediately hit the lever that sent the scope barreling up from its storage well. Getting down on his knees so that as little of the lens as possible would have to break the water, he hunched over the viewing chamber and peered inside.

He was afforded a spectacular view of the tug's stern that seemed to be only a hand's length away. Taking in the bubbling white froth left in the wake of the tug's propeller, Mikhail swept the lens to the northeast. Fortunately the weather remained good and he could pick out the flashing beacon that was situated on the eastern shoreline. Having seen enough, he sat up and pulled the lever that sent the periscope spiraling back into the *Sea Devil's* protective confines.

"Take us back down, Yuri," ordered the captain.

The sound of onrushing seawater filled the cramped compartment, and Tanya Olovski was quick to her CO's side with an unfolded chart.

"Well, Captain?" she breathlessly quizzed. "Were you able to see anything familiar?"

Mikhail took hold of the chart and pointed to a rounded section of coastline on the southwestern outskirts of the town of Gourock. "If you must know, my

365

inquisitive comrade, this is the location of the beacon that's passing to our starboard. We will continue traveling up the channel for another two and a half kilometers before turning off for Holy Loch."

"Then we've made it!" she exclaimed joyfully.

Mikhail again pointed to the chart. "Not quite, comrade. We still have the channel to cross. And since our friendly tug will most likely be continuing on in the opposite direction toward Port Glasgow at that time, we'll be doing so all on our own."

"This is still a remarkable feat," reflected the electrician. "To think that we've actually penetrated deep into the enemy's waters and are now approaching one of its most sensitive naval installations. It's incredible!"

"And the best is yet to come," offered Mikhail with a wink.

Suddenly remembering another concern, Mikhail called out to his Warrant Officer. "Comrade Zagorsk, do you still have the tug on your hydrophones?"

The headphone-wearing Siberian turned from the sonar console. "Yes, I do, Captain. In fact, we're almost right beneath them once again. They've seemed to cut back on their throttle some."

Ever thankful for the convenient cover of this vessel, Mikhail spoke up. "I would love to get the registration number of that tug so that we can send its owner a case of Russian vodka once we return home. What a great service he's provided!"

"Brother, would I like to see the face of that Scot when he unwraps it," returned Yuri. "He'd go to his grave wondering where in the hell it came from!"

The cramped bilge was thick with the stench of rotting fish and diesel oil as the two terrorists intently worked beside the massive cylindrical bomb bolted to the deck here. Trying his best not to gag on the nauseating combination of odors, Dr. Tyronne Blackwater watched as his colleague delicately removed the metallic cover plate that protected the nuclear device's detonator.

"I certainly hope that physicist wasn't feeding us a bunch of crap back at Cootehill House," remarked Bernard Loughlin as he pulled off the plate and viewed the complex grid of circuit boards and snaking wires that lay inside.

"He was too scared to lie," offered the physician. "I was just afraid that he was going to keel over from a heart attack before he spilled the beans to us."

"At least that would have saved us a bullet," returned the one-eyed terrorist, who used a dental probe to isolate the copper-coated electrode that Dr. John Maguire had pointed out to them.

"Why don't you just hand me that battery cable and we can blow it now," added Bernard.

"Patience, lad. Though we'd most likely complete our mission even from this distance, we might as well do it as planned. Besides, we've only got another two kilometers to go before we reach the definite kill zone."

Bernard replaced the cover plate, using only the two top screws to keep it in place. "You're right, Doc. I always was the overly anxious one. And it was that very character flaw that kept us from adding to the Brit body count on many a promising ambush. Once I even pushed the detonator of a remote-controlled mine too soon and just missed taking out the commander of the SAS. Now that would have been a real score!"

"You'll make up for it this time, lad," said Dr. Blackwater.

Bernard stood and climbed out of the bilge to drop down the battery cable. While he initiated this task, the physician scanned the decaying mass of fish that lay at his feet. He found himself longing for one last lungful of sweet air from the pine forest that surrounded his beloved Cootehill House. Tears clouded his eyes as he realized he would never walk the lush green grounds again; the drastic consequences of this suicidal mission had finally sunk in. And he couldn't help but wonder if his parents would have approved of his decision to die the death of a martyr for the sake of the ideals that they had instilled in him all so very long ago.

"I've got the tug, Captain! It's dead ahead of us. But I'm picking up the screws of another surface vessel as well."

The sonar operator's words sent William Foard scrambling over to the periscope. As he anxiously peered through its lens, he spotted the rounded transom of the vessel they were hunting down and placed it right in the scope's cross hairs. Yet before he could give the order to fire, he quickly scanned the surrounding waters in an attempt to locate the other contact that Chief Langsford had mentioned. It didn't take him long to spot the distinctive lines of this ship, speedily approaching from the east.

"Damn it!" cursed the *Bowfin*'s CO. "Of all the frigging times for the Gourock-to-Dunoon passenger ferry to pass by! Keep that fish in number one warm, Lieutenant Higgins. We'll get to use it yet."

From the wheelhouse of the tug, Sean Lafferty also watched the approach of the passenger ferry. Only when he was sure that the automobile-laden, flat-hulled ship would pass well behind them did he utilize the binoculars to scan the waters that lay in the opposite direction. The town of Gourock lay to their right, while ahead of them extended the jutting peninsula of land around which snaked Gare Loch. Anchored here was a frigate-sized ship painted dark blue with golden trim. A large Union Jack fluttered from its masthead, and Sean didn't have to see any more to lower the binoculars and shout into the intercom excitedly.

"We're here, comrades ! I can see the royal yacht, anchored before us only a kilometer or so distant!"

Quick to join him in the wheelhouse was Dr. Blackwater. The physician put the binoculars to his eyes and remarked, "So it is, Sean. And that Union Jack flying from its masthead means the Royal Family is currently on board, probably still sound asleep beneath their satin sheets. In a couple more minutes we're going to give them a wake-up call that they'll remember for all eternity!"

The physician affectionately patted Sean on his back and reached for the intercom.

"Bernard, it's the royal yacht all right, and the Queen's presently aboard. I'll get over to the transom and connect the cables to the battery. I'll knock three times on the deck when I'm finished. And then you're free to make room for us in the history books. For the glory of the Brotherhood, and at long last a united Ireland, comrade!"

Tyronne Blackwater hung up the handset and briefly caught Sean's concerned glance.

"Have no fear, lad. It will be over with so quickly that you'll never know what hit you. And besides, waiting for us at those pearly gates will be Bobby Sands and the thousands of other martyrs who willingly gave up their lives for the same cause. So be brave to the end, lad, and know that your sacrifice is a worthy one."

There were tears of pride in the physician's eyes as he hugged Sean, and then turned to get on with his duty.

Meanwhile, below deck in the bilges, Bernard Loughlin fought to keep his hands steady as he attempted to remove the two screws from the bomb's cover-plate. Until this moment he had always prided himself on his nerves of steel. He could lead a charge into an army barricade with rifle bullets whining overhead and not even break a sweat. But the simple act of removing the two screws caused his whole body to be soaked in perspiration. There was an alien tightness deep in his gut, and his right hand was shaking so badly that he had to support it with his left just to guide the head of the screwdriver into the proper slots.

Sweat dripped off his eyepatch and plopped down on the smooth steel surface of the bomb as he gratefully pulled out the last of the screws. Taking a second to wipe the moisture off his soaked brow with the rough palm of his hand, he peered inside the trigger mechanism and located the copper-coated electrode that he had isolated earlier. Just then, three loud knocks sounded from the deck above.

Bernard took a deep breath and reached out for the dual battery cables that hung from the hatchway. He grounded the black cable clip on the edge of the bomb. Now he had only to connect the red clip to the electrode, to trigger the detonator and cause the fission process to begin. Yet try as he could to make this connection, his hand was shaking so badly that this simple task was all but impossible.

"Come on, Bernard!" he urged to himself as he momentarily backed away to regain his composure.

Again he took in a deep lungful of the rank air that was getting increasingly foul with each passing second. Fighting back the urge to retch, he once more gripped the battery cable and leaned forward to complete his duty.

From the waters immediately below the tug Mikhail Borisov prepared to give the orders that would alter *Sea Devil's* course. The only thing that kept him from directing his chief engineer to leave the protective shadow of the tug and turn for Holy Loch was the passing of another vessel topside. Fearing that this ship was a frigate, or another type of ASW platform, Mikhail decided to play it safe and remain beneath the tug for a bit longer. And then there would be plenty of time to turn back to the west and get on with the completion of their mission.

Mac impatiently watched the *Bowfin's* CO peer through the lens of the periscope. It seemed to be taking forever for the ferry to pass. And he knew that the closer the tug got to Gare Loch, the more likely its deadly cargo would be detonated. Beside him, Major Colin Stewart seemed to share Mac's anxieties. The Scotsman's brow was damp with perspiration and his nervous gaze was constantly going to the bulkhead clock.

Suddenly the Captain's forceful voice filled the hushed control room. "You've got a clear firing angle, Lieutenant Higgins. Fire one!"

The weapons officer addressed his console, and seconds later a powerful jolt of compressed air shot the unarmed, wire-guided torpedo out of its tube.

Still hunched over the periscope, the captain added, "Now let's just pray that when our fish hits home, that bomb doesn't go off and send all of us on a voyage that we'll never return from!"

Dr. Tyronne Blackwater was perched beside the tug's transom in the process of watching the ferry steam off toward the town of Dunoon when he spotted the alien wake in the waters immediately behind them. He was puzzled by this sighting at first, and even wondered if it could be attributed to a fish of some sort, when a sudden shocking thought registered in his consciousness.

"Sweet Jesus, it's a blooming torpedo!" he cried as he ran off for the ladder that led to the bilges. "Bernard, what the hell's keeping you? We've got a damn torpedo on our tail!"

The stench of rotting fish was overpowering as he dropped down into the cramped compartment and turned toward the bomb. Kneeling beside it, his face ashen white and limbs trembling, was Bernard. Though he still held one of the battery cables in one hand, the physician could see from the terrified look on his face that he would be of no further use to them.

"My lord, Bernard . . . just look what a state you're in. Give me that cable you're holding and let me take over. This is our last chance, lad."

The founder of the Irish Republican Brotherhood looked up and spoke out a whimpering tone. "Forgive me, comrade . . . Because it appears that I just don't have the guts to do it."

Tyronne Blackwater never had a chance to respond. The bilge filled with an ear-shattering, buckling crack as the hull was ripped open. The deck wildly shook and rolled hard on its right side, finally tipping forward as the onrushing seawater poured into its shattered bow. Ripped free from its mount at this point, the 5,000-pound bomb went hurtling over the bodies of Bernard Loughlin and Dr. Tyronne Blackwater, killing them instantly. As it crashed into the forward bulkhead, it splintered the wooden planking, penetrated the crushed hull, and plunged into the awaiting depths below.

Mikhail Borisov was in the process of instructing his

chief engineer to break from the cover of the tug and bring them around to their new course when the frantic voice of Oleg Zagorsk interrupted him.

"Excuse me, Captain. But I'm picking up something strange on our hydrophones. It almost sounds like it's a torpedo!"

Sea Devil's CO proceeded at once to the sonar console to determine this fact for himself. No sooner did he put on the auxiliary headphones than a deafening crackling sound emanated from the waters immediately above them.

"I don't understand," reflected Mikhail. "Was that tug just hit by a non-detonating torpedo?"

The Spetsnaz commando never got a chance to learn the answer to this question, for the tug's deadly cargo smashed into *Sea Devil* with such a force that the mini-sub was knocked off its tracks and capsized. Mikhail Borisov crashed painfully into the mini-sub's ceiling, and the last thought he had before lapsing off into unconsciousness was that his well-ordered world had been abruptly overturned by the fickle hand of destiny.

It wasn't until the *Bowfin* surfaced and a single survivor was pulled from the water that Captain Foard, Mac, and Colin Stewart learned that their suspicions had been correct after all. Sean Lafferty was quick to confess the exact nature of their intended mission, and was shocked to find his own father among the sub's complement. They met with a warm hug, and Liam tearfully mentioned that this was the first time since childhood that his son had allowed him to take him in his arms.

While the two Irishmen continued their emotional reunion down in the wardroom, under the watchful eyes of the sergeant at arms, Mac and his Scottish colleague remained topside.

"Well, Major, it seems that we all owe you our undying gratitude. Not only does it appear that we'll get our bomb back, but we were also able to halt a tragedy of unprecedented scope."

Colin Stewart responded while watching a Sea King helicopter approach from the south. "Don't forget that without your support, this whole thing wouldn't have been possible. You're part of this just as much as I am. Now if that bomb casing only remains intact, and its plutonium is kept from scattering on the seafloor, we will all finally be able to rest easier."

Also gazing up at the blue Sea King was Mac. "We'll all know the answer to that as soon as that chopper arrives with CURV. Captain Foard's setting it up so that I can operate the ROV from the *Bowfin*'s sonar console. Its camera will show us if the bomb's still intact. Meanwhile, we've also got that salvage tug and those divers on their way from Holy Loch, with the DSRV *Mystic* coming in for good measure."

"I imagine that your ROV will come in handy checking out the remains of that submarine that we were forced to take out back in the channel," observed Colin Stewart.

"It certainly will," said Mac. "Though for the life of me, I still can't figure out what it was up to when it took those potshots at us. Sean Lafferty certainly didn't seem to know anything about it, and that would appear to rule out any Soviet-IRB connection."

"That remains to be seen," remarked the Highlander, who scanned the wooded shoreline of the Firth. His gaze finally halted on the distinctive blue hull of a frigate-sized ship anchored off the entrance to nearby Gare Loch. It had a Union Jack fluttering from its masthead.

"I wonder when they'll inform Her Majesty of these

goings on," said Stewart. "If she remains on schedule, she should be leaving the royal yacht any minute now to get on with the christening."

"I'd sure like to see her face when they do," returned Mac. "Though I doubt she'll believe it when they do tell her how close she came to the end of her reign."

Major Colin Stewart nodded thoughtfully. With his gaze still locked on the fluttering red, blue, and white Union Jack, he wondered if he'd ever be able to share this incredible story with his colleagues back at Edinburgh castle. Though even they would think that he was merely telling a tall tale as he described the events leading up to the tug's destruction. And in a way, he couldn't blame them, for he had trouble believing its validity himself.

Epilogue

Mikhail Borisov snapped back into waking consciousness with a start. The back of his bruised head throbbed painfully, and as his blurred vision cleared, a single sputtering candle illuminated a scene of total chaos. The *Sea Devil* was completely overturned. Smashed equipment and the prone, blood-stained bodies of two of his shipmates littered the ceiling that was now the mini-sub's floor. As he stiffly sat up, a hoarse voice broke the hushed stillness.

"Hello, Captain," greeted Yuri Sosnovo weakly. "Thank the fates that you too have survived."

Mikhail got to his hands and knees and located his chief engineer propped against what was left of the sub's gyroscope.

"My heavens, Yuri! What in the world happened to us?"

"Whatever it was, comrade, it took the lives of both Oleg and Tanya," managed Yuri. "They were both dead when I awoke several minutes ago."

Mikhail stood and made his way over to his shipmate's side. "That's a nasty gash you have on your forehead, Yuri. And it looks like your leg and arm are broken."

"That's not the half of it, Captain. I got caught up in between the sonar console and the helm when we went over, and it feels as if my guts have been ripped

377

open."

As the chief engineer was caught up in a coughing fit that brought blood-speckled spittle to his lips, Mikhail compassionately remarked, "Easy does it, my friend. It appears that the diving chamber is still intact. Do you think that you could manage to crawl over there with me?"

"What for?" retorted Yuri. "I'm finished, comrade. You go ahead and make good your escape, and I'll take care of activating the explosive charges to scuttle *Sea Devil*."

Mikhail shook his head. "I'll not leave you to die alone, Yuri Andreivich. Come on. I'll set the charges and we can take our cyanide capsules together."

"I'll hear of no such thing, comrade!" shot back Yuri. "Why waste your own life on my behalf? You must survive, if only to get news of our mission's outcome back to Admiral Starobin. Otherwise they'll fault *Sea Devil* and this brilliant operation will never get a chance to be repeated."

Knowing full well that he was right, Mikhail nodded. "Comrade Sosnovo, as always, your valued insights are correct. I'm going to miss you, my friend."

Yuri managed a fond grin. "We've certainly been in some tight ones together, Captain. Do you remember that time off Kiel when that German corvette had us cornered . . ."

Yuri's remembrances were abuptly cut short by another violent coughing fit that brought a renewed flow of bright red blood to his lips. Mikhail was also finding it hard to breathe, and realizing that the already foul air was quickly losing its oxygen content, he knew it was time to be going.

"Are you certain that you'll be able to hit that scuttle charge, Yuri?"

The chief engineer looked up and directly met his

CO's stare. "Of course I can, Captain. Don't worry. I'll get to it all right, on my last dying breath, if necessary."

Certain that he would, Mikhail began slowly picking his way back to the diving chamber that was now positioned on the ceiling. As he pulled open the hatch, he took one last fond look at his brave shipmate. Illuminated by the flickering candlelight, Yuri snapped his commanding officer a crisp salute. Fighting the tears that were forming in his eyes, Mikhail returned this salute, then pivoted and pulled himself up into the awaiting chamber.

And from the surface of the waters immediately above the overturned mini-sub, Commander Brad Mackenzie anxiously sat before the blinking monitor screen. The CURV was well on its way to the seafloor now, and it was with great anticipation that he activated the ROV's mercury-vapor lights. As he triggered its fiber-optic camera, the monitor filled with the swirling green waters of the Firth.

Mac carefully guided the ROV into the depths and soon located the channel's bottom. A curious salmon swam by, and as Mac began a broad sweep of the gravelly seabed, he sighted the wreck of the tug they had sunk. Remarkably, it was still in one piece, though there was a large hole in its forward hull, just below the waterline. While visualizing the two corpses that were trapped inside this vessel, Mac guided the CURV in a wide circle. It was during this maneuver that the monitor filled with a familiar cylindrical cannister that caused an excited roar to escape the lips of those who also watched the screen and were assembled behind Mac.

"We've got it, and it still looks intact!" shouted Captain William Foard. "We've got the damn bomb back!"

Though Mac was tempted to halt his search at this point and join in on the celebration going on behind him, his curiosity made him remain at the console. After slowly circling the nuclear device and finding it intact, he reinitiated the circular maneuver that he was in the midst of when he first came upon the bomb. Someone joyfully patted him hard on the shoulder, and he almost missed a series of unusual markings that were embedded in the gravel. His stomach instinctively tightened, his pulse quickened, as he closed in on these markings and found them to be an exact duplicate of the amphibious trail that he had previously viewed in such diverse places as San Francisco Bay, and most lately under the blue waters of Kwajalein Atoll. For this was the unique trail left behind by the mysterious tracked mini-sub that he had spent over a year of his life so desperately searching for!

His hands were slightly shaking as he addressed the keyboard and instructed the ROV to follow this track. CURV proceeded less than one hundred feet when the screen suddenly filled with an object that caused Mac to gasp in wonder. Lying overturned on the floor of the channel was a strange-looking vehicle, part submarine, part amphibious tractor, the very vessel responsible for the tracks! And Mac could only shiver in awareness with the realization that his long search had finally ended.

Totally unaware of the elation that *Sea Devil* was causing in the surrounding waters, Yuri Sosnovo leadenly crawled away from the bulkhead. The candle was almost burnt out now, and with its wick sputtering in the foul air, he locked his glance on the red striped box that was set into a nearby console. Inside this glass cubicle was a single switch. All Yuri had to do was